Praise for *New York Times* Bestselling Author

"A terrific tale . . . the s   *iew*

"Blazingly hot and erotic."
               —*Romantic Times BOOKreviews*

"Marvelously rich, emotionally charged, imaginative, and beautifully written."   —*BookLoons*

"A fantastic erotic vampire thriller."   —*Fresh Fiction*

THE COMPANION

"A darkly compelling vampire romance . . . the plot keeps the
reader turning the pages long into the night."   —*Affaire de Coeur*

"Bestseller Squires charts a new direction with this exotic, extremely
erotic, and darkly dangerous Regency-set paranormal tale. With
her ability to create powerful and tormented characters, Squires
has developed a novel that is graphic, gripping, and unforgettable."   —*Romantic Times* (4½ starred review)

"Travel through Egypt's deserts and London's society with two
of the most intriguing characters you will ever read about. You
will encounter a dark world that is intense, scary, and sexy, and a
love that will brighten it . . . powerful and passionate . . . captivating . . . Squires has a wonderful ability to keep her readers
glued to the edge of their seats."   —*Romance Junkies*

MORE . . .

"Squires has demonstrated a talent that few can surpass. Her descriptions and historical details are flawless. Her characters exceed their potential and the plot keeps you quickly turning the pages. Squires has joined the company of authors whose books are classics. Look for this book to become a classic in its genre too. *The Companion* is a gem. Obviously, everyone needs it."

—*Coffee Time Romance*

"A totally absorbing novel . . . the characters are brilliantly conceived and perfect for the gripping plotline. The author gives the reader a unique twist on what vampires really are, a tortured hero to adore, the only heroine who could possibly be right for him, a truly horrific villain—and a fascinating story that carries the reader through one exciting adventure after another . . . Squires's prose grabs you from the beginning and gives you a relentless ride through this complex, beautifully written book."

—*New and Used Books*

"A riveting story, the first of what I expect to become a fresh, unforgettable new vampire series."

—*BookLoons*

"A book to be savored, not torn through at breakneck speed . . . Squires is a talented author and *The Companion* offers the promise of more beautifully dark vampire novels to follow."

—*The Romance Reader*

St. Martin's Paperbacks Titles By
Susan Squires

One with the Night
The Burning
The Hunger
The Companion

One
WITH THE
NIGHT

SUSAN SQUIRES

St. Martin's Paperbacks

This is a work of fiction. All of the characters, organizations, and events portrayed in this novel are either products of the author's imagination or are used fictitiously.

ONE WITH THE NIGHT

Cover photo of people © Shirley Greene
Cover photo of castle © Corbis

ISBN: 0-312-94102-1
EAN: 978-0-312-94102-4

Printed in the United States of America

St. Martin's Paperbacks edition / April 2007

St. Martin's Paperbacks are published by St. Martin's Press, 175 Fifth Avenue, New York, NY 10010.

10 9 8 7 6 5 4 3 2 1

CHAPTER
One

Atlas Mountains, Morocco 1819
There was no denying her. She ran her long-nailed fingers
through his hair as he sat, naked, beside the chaise on
which she lay draped. His hair was as dark as hers. But her
eyes were almost black, while his were light gray-green, his
skin fair against her golden glow. She had chosen him for
his coloring. How long would he pay for the sins of some
French and English crusaders long dead? Until he died. He
had prayed for death so often. Blood oozed from various
cuts and punctures in his body, but she was careful not to
kill him.

Heat poured from a dozen braziers and a low fire in the
center of her tent. She liked heat. His skin was damp with
sweat. He fixed his gaze on the intricate carpet, trying to
avoid what would come. But she willed him to raise his gaze.
For the thousandth time he struggled. He clenched his fists
and grunted, panting.

Her laughter tinkled over him like shards of broken glass.
"You know you cannot win out, English." He wasn't really
English. She twisted his head up by his hair and showered
compulsion over him. The need to obey her surged through
him. His gaze jerked to her face.

Her eyes glowed with more than firelight as she chuckled.

How could laughter frighten him so? His chest heaved from the effort to resist her. The fine skin between her breasts gleamed with perspiration. Her nipples peaked under the diaphanous fabric of her burgundy gown. He found his own desire rising, whether he would or no.

His stomach clenched in despair as he lifted his chin to bare his throat to her. She would use him to slake several thirsts tonight. She was always thirsty.

She bent to his throat. He shuddered at the familiar twin pains just under his jaw. She stroked his nipple as she sucked at his neck and then slid down onto the rug beside him so she could grasp his swollen member.

"You still resist me," she whispered inside his mind. "How can I make you truly mine?"

She rocked against him, her breasts pressed to his chest. He moaned, partly with desire, partly in dread. He didn't want to know the answer to that question.

Edinburgh, Scotland, March 1821
The busy tavern came into focus around him with a shudder. Raucous laughter punctuated the hum of a dozen conversations. The smell of unwashed bodies, cooked cabbage, yeasty ale, and smoky whisky cascaded over him. It had been two years since he'd escaped her. He was in Edinburgh, on an entirely different continent than the desert mountains where he'd suffered at her hands. Yet still she haunted him. She had made him a monster in so many ways. He downed his whisky and slapped a gold coin on the shadowed table. Too much for the bottle, but he never cared about that these days. He pushed himself up. He had hope now. All activity in the tavern stopped as thirty pairs of eyes followed him to the door. They felt the energy that vibrated around him. He had a long journey ahead of him to find the one who might have the cure for what he was. But first he had an appointment with a bully.

Drumnadrochit, Scotland, March 1821

A scream rent the Highland spring night. Jane Blundell was just climbing into the gig in the village nestled on the shore of Loch Ness, ready to head back to the house she and her father had taken up the Urquhart River valley from the loch. Jane had spent too many years as a midwife among the poor of London not to recognize that scream. A woman was in labor and it was not going well. The sound died away into a moan. It was coming from that tiny stone cottage just off the lane that meandered through the village. She scrambled down. Papa could wait for his supplies. Figures had congregated in the tiny front garden. The sun had set more than an hour ago, but Jane saw extremely well in the dark these days.

The villagers wouldn't welcome her help. She and her father were pariahs ever since he offered to pay for blood donations, ostensibly to be used in his experiments. The words "unholy" and "sacrilegious" and "English monsters" were the ones most often bandied about when the newest occupants of Muir Farm were mentioned. The villagers were closer to the truth than they knew. The blood wasn't for her father's experiments. It was for her. Ever since she'd been infected, she had needed human blood to survive. And now, with her source gone, the hunger that horrified her scratched along her veins. Her father had offered to bleed himself for her. She couldn't allow that, of course, but what was she to do? She might resort to God knew what if the dreadful hunger got any worse.

She tried to put away panic. She couldn't think of that now. The cottage window revealed substantial silhouettes holding something down. In a village this small and remote they probably weren't even midwives. Outside, several men milled around a young man, who paced and ran his hands through his hair in distraction. Jane knew better than to approach the women.

"What is wrong?" she asked one of the men.

"Saw the monster, she did," the man said in that thick Scots burr she could hardly make out yet. "Put her right inta birthin' pains."

"She's early?"

But the man had realized who she was. "Get back, witch! Ye will no' hex this babe!"

Another scream tore through the night. In late March it was still cold in the Highlands, and the men's breath was clearly visible. The scream made the pacing young man moan in distress and look around wildly. "Evie," he cried. "Dinnae die, Evie!"

Jane pushed through the men. This was the father, surely. "Is she early?" she shouted, almost in his face.

He looked at her with frightened eyes and nodded, swallowing. Inside the cottage the women encouraged the girl to bear down and push. Jane grabbed the young husband by both biceps and shook him. "I'm a midwife, boy. And I tell you that if they make Evie push when she's not ready, the babe will break blood vessels and your wife will die."

The father, who looked absurdly young, blinked at her.

"Leave th' lad alone." A hand grabbed her shoulder and tried to pull her away.

"Ye've no business here, English," another said.

Jane twisted away and stood her ground. "I've delivered a hundred babies, boy," she said, staring right at the husband. "I know what I'm saying. *You* can make them let me look at her."

"Me? I can no' do anythin'!" he wailed.

"She's a Sassanach, Jamie," an older man warned.

"You're her husband. You vowed to protect her, didn't you? It's up to you." Jane laid a hand on his shoulder. It was thin under his rough flaxen shirt.

He looked into her eyes. She willed him to let her into the house. She felt a thrill along her veins, the thrill that had frightened her so since her sickness six months ago.

"Verra well," he said at last. His voice was strangely calm.

She nodded curtly and took his arm.

"Jamie, what are ye doin'? Ye can no' let an English witch into Evie's childbed!"

Jamie pulled away from the hands that tried to stop him. "Get back, MacDougal! All o' ye. Even ye, Da. If this woman can help my Evie, I'm bound ta let her."

Jane and Jamie pushed into the tiny cottage just as another scream made Jamie wince.

"What's she doin' here?" one of the women accused. "And ye, Jamie Campbell! We can no' ha' men here."

Jamie straightened his shoulders. "She's a midwife and she's goin' ta look at Evie," he said firmly. Jane was proud of him. "I am her husband. It is my bairn and it is up ta me."

Jane didn't wait for more authority. She pushed through to the woman with the distended belly writhing on the bed. She was hardly more than a child. She was sweating and heaving breath, her knees raised, plainly frightened. "Now, my dear," Jane soothed. "Let me just see how you're doing." Jane gently felt the distended belly under a sheet that covered the girl's spread knees. "I've attended more than a hundred births you know." She smiled. "You had a shock?"

The girl nodded. "I seen th' monster! I seen Nessie," she gasped, her eyes round.

"Well, never mind that now. You must breathe, slowly and deliberately. No pushing. We want that baby of yours to take his own sweet time." The child was in breech position. Jane moved to lift the sheet so she could see how far the womb had opened.

"What are ye doin'?" a woman screeched. "There's a man in the room!"

"I assume this man is already familiar with his wife," Jane remarked. "We must suppose he got the child on her." She smiled sweetly. "Unless you believe a stork brings them?"

"It is no' proper," one said, shaking a finger at Jamie.

Jane turned on the three women. "Enough!" They frowned at her, fists on their hips, looking ready for a fight. "Jamie, could you escort these ladies from the room? They're upsetting Evie." With relief she saw Jamie set his jaw and herd the women, protesting, from the room, looking for all the world like ruffled, clucking hens.

"Jamie, why don't you pull up a stool and just hold Evie's hand? I'm sure your strength would be a comfort to her."

Jamie grew taller by several inches. He pulled a stool under himself and grabbed his young wife's hand. "You're goin' ta be all right, Evie," he said with a voice almost sure of itself. Sure enough, at least, to fool Evie.

Jane wasn't so certain. She'd seen breech births come out well, but the combination of a breech position and the early onslaught of labor, made worse by those stupid women urging Evie to push, might spell disaster. Should she try to turn the babe? If she left the child as it was, the sac might break too early and suffocate the child—but if she turned it the babe might break the mother's blood vessels as it came out too quickly. Even if the child lived, Evie would likely die. But if Evie's contractions were so strong already that Jane couldn't get the baby turned one way or another, *no* birth was possible and Evie and baby both would die a painful death over many hours.

"Try to relax, Evie," she murmured as she removed the sheet and looked at Evie's womb. Not open enough yet for the head of a babe. Behind her, the door creaked.

"Da." Jamie's reedy voice had iron in it. "If ye've come ta help ye're welcome. Other ways, ye kin go."

Jane glanced back to see a rugged-looking man who was probably only forty-five, though work and a hard life made him look sixty. His face was deeply lined, his hair a shock of gray. He shared Jamie's prominent nose and pale blue eyes. Jane turned back to her patient. "I must feel if the babe is in the birth canal, Jamie," she muttered. "If you care to help, Mr. Campbell, you can sit at Evie's other side." She glanced to both men. "I'll need her still." They got the point. The older man looked grim as he sat down wordlessly with a hand on Evie's shoulder.

Jane examined her hands carefully. Any cuts or scrapes would heal almost instantly, but one must be sure. If even a molecule of her blood got into Evie's, she'd infect the girl.

Another contraction came. "Don't push, Evie," Jane said as the girl wailed. "Just breathe." The girl gasped and shrieked, but the contractions had moderated a bit. When at last she went limp, moaning, Jane looked again at the birth canal. "Evie," she said, "I'm going to feel exactly where the babe is." She smiled reassuringly and the girl managed a tremulous half-smile in return. Jane put her hand up the birth canal. The men looked appalled as they held Evie down.

"There! All done." Jane smiled again. Well, it wasn't the worst news. The babe wasn't crossways. Its feet were well into the canal. Birth was possible, but it would be wrong end round. It was still unlikely she could save the child. The sac would break and the babe would doubtless suffocate. All she could hope was to slow the birth enough to save the mother.

"Mr. Campbell." Rising, she motioned to the older man. He followed her into the corner of the tiny room. He was a tall man and his head nearly touched the low ceiling. "She's going to bleed, Mr. Campbell. The baby is feet first."

His face went white. "Ye're sure?"

She nodded. "I can't turn it now. She pushed too hard, too early." She didn't blame. She didn't have to. Mr. Campbell set his jaw. He knew.

"Jamie'll waste wi' grief if she passes," his father fretted. "Can ye no' save her?" His eyes held simple pleading. He had gone from distrust to faith in the last minutes. Perhaps he was responding to the life that seemed to throb in Jane since her infection. It made her seem . . . attractive to others on some level they didn't even perceive. That's what her father told her. And that attraction generated either fear or faith. Mr. Campbell had decided on faith.

"I'm not sure," she said bluntly. "But there is a chance. Can you go for my father?"

"Aye," he said, his mouth a grim line. "I'll go."

"Tell him to bring his Impellor."

"Inpeller," he repeated. It was close enough. Her father would know. Now if Mr. Campbell could pry him out of his laboratory . . . once he was embroiled in an experiment he had a remarkable ability to ignore the needs of others. Mr. Campbell nodded once and pushed out under the low lintel of the door. He looked like a man who wouldn't be denied.

Behind her, Jamie said, "Another one's coming, miss!" and Evie wailed.

Edindburgh, March, 1821

"Is there someplace ye can go?" he asked the group of young girls who clustered in the dingy hall, whimpering. They'd just watched him throw the master of this brothel and several brutal customers out a third-story window and yell to the street that the place was closed permanently. They'd probably seen his red eyes as well.

The oldest turned to Callan, mastering her fear. "Thankee fer wot ye did. But we'll likely end in another set o' rooms doin' pretty much th' same."

Callan fished in the pocket of his coat. "Money creates possibilities." He handed her the fat purse. She looked up at him, unbelieving, then untied the leather string and pulled out a winking gold coin. The other girls actually gasped.

"Buy a house," he growled. "Buy a shop. Yer bodies are no' all ye ha' anymore."

"Why're ye doin this fer us?" the leader whispered, her eyes intent on his face.

Callan shrugged. He couldn't tell them that. He turned to go.

"Wait! Let us take care o' yer wounds."

"No need." That at least was true. "Mere scratches."

"Then let us repay you in our own way." The girl stepped

up and ran a hand up to the nape of his neck. "Ye smell . . . like cinnamon. And ye ha' lovely blue eyes." His eyes weren't blue, but no one ever noticed that. Her breasts pressed against his chest. Another girl took his hand. Callan's member hardened. It was always ready these days.

He shook his head and put the girl gently from him. "I'd be as bad as they are, then. Ye should save that for th' ones ye care for, in any case."

"Seems no one cares about us but ye." One girl smiled through her split lip.

"Ye'll be surprised, I think."

The oldest girl took a breath and held out her hand. "Alice. And ye are?"

He was a monster, unless the good doctor in Scotland could cure him. "Does no' matter." He pushed past her, but turned back. "Dinnae hate all men, just ta' spite these, Alice." He plunged down the creaking stairs. These were useless gestures, like bailing the sea with a tin cup. He did these things to keep his sanity. Was that sane?

Drumnadrochit, Scotland, March, 1821

Jane ran her forearm across her forehead to wipe away the sweat and sat back. Where was Campbell with her father and his equipment? The babe would come with the next contraction, no matter what she did. She wasn't sure it would be alive. The feet had probably broken the sac by now and it had suffocated. Evie lay, half-conscious, soaked with sweat.

"Almost over," she whispered to Jamie. "Next one."

"Will it . . . ? Will she . . . ?"

"I don't know."

"She's in God's hands now." But he looked frightened.

"Well." She smiled wryly. "Let's give God a little help tonight." Actually she hoped some God somewhere was taking an interest. Evie was fading because she was bleeding inside. The night had taken a toll on Jane as well. The unnatural hunger that plagued her itched at her veins. She could smell Evie's blood. Jane's body, with its new and dreadful illness, was shouting at her, distracting her from the work at hand.

Evie moaned. Jane readied herself. The girl was fully dilated. Her moan cycled up into a scream, not as powerful as it had been earlier but still gut-wrenching for Jamie. He talked softly to her, trying to soothe her. Jane saw the tiny feet appear, slick with blood. This was it. She took hold, as gently as she could but firmly, and pulled. Nothing. Evie shrieked even louder.

"Miss Blundell," Jamie cried, panicked.

It all happened quickly, just as it always did. One minute Jane was tugging, trying not to break tiny limbs, and the next minute the babe just slid into her lap, a wizened, bloody mess. He was followed by a gush of blood. The smell assaulted Jane. But she had to focus on the baby. He was so still, so tiny. Jane held him up and opened the tiny mouth with her finger, scraping out the slime and fluid. Still nothing. Evie had gone silent. Jane could feel Jamie holding his breath. Jane wasn't breathing either. She held the baby upside down by his feet and patted his back.

The tiny, sputtering cough was deafening in the silence.

The door burst open behind them just as Jamie's son started to wail.

"Get me the knife," Jane cried, as her father and Mr. Campbell strode into the room. Jamie jumped for the knife Jane had made him sterilize in the fire.

"Well, Jane!" her father exclaimed. "I'm surprised you managed that. This good man said it was early and breech and the local women were making her push."

Jane nodded. He was always surprised at any of her successes. This time even she was surprised. She took the knife from Jamie and cut the umbilical cord. "Now we have another problem," she said quietly, nodding to the barely conscious Evie. All three men stared at the blood soaking the quilt and the bed.

Jane's father looked grim. His groundbreaking research into transfusion had been inspired by all the women he'd seen die from hemorrhaging. As a well-known obstetrician of thirty years, Papa didn't like to fail. Jane knew this would be upsetting to him. Especially since he had not yet solved the issue of why some blood seemed to do a patient good when transfused, and some seemed only to make the patient sicker. There was only one person's blood which seemed to work universally. Her father rolled up his sleeve. So far only his blood was a sure thing. But Evie was hemorrhaging so badly the blood her father could give might not be enough. Then it was Evie's gamble whether blood from anyone else would heal her or kill her.

"Jane, you take care of Mr. Campbell's son." He turned to the men. "This woman will die without blood from someone else to replace the blood she is losing."

"What're ye goin' ta do?" Jamie asked, white-faced.

Jane wiped the baby boy and tied the umbilical knot. Her father was busy setting up his equipment: a telescoping stand, some rubber tubing, and a squeeze bulb. The huge needles glinted in the candlelight as he laid them on the bedside table. "I'm going to suck blood out of the vein in my arm and push it into the vein in your wife's arm with this device. I call it the 'Impellor.' "

The banished women peeked in at the cottage door. "Against God's will," one muttered.

"The Sassanach'll be struck dead for tryin' to cheat Him," another whispered.

Mr. Campbell looked uncertain, suddenly. It was the equipment, so metallic and rubbery; out of place in the tiny stone cottage on the edge of a lake where dwelt monsters.

"This can work," Jane said urgently as she cradled the crying infant against her breast. "I have seen it. There are no guarantees, but she has no chance without it."

Jamie stood, toppling his stool. He was trembling. "Get out o' here, ye two-faced bitches," he cried to the apparitions at the doorway. "I'm goin' ta try everathin' ta save my Evie, if it goes against God or no'!" He turned to Jane's father. "Doctor, do what ye can."

The women in the doorway fussed as they withdrew. "If that child lives, it'll belong to Satan himself," one muttered.

Jane patted the tiny back and mourned the burden of suspicion just created for this small bit of life that would follow him as long as he lived in the village.

"Jane, give the child to his father. I need you to place the needle in my arm. Boy, your blood is next after mine, and then yours, Mr. Campbell." Jane was exempt, of course. If her father's blood was certain to help Evie, only Jane's was certain to kill her or worse.

Jamie paled, but took the now-silent bundle awkwardly. "I'll lend my blood if it will save Evie," he said. There was only a slight quaver in his voice.

Jane wondered if she could bear the sight of blood right now. She picked up the needle.

Their work was over at the little cottage. The last two hours had been a torment for Jane. The smell of fresh blood when she was so hungry for it was excruciating. That something that was in her blood rose up and demanded, and it was all she could to do concentrate on her work. Her father had given Evie blood and cauterized the vessels that were broken. He decided to chance using Jamie's blood, since Evie had lost so much. Jane was forced to leave the cottage. She set the needle and retreated to the cold night air to steady her nerves and escape the smell of blood. Thank God Evie had experienced no reaction to Jamie's blood. Only she and her father knew how lucky that was. Jane was shaking now with need, unsure how she would live through the next hours without losing what sanity remained to her. When she returned to the room, Evie lay sleeping, her face once more blushing, while a pale Jamie cradled his child.

Her father rose. "I think she'll be fine, Mr. Campbell,

perhaps a little weak for the next week. Be sure to make her drink some good dark ale so she'll have milk for the child."

Mr. Campbell was a simple man, not used to expressing emotion. But his eyes were full as he said, "I'll live in yer debt and that of yer daughter till the end o' my days, sir, and Jamie too. I know right well Evie and the boy would no' ha' lived without ye."

"I'll stop back by tomorrow and check in on them," Jane said, knowing her father would not want to take time away from his experiments. He gathered up his equipment. Mr. Campbell helped them take it out to the gig.

"So this is what ye're doin' with th' blood?" Campbell asked, speculation in his voice. "Practicin' how ta pass it, one ta th' other?"

Her father nodded, though that was not quite true. Papa apparently didn't have as much trouble with lying as Jane did. Or maybe he was just distracted. He often didn't listen to those around him if they weren't saying something he cared to hear.

Campbell nodded brusquely and handed Jane into the gig. It was late and perhaps three miles up the Urquhart Valley to Muir Farm. Jane still smelled blood. The thick, rich scent seemed to follow her. She pressed a palm to her forehead. Her hunger ramped up almost into pain.

Campbell nodded to himself. "If ye can save lives like ye saved Evie's, then it's God's work ye do, nae matter what those biddies say. I'll get donations fer ye, Doctor. Evera man in th' village owes me a boon."

Jane leaned over and took his large, work-worn hand. "Thank you, Mr. Campbell." Some would call feeding a monster the devil's work. Perhaps it was. She shook the reins and the gig rolled out of the village. Mr. Campbell didn't know he was doing the devil's work, so perhaps he would escape blame in his Creator's eyes. But what if it took Campbell several days to convince his friends to donate? Could she last?

The smell of blood made her giddy with emptiness. She

could sense the pounding of her father's heart that sent his blood careering through his body. She breathed and pushed down the thing in her blood that was so joyous at the scent. The mountains on each side of Urquhart Valley loomed up around her. She could see each brown bracken fern sending out green shoots from its root, and shale poking through the vegetation to make you realize the spine of the world lurked just below the surface. It was a sere land, the Highlands, a land she could not love. Even the softer valley, with its grass for grazing and the pines around the house at Muir Farm, was not soft like England was. It was not a land you could call beautiful.

"You shouldn't have tried to deliver that baby." Her father's admonition broke into her thoughts. "You should have called me immediately. That was work for a doctor, not a girl who's watched some crones catch a few babies."

He didn't think her capable. It hurt, as always. The irritation in her blood wound its way up into anger. "I've birthed a hundred babies myself, Papa. And some of them were breech."

"You!" her father scoffed. "Where would you have gotten such experience? Don't lie to make yourself seem more important than you are, Jane. It doesn't become you."

That was too much. "I got that experience in the slums of Whitechapel and Bethnal Green, Papa, while you thought I was embroidering pillow covers and gossiping with silly girls." She should have said "other silly girls," since he obviously thought she was silly too.

Her father knitted his brows. "Those are not places for someone like you, Jane. That was dangerous, reckless behavior. Why would you do that?"

She sighed. He couldn't help the fact that he would always see her as a little girl. Or how disappointed he was at that. She was tired, all of a sudden. "Because they couldn't afford an obstetrician like you, Papa. Someone like me was all they had."

"You will *not* expose yourself to such riffraff again, Jane. I expressly forbid it!"

She hoped someday to get back to her work. But she wouldn't say that. She'd already snapped at him. And first she had to get back to daylight, and normal living. "No, Papa."

"Do you want it now?"

"What?"

"The blood I took from Campbell. It's in the canteen under the seat. Can't have you getting wild. It's been a fortnight."

Jane mastered herself, and managed a smile. "I shall wait and sip it from a china cup as I always do." She squeezed his arm. "Even a vampire can be civil."

"Don't take that mocking tone with me, young lady," he said severely.

She willed herself to silence, thinking about the horrible things she had discovered about herself ever since she had been infected. It wasn't only the blood. There were the . . . urges in her body that were almost uncontrollable, and the fact that sunlight burned her. She lived in dread of discovering some new effect.

Still, vampires could be civil. *At least I hope so,* she thought.

CHAPTER
Two

Urquhart Valley, Scotland, April 1821

Callan Kilkenny tied Faust to a tree in the copse behind the farmhouse. The smell of fir mingled with the rot of cones beneath his feet. There were lights on in the house, a large stone affair made of the local slate, and also in one of the outbuildings, the largest except for the barn. The horse snorted and blew, restless. Callan stroked his shoulder. That wasn't like Faust.

This was Muir Farm, all right. He hadn't even had to use compulsion on the woman outside the village. She was so frightened by her unconscious sense of his vibrations, she told him where the doctor and his daughter lived straightaway, just to get rid of him. Highlanders had no use for the English and they regarded Lowlanders like him as English once removed, so this woman had felt no compunction in passing the object of her fears along to an English visitor.

He'd been on the road for nearly three weeks, hunting down the author of an article on human vampirism. Dr. James Blundell thought there was a cure, and the article was meant to solicit help from fellow doctors and scientists to find it. It was the hope that the good doctor had discovered what he sought that had driven Callan on. If he could get rid of the thing in his blood, he might get back to who he'd been before *she* had made him a monster. And if he couldn't . . . if she had destroyed his soul as well as made him vampire . . . well, at least if he was human, suicide would be possible. He steeled himself and blocked out memories of that time in the desert, as he did countless times each day, sometimes with more success than others. The doctor and his daughter had been forced out of first London and then Edinburgh by horror at his experiments with blood and his theories that human monsters did exist. But Callan had found them, here outside the tiny village by the shores of Loch Ness. He only hoped Blundell had found the cure.

A woman's figure moved about in the room at the back of the house. The outbuilding had a tangle of what looked like poles and flasks silhouetted against the light. A laboratory, surely.

Wait. What was that faint smell? Cinnamon and ambergris. He stepped into the concealing branches of the fir tree, and peered around. There was another vampire here.

Callan spotted him moving around the barn to the outbuilding with the laboratory. He was a blacker splash of darkness on the night, a big man, carrying a heavy cudgel. Callan wasn't the only one who had read Blundell's article.

Still, he did not greet the newcomer. Callan's vibrations, that energy about him even humans could sense, were slow. That branded him as young, and made by infection with a vampire's blood, not born to his nature. And born vampires killed those who were made on sight, without asking for character references. Was this vampire born? The vibrations he felt were confusing. One moment he thought they were slow and new, the next they seemed old and powerful, operating just at the edge of his senses. He must be too far away.

The vampire made his way around the outbuilding to the door. He didn't appear to be making any effort to conceal his presence. Callan didn't care if he wasn't first in line for the cure, as long as there *was* a cure. He'd wait to see how the old doctor greeted a potential patient.

· The vampire kicked in the door to the laboratory, growling. Callan stiffened in shock. He felt the power in the air ramp up to impossible heights. The old man in the laboratory shouted something unintelligible.

"You have no right to meddle!" The vampire's voice boomed in a vaguely Eastern European accent. He began swinging his cudgel. The crash of breaking glass shattered the night.

Callan burst from the copse at a run. The creature was mad! He crossed the short meadow in long strides. He didn't know he could run that fast. The vampire was advancing on the old man. Callan pressed himself for more speed. The girl came out of the house from a back door at a run. He crunched across gravel spread in a path to the house and lunged through the door to the laboratory just as the vampire raised his cudgel to brain the old man.

Jane saw the big man tear across the yard toward the creamery, arms pumping. Was he going to join the attack on her father? She was strong these days, but she had never known how to fight. Was she a match for two men? She ran toward the laboratory. She'd soon find out.

But the tall man was ahead of her. He pulled the attacker's shoulder round. Jane stopped in the doorway, panting. Her father shrank back against his workbench, now covered with broken glass. The creature who had been attacking the laboratory and her father had black hair and black eyes. His features were craggy, his expression callous and jaded. The air was filled with the scent of cinnamon and something sweet she didn't recognize.

"What are ye doing, man?" the one who accosted the attacker cried, stepping back. "Dinnae ye know he's workin' on a cure?"

"And why would those born to the blood want a cure?" The man's voice reverberated with power. The air was electric with it. He was a vampire just as she was. A thrill of fear made her gasp. Did the man trying to stop him not know that?

"Sa ye dinnae ha' ta kill th' ones ye made," the newcomer said.

"Some don't find that killing onerous." A smile that turned Jane's stomach lurked in the attacker's eyes.

The newcomer tried again. "Even those born get tired of livin'. A cure would be a blessing."

"Fool!" The creature's eyes went hard. All Jane could see of the man who was trying to stop this attack was a broad back clad in a black caped cloak and black, curling hair. "You're new," the vampire said. What did he mean? "So I shall get the pleasure of killing one who was made while I destroy this cure." He took a step toward the newcomer and . . . and his eyes glowed red. There was no other word for it. They gleamed a clear, true red that deepened into burgundy. Jane had never seen anything so chilling. The air vibrated with power. The newcomer didn't seem to be frightened though. He stepped in to grapple with the creature. He was going to fight a vampire to protect her father? Didn't he know how strong they were? Behind them, her father approached the two.

"Get back, Papa!" she screamed.

The newcomer glanced behind to her, startled.

His eyes were red too.

Damn! The creature's power drenched Callan. He was no match for this one. The pistols in his pockets were useless. Was he strong enough to decapitate one so much older than he? But that was almost the only way to kill one of his kind. *Companion!* he called to the thing in his blood. His power ramped up and the room was veiled with red. He threw himself at his adversary. If he could get a grip . . .

Behind him, the girl screamed to her father. He glanced back. She stared at him in horror. Then she set her mouth decisively and ran for the house. The vampire beat at Callan with his cudgel, a fierce grin on his face. Callan stepped back, trying to draw the creature away from the old doctor. Broken glass crunched under his boots. Metal scaffolding hung at crazy angles everywhere. He shrugged off his cloak. The vampire had backed him up enough so the brute could draw a light sword. That was bad. Well, if bullets wouldn't kill the man, they might weaken him. Callan pulled out both pistols and got off one shot from each at point-blank range. The creature jerked with the impacts. Blood blossomed in twin flowers on his waistcoat. But he only growled and lunged forward.

Companion, Callan thought, *more power!* The vampire hefted his sword. Callan put up his forearms to protect his neck. They wouldn't be enough. The vampire cut down ruthlessly with his sword. Callan twisted. Pain shot through his shoulder. He lunged for a piece of dangling metal pipe and wrenched it down. He felt the sword slice into his back and side. Somehow he got the metal up to keep the sword away from his neck. Sparks flew as the blade hit metal.

With a roar of frustration, the vampire began hacking at Callan's body.

Behind him he heard the girl screaming again. The old man had fallen to his knees. A burner tipped and spilled its tiny flame onto the floor. The vampire was cutting at Callan's hips and thighs, trying to make him protect them and leave his neck exposed. He was losing blood fast now, though the pain had dimmed. What chance was there to kill the creature when he could hardly defend himself?

"Sword! Sword!" That was what the girl was yelling.

Of course the creature had a sword. The damn thing was making the floor slippery with Callan's blood. Wait! He chanced a glance backward. The girl clutched the hilt of a huge claymore. The weapon was longer than she was tall. The vampire's blade cut into his shoulder dangerously close to his neck. He threw himself backward, leaving himself vulnerable as he fell to his knees. She tossed the claymore to him. How could she toss such a heavy sword? He caught it. The hilt felt good and solid in his hand.

The vampire descended with a roar, knowing Callan's odds had just improved.

He swung upward between the vampire's legs and felt the blade cleave bone. The vampire shrieked in pain, giving Callan the moment he needed to scramble to his feet. He swung the weapon up. *Keep it moving,* he admonished himself, *for however long you can.* The vampire blocked his blow with the lighter sword. Callan tried to break the other's blade, but it was flexible. Behind the vampire, Callan saw the old man scuttle around the large table that held his equipment, trying to escape the flame that licked through the broken glass.

The vampire backed toward the flame. Callan swung the giant sword. Only the strongest humans could wield the claymore, but it would be nothing for Callan in normal circumstances. Now, however, he was wading in his own blood. The thing was getting heavy. He swung it again, and again the vampire parried the blow. The only sound was the clang of steel, the grunts of effort, and the crackle of flame. The end was coming soon, one way or another.

Then he had nothing to lose. Callan gritted his teeth and dropped his sword point. He put his head down and simply drove at his adversary. The vampire cut at Callan's back and buttocks as he stumbled backward. Callan pushed his head into the creature's midsection.

And then it happened. The vampire stumbled and fell backward. Callan straightened. He stomped on the man's wrist, locking his sword hand to the floor. Straddling him, Callan raised the claymore high above his left shoulder. He could see the vampire accept what would happen even as he struggled to free his wrist. His arms trembling, Callan brought the sword down.

He stepped back, chest heaving, and kicked away the severed head. Unless it was separated, the vampire might still heal. Life in his adversary drained away, protesting. The room seemed to echo with shock. Callan's gorge rose. The thing in his blood shuddered in revulsion too at the death in the air.

Coming to himself, Callan looked around. Flames were spreading through the laboratory. The creature would accomplish his goal even in death unless Callan moved quickly. He stripped off his coat.

Behind him, the old man yelled, "Careful, my dear!"

Callan turned. The girl had a bucket sloshing in each hand. She darted across the broken glass and the blood, purposely not looking at the vampire's corpse. "Stand aside!" She tossed first one bucket and then the other into the flames. Callan swung his coat at a flame racing along the floor. The girl whirled with her buckets and dashed out the door. Fire licked at the heavy curtains, made out of some kind of sacking. Callan pulled them down and smothered the fire at their base. He used the smoldering fabric on other patches of flame. The girl came running back with two more buckets of water and sloshed them across the floor. Her father looked on helplessly as Callan stomped on several last flickers.

The fire was out. Callan looked around. The laboratory was a shambles of broken glass and twisted metal. Oily concoctions in vibrant hues swirled in the sooty water on the floor. The place reeked of smoke and blood, alcohol and pungent herbs, all combining in noxious fumes that made him cough in protest. Had the vampire succeeded in destroying the cure after all?

He turned to the girl. Her own eyes were big and frightened. He noted somewhere at a distance from himself that she was quite beautiful in an English sort of way; eyes so dark blue they looked violet, light hair a thousand colors of blonde, fair, fine skin now pinkened with her exertion. But all that paled as the slow vibrations washed over him. Even through the other odors he could detect her distinctive personal version of cinnamon and ambergris. It had been her vibrations that had confused him in the copse. The girl was vampire.

Jane looked up at the creature who had just defended her father and his laboratory. He might be as bad as the one who had attacked them, but she had realized immediately that she and her father had few choices. Monster or not, they must cast their lot with him. He at least wanted the laboratory and her father saved. That's why she had run for a weapon. Now she wondered what she had done. The air was filled with the scent of cinnamon and that something else she couldn't quite describe. His eyes weren't red anymore. They were some light color between green and gray. But she couldn't forget the red glow that was absolutely not human or the incredible strength he had displayed. And . . . there was something more *alive* about him than any other man she had known, in spite of the fact that he was covered in his own blood.

Indeed, he stood in shirtsleeves and waistcoat soaked in blood, his wild, dark hair matted with it. His expression was desperate just now. Then she saw him recognize her for what she was. His eyes became watchful. He might see her as a rival for the cure. She swallowed. She was no match for him, even injured as he was. So she held out her hand.

"Jane Blundell," she said, "if you will permit so unorthodox an introduction. And this is my father, Dr. James Blundell."

"Well, I know why he's workin' on a cure," the stranger muttered. His accent was like the ones she'd heard in Edinburgh, not nearly so broad as the Highlanders in the village. His lips were very mobile and expressive. Words seemed to ripple out over white, even teeth. Definitely not like the villagers, and really quite . . . fascinating. His nose was straight. Under a two- or three-day growth of beard she thought his chin was cleft. There were streaks of gray, obviously premature, at his temples. His dark eyelashes were lush, almost like a girl's. And now that she was so close, she realized just how big he was, over six feet and powerfully built. The thrill between her legs was unwelcome. Lord, but she was untrustworthy these days! This creature might well kill her and here she was lusting after him. She could thank her infection for that.

He looked uncertainly at her hand before he extended his own. When he saw that it was smeared with blood he jerked it back. "Pleased," was all he said. Indeed he turned away, grabbed his cloak and threw it over the headless body. He swayed on his feet as he turned back to her.

Her father wandered through the debris to her side. He carried the slate on which he chalked his formulas. It was cracked.

"Is th' place wrecked past savin'?" The vampire's eyes burned with hope and fear.

Her father sighed, and pushed a broken beaker from the table with one finger. It crashed to the floor. "No. Replacing this glassware will stretch my store, though. And the delay for repair will set me back at a crucial time." He frowned.

"Ha' ye found it, then?" the stranger insisted.

Her father glanced up to him. "What? Oh, the cure. No. It has proved rather elusive. The trick, you see, is killing the parasite without killing the host as she becomes human again."

The stranger's look of hope dimmed. He set his jaw. "Well, then . . ." He moved to the table. His boots squelched with blood. He fingered a beaker with a green liquid still sloshing in it to cover the fact that he was bracing himself against the workbench just to stand upright.

Her father glanced at him with an avaricious gleam for knowledge in his eye. "So, can you heal even these wounds?" Her father knew he was vampire, of course. It was the red eyes and the cinnamon. Could her father feel the vibrations, as Jane did?

The stranger nodded. "Aye, I'll heal." He sounded disgusted with himself.

"Aren't you in pain?" her father pressed.

"Some," he acknowledged. He looked around as though bewildered. And then his eyes rolled and his legs collapsed under him.

Jane lunged forward and grabbed at his body before he could fall into the broken glass. "Perhaps more than some," she noted dryly. She shrugged the unconscious man's arm up over her shoulder. What should she do with him? Could they take in a creature who had red eyes?

"Well, get him into the house, my dear. He's too big for me." Her father was right. They must help him. He had saved their lives tonight, at great personal cost.

"All right, Papa." He accepted her strength and the acuity of her senses so much better than she did. Of course she had never told him of the increase in her sexual response. One didn't tell one's father about things like that, even if he was a scientist.

"We shall witness the healing process," her father said, rubbing his hands in anticipation. Perhaps her father's impulse had not been entirely humanitarian.

Jane wasn't so sure there would be any healing to witness, no matter what the stranger said. She knew she could heal cuts and abrasions almost instantaneously. But could anyone survive with so little blood as this man must have left, and with so much damage to internal organs? His shirt gaped where their attacker had slashed at him over and over again. Could the parasite in his bloodstream heal such damage? She put one arm around his waist and clasped the hand that draped over her shoulder. Warm blood soaked her dress. *I'll never get the stains out,* she thought, as she dragged him out the laboratory door and up toward the house.

It was a good thing her father couldn't know about that sexual response, for the feel of the stranger's hard body pressed so closely against hers, the cinnamon scent, the droop of his head on her breast, were making her throb. *How can you?* she scolded herself. *The man is more than half-dead!*

But apparently that didn't matter, for the wetness between her legs increased.

Her burden was awkward, but by no means too heavy for her. She probably could have picked him up like a baby had he not been so large her arms wouldn't encompass him.

Her father held the door to the kitchen open for her and lit a lamp. The room glowed golden. It was big, and would be awash with light during the day, except that Jane kept the windows carefully covered against the sun. The peat fire in the great hearth was banked around an iron caldron. A large dark wooden cabinet sat in one corner with dishes neatly stacked behind the leaded glass of the top portion. The fresh loaves of bread she'd baked today were laid out on the big central table designed for working or eating. Pots and pans hung from a metal rack suspended from the high ceiling and dried herbs dangled from hooks in the rafters. Their exotic scents hung under the yeasty smell of bread. Under the windows sat a large basin for washing up. Shelves under another window held her books. It was her favorite room at Muir Farm.

"Put him on the table," her father ordered.

Jane turned him and dragged him up on to the huge trestle table.

"Just you undress him while I get my medical bag. I wonder if I should consider sutures at all in such a case?" he muttered as he hurried away. "Will the process begin at once?"

He doesn't want to miss a minute of the show. Jane sighed. She was going to have to strip this man naked. The very thought excited her body. *Stop it!* She started with his neckcloth. It was tied simply but it was clean; at least it had been clean before the blood. He was deathly pale. As she worked, a cut on his forehead slowly closed. Papa would be sorry to have missed it.

She should take a tip from her father's attitude. This was science. They were impartial observers. She ought to be able to observe a naked man calmly. She had done so many times, as her father dissected cadavers and she had handed him instruments while she absorbed as much anatomy as she could. She tossed the cravat to the floor and grabbed the neck of his shirt. It ripped easily with her strength. She tore the sleeves then pulled the whole thing out from under him. Nasty sword wounds. Shoulders, sides, chest, arms, belly. Several were deep enough to show bone or intestine. Sweet Lord, but she had never seen a man cut up so! Under the gore he was certainly well made. His shoulders were broad, his chest well defined with muscle. Dark hair curled over his breastbone and then cradled his pectoral muscles in twin crescents. His nipples, pink and soft just now, made him look more vulnerable than did the wounds . . .

Never mind that! Boots. She couldn't get his breeches off unless she removed his boots. She grasped first one and then the other. They were finely made but worn, not dandyish with white tops but serviceable, though they were soaked with blood. She tossed them aside and pulled off his stockings. His head rolled to one side. His neck was strong. His throat still beat with a pulse, though where it got the blood for that she wasn't sure. There were small white, round scars just under his jaw. But this was no time to examine them. A vee of dark hair on his belly seemed to point downward, across the gaping wound there. The throbbing in her loins was becoming ridiculously insistent. Where had he come from? They might never know, if he were to die. Could he die? The vampire in the laboratory had died. And his passing had caused her a tremor of revulsion that seemed to come from the parasite in her veins. She worked the buttons on the stranger's breeches, just below the gaping wound in his belly. Her fingers touched the flesh below his navel and that light dusting of hair. The jolt she felt—could that be actual passing of energy between them? Never mind! She ripped the fabric, sending buttons flying. Breeches were pulled out from under him, tossed aside. His smalls were the work of a moment.

She sucked in a breath and stepped back. *Oh, my*.

Her father scurried in, his bag in one hand and the writing box in the other. "It was in my room of all places." He stopped. "Interesting. I shouldn't think he'd have enough blood for that."

Her father was reacting to the impressive erection the stranger was exhibiting. Heat spread to Jane's face from somewhere at her core. Luckily, her father was too preoccupied to notice. He lit another lamp as she went to get some hot water from the caldron sitting in the coals of the peat fire. The room brightened from a romantic glow to stark surgical light. Jane shook her head to clear it. Her only experience with a man had not prepared her for this stranger.

Her father peered closely at the stranger's body. "The wounds have stopped bleeding already," he muttered. "I'll wash him, Jane, as I examine him. Can you just take a note or two? I mustn't be distracted from my observations."

Thank the Lord God he hadn't asked her to wash the man. She didn't think she'd survive it. Somehow, Jane moved to the little box in which her father kept his writing equipment and took out his notebook, the stoppered inkstand, and a quill. She glanced at the watch she wore round her neck and noted the time. It was nearly ten.

"Just put down 'firm erection.' We'll see how long it lasts," her father murmured, adjusting his spectacles. He scrutinized the stranger's body. "Fourteen wounds. Bone clearly visible in most. Entrails revealed"—he peered closer—"and damaged in at least three wounds. Jane, can you lift him?" She put down her quill and lifted the stranger by one shoulder and hip. There was definitely some exchange of electrical current between them. Should she note it down? Her father peered at his subject's back and buttocks. "Make that twenty-nine wounds."

Over the next hour, they catalogued the healing. Her father tried sutures in the deep belly wound, but they popped out as the wound sealed itself and resolved into a pink line of shiny new flesh. Jane did not touch the vampire again. After about twenty minutes, his erection subsided. Jane noted the time, suppressing all other thoughts ruthlessly.

Her father was very excited, though not, she trusted, in the way Jane had been. "Well, I've never seen anything like it," he announced, after nearly two hours, hands on his hips.

Of course you haven't, Jane thought, equally struck. *Is this what I am?* If the parasite allowed one to heal injuries like this . . . A thrill of fear wound through her. Of course, the vampire in the laboratory had been killed tonight by decapitation. But this one was whole again. His flesh was pink. The remaining lines of new skin were disappearing fast. What did it mean?

Now that the blood had been washed away and the wounds were healing, she saw that he had many white scars, both round circles and jagged lines, over his body: circles at the inner crook of his elbows and at the joint of groin to thigh, as well as on both sides of his throat, jagged lines over both shoulders, both biceps, his pectorals, thighs. Why would he have scars if he could heal wounds to a point where his flesh was virgin? And what kind of scars were these? They were symmetrical on his body, as though they had been inflicted purposely.

The stranger's head rolled. A small moan escaped him. He was waking.

Jane had no desire to face those eyes, red or not, while the man was naked. She hurried upstairs for a blanket. By the time she returned her father was helping his patient to sit. She stopped just inside the door. He was still most definitely naked. The play of muscle under his broad back was spellbinding. How had she never noticed how strangely triangular men were, with their broad shoulders and narrow waists? His back was crisscrossed with fine white lines. More scars. It looked as though he had been whipped. A lot. What had happened to this man? He was still a little shaky. He ran his fingers through his hair. They came back sticky with blood.

"I dinnae want ta be a charge on ye," he murmured, staring at the blood on his hands as though he couldn't be certain the struggle in which he'd so recently engaged was real.

"Nonsense, man," her father harrumphed. "You are no burden. It is a pleasure to observe your unusual physical qualities, isn't it, Jane?"

The stranger turned his head over one shoulder, shocked to see her. Jane felt herself blush and saw with some interest that the stranger did the same. Her body responded with more than a blush, but at least there was no evidence of that. "Here," she said, holding out her blanket awkwardly. He snatched it from her and drew it across his lap, his expression clearly alarmed.

Her father patted his thigh. "Don't worry. Jane assists me often. She's seen male patients before, though perhaps not in quite so interesting a state as you were in."

That didn't reassure him. "Ye dinnae mean . . ." His voice was panicked.

"Actually," her father remarked as he scribbled a final notation, "erections are not uncommon in the recently deceased, but I've never encountered one in a badly wounded man."

The stranger looked as though he wanted to sink into the floor. Jane thought she might join him. He swallowed. Then he shot her a self-deprecating glance over his shoulder. "Sorry."

"No apologies necessary. My . . . my father forgot to thank you for saving our lives. We are in your debt. Uh . . . can I get you food or do you want to retire directly for some rest?"

He got up off the table, careful to pull the blanket about his waist. There was a noticeable bulge at his groin. Then he jerked his head up. "Faust!"

Jane and her father both looked blank.

"My horse," he explained. "I left him in th' copse." He glanced to the blanket. His eyes strayed to the pile of bloodied clothes on the floor. "I ha' some extra gear tied ta th' saddle."

"I'll go for him," Jane said. "I see well in the dark." She colored. Of course he knew that.

"Better let me," he said. "There could be others. Th' claymore?"

She raised her brows in question, not certain what he meant.

"Th' great sword, lass."

Is that what it was called? "In the laboratory."

He nodded, clutched the blanket about himself, and strode out, half-naked, into the night.

"Should . . . should we let him go in his condition, Papa?"

Her father raised his brows. "You may be able to stop him, but I certainly could not." He turned to her. "Perhaps you should just go with him, though."

Jane nodded. She swung her cape around her shoulders, picked up the stranger's boots in one hand and her skirts in the other. Her dress was sticky with blood and fast stiffening. She hurried into the night after a man who was still, for all the vulnerability he had shown tonight, a monster with unknown powers who drank blood and had red eyes. Could she have red eyes, too? Her father had never said anything about it. Still, she had something in common with this man. Jane had no idea how to feel about that except frightened, and excited. He excited her because he had the key to all the secrets she didn't know about herself. Only that.

CHAPTER
Three

Cold bit at Callan. April in the Highlands hadn't quite forgotten the chill of winter. The crescent moon was pregnant with a shadow belly where it hung low over the loch. The laboratory was dark, lit only by that sliver of moon and the glitter of countless stars. That didn't stop Callan, of course. His night vision was perfect. The door swung crazily on one hinge. Inside, butter churns and paddles were piled in a corner behind the shattered laboratory equipment. This must once have been the farm's creamery.

Why did the damned doctor have to have a daughter like that? He must protect the laboratory and the doctor until he could produce the cure. The last thing Callan wanted was a beautiful woman near him, distracting him, tempting his unruly body. He'd managed to refuse temptation for nearly two years even though he was a vampire, but Lord knew he was not to be trusted since his experience with . . . *her.* He hated what he had become. But that was why he was here. How long would it take Blundell to find the cure? Would Blundell be willing to let him have a dose? He'd treat his daughter first. That was his right. Callan only hoped the doctor could make enough formula to cure him too. If the ingredients were not too rare, perhaps there would be enough for any vampire who sought it. Making it widely available just might be a cause that could provide him purpose.

His life had been one long search for such a cause. Probably he just used causes to borrow an identity. He wanted now to get back to who he was before he'd been infected. But did he really know who that was? As the youngest son of an impoverished fourth son of an impoverished Irish earl, he came from a long line of failures. His father had brought his hopeful family to Scotland, believing he could earn a living with his pen and making Callan an instant outcast among his peers. Was he Irish or Scots? He'd had to renounce the Catholic Church to get a scholarship to the University of Edinburgh on the recommendation of the local Presbyterian cleric. It was the only way he could afford an education. Catholicism wasn't much loss. He wasn't a Protestant either, at least in his heart. So he'd carved out an identity as a charming Irish rogue by day, drinking more, wenching more, and sharper of wit than his fellow Scots students, while by night he'd labored over pamphlets supporting his latest doomed political cause. He just never quite believed in them either. Now what he believed was that there were monsters in this world. Maybe he would never be that charming rogue again. He couldn't imagine laughing that much, or trying that hard to be liked. He couldn't imagine casual relations with women either, not after what *she* had done to him. His only cause now was trying to avoid becoming a monster just like her. And to that end, he needed this cure, if the doctor could find it.

He heard the girl's footsteps behind him.

"If there are others, I can help."

He didn't look at her, but reached for the claymore, lying in the broken glass. Why did she have to follow him? Even now his body responded to her presence. "Not likely," he muttered and strode off toward the trees, still barefoot. Perhaps she would just let him go. Not the time for his vaunted luck to desert him. But it did, for he heard her scurrying after him. Maybe she didn't want to be alone. Better the monster you know . . . He headed to the left side of the copse, then worked his way quietly along the perimeter, trying to remember where he had left Faust. Damnation! All he could think about were those slow vibrations. They were her blood calling to his. He'd never find Faust at this rate. So he just stopped and listened. The girl stopped behind him. There—he heard movement. A grinding sound. He relaxed and let out a low whistle. A soft whicker sounded in return. He started toward the noise, the girl trailing in his wake.

Faust was all pricked ears and flaring nostrils, waiting where Callan had tied him to a sapling alder. Callan leaned the claymore against the bole of a large oak and ran one hand over the horse's hide. "Ye're well?" he asked the animal. Faust blew softly on his neck. When Callan had satisfied himself that Faust had not been harmed, he dropped his blanket to unfasten the valise tied to the back of the saddle.

He heard the girl swallow and went still. What was he, daft? The battle and the process of healing must have taken more out of him than he thought. He had two choices—grab for the blanket and look ridiculous or brazen it out and put the onus on her.

He turned his head just enough to see her and raised his brows in inquiry.

She whirled, turning her back to him. "Sorry."

Callan dressed as quickly as he could in his other breeches, stockings, shirt. Too bad he hadn't brought his boots. He threw the blanket over Faust against the chill.

As he turned to the girl, he saw that she was carrying his boots. He'd been wishing her away when she'd just been trying to help him. *Ignore her effect on ye. She does no' ha' ta know about it.* His touch on her shoulder made her jump.

"Oh!" she exclaimed, turning round. Her eyes ran over him. He felt a flush rising and brusquely exchanged the reins he held for his boots. She stroked the gelding's soft nose as she watched Callan pull on the boots. *Get hold a yerself, man!* he admonished. He hefted the claymore and took back the reins. She fell in step with him as he strode from the copse.

Everything about her was feminine, in spite of the fact that she wore a gray gown with a round collar that did nothing to flaunt her femininity. And at the moment she was far too close. He thought he had better control. He looked down at her blonde hair streaked in a dozen shades of gold and tied in a knot at her crown, with wisps at her temples and her nape. She was a good eight or ten inches shorter than he was and had a handsome figure, worse luck. In spite of his best intentions he couldn't be trusted around her. Even now his body betrayed him. Best he hope Blundell found the cure quickly, so he could get what he came for and get out.

Blundell hadn't agreed to share his formula with Callan though. He glanced at the girl. He could take it by force, but that could be ugly. The girl might stand in his way. He could kill if it suited his purposes. No one knew that better than he. He pushed down the wash of guilt that threatened to drown him. Best find out where she stood on the subject.

"Ye're new," he said without preamble.

It took her a moment to know what he meant. "Oh. Nearly five months."

"How?" He slowed, so that she could keep up with him better.

She took a breath and let it out. "My father had several vials of infected blood from a patient. Someone vandalized his laboratory. I was cut by a broken vial of the tainted blood."

She was lying. He stopped and turned. "Tell me the truth. Who made ye?"

She looked taken aback. "No . . . no one made me."

"Dinnae lie ta' me. Ye need vampire blood ta give ye immunity, else being infected with th' parasite kills ye. A vampire made ye with his blood."

"Oh," she said. "I see what you mean. In that case I suppose Ian Rufford made me. He was Papa's vampire patient.

It took Papa some time to realize that my only choice was to
acquire immunity or die and that I could get immunity from
Mr. Rufford's blood. Rather like a foal getting immunity
through its dam's first milk. Papa infected more blood with
the parasite from the remaining vial of Mr. Rufford's blood,
and fed that to me." Her eyes darkened, remembering. "I
shouldn't like to go through that again."

"Turnin' is painful," he agreed, keeping his voice neutral.
He envied this girl. If one had to be made vampire, better to
be made by a vial and nursed through the experience by
someone who cared for you, than be made as he had been.
She was a vampire once removed. How much did she even
know about her condition? He thought back. She hadn't
drawn her power tonight when the vampire attacked. Unless
she had been taught by her father's patient, she might know
very little. What was his name?

"Wait, I know this Rufford!" The pain came washing over
him. He mustn't let her see it. "He freed me from th' woman
who . . . who made me." What possessed him to tell her
that? She might know of Asharti from Rufford. He looked
away before she could see his devastation. The last thing he
wanted was her sympathy. She said nothing, just looked
thoughtful. *Damn me for a fool!* He'd be spilling his guts
and mewling like a babe in another minute, likely. He started
back to the house before he could reveal anything more. He
was tired, that was all.

"What is your name?" she asked, practically running to
keep up with him. "You never returned my introduction."

He sighed. Well, he was going to be here until Blundell
found the cure. He might as well tell the girl his name. It
wasn't much of himself he was giving. "Callan Kilkenny."

"Why, that's an Irish name, isn't it?" she asked with surprise.

"Aye," he muttered. Now would come the questions.
How is it that you have a Scots accent? Why didn't you
grow up in Ireland? Do you think of yourself as Irish or

Scots? To forestall her, he exerted himself in conversation more than was his wont these days. "I dinnae remember yer name, miss. I was a bit under th' weather when ye introduced yerself."

"I'm Jane Blundell." Her voice was strong and steady, her manner firm.

"Pleased." He wasn't of course. He glanced over to find her regarding him candidly with those great, dark blue eyes. It occurred to him that the only thing worse than having only power-mad evil to teach you about your new condition might be having no one to teach you at all. She must have courage to confront the horrifying effects of vampirism with no one to tell her how to go on. He felt sympathy rise in his breast, and pushed it down. It was not his job to play nursemaid to new vampires. He was only here for the cure. Once Blundell found it, if they didn't want to share it, he'd just take it. No matter who he hurt.

He must have loved the woman who made him very much, Jane thought as she hurried beside him back toward the house. She had never seen such pain in anyone's eyes. She felt small and petty for the lust that was circulating in her body even now. He had loved enough to transform him, and devastate him when it went wrong. Had the woman left him? Was she dead?

Lord, Jane, you simpleton! What use such speculation? He knows everything about your condition, and yet here you are wasting this opportunity. Well, that could be rectified.

He turned up the path to the barn. "I'll just take care of Faust."

He wouldn't get rid of her so easily. "I'll help you."

She pushed open the barn door. Inside she smelled animal hide and manure, the sweetness of summer captured in the hay, tanned leather and sweat, all the subtleties her new senses had revealed. A mouse darted into a hay crib and big animals shifted in the darkness, reacting to the scent of blood on his boots and her dress. He led Faust in past her. Too near! She could smell him; feel him moving inside his clothes. The throbbing became more insistent. *You are pathetic,* she told herself. *You don't even care about men. You certainly didn't feel lightning and thunder during that experiment two years ago.* But that was before she became vampire.

"The fourth stall is empty there on the right," she said, and followed them.

He lifted off the saddle and bridle, saying nothing. She moved behind him, watching him. He bent to pick up some straw, then cleared his throat as he worked the twin handfuls of straw over Faust's croup. He was uncomfortable. Perhaps he knew she wanted to ask him questions. She grabbed an armload of hay and let herself into the stall with horse and man to lay it in the manger. He had to move closer with the horse as the greedy creature stuffed his nose in the food.

She too cleared her throat. She had no idea where to begin. Perhaps with the events of this evening . . . "Why would a vampire want to destroy the cure? I would give anything to go back to the way I was."

He set those marvelous lips. "I expect those born to th' blood would no' want ta be cured." He thought a bit. "But that's no' true. Some would. They get heartsick or crazy and retreat ta' th' refuge of Mirso Monastery if th' Elders who control th' place let them in."

"What is Mirso Monastery? Who are the Elders? Why is it a refuge?" Her questions tumbled over themselves.

For a long moment she thought he wouldn't answer. At last he sighed. "Mirso Monastery is in th' Carpathian Mountains. Th' Elders who run it are verra old and powerful, I'm told."

She patted Faust absently. The horse paid no attention, being wholly absorbed in his oat hay. The grinding of his great back teeth filled the stall. "Why do vampires want to go there?"

"They ha' some secret chants that let ye go without blood

for a long time. And through meditation, ye can maybe get peace with yer Companion." He rubbed Faust briskly.

"Companion?" She pounced upon the word. He did know everything!

"It's what they call th' thing in our blood."

She paused, mulling that over. "That word seems so . . . comforting." It didn't seem right. "I certainly don't find it comforting."

"Nor do I," he said, glancing at her. His head dipped in deprecation. Was that a wry smile? It was so fleeting, so hesitant, she could hardly be sure. But she had seen a gleam in his eyes, had she not?

"Well, I hope I never have to go there," she said firmly. "It sounds dreadful."

"I hope sa, too," he returned, raising his brows. "Because th' likes of us are no' welcome. It's only for th' born."

Hmmm. "The man who attacked us said vampires who were made must be killed. Do they all think that?"

"Pretty much."

"So we belong neither to human nor vampire society." She took a breath. "Unfortunate."

"Aye." His voice was . . . wry? Rueful? Did he think her naïve?

"So you think the Elders sent someone to destroy Papa's laboratory so that there would be no other solace for their own kind and they could retain their power?"

"Somethin' like that." Again the fleeting expression that might have been a smile and the gleam in his eyes as he glanced at her.

"If they grow to hate their condition so much, why don't vampires just commit suicide?"

He gave her a startled look.

"I mean, I know it's against the laws of God, but . . ."

"Ye've never tried it, ha' ye?" he asked.

"No." She fought the urge to defend herself for not having tried suicide.

"Th' Companion loves life." His tone grew harsh. "Why d'ye think it heals its host and prevents aging? It rebuilds its host constantly because it dies when we do. I dinnae know if ye've noticed, but th' thing is pretty persuasive." Now he was mocking her!

She sucked in a breath. "I've noticed." She paused. "So we can't commit suicide?"

He heaved the saddle off the stall door. "It will no' even let ye try, once it's taken a firm hold of ye."

She turned away. He knew that because he'd tried it. She was willing to wager on it. But this had another consequence. "How . . . how long can it keep healing us?"

"Ye mean, are we immortal?" His bitter chuckle was jarring in the glow of the lanterns and the soft sounds of the animals in the barn. "Short of decapitation, I think sa. It can even regenerate limbs."

She turned back to him, pressing. "No disease?"

He shook his head.

"No scars, no marks of age?"

He glanced up at her and a muscle moved in his jaw. He knew she'd seen him naked and was asking about his scars. Would he tell her how he had come by them? "None but what we ha' before we're made. Th' born grow up and just stop aging. No marks at all, I'm told."

No he wouldn't tell her about the scars. Wait—immortality! "Oh, my God." Her gaze flicked about, unseeing, as the concept careened around in her head. What would you do, in the next minute, in the next year, in the next thousand years, if you knew you couldn't die?

"I ha' no' found much of God in it at all . . ." he remarked, pushing through the stall door.

She grabbed his arm. Even through the sleeve of his coat she felt the contact like a blow. "They'll be back, won't they?"

He looked down into her face. His gray-green eyes had an expression that said he was sorry he couldn't lie to her. "Aye, Miss Blundell. They will."

"Don't tell Papa," she said, trying to put command in her voice. "It will only make him more nervous about finding the cure." She should remove her hand from his arm. Sensation was charging right down to that point between her legs. She felt herself grow wet there.

"As . . . as ye wish. He's yer father." His voice shook.

She looked down to her hand on his arm as though it was a foreign object. If she didn't move it she was going to . . . she didn't know what. Burst, maybe. And him—did he feel it? Her eyes strayed lower. His breeches bulged. He did feel it!

She pulled her hand forcibly from his arm. They both let out their breath.

"Get . . . get on ta th' house, Miss Blundell. I'll bury yer unwelcome visitor."

She shook her head. "You've already done enough for us. My father shouldn't be exposed to this . . . this situation. But I'll . . ." She swallowed resolutely. "I'll do it."

"Nae. A gently bred girl doesn't bury headless corpses." She was about to protest when he added, "Besides, I'll be faster at it."

That was true. She couldn't admit she was relieved. "Are you certain you're up to it?"

He nodded.

"There's a spade in the corner. Come to the kitchen when you are done. The least I can do is manage some supper for you." She crunched away down the gravel path toward the house, feeling lucky to have escaped with her senses. What was she going to do with Mr. Kilkenny in the house? The prospect was frightening. And exciting.

CHAPTER
Four

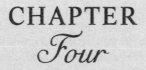

In spite of the crisp April night, Callan was sweating, his shirtsleeves rolled up. Blundell had better find this cure soon. If the vampires who wanted to destroy it didn't kill him, his response to Miss Blundell would. She had felt exactly what he had in that barn tonight. He could smell her woman's musk. Two vampires with the heightened sexual appetite given by their Companions in the same house was likely to be a torment for them both.

The grave behind the barn was nearly complete when he heard movement. He leaned on his spade as the old man toiled up the rise, carrying a lantern.

The doctor held the lantern high to peer at the corpse and its severed head. "It seems a shame to bury the creature before I have a chance to examine the body." Miss Blundell's concern that her father needed protection from grisly reality was apparently much mistaken. He'd called the vampire a creature. Did he feel that way about his daughter?

"It would no' do ta have th' servants find him."

"We don't have servants. They took fright over our need for blood."

Callan could believe that.

"But Jane does for us," Blundell continued. "It is really more convenient that way." He reached for the head.

"Dinnae touch it! Ye might infect yerself."

The doctor jerked back and sighed. "I suppose it is too dangerous to leave unburied."

Callan frowned. "Ye and yer daughter take care o' th' house and th' animals yourselves?"

"My research takes up all my time," the doctor said, pushing himself up. "Jane takes care of the whole. Very handy, Jane."

A gently bred girl who cooked and cleaned and took care of the horses and milked the cow? He'd seen a goat too, hadn't he? No help, no visitors. "Must be a hard life for her."

"Oh, Jane has her books and her journal, and she paints studies of the local flora. Very amateurish, of course. She's very content on her own." Blundell waved a hand dismissively.

Callan tossed the shovel aside. The grave was deep enough. He rolled the body into the hole with one boot. Now it was time to get a commitment from the doctor. "Are ye close ta findin' th' cure?"

"I . . . I wanted to talk to you about that, Mr. Kilkenny." Blundell cleared his throat. "Jane mentioned your name." He paused again as though unsure how to proceed. "I have encountered a problem in completing the cure I think you may be able to resolve."

"I'll stay on ta protect ye from others in return for yer word I can ha' some of th' potion after ye've treated yer daughter."

"I'd be grateful, of course." Blundell lowered the lantern as though to conceal his expression. Didn't he know Callan could see his agitation even in the dark? "But the problem is empirical testing. In order to make real progress, I must test my formulas on an infected host." Blundell rushed on. "Well, you must see that I can't test a concoction on Jane. Of course, if it *doesn't* kill the parasite, the parasite itself will heal any damage. But . . ."

The formula might kill both parasite and host. What did

Callan care? Hadn't he longed for death? Was there anything he would not risk for a cure? He picked up the head by its hair and tossed it into the grave. It landed with a thunk. "Ye can test yer formulas on me," he growled. It looked as if he'd be the first to receive the cure, if he lived.

"Excellent." The doctor beamed. "Just excellent. I'm sure I'll make much faster progress." His mission accomplished, he nodded briskly and raised his lantern to head down the hill. Callan shoveled a spade full of dirt into the hole. "Uh . . . Mr. Kilkenny?"

Callan straightened. Blundell had turned back.

"Don't tell Jane about our little arrangement, will you?"

So, if she knew, her father thought she would insist on sharing the risk. He couldn't blame a father for not wanting to poison his daughter. And he thought better of her because her father had to lie to her to achieve his goal. "I will no' tell yer daughter."

The doctor nodded, his jowls moving over his neckcloth, and hurried back to the house.

Jane had been preparing dinner when the vampire attacked, so she could provide a kidney pie and a brace of partridges, potatoes and early sorrel with butter sauce, to sustain Mr. Kilkenny. Though her father liked eating in the kitchen, she had moved the meal into the more formal dining room until she could clean up after their ministrations to Mr. Kilkenny. Her father had picked at the kidney pie and retired, exhausted. She had just finished laying a fresh place at the table when Mr. Kilkenny came into the kitchen, rolling down his sleeves over forearms corded with muscle. How she did like forearms! His were covered lightly with fine black hair. His shirt was open at the collar, revealing a pulse throbbing in the vulnerable notch of his neck.

"The dining room is just through there." She heaped a plate with food and took it in while he washed his hands. As he fell to his dinner, she fetched a bottle of claret.

"I dinnae expect wine," he protested.

"You'd prefer whisky?" she asked. Scots always liked their "wee dram."

"Ale is good enough for th' likes 'o me."

He didn't seem to think much of himself. She smiled. "But we've a cellar full of this French claret my father has had for twenty years. It ought to be drunk before it goes bad. Surely you can choke some down?"

He looked taken aback. Perhaps vampires were unused to mockery.

"We may live on a remote farm in the Highlands, Mr. Kilkenny," she continued with feigned severity, "but my father likes to command the elegances of life. And we aren't poor. No, no, no. A Harley Street doctor who attended the *ton* on their beds of pain? We can spare you a bottle or even enough to get thoroughly foxed if you like." She raised her brows.

"Sorry," he muttered, and shrugged with that tiny thinning of the mouth that might be a self-deprecating smile, so attenuated as to be almost unrecognizable. "I am no' used ta . . ." He trailed off. Had he been going to say "kindness"? She poured the ruby liquid. He was about to return his attention to his plate when he seemed to recollect himself. He stopped and gulped the wine. "It's verra good," he muttered.

Well, that seemed dragged from him! She fetched her own plate and sat across from him. "Papa says you've agreed to stay on in case any others come," she said, toying with her sorrel.

"Aye."

Would he volunteer nothing? He had been forthcoming in the barn. She had a thousand questions she wanted to ask him! "Are there . . . many of the . . . the born?"

"Enough."

How annoying! "You're not very talkative, are you?"

He stopped and sat back, chewing, and took another drink of wine. His gray-green gaze roved over her, a certain hunted look in his eyes, and beneath that a heat that felt only too familiar. She flushed. He saw it and looked away. "I talked once. A lot."

"You . . . you don't anymore?" She picked at her partridge breast.

"Nothin' worth sayin'."

"Ah." Had he resolved not to answer her questions? She noticed that his hand shook almost imperceptibly as he reached again for the glass. But of course he was exhausted. He'd engaged in a fight to the death, healed wounds that would have killed a human man a dozen times over, then cared for his horse and buried a vampire. She felt small and selfish. Indeed, as he sat back, he seemed to have used the last of his strength. He blinked and licked those marvelous lips, half-dazed.

"You should rest," she admonished. "I've put your things upstairs. First room at the left."

"I . . . I should sleep in th' barn . . ." He pushed back from the table and stood, wavering on his feet and looking around.

"Nonsense! When we have four perfectly fine bedrooms unoccupied?" How did he think he'd get up to the barn in this shape? She got up from the table and steeled herself. "This way," she said firmly and took his arm. The effect of feeling his biceps beneath the fine linen as they clenched against her touch produced an effect that hadn't diminished with repetition tonight. He looked down at her, a question in his eyes. He felt it too, she was sure of it. And then his eyes swam. She braced herself.

As he passed out, she let him fall gently to the floor and then got round and put her hands under his armpits to drag him up the stairs and into his room. She heaved him onto the bed and pulled off his boots for the second time tonight. She didn't feel up to undressing him. Not with the current that was running between her brain and her woman's parts. She lifted his stocking feet onto the bed, pulled a quilt from the chest and laid it over him. She grabbed his boots. They smelled of blood and the leather would soon stiffen. There was time to clean them yet tonight, along with the kitchen.

At the door, she paused. The light from a candle on the small hall table leaked through the half-open door, bathing his face in faint, golden light. His dark, thick lashes brushed his cheeks. His lips had relaxed into fulsome sensuality. She breathed in. Cinnamon, and something else, overlaid on a smell that she could only describe as intensely male. Sweat? Yes. But also a faint smell of . . . something primal.

It was all she could do to break the spell and close the door.

Having him in the house was going to be torture. But it would be worth it if she could get him to tell her about being a vampire. If her father failed and there was no cure, then she'd need all the information she could pry out of the laconic Mr. Kilkenny over the next days. She took the candle along to her own room. She just hoped she could survive the experience.

His eyes opened on darkness. He tried to get his breath. His body was bathed in sweat and tears ran down his temples. He had been dreaming of *her* again. He swallowed, trying to moisten his dry mouth. Could he not have resisted her? Was there not some way to go back in time and find a way to save even a small portion of his soul?

Marrakech, August 1819
Callan came to himself slowly, trying to remember what had happened. He blinked. He'd been captured trying to fight his way to the gates of the city. The invading army had red eyes. Had that been his imagination? Now he seemed to be lying on the floor of the Dey's audience room. Once it had been crowded with supplicants when he'd been here before as part of the Irish legation looking for support from Morocco in their quest for independence from England.

He pushed himself up on one elbow. His head spun until

he shook it and his vision cleared. Now the vast room was empty. The hangings on the walls could not make it comfortable. It was lit dimly, with smoking wall sconces around the perimeter and candles in tall holders standing around a carpeted dais at one end. He lay in front of the dais, naked. The marble was cool on his bare flanks. On the dais, draped on a kind of low, pillowed sofa lounged a woman, her head thrown back over the pillows to bare her graceful throat. She had a classic profile and perfect skin. Her kohl-lined eyes were closed, one arm flung up over her forehead. She was hardly dressed. A diaphanous red gown was slit to her waist and held there by an intricate golden girdle. He could clearly see her nipples and the dark triangle of hair below the girdle. It was rumored that the leader of the army that had captured Marrakech was a woman. Was this her? He could hardly credit it. But who else would occupy the Dey's palace?

She turned her head slowly. Her eyes opened. They glowed red like smoldering coals. Not human! Callan wanted to struggle, but he did not. The eyes examined him. She smiled. Fear trembled down his spine. "Your blue eyes saved you," she said, in Arabic. "My servants knew you would please me."

He didn't have blue eyes. They were gray-green. But no one ever looked closely enough to notice that. The woman had no bodyguard. Callan was a big man who had fought against her invading army. Yet she thought herself secure alone with him. He must get out of here!

But he made no move to escape.

"Kneel up," she said. Or maybe she had not said it at all. Her voice was inside his head. His skin crawled. He wouldn't kneel to her! But the impulse to obey gnawed at him. He clenched his muscles in resistance. She smiled and her eyes went redder still. He gasped and doubled over. Pain burst in his brain. But he couldn't look away. Slowly, jaw clenched, he got to his knees. She wanted his knees spread wider. His chest heaved with effort, but still, God help him, he spread them. His balls grew heavy and his cock swelled.

How could he get an erection now, full in her view? The scent of cinnamon filled his senses.

"You are well enough," she said, surveying him. "Es tu Anglais ou Français?"

He could not refuse to answer, but he hardly knew what to say. Scots by upbringing, Irish by birth. The last thing he would say was British. "Scots-Irish." Close enough.

She switched to English. "You have the Celt in you. You remind me of Robert Le Bois." Her eyes darkened to burgundy. Callan's loins pulsed. The audience room was hot. Sweat trickled down his back. Wasn't Le Bois the Frenchman who had taken Jerusalem in the First Crusade? Yet she talked as though she knew him personally. "He taught me that cruelty could be pleasurable by taking pleasure in his cruelty to me." She beckoned Callan with one long, gilt-painted nail. He crawled up to the dais and knelt beside her. He was fully erect now, his balls almost bursting. "I may be developing a taste for British men." Her voice was a seductive whisper in his ear. Her breath on his neck made his right side erupt in gooseflesh. He raised his chin, baring his throat, because she wanted that.

"The first taste," she whispered, "is always the sweetest." Her eyes went carmine. Her lips caressed his throat. Something sharp scraped there. Fear washed over him. Two sharp points of pain just under his jaw made him want to cry out in revulsion. She had bitten him! But he did not cry out. She held him by the nape of the neck as she sucked at the great artery in his throat. How could sucking his blood be sexual? Yet his cock throbbed in unison with the pull of her lips. He moaned, not sure whether it was in pleasure or in pain.

When she withdrew, blood smeared her mouth. She licked her lips, smiling over canines that were longer than human teeth could be. "I like blood salty with a man's sweat."

In his mind she bid him come to her. With revulsion in his heart he pulled himself up beside her and moved aside the diaphanous red fabric over her breast. Her nipple was tight

*in anticipation. He licked it softly as she let out a little moan.
That was what she wanted. She tasted of salt and smelled of
cinnamon. He moved to the other breast. She ran her fingers
through his hair. He sucked at the nipple. She wanted him to
suck harder and he did, rolling the tip between his lips. She
allowed his hands on her body, cupping the other breast,
moving over her belly and hip. Damp skin slid over damp
skin. She wanted his cock now. She spread her knees. He
parted the panels of her skirts and lay between her golden
thighs. She pulled his buttocks down with both hands and he
pressed into her as she lifted her hips to grind against him.
She controlled the pace of his thrusting, dictated the arch of
his back, the kisses he lavished on her neck and breasts. He
thought he would burst, but he didn't. His erection became
nearly painful. With horror he realized she could somehow
make him hard but keep him from coming, just as her will
could creep inside his mind. He thrust again and again, until
she moaned with her release. Her womb grasped at his cock
as it contracted. At any other time he would have been spurting in unison with his partner. But this was not a partnership,
and she did not allow that.*

*When she was done with him, it was she who rolled him to
the side. She was too strong for a woman. His mind fluttered
in disbelief at what had just happened. His cock still
throbbed with need against her thigh.*

*After a while, she raised herself against the pillows and
poured some wine. "You'll do nicely," she remarked. "A
good, strong cock, straight and thick, bigger than most." She
took his shaft in one hand, examining it as she sipped. "Your
sac is tight and high. It presents your stones well." She
glanced up at his face. "You look so horrified." She smiled
that smile again, secret with satisfaction. "Broad shoulders,
a tight belly, powerful thighs and buttocks. And blue eyes
into the bargain. Excellent. You're strong. I'll wager you last
a long time."*

She could make him do anything. *The realization went*

beyond horror into a spiritual numbness that might be despair. He couldn't afford despair. He shook himself mentally. He must escape, bide his time until her attention was not on him, and escape.

She opened her eyes. "You respond nicely as well." She tossed him a cloth that had been tied about a jug of wine and he wiped his mouth. "But there is the matter of punishment."

Had he not just abased himself beyond belief at her command?

"Ah, but you did not submit without an effort on my part. That is not acceptable."

His mouth was dry. If what she had just done to him was not punishment, what was?

Callan flung an arm over his forehead and turned his head, trying to suppress the sound in his throat. Slowly he got his breath. He wiped his face, ashamed of his tears, ashamed of far more than that. He wouldn't think about that time. He wouldn't let thoughts of Asharti into his life at the very moment he might have a chance to become human again. He was not like her. He was *not* . . . like . . . her . . .

That had not been the worst of it, of course. But he had escaped Asharti. He had hope of a cure for his condition.

His stomach turned. What a fool! He would never escape what he had done in the desert, for her, and in her name. The doctor might cure him. But he was afraid there was no cure for the damage he had done to his soul.

CHAPTER

The bed was hot. She was sweating as though it were July in Siena, where her father took her when she was twenty. But she was naked. The heat was inside as well as outside. She ran her hands through her hair and felt the dampness. And then she smelled it; cinnamon and something else she could not name, a sweet undertone, and underneath that, the smell of a man, sweating. He came out of the darkness and he was naked too, his muscles heavy even in quiescence, his hair curling round his shoulders. The gray-green of his eyes should have been cool, but it wasn't. She should have been modest or embarrassed, but she wasn't, God help her. She arched her back to lift her hips from the tangle of sheets, feeling her nipples peak on swollen breasts. Her eyes strayed to his loins. His member swelled and straightened. The throbbing at the place between her legs grew almost painful. She stretched out a hand, inviting, though adding his heat to hers might well cause spontaneous combustion. He touched her outstretched hand . . .

And his eyes went red.

Jane gasped and sat straight up in her bed. Her heart was pounding. She could hardly draw breath. Fear sat in the dim room, palpable. Her gaze darted from corner to corner. The heavy velvet curtains were drawn tightly across the windows.

Just her room. No eyes either—gray-green or red. The dream faded, leaving only the throbbing wet between her thighs.

Dear God! What is happening to me? Have I lost all control over my body, that I have such a reaction to a man in the house? One whom I've seen naked? And erect . . .

Just a dream. She swallowed and shook her head. It seemed to pound.

No, that wasn't her head. It was the sound of boot heels on a wooden floor. The events of the night before came rushing back. Mr. Kilkenny was moving about in his room only a few feet from where she lay in her thin night rail. She was trapped in the house by the daylight with a man who had been a red-eyed monster last night and who made her have dreams mixed equally of lust and fear. She hugged her body. *You are just like him,* she admonished herself, *and he knows more about your condition than you do.* She had not had the courage to ask him last night about the red eyes. Her father had never mentioned her having red eyes. Perhaps he daren't. A flicker of fear spiraled down her spine. Was she afraid of Mr. Kilkenny or of herself?

Nonsense! She must look at this as interviewing a subject. She would take the scientific approach. Practitioners of science were not afraid. She grabbed her journal from the night table. She had been up most of the night making notes about her observations. And she had kept them perfectly scientific. The only mention of the strange effect Mr. Kilkenny seemed to have upon her was . . . She flipped some pages . . . "The subject is a fine specimen of a male in his prime." She hadn't said male what. She couldn't decide between "man" and "vampire." Had his disease brought him beyond being human at all?

She needed information. She must gather the courage to ask for it. And if he was reluctant, she must pry it out of him.

She threw back her tangled, damp bedclothes and hopped out of bed. She pulled open her wardrobe. Hmmm. All her dresses were shades of gray and black, severe in style as befitted a serious student of scientific method, even if she was only a midwife and not a doctor. A tendril of regret wound through her thoughts. It didn't matter. After all, she had no desire to impress Mr. Kilkenny except with her professionalism. She chose a dress at random. She pulled on her half-corset and her skirt, then the sleeves and bodice. She had added some ingenious buttons that allowed her to dress herself. She brushed out her hair. It was thick enough, and shiny. If only it were guinea-gold instead of all those different, streaky colors. Well, he wouldn't be able to tell much about the color anyway with it all tied up in a knot. She twisted ruthlessly, pinned, and then pulled out some curls at the side. There.

Jane marched out of her room and down the hall. She gave herself no time to think but knocked on the door behind which the pacing had suddenly stopped. "Mr. Kilkenny?"

No sound.

"Mr. Kilkenny?" She put her hands on her hips. She knew very well he was awake. "I am not going away." There were two abrupt strides inside and the door jerked open.

Jane took a step back. He looked fierce. His hair was tousled. His three-day growth of beard was now four. His eyes were red rimmed and there were circles under his eyes. He wore only a shirt and breeches with the boots she'd cleaned and the shirt was open at the throat, revealing the dark hair of his chest.

"What d'ye want?" he growled.

Well! "To . . . to ask how you did!" she sputtered. "Though I see my solicitude was quite misplaced!" She made a half-turn to stalk down the stairs, not sure whether she was more offended or frightened.

Before she could go, she heard him mutter, "Get hold o' yerself, man," under his breath.

She frowned and turned. He had dipped his head and now ran one hand through his dark curls, his other palm braced on the edge of the open door. And . . . and now that she looked more closely, he was breathing hard. A sheen of sweat slicked his neck and chest. The scars she'd seen last night stood out whitely. "What's wrong?" she asked.

He straightened. "Nothin'. I . . . I need ta go out for a bit is all." He reached for his coat.

"It's still light."

He chewed his lip. "An hour. I'll go in an hour." He looked around as if wondering what he could possibly do with himself for an hour. His hands definitely shook. He looked down at them and clasped them forcibly together.

Everything became clear.

"You need blood, don't you?"

He looked up, startled. She raised her brows. He must know she of any would understand. But she hesitated to think what he might be willing to do to get it.

His eyes said he realized she knew at least some of his secrets. He shrugged as though it didn't matter to him. "Last night seems ta ha' drained me."

"Well, I should think so." But she must make one thing clear. "You can't take your blood in the village." She imagined panic over stories of a strange man-beast lapping at knife wounds.

He nodded. "I'll find a shepherd's cot."

"No," she protested. "You can't take it forcibly from anyone!" But she couldn't stop him. She changed her approach. "And you needn't. I have several bottles cooling in the well. Only wait until the sun sets and I'll get you some."

His eyes narrowed. "Bottles o' . . . blood?"

She nodded.

"How do they get there?"

"Well . . ." She cast about for an answer. "I lower them in the bucket."

"Nay, lass," he said impatiently. "How does th' *blood* get in ta th' bottles?"

"Oh, sorry." He wanted to know about her father's invention. "Papa connects a tube to a needle. We insert the needle just here." She held out her arm and pointed to the vein in the crook of her elbow. "You make a fist and squeeze and the blood flows out. He then uses a squeeze-bulb to push it into the arm of a patient or into a . . . a bottle. He calls his device an Impellor."

"People . . . *give* th' blood without compulsion?"

What did he mean, "compulsion"? Overpowering them with her strength? She shrugged. "They didn't exactly line up for the privilege at first. That's when we lost the servants. But Papa and I helped at a difficult birth, and . . . and the lucky grandfather helped us get donors. Of course we pay for the blood. They think it's for Papa's experiments. Which it is, in a way," she added, lifting her chin. She and her father hadn't really lied to the villagers.

"D'ye . . . d'ye have enough ta share?"

"They give more than I need. One can hardly stop them. Papa doesn't like to be interrupted, so I ask them to come up in the evening and take the donations myself."

He looked at her strangely. She wasn't sure why.

"Come downstairs," she said. "I can heat water for a bath if you like."

He rubbed his beard convulsively. "A bath is good. I can smell th' blood on me."

That would be hard if he was hungry. "The hour will be up before you know it."

As he walked down the stairs behind her she suddenly realized the next hour might be difficult for her too. He would be bathing in the little room off the kitchen with a solid wood door between them. But just the thought of his naked body with rivulets of water sluicing off the slick soap . . . . Oh, dear.

Callan folded his clothes and set them in a neat pile on the stool. The room was warm because it backed up to the kitchen hearth. The hunger itching in his veins was painful. His Companion demanded sustenance. *Soon,* he promised it.

Watching the blood beat in the girl's throat as she poured the huge pot of boiling water into the bath had been torture. He stepped into the hot water and eased himself down, feeling some of the tension go out of his body. He could last. At least his need for blood took his mind off the other effect she had on him. He slid down to duck his head and came up streaming. He lathered his hands. The soap smelled like lavender, and more subtly, her, where she had held it. Her own particular brand of cinnamon and ambergris was delicate, seductive. He rubbed the soap over his body briskly, scrubbing at the remains of dried blood. He lathered his hair as well, ducked several times to rinse it. He put off washing his genitals because it always reminded him . . . *Nonsense, laddie. A man has ta wash.* He slid his right hand under his balls and washed his cock briskly with the other. At least with hunger running in his veins, he wouldn't rise. But he did. His cock swelled instantly. Lord, but he was a low creature. He wished he could give up all sexual response. He would have been glad to be a eunuch since *she* had finished with him.

"Nay, lad," he breathed, fighting back the memory, "Think o' th' blood. Th' girl's got blood and she's willin' ta share with ye." But he seemed to think more about the girl than the blood and his erection wasn't easing at all.

He stood and grabbed for the towel she'd left. He rubbed himself down as though he could rub away the evil. That's what he'd been attempting to do all this last year. He'd taken the advice of a man sent to kill him who told him to find meaning in righting small wrongs. Ever since, he'd been trying to keep from turning into the creature he knew he had it inside him to be. In each new town on the way up from the south of England, he'd locate a bully by talking to the town gossip. Then he'd break the bully's hold on the prostitutes or working men in his thrall by main force and fear. He showed the tyrant that the problem with being a bully is that there is always someone worse than you are. In his case, immeasurably worse.

And he sealed the command to cease and desist with a good dose of compulsion. It was useless, of course. There would always be another bully. The world was a dreadful place. And it hadn't given his life meaning. Maybe it had prevented him from turning into Asharti. He wasn't even sure of that.

Keep yer attention on today, he told himself. He had only two shirts now. He'd have to find some clothes if he was to stay here for any length of time. He couldn't have the girl washing his shirts every other night. Even now he could hear her moving about in the kitchen. She shouldn't have to take care of this place all by herself, let alone him into the bargain. He toweled his hair, then stropped his razor, trying to focus on the snap of the leather.

She was a strange girl. How she had mocked him last night over refusing the wine. The laughter was plain in her eyes and the wry twist of her mouth. How could she laugh, infected as she was?

He lathered his beard in front of the small mirror. His hand trembled, but any cuts he made would heal. He shaved without meeting the eyes in the mirror. He didn't look into them anymore. He wouldn't think why. He'd think about the coming blood.

When he came out, the girl looked up at him from where she knelt at the hearth for a startled moment and then flushed. That flush sent blood racing about his body, too, but not to his face. She was shaking almost as badly as he was. Maybe she hadn't had blood in a while, either.

Outside the sun sank below the horizon. He always knew where the sun was.

She must have felt it too. "All right, sir. Let's get you what you need." He followed her out into the soft light of the gloaming. She struck out across the yard to a stone circle fitted with a windlass. Callan sprang to the handle and began turning. There was definitely a weight at the end. She peered into the dim echoing well. As the streaming bucket came up she reached for a carmine-colored bottle stoppered with a fat cork, one of several, and turned back to the house.

"Let the bucket down slowly," she called back. "We wouldn't want to break a bottle."

He wanted to let the bucket fall and dash after her, grab the bottle, pull the cork, and upend it over his mouth. But she was right. Such a supply of blood was a treasure. Somehow he unwound the windlass handle slowly, heard the plop of the bucket, and went after her at a run.

"Just give it to me," he demanded, trotting beside her.

She frowned at him. "It does no good to give in to the bestial nature of our affliction, sir," she said with asperity. "Have patience a moment more."

Didn't she know that the hunger was clawing at his veins this minute? But he couldn't just grab the bottle. She was being generous to give him any blood at all and Lord knew how he would have lasted while he searched the hills for shepherds. He forced himself to a walk beside her. When they reached the kitchen, she gestured toward a chair and got out a silver salver, two delicate china cups, and a silver teapot. Into the pot she poured the blood. Its rich scent filled the kitchen. He wanted to moan. His Companion surged in his veins, demanding repayment for the energy it had expended last night. She brought the tray to the table and sat. He clasped his hands in his lap. He could hardly swallow his mouth was so dry. She poured out one cup and passed it to him. It rattled against its saucer in his trembling hand. He set it down and watched it, stomach heaving with his need. Somehow he waited for her to pour out her own cup and lift it to her lips. He reached for the cup. He mustn't crush the delicate handle. She was saying something about the set belonging to her mother.

He raised the shaking cup to his lips. Ahhh! Sweet viscous liquid, copper-tinged! It slid down his throat. The well water had kept it cold, which made it even thicker than normal. He had never tasted blood so good. He closed his eyes, and gulped the whole.

His Companion shuddered in his veins in ecstasy. The painful itch receded. He sucked in a breath and felt the life within him rejoice. When he opened his eyes, the girl was just patting a napkin to her mouth. Her cup was not drained as his was. She had only sipped.

"More?" she asked.

He nodded. She poured another cup out. This time he managed to take a gulp and set the cup back down. "So this is how ye take yer blood? Someone gives it ta ye with a needle and ye drink it from a china cup?"

She nodded and lifted her chin. "Better than stabbing someone and holding them down to lick the wound. We must preserve what humanity we have, sir."

"I'll give ye that," he said ruefully. "But . . ." It struck him again just how much she might not know. He examined her face, in some ways so innocent, in some ways so strong. Was it the look in her eye or the set of her jaw that made it so? Both and neither. And which said innocence, which strength? He had taken pity on her at the barn last night, and told her what he could of her vampire kind. But this . . . "If ye dinnae ha' a needle or a knife, what would ye do?"

She flushed. Her fair complexion flushed easily. She pursed her lips. She obviously hated that fact. "Well." She cleared her throat. "I suppose . . ." She trailed off.

"Ye dinnae know, do ye?"

She considered brazening it through. He saw it in her eyes. She didn't like to admit she didn't know something, but lies didn't come easily to her. And then she looked away. She took her teeth between her lips. When she looked back up at him her eyes were brimming with tears. "No. No, I don't. I was hoping you could tell me about my disease."

"Disease, now, is that what ye think it is?" Well, that was convenient. You couldn't be guilty if you could lay the whole fault on a sickness.

"And why not?" she challenged, lifting her chin. "The condition starts with an infection of the blood by a parasite. It changes its victims' physiological state. Any doctor worth his salt would call that a disease. There is nothing supernatural about it, I assure you. Our condition apparently gives us much in common with a species of South American bats."

He was about to protest, but what would he tell her, that she was not a victim of a disease but a monster who inhabited children's nightmares? South American bats might drink blood, but they didn't live forever, or have the ability to compel men's minds or move about in space unseen. They weren't ten times as strong as others of their kind. And their condition was not due to a parasite in their bloodstream that fused with their souls. It would do no good to torture her with facts. "Verra well. It's a disease." He drank his cup of blood. "Are ye goin' ta finish that?"

"I . . . I had some day before yesterday." She pushed it toward him and after a slight hesitation he took it. He had been seriously depleted. He upended the cup. No use denying what he was and what he needed, as she did. Their Companions made them more than human and less. China cups couldn't change that. Still, as he put the cup down, he sucked his lips to make sure they were not stained with blood, though he drew the line at using the napkin.

She loaded the tray with the empty cups and took them to the sideboard. With a corner of her apron, she dabbed at her eyes. Then she set her shoulders and turned back to him. "So, will you tell me about my . . . condition? What would I do if I didn't have a needle or a knife?"

He took a breath. And he couldn't do it. No matter how much she wanted to know. He wouldn't be able to bear her revulsion and he didn't want the guilt of spoiling her innocence. "Nae, I'll not tell ye, Miss Blundell." He put up a hand against her protest. "Ye've nae need. Ye drink yer blood from a china cup and yer father will find a cure for ye, and that's th' end of it." He stood, as a defense against the protest he could see rising to her tongue. "I'll take care of th' animals and th' outbuildings while I'm here." Before she could say more, he turned and escaped out the back door.

Well! What an arrogant creature. And he stalked out without another word and left her standing there with her apron wet with tears. Tears. She had shed *tears* in front of the horrible man. She sank to the chair. How humiliating. It was all because she was set on edge by this dreadful reaction she had to his presence. When he had come out of the bath, after she had been imagining him washing himself all over, he was shaven and pink cheeked, smelling of lavender soap with that damp, dark hair curling almost to his shoulders and that surprising cleft in his chin revealed. She realized just how attractive he was. Well, it had been all she could do to tend to his need for blood. But she had. She'd given him blood and all she asked in return was information, which he refused outright to give her. Actually, she had very nearly begged.

Oh, dear. How had it come to that? And with a maddening man like Kilkenny!

She paused, her whirling thoughts clunking into place and slowing. The information must be very dreadful if he couldn't bring himself to tell her.

She took a breath. Well, she wouldn't think about that. Very likely it wasn't terrible at all. He just wanted to hold over her head that he knew things she didn't know. And very likely he was right. Papa would find a cure at any minute.

But she needed to know about the disease of vampirism in the spirit of scientific inquiry anyway, whether Papa found a cure or not. Why, if one knew all about the disease, perhaps one could help others mitigate their symptoms, even if they didn't want to be entirely cured. Or, if finding the cure took a while. Which it might, at the rate her father was going.

She'd have to find a way to make Mr. Kilkenny tell her. And until she could, she would study the one phenomenon she had observed in herself. There was no question that her sexual needs had somehow changed when she was infected. Look at her deplorable reaction to Mr. Kilkenny. And she suspected strongly that his sexuality was also intensified. She had detected an erection on several occasions besides the obvious one, including just after he had come out of the bath. She felt herself blushing in memory of his naked body, smeared with blood, gashes everywhere, but still so throbbingly erect. She . . . even now . . .

Stop it, she commanded. *You'll never get anywhere like this.*

What she needed was a baseline of her sexual reactions prior to infection. And she had just that. She went to the sideboard and pulled her journal from the drawer where she always kept it. She'd just review the section about her experiment with Tom Blandings.

Relations between men and women had always been a mystery to her. At twenty-four she had been a virgin and likely to stay so. No man vaguely marriageable wanted a girl addicted to reading books on anatomy and determined to be a midwife, or even one with ideas of her own, for that matter. Jane found them as boring as they found her. She had quite resolved to be permanently on the shelf. She flipped through the pages of her journal.

And yet, she had felt she was missing something in life. Her friend Miss Fern Sithington, who had lived in tropical climes with her father, thought that physical relations between the sexes were a transforming experience. Jane made a survey of her patients. Some agreed with Miss Sithington. Others talked of the sexual act as something to be endured. Jane thought solving that mystery might make her better able to advise her patients. She could not share the experience of having and raising children, since no one would marry her. She sighed and pushed down that familiar pain. She couldn't remedy that. But she could share her patients' experience of carnal relations. How could a good midwife be a virgin?

She had resolved to conduct an experiment. Even then she had been a little frightened of the consequences. Not of the act itself, of course. She had read her anatomy books and she understood the organs and their physical responses. But if the act *was* transforming, that meant one lost control of the situation and oneself, and loss of control was always frightening to her.

However, a scientist could not let fear stand in the way. And she had not let her virginity stand in the way of her chosen path, either. So she constructed the experiment . . .

Ah, yes, here it was . . .

My preparations are now complete. I have reviewed my father's notes on the anatomy of reproductive organs and the copy of the Kama Sutra I borrowed from Miss Sithington. How lucky that Miss Sithington lived in India! I have interviewed Meg Carruthers, a seasoned prostitute, who, for a small fee, allowed me to watch her at her trade (see notes, page 56).

She skipped ahead, through the descriptions of possible candidates for a partner. She must have chosen Tom Blandings for a reason . . .

Tom Blandings: third son of Sir Sheffield Blandings. Has been on the town for three years. Presumably has excellent level of experience with women by now. A sportsman, by his own account he has touched Mr. Jackson in the ring and rides admirably with the Quorn when in the country. Physique therefore no doubt in excellent condition.

Was that all? And were those the right qualifications? She suddenly wasn't sure. True, he was experienced and physically fit. How else could he have performed so quickly and efficiently? And he had been almost as adept at disrobing her as her dresser, Molly, so he was certainly experienced with women. He'd been a perfect gentleman about it, agreeing that since she was a dreadful bluestocking and unlikely therefore ever to marry, this was an excellent way to acquire the same experience as her patients.

When approached, he agreed to the scheme. However, since he is of higher social standing than I am, he required a statement of my purpose and a release from any matrimonial aspirations I might have. He prepared a release, and I signed it.

She had coupled with him three times, and all three times were essentially the same, barring the loss of her virginity the first time, which had been a little more painful. All three times were uncomfortable. She would describe the experience as dry or rasping, at least until Mr. Blandings ejaculated, but mercifully short. She had found nothing transporting about it. It was an act that reduced both partners to their least transcendent. Perhaps her hip movements were incorrectly executed. But all in all it was rather . . . disappointing. Afterward she'd felt nothing but the need for a bath. A voice intruded on her thoughts. *More disappointing or relieving? You never really wanted to become someone different, or lose your sensible nature.*

The question was—could one consider her experience with Mr. Blandings as a baseline of sexual response before her infection? The only way to know for certain would be to repeat her experiment with Mr. Blandings again now, and she couldn't imagine doing that even if it were possible. She took up her pen and her inkwell and sat down at the table. Dipping her pen, she paused for a moment, thinking how to describe her predicament.

April 24, 1822
  I shall start with what I know, and provide an accurate description of my symptoms. Since my infection, I have had increased interest in males of sexually active ages. I experienced

*an urge to touch the arm of the driver of the post chaise we
hired from Edinburgh. I also had several vague dreams about
men of my acquaintance that left me dissatisfied upon waking.
But these are hardly conclusive evidence of a change.*

    *However, in the last day I have experienced something
more nearly similar to my experiment with Mr. Blandings; to
whit, my response to the sexual stimulus of seeing a naked
and aroused male. This response was markedly different than
my reaction four years ago. My reaction to Mr. Kilkenny
could only be described as much . . .*

How should I say it?

*"wetter" than that to Mr. Blandings. I have found myself on
several occasions wet between the legs with a viscous liquid
which has issued from my womb area. (Indeed I feel this even
now!) Secondary symptoms include a tendency to blush, a
tightening of the nipples on my breasts, and an aching in my
loins which can approach pain.*

    *But could these symptoms be the result of the physical
differences between the two subjects? Mr. Blandings had
rather narrow shoulders, a flat chest, and one would say, a
stringy habit of muscle. He had little or no hair on his body,
except about his genitals. Mr. Kilkenny is older, probably in
his mid-thirties. The difference in Mr. Kilkenny's body might
be attributed only to the fact that he is a fully mature specimen. He seems much—well, bulkier. His musculature is pronounced over chest, shoulders, upper arms, and thighs, in
fact even his buttocks. He is constructed more broadly
through the shoulders and chest, though his hips do seem as
narrow as Mr. Blandings'. Mr. Kilkenny has some hair over
his chest and down his abdomen, a little on his calves and
lower arms. One would suppose that this would make him
seem coarse, but it does not. Mr. Kilkenny is also endowed
with a larger penis and testicles both resting and aroused.*

His expression may also have a role in my attraction to him. It is closed, as over a great pain or sadness which keeps him from being open to the world. And yet I have seen a flicker of humor in his eyes. He must once have laughed easily. I find that courageous, and this courage is attractive to me.

There is, however, one additional variable. Mr. Kilkenny is a vampire, as I am. Could his condition itself have an effect on me? There is something about him that sings with life. Could this energy exert a sexual influence over me? Does it connect to the surge of life I feel in my own veins, or would his energy affect any woman in this way? And what of his unique scent? Could this be related to the musk emitted by some species of animal when desirous of mating?

These are questions I cannot answer. Therefore I feel any comparison of my sexual response pre- and postinfection is doomed by too small a sample of partners, and the number of variables that have been introduced. Since I cannot reach a satisfactory conclusion at this time, more observations are necessary, though I am sure to find the continued effort to evaluate my response stressful in the extreme.

Jane blotted her quill and sighed. The only person who might know for certain what was happening to her was the subject of her observations himself, and he would never hear a question from her lips on *this* subject. She was on dangerous ground, though. If she could not keep herself in check . . . well, who knew what might happen? She might end like those patients of her father's who couldn't help but rub themselves raw if they couldn't find a man to do the deed for them. If she had felt little but the need for a bath after her experiment with Mr. Blandings, now feelings seemed to be washing over her like a tide, unwanted, inconvenient, and possibly even dangerous. She had been reduced to tears in front of Mr. Kilkenny tonight. Dreadful!

She puffed out a sigh. Better get to work. Her father would be in soon and need dinner. Maybe Mr. Kilkenny was right—she didn't want to know any more about this frightening condition than she must to know to live, just until her father found a cure.

And let it be soon.

CHAPTER
Six

Callan set the last nail in the wooden frame he was constructing to hang Dr. Blundell's equipment. A single strike of the hammer sent it home. He had to be careful not to crush the post itself and splinter it. It was near dawn. Blundell had made good progress in reconstructing the laboratory during the day. His vials and small burners had been set up on the long table again but he'd taken no pains to remove any of the debris from last night. So after Callan had taken care of the animals and cleaned all the stalls, he'd had swept up all the broken glass and buried it in a grave of sorts next to the one he had dug last night for the vampire. He'd torn down the half-burned draperies and nailed up blankets Jane Blundell had bought in the village. She'd left them just inside the door and practically run back to the house. Just as well. He didn't want her or the feelings she raised anywhere near him. He had scrubbed the blood from the wood floor as best he could. Good thing he'd grown up poor in a big family with only one sister and a sickly mother, he thought grimly. He knew how to clean and scrub floors.

He jumped down from the table where he'd been constructing the rack. How distant all that seemed. Even his mother would disown him now. But she was twenty-five years dead, and his father ten. Best he get down to the house before the sun rose. Yet he was strangely reluctant to go. She would be there, no doubt, just ready to go up to bed.

Finally, when the sun was moments from rising, he dashed down to the house to find the kitchen mercifully empty. He shut the door with a sigh of relief. She'd left the windows covered against the coming sun and bacon was laid out on the table with some fresh eggs. He was starving. He went about cooking his breakfast. A tankard of ale had been thoughtfully left next to the loaf. That meant she had touched it. He slid his palm around the cool metal of the handle, imagining he could feel the lingering presence of her palm. *Ye'd better start takin' things inta yer own hands, lad,* he thought bitterly, *before ye burst inta flames and take her with ye.* After he cleaned the stable tonight, he'd go out behind the barn and release some of that tension.

When he had a plate heaped with bacon, eggs, and thick slices of bread and jam, he took it over to the table, and sat. Before he could take many bites, though, his eyes strayed to a leather-bound book at the end of the table. It was a smaller version of the one Dr. Blundell carried for his notes. It must be hers. He focused on his food. Likely a journal or a diary. One couldn't read a diary. Still, Dr. Blundell's was not a journal. It was a notebook of his scientific observations. One could read observations, couldn't one?

He drew the notebook closer. He chewed the bread, still warm, drenched with melting butter, hardly tasting them. He'd just see if it was a diary. If it was, he'd close the thing up straight away. He flipped open the cover and paged through. It was hers, all right. Each page was covered by a tidy, sloping hand. One page held notes about some flower or other. It wasn't a diary, then.

He turned the book with one finger to a better angle. If she came down, he would hear her in plenty of time to close the book. Before he knew it, he was flipping through the pages. She was a midwife. Odd. And her father didn't know she delivered babies in the poorest parts of London. She felt guilty for keeping it from him. But really, he never seemed to know or care where she was. He flipped ahead. *Kama Sutra.* What? He pulled the book closer. What was an innocent girl doing writing about the Indian book of sexual relations?

His eyes flicked over the pages. Sure she would never marry . . . wanting to be like other women . . . an experiment . . . watching whores service their clients . . . picking out the lad . . .

What a cad. He'd like to land that loose screw a facer, draw his cork, and watch the blood spill over his no-doubt ridiculously high collar points. Agreeing that she would never appeal to a man enough to marry? Making her sign away her rights when he had ravished her? For it was little more than ravishment. The way she talked of the experience, the cub obviously hadn't even brought her to her pleasure. She'd given away her virginity and didn't even receive the simple recompense of sexual satisfaction. And with her resolve to give her life to midwifery and doing for her father, she might never know it, even if she found the cure for her condition. She had gone looking to see whether love could transform you. She was that naïve. But had she deserved what she got? Tom Blandings found a good thing thrust into his lap and used it. Used her. And she thought that was lovemaking. She'd never believe in love at all with that as an example, and what must she think of the sexual urges that surely accompanied her vampire state?

What was he saying? He didn't believe in love, either. She had been used more blatantly than most. He knew about being used. And he had had his way with women in his younger days. He hadn't forced them. They were more than willing to spread their legs for a comely lad and they got their pleasure of him. But he hadn't cared much about them. Now, whether love existed or not, it wasn't possible for him. The kind of use he had experienced at Asharti's hand erased all possibility of tender feelings. And he had responded to

Asharti's lust. He could no longer pretend he didn't know just how base a man's inclinations were.

He flipped through the notebook. The writing got shaky. He peered at it. Ahhh. The time she'd been infected. Sparse notes . . . how ill she was . . . no entry for nearly two weeks. And this one . . . it was splotched with . . . what? Her tears?

> _Papa told me tonight that the infection appears to be permanent. I have a parasite in my system now, and the only way to keep it at bay is to drink (a large splotch here that ran the ink) human blood. Indeed only Papa's infecting donor blood with Mr. Rufford's tainted sample has made enough to keep me alive to this point. My saliva has properties in common with South American bats. He didn't like to tell me. But at that point I knew. I have become vampire. I will never be the same again._

Poor lass. He knew how she felt at that horrible realization. Only she had no one to tell her even what it meant. At least he had the society of other vampires made by Asharti, freed by her death and on the run in the desert of North Africa, adrift without her personality to drive them. Jane Blundell had nothing, no one. He paged ahead.

> _I shall strive to think of it as a disease. I cannot help but think myself star-crossed or ill-fated to have caught it. But I cannot believe it makes me the stuff of nightmares, unless I allow it to do so. Are not lepers vilified for their condition and exiled from human companionship? Surely, their disease is a trial, but I will not believe it is a judgment on them. Nor is my disease a judgment on me. I will find a way to go on. I will find a way to turn my fate into a force of good._

Callan found himself hoping that Blundell found the cure as much for the girl as for himself. He should not have mocked her for calling it a disease. That was her way of dealing with her tragedy. She had courage. More than he had, perhaps. And for that very reason, he hoped she might be spared as many horrors as possible.

He heard footsteps on the stairs. He snapped the book shut and braced himself.

But it was only Blundell. "Well, boy, are you ready for a day of testing?"

"You're up early, Doctor," Callan said in relief.

"Strike while the iron is hot, so they say," the doctor replied, looking around and rubbing his hands. "Can you make it up to the laboratory in the daylight?"

Callan nodded. "I'll wrap myself in a blanket." It would be painful. But he was eager to get on with it. Death or redemption was at hand.

"Sit." Blundell gestured to a stool that might once have belonged to a milkmaid churning butter. "I'll just heat up my mixture." He turned to the forest of glassware and lit a lamp set under a flask filled with a vaguely green liquid.

Callan sat and tried to quiet his mind. "What's in it?"

"No, no. I won't tell you that. It might prejudice your reaction."

More likely Blundell thought he'd refuse to drink it. The green liquid began to bubble in its flask almost immediately.

"Excellent," the doctor muttered. He removed the vial and poured the liquid into a thick pottery cup, blowing on it to cool it. "Now spread out that blanket on the floor over there. I don't want you near the glass, in case of thrashing."

Thrashing? Callan swallowed. He stood and spread out the blanket as instructed.

"I'd tie you up, but I can't think what would hold you, as strong as you are. Still, you'd better take off your clothes before you lie down."

"Ye want me ta strip?"

"Well, in case you soil yourself, you won't want to ruin your clothing."

Callan set his mouth and took off his clothing while Blundell pulled out a leather book. Blundell handed the cup to Callan, then dipped his pen in an inkstand. Callan laid his length along the blanket. Excitement warred with fear in his belly. He propped himself on one elbow and, allowing himself only a pause to suck in a breath, he upended the beaker and gulped the bitter liquid.

The burning in his chest as the liquid made its way down his gullet made him drop the beaker with a gasp. It shattered, spraying glass. He curled over as the first wrenching spasms hit.

"What are you feeling?" Blundell barked.

"Twisting . . . twisting in my gut," he gasped. "Burning." He broke out in a sweat.

"That's the strychnine." Blundell scribbled furiously.

"Strychnine? Man, ha' ye . . . lost yer . . . mind?" Callan was finding it difficult to breathe.

"The poison must be strong to kill the creature. I distilled this from rat poison."

Callan writhed and cradled his belly with both arms, groaning. "Ye've killed me, man."

"There's always that danger, of course." Blundell peered at him. "But I added other ingredients to mitigate the effect, as well."

Callan couldn't respond. He twisted his body, groaning and straining against the pain. He was afraid he'd die in the next thirty seconds and then afraid he wouldn't. He dared not call to his Companion. He didn't want it to save him, or itself. Still, he felt it rise inside him. The pain went on, though, on and on. It seemed as though his intestines were being drawn out and hacked about. He strained against the pain. He could feel the veins standing out in his temples, his neck. He was about to burst. And then the room went slowly red.

With a kind of silent whoosh, the pain ramped down to manageable. Callan collapsed, barely conscious. The red film drained away from his eyes. Blundell was kneeling over him, saying something. The old man's figure was blurry, as though seen through water. Blundell pulled up Callan's eyelids and peered into his eyes. He . . . he was asking a question. Callan didn't care. The pain receded further. Or was it Callan who receded? Everything receded until all he could see was a tiny dot of light in the blackness. And then only blackness.

Someone was making noise. Clinking. The clinking echoed dreadfully and made his head throb. He wanted the noise to stop. He opened his mouth to shout at whoever was making the noise, but only a faint moan issued forth. That was strange.

He cracked open his eyelids. Blurry light resolved itself into a lamp. The flame was reflected everywhere. The clinking stopped. A figure blocked out the refracted light.

"Are you all right, man?" the voice boomed. It made him shut his eyes again.

Wait! That was Blundell's voice. And Callan lay on a blanket on the floor with another thrown over him. Glass flasks and tubes were refracting the light.

"Am I cured?" he croaked, trying to get up on one elbow. Hands pushed him down.

"I'm afraid not." The voice sounded more normal.

With a supreme effort, he made it up on his right elbow. "How d'ye know?" The doctor was wrong. He had to be wrong! All that pain *must* have killed his Companion, and he was definitely still alive. His aching head told him so.

"Empirical evidence, my boy." Blundell took a small knife, grabbed Callan's left wrist and cut his forearm. A single sear of pain seemed unimportant compared to what he had just endured. A cut. No more. What evidence was that? And then the cut slowly sealed itself.

Callan's shoulders sagged.

Blundell patted his bare shoulder. "That was only the first trial. I never really thought it would work. But studying the reaction of your body was extremely useful. The poison seems to take its normal course. Then the parasite raised its power, and neutralized the poison. Was there still some pain at that point?"

"Aye," he muttered. "Though no' sa bad as at first."

"The intestines were still damaged, I expect. It no doubt took some time for the parasite to regenerate the lacerated tissue."

"Nae doubt," Callan said, trying to achieve wry.

"How do you feel now?"

"Tired."

"Don't worry, boy. I have some ideas. We'll keep at it until we find the right formula."

Callan found that prospect daunting.

"Rest now," Blundell instructed. "We'll get you back to the house before Jane wakes."

Callan fell back onto the blanket.

God help him.

But he had no hope of that.

Jane woke in the late afternoon to sounds of movement in the house. They came from the kitchen below. She could hear men's voices. Papa and Mr. Kilkenny.

"I need some herbs gathered tonight. Are you up to it?" her father was saying.

"Aye. But I dinnae know much about plants."

Jane jumped out of bed and began to dress as quickly as she could.

"Jane knows her plants," her father said.

"Then she can go."

"I'll not have her wandering about alone with those creatures about." Didn't he know that she and Kilkenny were "those creatures," too? "You'll have to go with her."

"Th' point of me staying was ta protect ye and yer laboratory."

Jane pulled on her shoes and dragged a brush ruthlessly

through her hair. She had no time to dress it. She would not be talked of as though she were some dreadful obligation.

"Jane is my only reason for finding a cure." Her father's voice was hard. "If anything happens to her, I warn you, I shouldn't feel obligated to continue."

Jane hurried down the stairs.

"Verra well." Kilkenny sounded tired. "I'll go with her. I'll rig up a whistle. Ye blow it, if ye need me."

"I doubt you could get here fast enough to do any good, Mr. Kilkenny," Jane said, pushing through the kitchen door. They were sitting at the long table. Her father had a cup of tea, and Kilkenny a tankard of ale. She was struck immediately by how haggard Kilkenny looked. His hair was a tangle of dark curls, his shirt was stained with sweat, and there were faint circles under his eyes. His fight with the vampire must have taken more out of him than he let on. There was a half-empty bottle of blood on the chopping block. Her father must have gotten it in the daylight. That should have refreshed Kilkenny.

"I'll get here, as long as we're nae farther than five miles," he said grimly.

How? He was hiding something again. However would she get him to answer all her questions? The man was stubborn: a very unattractive trait. "I'm more than capable of getting whatever you need, Papa. Haven't I walked all over these hills and valleys?"

"Carns and glens, if ye dinnae want ta sound foreign."

Maddening man! "I have no desire to blend in with the locals," she said with some asperity. "As soon as Papa finds the cure, we will be shut of this dreary place."

Kilkenny chuffed a scornful laugh. "I would no' be packing just yet."

"Well, then, I should think it important to get Papa whatever he needs." She turned to her father. "I don't need any help from this . . . person, Papa. What shall I search out?"

Her father stood. "I'll not tell you Jane, unless you give

me your solemn word that you won't stir from the yard without Kilkenny. I can't be worrying about you. It distracts me."

Her father would never believe any objection Jane might make to Kilkenny's company on account of propriety in light of the way she had always railed against the restrictions placed on females. Jane sighed. Walking the hillsides alone with Mr. Kilkenny would be difficult for more reasons than she could count. "Very well, Papa."

He slapped the table with both palms, rising. "Excellent. I think . . . *Amanita virosa* and *Amanita phalloides*. Either or both. As many as you can find."

That made Jane open her eyes. Those were probably the most poisonous mushrooms in the British Isles. She forced a smile. It wouldn't do to let Mr. Kilkenny know about that. Why make him fearful of the cure he wanted so badly? She nodded to her father. "Let's see. They need damp but acid soil, and they grow in the leaves under trees. Perhaps by the river or . . . up at the Falls of Divach?"

"I'd try the falls. The moisture in the air would make a good environment for *Amanitas*. And can you find me some *Atropa belladonna*?"

Deadly nightshade? What dreadful concoction was he brewing? She nodded. "First thing after dinner, then," Jane said shortly, glancing to Mr. Kilkenny to dare him to protest. He only lifted his brows.

"I'll take dinner in my room, my dear. It's been quite a day." Her father sighed and rose.

She stood on tiptoe to kiss his forehead. "I'll bring it in directly."

She tied on an apron and bent to check the pot of hare stew she had left simmering all day on the coals as her father headed upstairs. She could feel Kilkenny behind her. She stirred it. Good, it hadn't stuck to the bottom. It had parsnips and carrots in it. With some roasted potatoes that would make a fine meal. She went down into the root cellar, relieved to escape Kilkenny's eyes. When she came up with an apron full of potatoes, he was sipping his ale, considering.

"Where did a lass like ye learn housekeeping?"

"Oh, it's a question now, is it? You who don't answer anything want answers?" She lifted her brows, mocking.

He looked down at his tankard. He seemed embarrassed or ashamed. As well he should. She had already answered questions about how she was made vampire. But had he? He had not. And what of the scars on his body? He kept himself a mystery. All she had wanted yesterday were the facts related to being a vampire. But there were more than facts involved, weren't there now? There might be suffering and doubt. Suddenly she thought she might want to know about Mr. Kilkenny's feelings and experience as much as she wanted the bare facts about vampirism.

In truth, she was going about this all the wrong way. Instead of antagonizing him, she should draw him out about himself; let him get to know her in return. Then he'd feel comfortable enough to tell her anything she wanted to know.

"That wasn't kind of me." She took a breath. "I learned housekeeping from books."

"From books?"

She glanced up and saw she'd caught his interest. "Those books." She gestured with the knife to the bookshelf that looked so out of place in the kitchen. He rose and bent to peer at the titles. She knew what he'd see: *Economical Housewife: A Treatise on the Homely Arts, Cuisine de Campagne* and all her books on midwifery, as well. "One can learn almost everything from books."

"Not everythin'." His voice was bleak.

She continued on lightly. "I already knew how to sew. One of the few practical things out of the so-called education they give to women today. Speaking of which, we should stop in the village and see if we can procure you a shirt. Old Mrs. Dulnan's son was killed last November. She might sell you his clothes." She thought about his threadbare coat. "I can buy them for you, if . . . if money is a temporary problem."

"Our kind always has money."

"Really? How? Why?" Oh, dear! Where was her vow not to press him too soon? She'd let curiosity overcome good sense. He'd never answer her. Indeed, his expression closed, and then . . . to her surprise he consciously gathered himself to answer.

"I'm lucky. And I invested in th' funds. David Hern gave me a tip."

"You knew the Chancellor of the Exchequer?" He had died in a spectacularly grisly way.

Those gray-green eyes measured her. "He was one o' us. A member of a lost cause."

That took her aback. She wanted to ask what the lost cause was. His eyes said that was not allowed. But she had to keep him talking "You believe in lost causes, then?"

"No' anymore."

Now *that* was a bleak tone. She smiled. "Of course you do. You're here, aren't you?"

"Point taken." Were there crinkles around his eyes? They certainly had a gleam in them. She liked provoking that gleam.

She laid the potatoes in a large pot with a little of the bacon grease from her father's breakfast yesterday, rolled them about in it and put the pot into the coals. Half an hour until they were done. That meant half an hour with Mr. Kilkenny and nothing to distract her . . .

"Ye dinnae ha' a dog whistle, do ye?"

"I have no idea," she said, raising her brows. "There aren't any dogs here now."

"Ah," he said, disappointed.

"Oh, you mean to give that to Papa! Will . . . will you be able to hear it?"

"I should think sa."

"Well, we have the original furniture. The drawers are filled with all sorts of things. And a farm like this ought to have had dogs once, should it not?"

"D'ye mind if I've a look round?"

"Of course not." He got up. How could she ask him questions if he was leaving?

CHAPTER
Seven

Callan found himself in the front of the house. He puffed out a breath. It was easier when he wasn't so close to her. Glen Urquhart was settling into the long gloaming. This far north, there would be less and less night as the year drove on to the summer solstice. He'd be trapped in the house, with her, for long hours if he hadn't moved on. He'd better have moved on. By then they must have a cure. Would the doctor try some terrible new concoction on him every day? Could he survive that for long without going mad? He set his jaw. He'd survived worse.

To the task at hand. The chances of finding a dog whistle weren't good. He looked around. The old stone house was richly furnished. It had probably been a laird's hunting box, and not a true farm. Turkey carpets covered the floors, comfortable wing chairs sat in front of the fire, rather than the usual Scottish settle, hard and unyielding. He could imagine how cheerful the room would be with a fire crackling and snapping in the grate, a dog or two dozing in front of it, and Jane Blundell, sewing by lamplight or reading. She seemed to read a lot. Housekeeping out of a book? Inventive. He'd give her that.

He went to a scarred desk and started opening drawers. Old bills, balls of string, unmended quills . . . this didn't look promising. Accounts from ten years ago, a miniature of a young man in uniform, no doubt dead in a war long over. The desk yielded nothing. The gaming table had a drawer, but it held only chessmen.

He went into the other room. This had been made into a library, with bookshelves to the ceiling on one wall. Botanical treatises, anatomy books . . . On the other wall were hung a series of startling paintings. They were botanical studies of the very first order, flowers and leaves in intricate detail, just as you would see in drawing rooms all over Edinburgh or London, though of better quality. Except for the fact that they had obviously been painted at night.

Normally botanical studies were painted without the distraction of a background on plain white paper. But these paintings had backgrounds shaded of black and gray, perhaps faintly washed with color and intricate themselves in detail. A pine cone stood against the background of green needles and starry sky. And there, a white flower (he didn't know its name) was shown against a cloudscape and moon. Whites glowed with life. Colors snapped. They all seemed to vibrate with energy an energy he recognized immediately. They had been painted by a vampire, who saw that clearly, that vibrantly, at night.

She had painted them. It was if she were standing in the room with him. So it was with little surprise that he heard her say, "Did you find . . ."

He glanced around. She was looking abashed. "Ye painted these."

She nodded, then shrugged in deprecation. "The other useful thing about a ladies' education. They teach us watercolor. Frivolous, of course, for most girls, but it has its scientific uses. The lily is from our greenhouse in London. And when we first came here, before the local folk got frightened, we had help around the farm. I had time to roam the hills and valleys . . . excuse me, glens and carns, with my paints."

."These are more than scientific studies." The woman who painted these loved beauty.

"No, they aren't. But that's all I wanted, just competent studies."

"If ye'd wanted only scientific studies, ye'd no' ha' bothered with th' backgrounds, or ta give them such life." He looked around at them. "These are th' world as only we can see it."

"Well, that's a compliment coming from you," she remarked dryly. "I don't get the feeling you're in the habit of doling them out."

He felt himself flushing. In spite of the dim light she would be able to see it. He cleared his throat. "Ye should be proud." He stalked by the mirror over the mantel toward a small cabinet in the corner.

"I always thought vampires couldn't be seen in mirrors," she said, tentatively. "That appears to be a myth." She was trying to draw him out again about the properties of vampires.

He wouldn't be drawn. "Mostly."

The cabinet was triangular to fit the corner exactly, one of those pieces of furniture he'd never seen a use for. He pulled open the door. Inside were a collar, long empty, and a little silver dog whistle. He held it up. A very small miracle, but maybe only small miracles were available.

"It seems you have the luck of the Irish, Mr. Kilkenny," she remarked, a glint of mocking laughter in her eye. "Dinner's ready." She slipped from the room.

It occurred to him that she had taken what her condition gave her, seeing well at night, and turned it into something beautiful. His gaze roved over the paintings once again. He hardly even minded her teasing him about being Irish.

Jane was just clearing up the plates when she heard it; the clatter of wheels and the thud of horses' hooves on the soft earth of the road. She glanced to Kilkenny. Their eyes met, as she sifted possibilities through her mind and rejected them.

Not the rumble of a cart, therefore it wasn't someone from the village. No one owned a carriage there. An outsider, then.

Kilkenny stood, tension radiating from him.

"Who could that be?" she wondered. She shrugged at Kilkenny, trying to dispel his obvious anxiety. "Probably one of Papa's colleagues come at last to consult with him about his research. He's been expecting his article to generate some interest."

The carriage rolled up the circular drive as they made their way to the front of the house.

"Jane," her father shouted from upstairs, "who comes calling so late?"

Jane almost gasped. She could think of one brand of visitor who would only come at night. Kilkenny was striding toward the front hall. Outside gravel crunched and horses snorted. Jane heard her father coming down the stairs. Kilkenny pulled open the door with a jerk.

The scent of cinnamon overlaid by something else she could not name washed over them. Vampires! She glanced around. There was no weapon to hand. The great claymore was not hanging over the fireplace in the library. It was probably upstairs in Kilkenny's room. A thrill of fear made her throat close. His big frame filled the doorway. Jane had to peer around him to see a strange figure leap down from a very stylish barouche, its wheels picked out in an odd shade of lavender against shining black. The figure appeared to be a monk. He wore a habit of rough brown wool tied with coarse rope, his cowl thrown back to reveal the face of a man in his prime. He had a prominent nose and thin lips, black hair cut short but not tonsured, eyes so brown they were nearly black. There was a look of surprised disappointment about him, as though he were shocked that life held so little. He glanced their way, but went directly to open the carriage door.

Out of the carriage came another surprising creature. Her lilac traveling costume was rouched and braided down the front and on the sleeves. It was made by a modiste of the first stare. And the lilac kid half-boots that encased the visitor's dainty feet must have been shockingly dear. On her head sat a hat with no less than four lilac ostrich plumes. Such marvelous clothing matched and accessorized so perfectly made Jane cringe in envy. And that wasn't all. The woman was, quite simply, the most beautiful creature Jane had ever seen. Her black eyes and black hair set off creamy skin. Her cheekbones were high, her eyes slightly slanted. She was shorter than Jane, and more delicate. She looked exotic, fragile. But the fragile part, at least, was a lie. Her cinnamon scent overpowered the more masculine version of the monk, and she brimmed with life. She took the monk's offered hand and stepped to the ground.

Behind the ravishing creature was a young-looking woman, plain and drably dressed. She had the look of a servant girl to a demanding mistress, eyes downcast and self-effacing.

"Elyta Zaroff," the beautiful woman said, as she moved toward the door, holding out her hand to Kilkenny with a regal air. Her accent was . . . Austrian? Hungarian? Balkan? Jane wasn't sure, what she was sure of was that her vibrations were both powerful and so intense they seemed to be operating at the edge of consciousness. Kilkenny made no move to take the woman's hand, so she dropped it. Her eyes flicked to Jane, then back to Kilkenny. Her gaze roved over Kilkenny's body as well his face. A sly complexity crossed her eyes and was gone. "I'm sure I did not expect the doctor to be so young, and . . . handsome." Then her great, dark eyes narrowed. "But you are *both* vampire . . ."

"Sa there's five o' us," Kilkenny said shortly. "What d'ye want?"

Behind Jane, her father bustled up, a robe hastily pulled over his nightshirt, his feet bare. "Who is it, Jane?"

Everyone ignored him. The tension in the air was palpable. "Ye ha' no' answered." Kilkenny threatened.

"We come for the cure, of course," Miss Zaroff said, finally glancing at the doctor.

"One o' yer brethren was here th' other night," Kilkenny rasped. "I buried him behind th' barn." Jane could feel his power ramp up. But he would be no match for three of them.

"I thought Khalenberg would send someone. He wants to see the cure destroyed. We, however, do not." The woman's voice was matter-of-fact. "Are you going to invite us in or not?"

"Of course we are," Jane said, pushing past Kilkenny. They really had no choice, after all. "I'm Jane Blundell." Jane held out her hand. "And this is my father, Dr. James Blundell." Energy· shot up Jane's arm as the newcomer shook it. "And Callan Kilkenny, our . . . our guest."

"How do you do?" Miss Zaroff said, her gaze fastening on Jane's father, then flicking back to Kilkenny. "This is my maid, Clara." Miss Zaroff waved vaguely at the girl hovering in the background by the carriage. Clara dropped a curtsy. "And this is Brother Flavio."

"Brother Flavio." Jane made her curtsy. Kilkenny did not extend his hand or make his bow to any of them. He stood aside only grudgingly as they entered. Jane led them to the sitting room to the left of the entry

"I'm surprised one of your age and strength could dispatch one of Khalenberg's followers," Miss Zaroff remarked. She peered at Kilkenny as she sat. "Or perhaps not, if you are whom I think you are."

"And what d'ye want with th' cure?" Kilkenny had folded his arms across his chest.

"To give hope to lost souls." Miss Zaroff's eyes went limpid. Was her emotion real? "As hard as it is to believe for those new to our state, there are those who would give up eternal life."

"We who're made dinnae think it such a blessing, either." Kilkenny's voice was raw.

She nodded. "So you want the cure, as well. It has been found?"

"Not yet." Her father sighed. "But I am close, I know."

"Then our mission is clear: to protect Dr. Blundell and the formula once it is found," Brother Flavio said. Jane had forgotten all about him. He came now to stand in the group that surrounded Miss Zaroff. "Khalenberg and his faction won't give up. They can't bear to have our condition changed. They are true conservatives." He too studied Kilkenny intently.

"Aye. A cure would change everythin', would it no'?" Kilkenny asked grimly.

"I wonder if you are trustworthy, Mr. Kilkenny? I rather think he should not be trusted around the cure, don't you, Flavio?"

"He suffered terrible wounds to protect my father and the laboratory," Jane protested. "Those actions serve as his credentials."

"Hmmm, I rather think he is dispensable now that we are here, though." Was that beautiful face suggesting murder or simply banishment for Kilkenny?

"But he is quite indispensable to my experiments," her father chuffed. "No, I couldn't possibly do without him at this juncture."

Jane turned in surprise. She had almost forgotten her father. That wasn't true of course, but it was kind of him to defend Kilkenny.

Miss Zaroff asked sweetly, "And why could he not be replaced?"

"Kilkenny is my test subject. I tested my newest formula on him today. I intend to test the permutations every day. There is a significant amount of pain involved. It's also possible the subject might die, so of course I could not use Jane." He raised his eyebrows at the others. "Unless one of you would care to play that role?"

Jane saw from the grim line of Kilkenny's mouth that it was true. "You let him poison you?" No wonder he looked haggard earlier this evening. They had concealed it from her. Her father must have known she'd want to bear her share. Which she did! She felt betrayed.

"Well, I can't do without Clara. Your daughter is precious to you." Miss Zaroff shrugged. "So Kilkenny has his role. We will see he does not shirk it."

"I dinnae need compulsion." Kilkenny was white around the mouth. What did he mean, "compulsion"?

"We'll decide that." Miss Zaroff's smile was knowing and smug and . . . cruel. She only looked the frippery female in her modish clothes. Jane wondered just how old these vampires were. Miss Zaroff looked to Jane's father. "You work in the daylight, I suppose?" Her father nodded. "Then we have interrupted your rest. Jane can show us to our rooms."

"Ye'll not stay here." Kilkenny issued it as a challenge.

"How else can we protect the effort?" Brother Flavio asked. "There will be more the next time. Khalenberg and his followers are quite determined not to let the cure survive."

Kilkenny set his lips.

"Can you accommodate us, Miss Blundell?" Miss Zaroff asked.

Jane nodded. "We've six bedrooms but no servants. Not what you're used to, I'm sure."

"Clara will help with whatever we need." Miss Zaroff rose gracefully.

"In the matter of . . . blood." Jane cleared her throat. "The villagers make blood donations to my father's work. I can provide. But I would ask you not to take it in the village."

"As you will." Miss Zaroff nodded. "We have no immediate need. Flavio, my trunks?"

Kilkenny looked as if he would protest, but thought better of it and spun on his heel. His boots echoed through the kitchen. Jane heard the door to the yard snap open and slam shut. Brother Flavio left by the front entrance.

"Well," Jane said with feigned brightness. "Let me just go up and air the sheets. Then I'm afraid Mr. Kilkenny and I must go out and gather the herbs my father needs for his experiments. Rude, I know, to leave you to your own devices."

Miss Zaroff smiled. "Do what you must. Do you need Kilkenny with you?"

Strange question. "Yes, I'm afraid my father does not rest easy if I am out alone. We mustn't let worry distract him from his experiments."

"Very true," Miss Zaroff said. She smiled again and motioned for Jane to precede her.

Kilkenny strode up to the barn, fuming. These three were from Mirso Monastery without a doubt. He knew of Brother Flavio from Stephan Sincai, the Harrier Mirso had sent to kill him. He should be grateful for more protection for Miss Blundell and the doctor. But he never felt easy around born vampires and if these were from Mirso they were born, not made. The only reason he was still alive was that he was needed to produce the cure. He thought from their intense scrutiny that they knew who he was. What born vampire did not know of Callan Kilkenny and his reputed army of vampires? To them he was a traitor, carrying on Asharti's mad scheme. They wouldn't kill Miss Blundell. That would upset the doctor, and they couldn't afford that, at least before the formula for the cure was found. Even killing Callan would upset the doctor, and worse, delay the coming of the cure.

They hadn't told the Blundells what they knew of him. Probably, they thought the doctor would throw him off the farm if he knew the depth of Callan's depravity. Whatever the reason, the result was good. He didn't want the Blundells to know his past. They couldn't deny him the cure since he'd be the first to experience it. But they might refuse to trust him with the formula so he could distribute it to others, and then he'd have to take it by force. The look of betrayal he would see in Miss Blundell's eyes when she discovered he had stolen the formula and left . . .

He pushed into the stall and began to saddle Miss Blundell's mare. Still, he now took his promise to the doctor even more to heart. He wouldn't leave Miss Blundell alone and vulnerable with born vampires about, no matter the torture to his damnable cock to have her near.

He heard the footsteps long before they entered the barn in spite of the shushing movement of the animals through their straw and the skitter of mice looking for grain. The smell of cinnamon and ambergris did not have Jane's peculiar twist, and the footsteps were too heavy.

He glanced behind himself. Flavio was silhouetted against the square of lighter midnight in the barn door. The monk was breathing hard, but not from the gentle slope up from the house. He had the reins of a carriage horse in each hand. Callan motioned to two empty box stalls.

The monk seemed to come to himself and led each animal to a stall and slipped off the bridle before he closed the door on them. Callan cinched the mare's saddle and moved to Faust's stall. Behind him, he heard the monk, still breathing hard.

"Is he dead?" Flavio's voice was a coarse rasp. He meant Stephan Sincai, of course.

"I dinnae know."

"God, man, tell me true! Did you kill him?"

"Nae. I told ye that."

The monk ran a hand distractedly through his thick, dark hair. "Did your . . . army kill him? Don't fence with me!"

"Army?" Callan snorted. "We were twelve. He was a Harrier. He killed all but me."

"There was no army? I thought . . ."

"Ye thought what th' Elders wanted ye ta think." He lifted the saddle over Faust's back.

"Then why didn't he return? He wanted the refuge of Mirso more than anything."

Callan sighed. "Why should I tell ye? So ye can hunt him down?" Flavio might have raised Sincai, but he still served the Elders. Callan felt the monk's silence behind him. He snapped out the stirrup leathers and cinched the saddle.

Flavio sat heavily on a wooden stool. Callan glanced back to see that the monk's eyes were raw.

"I can't believe you won. We made him stronger than any of us. You were newly made."

"He took pity on me, if ye must know." It was hard for Callan to admit, even now.

"He spared you?" Flavio was incredulous. "The Elders will never let him back into Mirso if he betrayed his mission."

What did Callan owe this man? Nothing. He had no obligation here. And yet . . . Stephan Sincai had loved Flavio like a father and Callan had come to value Sincai. "He knew that. Mirso did no' matter ta him in th' end."

"Why not?" Flavio's mouth turned down.

Callan shook his head. "There was a girl. She . . . told me about him." He took a breath.

Wait! Callan stiffened, thinking back to what he knew of Sincai and what Sincai had experienced of this man. He turned slowly. The rag dropped from his hand. "It was you who let them make him a Harrier. He . . . he suffered so in the training . . ."

Flavio sank his head on his chest. "You do know. I betrayed him. I thought . . . I thought he was our kind's only hope against . . . you."

"He did no' blame ye. Only himself."

"That was like him. He spared Asharti once and blamed himself for what she became."

Callan winced at Asharti's name. His suffering at her hands seemed like it had happened yesterday. But he never blamed Sincai for an old act of generosity.

Flavio took a breath. "It's hard to think of him, wandering, alone, far from any refuge."

Callan relented. "I dinnae think he's alone. I told ye, there was a girl." He grabbed a bridle from the stall door. "He found somethin' more important ta him than Mirso."

"Love? He found love?" The hope in the man's voice was too tenuous to be crushed.

Sincai and the girl loved each other, all right. They both seemed . . . transformed. Was that possible? He hadn't thought so, and yet . . . "Aye. He found love."

Flavio relaxed his shoulders. A small smile played over his lips before he sighed. "No thanks to me. Still, I'm grateful." He looked up. "Thank you. Thank you for telling me."

Callan nodded once and buckled the throat latch of Faust's bridle.

Behind him, he heard the monk rise, sigh once more, and leave the barn.

CHAPTER
Eight

"Mrs. Dulnan," Jane called, knocking at the tiny cottage's wooden door. She hoped the woman would admit her. "It's me, Jane Blundell." She pulled her cloak around her. She had thought she and Kilkenny might as well stop by Mrs. Dulnan's cottage on their way to the falls.

The door opened a crack and the fearful face of a dour woman peered out just above the latch. "It's late," she complained.

"I'm sorry, Mrs. Dulnan. The sun bothers me, you know. I couldn't come earlier."

"Aye, I ken ye dinnae like th' sun." She opened the door a crack wider. She must have seen Kilkenny standing at the horses' heads in the road. "Who's that?" she asked, suspicious.

"A patient of my father's," Jane soothed. This had the virtue of being at least a half-truth. "His condition is not contagious. He's perfectly harmless." Well, *that* was a lie.

The woman pursed her lips, unsure. Her wrinkles said it was a habitual gesture.

Jane smiled. "Could I come in and speak with you?"

"If ye must." She peered out into the dark. "Him, too, if ye'll vouch fer him."

"He'll be docile as a lamb."

"I ha' no' got any tea hot," the woman warned.

"Then we'll be satisfied with your good company," Jane allowed, smiling. She raised her brows. Mrs. Dulnan hesitated, then nodded once. Jane motioned to Kilkenny who tied the horses' reins to a holly bush. She ducked inside as Mrs. Dulnan opened the door.

Kilkenny bent to get through the door. The cottage was lighted only by a lamp set on a scarred wood table in the main room. Two straight-backed chairs sat at the table. A narrow bed served as extra seating along with a settle by the hearth, which was cold now in spite of the chill. A rag rug covered much of the floor. Through the two doors that gave off the room Jane saw a tiny bedroom, the bed covered with a finely stitched if worn quilt, and what must be a kitchen. That appeared to be the extent of the cottage. Mrs. Dulnan gestured toward a chair, her eyes never leaving Kilkenny. It occurred to Jane that Mrs. Dulnan might not be able to afford peat for her fire now that her son was dead. Jane knew the woman took in sewing when she could, but most families in the village were poor and had to make do with what their women could sew themselves. That didn't leave much business. It was a hard life for a woman alone.

"Mrs. Dulnan, may I introduce Mr. Callan Kilkenny?"

"I . . . I ha' a sweet cake, if ye've a mind . . ." Mrs. Dulnan said.

Jane didn't want to take what little the woman had and was about to decline when Mr. Kilkenny rumbled, "That'd be verra nice." He sat in one of the straight-backed chairs.

Mrs. Dulnan reappeared in a moment with a plate of tiny pastries, and surprisingly, a tankard of ale. She set them down on the table. "My boy always liked a bit of ale with his cakes," she murmured, and then turned suddenly away.

Mr. Kilkenny took a bite of one of the cakes and washed it down with a swig from the tankard. "It's been long since I had sweet cake," he said, sighing in satisfaction.

"Very good," Jane agreed, though the cakes were not quite fresh. "Mr. Kilkenny's treatment is taking longer than he expected, Mrs. Dulnan. He finds himself short of clothing. I was thinking . . ." There was no way to say this without offending the woman or stirring her sorrow. "I thought you might have some for sale."

The ghost of grief flitted behind the woman's eyes. Mrs. Dulnan heaved a breath and steadied herself, then turned to Mr. Kilkenny and eyed his person. "Ye're about th' size." She pulled a rough wooden box from under the bed, opened it and smoothed the clothes within. "I ha' no' got use for these now," she said roughly. She took a linen shirt by the shoulders and shook it out, then tossed it on the bed. It was followed by three of its fellows and several wool waistcoats before she came to the tartans. "His plaid." Her hand hesitated before she picked up the red and blue cloth. "D'ye object ta wearin' a tartan not yer own, Mr. Kilkenny?"

"I'm Irish by birth, good mother. I dinnae ha' a tartan ta call my own."

"Ah," she said, sharing his sorrow. She dug into the makeshift trunk. "My boy wore one not his own on occasion." She pulled out a black and blue and green plaid cloth. "Forty-second Regiment of Foot, he was," she whispered. "They called their tartan th' Black Watch."

"I hope ye will no' think an Irish Lowlander unworthy ta wear it."

She looked at him, appraising. "I kin spare it. But I will no' accept a shilling fer it." She tossed it on the pile and fished out heavy wool stockings and stout brogue boots that laced up the calf. Finally she added an ornate metal pin about two inches across and a leather belt.

"I canno' thank ye enough, good woman," Kilkenny said, his voice a low growl.

Mrs. Dulnan closed the trunk briskly and shoved it under the bed. Then she stood and took their plates into the kitchen without another word. Jane saw her wiping at her eyes.

"You have to pay her for them," Jane whispered urgently.

"She's made me a gift," Mr. Kilkenny said under his breath.

"A gift in return, then. I can't stand to see the poor woman in want. I've enough in my reticule to keep her for a month," Jane protested, pulling open the small embroidered bag.

"Put yer charity away," Kilkenny hissed as Mrs. Dulnan came in from the kitchen. He cleared his throat. "I was wonderin' if ye might know someone who could help out at Muir Farm. Th' doctor mentioned five shillings ta come three times a week. They've a sore need."

What? What was he thinking? It wasn't his place to contract for a servant for them. But it wouldn't matter. Even for so handsome a wage, no one would come to Muir Farm.

Kilkenny looked at his nails as though they needed paring. "Th' place is just too much fer Miss Blundell alone, though she does no' like ta own it, and now they ha' several guests."

Jane blushed. She was about to protest, but a glare from Kilkenny kept her silent. Mrs. Dulnan chewed her lip and studied him. "It's a fair walk," she murmured.

"The doctor could leave a cart in the village." Now he was volunteering their only gig? That left her only her mare for transportation. How would she haul supplies up to the farm?

The woman nodded. "In that case . . . I'll take ye on meself." Her eyes gleamed with tears.

Jane groaned inwardly. "People are . . . afraid of Muir Farm. If you'd rather not . . ."

"Ignorance," Mrs. Dulnan said briskly, blinking. "Men ha' been comin' up recent ta give blood, and none ha' died yet." She peered up at Jane. "Unlike some others I could name, I dinnae think birthin' that baby when it was like ta die were against God's will."

Ahh. Mrs. Dulnan must not like the women who had spoken against Jane for delivering Evie's boy. She'd help at Muir

Farm just to spite them. Well, Jane couldn't gracefully refuse, under the circumstances. She smiled and held out her hand. "Thank you so much. Would tomorrow be convenient?"

"Tomorrow be fine." Mrs. Dulnan shook Jane's hand. "I'll send a boy up fer th' cart." She glanced to Kilkenny, who was just getting up from the table. He towered over her. "And ye, lad, dinnae be careless with my Lachlan's plaids. Now I'll be there ta brush 'em fer ye."

Kilkenny bowed. "I'll be honored ta wear thém." Still he made no move to pay her.

"I expect th' place is in a state," Mrs. Dulnan remarked.

"It's probably not what an expert housewife could do," Jane said, only to be courteous.

Kilkenny gathered up the clothes. Jane reached again to her reticule, staring pointedly at him. "We've imposed on Mrs. Dulnan long enough," he muttered, and pushed Jane in the direction of the door. Mrs. Dulnan led her into the tiny yard. He trailed them to the gate and tied the clothes into a bundle he fastened behind Faust's saddle. Jane mounted her mare, Missy, by herself while he was busy, just to avoid having to put her boot in his cupped hands. She had managed to avoid his touch so far tonight. Mrs. Dulnan disappeared inside. Kilkenny glanced over and frowned.

"I can't believe you didn't pay for her son's clothes," she accused.

"And shame her for settin' a price on his memory? I dinnae think sa."

Jane sighed. "I suppose I now employ a housekeeper I don't need at the cost of a cart I do need in order to provide for her without making her feel like she was accepting charity."

He didn't disagree. "But ye do need her." They moved off into the night.

"I do just fine," Jane muttered as the village disappeared behind into the darkness.

He said nothing. Maddening man! How could one argue with him? Very unsatisfying. And distracting. She couldn't

help but watch him. She had to pull her thoughts away from
the muscle she knew moved under the shoulders of his coat.
Mrs. Dulnan would no doubt make a racket about the house
while Jane wanted to sleep and disturb her father at his work.
That is, if she didn't find out that the house was full of vampires and run screaming into the village. They'd probably
end up being burned out by an angry mob. Painful surely, if
it didn't kill them.

Of course, if the woman just cleaned and perhaps washed
clothes and Kilkenny took care of the animals, she'd have
time again for her painting. And now she had to make time
to traipse all over the countryside looking for plants for her
father's experiments. Perhaps it wasn't such a bad solution
after all, if the woman would keep to herself.

She'd never tell Kilkenny that, of course. Off to their
right, the waters of Loch Ness seemed to heave and sway.
Missy let out a worried whinny. "What was that?" Jane asked.

"I dinnae know . . ." Kilkenny muttered as he struggled
for control of Faust. Jane turned to look, but the water was
smooth and still again. Clouds were coming up from the
west. They passed in front of the waxing moon, and the
landscape darkened. The horses quieted as they started up
the road away from the loch.

The silence stretched. They wound up into the hills on a
track hardly more than two ruts. The horses' hooves thudded softly in the loam. A stream, not quite a river, chattered
to their left. The darkness felt . . . intimate. She had never
been afraid of the night. In fact, the night had always been
almost comforting. But now, its seductive undercurrent felt
menacing.

She cleared her throat. "You must be looking forward to
wearing kilts again."

"I'm a Lowlander," he said, an edge to his voice. "Ye English might not ha' noticed, but kilts are Highland dress."

"King George himself wore the kilt when he came to Edinburgh two years ago. They're a symbol of the Scots now."

"Dictated by th' English."

"The clan leaders all wore them," she protested.

He snorted. "Nae doubt descendants of th' same lairds who voted away their country."

His growling intensity was disturbing. But here at least was something with which she could argue. "I don't see Scots clamoring for freedom."

"Nae, ye dinnae see that." His voice was flat. Oh, dear, she had touched another nerve.

She had a thought. "Did *you* speak out against the Union?" An Irishman more patriotic than the Scots he lived among? How interesting

"Aye," he said grimly. "More than a hundred years after th' Treaty, and fifty after Culloden. I wrote foolish drivel nae one wanted ta hear."

"Why did you write it, then?"

"Genetic, probably, from m' father." His lips sneered. "Fourth son o' an impoverished Irish earl who moved to Scotland and wrote political tracts. Nothin' quite sa useless, is there?"

But she didn't care about his father. She wanted to know what he had believed in and why he no longer believed it. "Not good enough. Why did you write against the Union?"

He spared her a glance. His lips were a thin line and she thought he wouldn't speak. But finally he said, "Maybe I was tired o' the English lookin' down on us."

"Really?" she asked, surprised. "The English are positively infatuated with Scotland."

"No' for what it is. They ha' an idea o' Scotland— sublime beauty but primitive people." He snorted derisively. "We're no' primitive. And sublime beauty?" He shook his head in disgust. "Th' land is poor and cold and hard. Lord, th' way they talk of heather, like it was soft instead o' just a bramble!"

She had to laugh, as much for his torrent of words as for the words themselves. He looked at her in surprise. "I agree with you there. How someone who lived in England could think such a hard land beautiful, I don't know. It's all just propaganda put about by the Scots themselves. My friend Miss Sithington always talked about Scotland as though it were right out of a novel by Sir Walter Scott."

"Mr. Scott has much ta answer for," he agreed. There was that gleam in his eyes again. "But no' sa much as Bobbie Burns." Were those crinkles around his eyes all he had left of a smile? She had never seen him straight-out smile. He sobered. "It's a hard life th' people ha'."

He was proud of them, though they were an adopted people. She cocked her head. "Scots have contributed far more to science and philosophy than the country's size warrants. And there is, of course, the brave performance of the Scottish regiments at Waterloo. That certainly endeared you to the English."

"Aye," he said. "If there's one thing a Scot knows, it's how ta die fightin' against odds. But I canno' say I'm a Scot."

Ahh. He was proud of them, but he didn't count himself one of them. "Of course you can. Scots were Picts and Celts and Vikings and Normans and Irish. Why, the area first called Scotia was inhabited by settlers from Ireland. And Ireland is also Celt and Viking and Norman. Not much difference, when you come down to it."

He glanced over at her, glowering. "Then how is it Scots seem ta hate th' Irish sa much?"

Here was the point of all this. He had grown up living with prejudice, an outsider. He still felt it. Only now it was magnified by his condition. She shrugged. "Well, now, I can't imagine why people who are the same might take an irrational dislike to each other. That's never happened before. But let's see . . . how about territorial disputes, old grudges, or the ever-popular doctrinal disagreements inside the same religion? Would those do?"

He set his lips. He didn't like to be mocked, did he? Still, his eyes did gleam.

"You wouldn't happen to be Catholic, would you?" she asked sweetly.

"No' sa ye'd notice."

That meant he was, or had been once. He pulled up. The track petered out into a path as the hills steepened. They would have to walk from here. She pulled her cloak up and brought her knee over the pommel of the sidesaddle so she could slide to the ground. She unhooked the basket she had brought for the mushrooms, and tied Missy to the bole of a larch tree in range of some sweet green grass. "You think the Scots are an oppressed people?" she asked.

"Poor people are always oppressed." He tied Faust to a birch and started up the path.

"And women," she said. "That's general, too."

"Women? I dinnae think sa."

"Of course they are," she said hotly. "A woman is sold into marriage. All she has passes to her husband's control. He can beat her or rape her, take mistresses. She has no rights. If we give our bodies elsewhere we are called sluts. Have you noticed there is no derogative word like that for men who bed multiple women?"

There was a long moment of silence as they climbed around a boulder. He reached back to hand her up. His touch roused that feeling that always seemed to lurk inside her these days. Was there no respite from it? He felt it, too, because he pressed his lips together and frowned. She thrust herself into the breach. "And often our bodies are the only living we can make. We trade them for marriage, or if we can't, then for money."

He looked grim. "I'll give ye that. But women parade themselves in their finest ta catch a husband." She couldn't argue with that. "They seem ta me like spiders in a web, waiting for th' unwary fly."

She had to smile, in spite of the shadow she saw pass behind his eyes. "Do we really? I hadn't thought of it like that. And you men are the poor unwary flies?" She considered.

"I think we adorn ourselves because it is the only power we have." She sighed. "It does seem vain."

"Ye dinnae indulge that vanity."

If he only knew how she longed to indulge it. She was jealous of Miss Zaroff with all her perfectly matched, expensive clothes. But no one knew that. "I'm not looking for a husband," she said with asperity. Or did it rankle that he thought she dressed plainly? "You must admit that the power to please is a small kind of power."

"Some women ha' more power than is good for th' world. There are those that are stronger than men. And if one *is* stronger . . ." He took a ragged breath. "Then she takes revenge fer all th' crimes o' strength against her sex."

A woman who was stronger? "Oh. You mean like an aristocrat who has social leverage over her servants or a queen over her subjects?"

"Somethin' like that." His voice, drifting back, sounded defeated.

Or maybe women like Miss Zaroff. She would be stronger than human men even in a physical sense. Jane decided, however, that she didn't want to talk about Miss Zaroff. She wouldn't think why. "I . . . I don't disagree with you," she said. He glanced back at her in surprise. "I've felt that anger against men. But men can be just as bad to other men."

A pause. Was he considering? "Aye."

"That's just the way of the world. Powerful against powerless. I wish it wasn't."

She thought he had decided not to respond but after a moment he continued. "Sometimes ye can balance out th' scales a little." He sounded so tentative.

But this was fascinating! She took three breaths so it wouldn't look like she was pouncing on his words. "You mean you take the side of the powerless?"

"Dinnae make it sound like Robin Hood." She heard the snort over the noise of the falls. "Whatever I am, I am no' English, and no' a hero." Again he paused. "But if ye're strong or rich or ha' a skill . . . there's an obligation ta go with that." He chuffed a derisive laugh. "Comes ta nothin' in th' end, any road. Ye clean out a nest o' vipers, and a new viper moves in."

"So what do you do?"

"Frighten the bullies. Give th' weak some leverage in return. With women it's usually money. They only sell their bodies because they dinnae ha' anythin' else. Ye're right about that."

He gave prostitutes enough money to leave the trade? "Sounds like a good tactic."

"Nae. They'll be back at it." A silence. She let it stretch. "There was one named Alice. She might make it out." His voice drifted back, wistful, through the darkness.

"I hope she does." She had pressed him enough. She dared no more. So she lightened her tone. "Perhaps the hardest part is that we women are not allowed to use our brains."

"Oh, sa ye ha' brains? I never knew." He had his voice under control now. It betrayed nothing. She was about to be outraged when she realized he was joking her. This was a first.

"You may scoff, sir. But it is very hard to be hedged round and kept from being what you can be. I want to be useful. But even my father lets me help only in menial ways. I hand him instruments. I clean the laboratory." She felt the old pain rising. "I could be a doctor—I know I could. But women aren't allowed to study medicine. So I must be content to be a midwife and learn what I can of anatomy by watching him."

He glanced back to her and then away. "I was no' scoffing. I only meant it's daft ta think all men dinnae want their women ta ha' a brain in their heads."

"As daft as thinking all women are spiders trying to trap men and eat them?"

He hesitated. "Point taken." He was practically shouting

to be heard above the noise of the falls now, which had been growing louder with each step. Well, at least he wasn't the kind who couldn't admit being wrong. That raised him in her estimation. She found herself wanting very much to know what Mr. Kilkenny would say next.

CHAPTER
Nine

Jane and Callan sidled round a bend where the path was narrow and muddy, squeezed between a high rock on the right and the rush of water on the left. The Falls of Divach poured down a sheer side of bare rock thirty feet into a black, roiling pool. The air was heavy with water vapor. The pool in front of the falls edged up to old trees, broad leaved and immense. Under their shelter moss and fern in midnight-green spread for perhaps fifty feet before they met steep hills covered in bracken where trees jutted out in crazy angles. If there were *Amanita* mushrooms to be had, *phalloides* or *virosa,* they would be here, in the damp under these trees.

She looked up at the night sky. The stars had disappeared. The clouds had lowered. "All right!" she shouted. "We're looking for mushrooms. One variety has a white umbrella cap about three inches across. Those are the *virosa*. The other has greenish caps about five inches across. Those are *phalloides*." She didn't tell him that one was called Destroying Angel and one Death Cap. "I'll take the top of the meadow near the falls. You start over there. Sing out if you find them. They grow in clusters."

She started toward the falls, poking under clumps of fern in the damp leaves with a stick she'd found. It took her an hour to work back down to the path. She'd found no trace of the deadly mushrooms. She straightened, putting a hand to the small of her back, and looked for Kilkenny. He had searched close to the hillside, but now he was coming out of the trees. She raised her palms in question. He shook his head.

She gripped her lip in her teeth. She hated to fail her father. She was failing herself and Kilkenny, too. She looked around. There! Across the pool. Wasn't that a knobby clump of small umbrellas among the green, and there, another! The cursed mushrooms were growing in the open on the other side of the pool. She turned to motion to Mr. Kilkenny and found him by her side. She hadn't heard him approaching in the noise from the falls. She pointed to the mushrooms.

He nodded, surveyed the problem, and began pulling off his boots.

"You don't mean to swim the pool," she shouted.

"If I dinnae swim, we dinnae ha' mushrooms," he shouted back, taking off his stockings.

"You'll catch your death."

First his eyes crinkled then a slow grin spread across his face. His teeth were white and even in the darkness. In that moment, she truly saw the charismatic rascal he'd once been. It was a revelation "Nae, ye canno' believe that, lass!" he chided.

Oh. She suppressed a sheepish look. He pulled at his shirt. She was so fascinated by that anomalous grin, it took her several seconds to realize what was happening. She spun around. Did the man insist on being naked in her vicinity? She flushed.

"Dinnae worry, I'll no' take off my breeches." Did he mock her? She wanted to see his eyes. "Hand me yer basket."

She took a breath and turned. It wouldn't do to let him know that even his bare torso did things to the part of her between her legs that made breathing difficult. In the moonlight his pale skin stood out against the dark of water, fern, and trees, his scars shining whiter still. The mist in the air made him gleam as though he was sweating lightly. She

handed him the basket. He fixed the handle to his belt, then
turned and walked into the pitch-black water. The scars on
his back were like the spiderwebs they had been discussing.
The bottom of the pool receded quickly, for he struck out to
the other shore after only two steps. The water must be like
ice. Jane shivered just to think about it. He was a strong
swimmer. He stepped up the far shore, dripping as he went,
and surveyed the meadow. He headed for the nearest clump
of mushrooms. She watched the play of muscles over his
back and shoulders as he bent. He went from clump to
clump. It wasn't long before he had the basket brimming
full. He held it up for her inspection. She nodded. That was
much more than enough. Her father couldn't think to use
very much of such a poisonous plant. This time Kilkenny
paddled back with one arm, holding the basket out of the
water.

He was shivering as he came out of the pool. His nipples
were pinched with cold. She held up his shirt and he used it
to wipe himself down.

"Thank you," she said, as he sat to pull on stockings and
boots. His breeches were doeskin and would hold the water.
"I don't know what I would have done without you."

"Ye'd a been cold and wet from swimming or ye'd ha'
gone home empty-handed," he agreed, that glint in his eyes.
He pulled his shirt over his head. It was hardly dryer than his
breeches at this point.

"What you need is a nice warm tartan," she said, picking
up the basket.

He rose and took it from her. "If ye lose yer footing and
dump th' mushrooms inta th' river, th' current'll take them.
And I'll no' ha' my swim wasted."

"I . . . I can carry a basket," she sputtered, but he had already started down the path.

She was silent on the way back. The wind had come up
and was pulling at her hair. And he took all her attention. His
every movement had a weary grace she had not recognized

before. When they got to the horses, he tied the basket to Missy's saddle while she pulled out one of Lachlan Dulnan's clean shirts, a vest, the Black Watch plaid, the warm green woolen stockings, and the boots that laced up the calf from the bundle he'd made. She laid them out on a rock and went to nuzzle Missy, her back to him. He could just take off his clothes and be done with it. She was not going to imagine the ribs of muscle over his flanks or the white curve of buttock as he bent to pick up the shirt. She needed a distraction. "Do you know how to wrap a plaid?" she called. She pulled herself up into her saddle and tucked her knee over the horn of the sidesaddle.

"I've seen it done a time or two."

She waited, arranging her skirts and careful not to look in his direction as Missy sidled.

"Ouch!" he exclaimed. "Damned pins."

She smiled and looked at her hands. She felt him come up beside her and swing up into his saddle. Now she could not help but stare. The green and blue of the tartan looked well on him, over the white of the shirt and a hunter-green waistcoat. The thick leather belt kept the pleats of the plaid secure around his loins. He'd pulled up the excess cloth over his back and fixed it with the pin of twining, stylized animals to his waistcoat over one shoulder. His collar was open at his throat. The twin, circular scars up and down both sides of his neck were usually covered by his cravat. She wondered again what could have made them. The glimpse of strong bare knees and the curve of muscled calf under his stockings might make the ride home long. "You look well in it," she said, just to be saying something. "The green goes with your eyes."

He looked at her sharply but said nothing. He took up the reins and gave Faust his office to start. Missy turned naturally in behind him.

It must be close on midnight. The clouds boiled above them and the wind was rising. She hoped they got home without a soaking—not that she was not already wet in certain places. What was she becoming, that just knowing Kilkenny was naked fifteen feet away could set her into a lather? Was she becoming one of her father's nymphomaniac patients? If he did not find a cure soon she might well lose herself, and not find her way back.

"Penny for yer thoughts," the man whose bare knees were riveting her attention said. The horses were walking side by side again now.

"They aren't worth a penny." They were coming down into the village. But their night's work was not done. "Turn right up ahead, Mr. Kilkenny."

He looked his question at her.

She did not answer directly, but only said shortly, "We've another stop to make."

Their destination soon became apparent. Ahead Callan saw the outline of ruined castle walls. He'd seen them the night he arrived as he turned up the glen toward Muir Farm. A tower of some five stories had its roots in the loch. Half-ruined walls, and the outlines of other towers, clung to the rock. Why would she want to go there?

"What is it?" he asked.

"Urquhart Castle," she said. "It's the reason for the village."

"Is there anythin' up there?"

"A fine specimen of nightshade as I recall and an excellent view of the loch."

They wended their way upward through the trees, losing sight of the castle several times. When at last they burst out of the woods the vast extent of the ruins was fully visible. Mist rose from the dark trees on the far shore of the loch, and nearer, the icy black waters spread small ripples ahead of the rising wind. Callan pulled up Faust beside a grassy ditch that must once have created a barrier to invasion by land. All that was left was a small stone bridge across it now.

Beyond lay stone walls no higher than a man in some places and roofless outlines of the many outbuildings it took to house garrisons of soldiers; smokehouses, root cellars, armories, and kitchens. The only building left intact seemed to be the tower.

"Looks like there's no' much left."

She climbed down and surveyed it. "Well, it's old. Built in the early twelve hundreds so they say."

"Sa was th' castle at Edinburgh, and it still stands." He hopped down. She started across the little bridge and he followed.

"This one changed hands about a hundred times, from Scot to Scot and English to Scot and back again. It commands the water passage to the Highlands. The last garrison was starved out but they blew it up as they left to prevent it being used against them. That was two hundred years ago, I think." She pointed to a bush growing along the outer wall. "There's our quarry. *Atropa belladonna.* Quite poisonous. It grows in lime. Hmm. I wonder if it grows just here because that's where they used to douse the soldiers with lime to kill their lice?"

"Well, that's an attractive thought," he muttered.

"Duncan is rumored to have killed a whole Danish army with it."

He looked around then glanced down toward the village on their left, dark now, its God-fearing people asleep. "Blowin' the place up was just th' first step in its demise. They took th' stones ta make their cottages."

"Much easier than quarrying more."

They dismounted. Jane was thankful she knew exactly where the specimen grew, for the clouds were really quite lowering, and there was an eerie, almost green light to the blackness.

"Leaves or roots?" he asked, untying the second basket from Faust's saddle.

"Both." She retrieved her trowel. Kilkenny walked over

to where the bush grew against the ragged stones of the ruined wall, Faust trailing in his wake, and got out his pocket
knife.

"Wait!" she called. "Let me." She hurried over, pulling on
some gardening gloves. "We shouldn't touch it with our bare
hands."

"That bad?" Kilkenny asked, his lips pressed together
grimly.

"Not a pleasant plant."

"Yer father seems ta have a penchant for th' poisons."

"Daunting, isn't it—that we might have to take something made with these ingredients?" She took his knife and
began cutting leaf clusters.

"A wee bit." His tone was ironic. Was he laughing at her?
He held out the basket.

It began to sprinkle. Jane cut faster. The sky split with
lightning. The flash made Jane squint. Each stone of the
wall, each leaf of the nightshade, stood out in relief. This
was as close to daylight as she and Kilkenny were likely to
get until her father found the cure. She counted two before
the thunder thudded in her chest. Kilkenny took the trowel
and dug until he got up a section of gnarly root. The basket
was almost full when the sky opened up and the deluge began in earnest. The drops were so large and so close together
that they sent up a haze of water as they bounced off the turf.
Lightning forked again, followed almost immediately by
thunder. It was getting dangerous out here in the open as
well as wet.

"Does that tower still ha' a roof?" Kilkenny shouted over
the clatter of the rain.

"Yes!" she yelled back.

"Come on, then!" He pulled Faust into a trot as he ran
across what was once the open castle yard. Missy needed no
encouragement to follow.

By the time they reached the tower, the rain had soaked
through her cloak. Kilkenny's kilt and shirt clung wetly to

his body. Their hair was streaming rivulets down their necks. The wooden door to the arched stone entry hung askew. They ducked inside to relative dryness. Jane clucked to Missy. After a hesitation, the mare walked into the darkness.

"Come on, Faust." Kilkenny's horse hung back at the end of his reins. "It's in or out, boy." Faust wasn't sure he liked the looks of the darkness. The rain on his croup made a halo of water. Kilkenny clucked and Faust used that as an excuse to surrender to dry stabling.

The tower only looked to be two stories high from where they had entered, but that was because three floors were below them, stretching down to where the stone rose from the loch. The room they were in was about twenty-five feet in diameter and roughly octagonal. The floor of thick timbered beams still stood firmly after centuries. The crash of the rain against the stones seemed comfortingly futile from inside these thick walls.

Jane went to one of three narrow slits that served for windows and looked out onto the loch. Kilkenny prowled the space behind her, peering out of each narrow slit. Then he went to the mare and began uncinching her saddle.

"What are you doing?" Jane asked.

"This looks ta last a while. They might as well be comfortable." He tossed the reins over Missy's head and tied a knot, so she couldn't tangle her feet in them, then moved to Faust.

Jane watched him in the darkness, feeling his body move and the animal energy that pulsed just beneath his surface. The tower seemed much too small, not because of the horses, but because of Kilkenny. He smelled of wet wool and wet hair.

Gusts of wind blew sprays of rain across the floor. Freed of their saddles, the horses moved together, nose to tail for comfort and warmth against the wall farthest from the open arch of the door. Missy didn't even squeal at the gelding. Kilkenny's boot heel thunked once as he moved the saddles out of reach of the rain. He put down her sidesaddle, then went back and stomped over the place again. He lifted his brows and leaned over to examine the timbers. "Aye, here it is," he muttered, grasping a ring set in the floor. He pulled. A section of floor creaked up, apparently on hinges, revealing a ladder.

"Some observer I am," Jane exclaimed. "I never noticed those."

Kilkenny stared into the abyss then descended the stairs, testing each one before he put his weight on it. They creaked, but held. Jane peered into the darkness. "What's down there?"

"Much th' same." His voice echoed up to her.

Lightning cast brilliant light through the windows. She put a foot gingerly onto the ladder and followed him down. "I wonder if there are stairs to the other levels."

"Likely. Are ye wantin' ta explore?" His voice was a hoarse whisper in the darkness. He was close. Now that the horses were above them, the space seemed even more filled with Kilkenny. It smelled of dust and stone. He smelled of cinnamon and something else. The fecund wet of spring rain wafted in through the windows.

"No. This is fine. Dry is as much as we can expect. Warm is too much to ask."

"Up with th' horses'd be warmer." He paced away from her, stamping his feet to test the sturdiness of the flooring. Did he really doubt it, or was it merely an excuse to move away?

"Not with wind gusting through that open door frame." Actually, she was thinking this room was fairly warm after all, what with Kilkenny giving off heat like a bonfire. Or maybe it was her body that was burning. She had begun to throb. She untied her cloak and swung it off, shaking as much water as she could from it. She laid it out on the dusty wood to dry, then wandered to the window embrasures, careful to avoid his restless pacing. The walls were so thick the rain couldn't gust in through the narrow slits. Outside, the loch was almost invisible through the roaring downpour, except when it was shot into brilliance by the lightning.

"I expect the soldiers thought this tower gloomy," she murmured. "They couldn't see in the darkness." She made her voice light. "You see? There are advantages to being vampire."

"I will no' miss it when it's gone," he said gruffly.

"Is there nothing about our condition worth missing?" She meant it as a real question. He must have heard that she wasn't feigning. He stopped his pacing. He'd have to answer her truly now or refuse her direct. Somehow, she didn't think he'd lie to her.

She saw him set his jaw. "There is a feeling o' being alive . . . Probably just ta seduce ye inta livin' with th' thing until it can get its teeth inta ye, or ye'd hire th' first ruffian ye could find ta chop off yer head." She found the lilting burr attractive, no matter the harsh words.

"Would it be that easy?"

He shook his head. "Nae. Th' thing makes ye fight against death. It'd only be possible, maybe, right after ye've turned and even then . . ." He trailed off.

"I know that alive feeling. It is wonderful, and . . . frightening," she whispered. "But is there nothing else to treasure?" Would he mention what it was like to make love when your body wanted it so badly and every sense was heightened? *God, where did that thought come from?* Perhaps from the heaviness in her core and the tightening of her nipples.

He shrugged, trying to deflect her question: "I like winning when I gamble."

"The infection makes you lucky?" Now that was a surprise.

"Aye," he said, disgusted. "I ha' supported myself since my . . . change at cards and dice. That's how I got th' money ta invest on the 'Change."

"How lucky?" she asked. This was intriguing.

He strolled closer. "I always win, sharps and Jack Flashes—it does no' matter. If I need a huitième at piquet, I get one."

Her mind began to whirl. "Why, the mathematical odds against getting a huitième must be . . . How many have you had?"

"Dozens."

"How could you influence the cards that way? Can it be that the energy . . . ? But how would the Companion know what cards were apropos to the game?" She tapped her lip with one finger. "Because *you* know, of course. That is the closest argument for a truly symbiotic relationship between the host and parasite yet. Does it always work?"

"I canno' win from poor men. Dinnae ask me why."

That started her to thinking in earnest. "Because you know who is poor from how they're dressed and you don't want to take their money. So that effect may not be universal to our kind, it comes from your personal ethics . . . It would be almost unconscious, of course . . ." She looked up at him. "We must have a game, so I can see it work."

His eyes crinkled, so faintly . . . "But ye would no' be a fair test, now would ye?"

She sighed. "I keep forgetting. Still, I must observe this phenomenon . . . why, it could have all sorts of consequences." If the Companion could meld its power with thoughts in its host's head . . . This was exciting!

"Scientific spirit o' experimentation?" Was his tone rueful or wry?

"You're making game of me. But we *should* strive to know about our condition."

"I just want it over."

She didn't berate him or ask him to find more good things about being vampire. The bleakness underneath that flat declaration bade her take pity on him. The momentary diversion of the fact that vampires somehow influenced the fall of cards and dice was gone. She realized she was staring at him. She turned away and leaned against the wall, looking out at the furious rain.

He came to stand behind her and cleared his throat. "I ha' been meaning ta thank ye for what ye did for me that first night, and fer sharing th' blood ye collect. Ye're verra kind."

"It was nothing. You would have done the same." He was too close.

"Ye dinnae know that." He shifted awkwardly. His eyes were light in the darkness of the tower room. Did he feel his mistake in standing too close? Would he move away?

"Yes I do." Her body was reacting as if it had been struck by the lightning that illuminated the loch. The thunder was rolling farther away now. Or maybe that was just the thumping of her heart in her chest. Her thighs were slick. She had been running from the feelings he raised in her ever since he got here. But in truth, she wanted very much to know what it would be like to make love to Callan Kilkenny. Why had she been avoiding him? Was she not a grown woman of nearly thirty? And she was not a virgin. She'd made sure of that. Was he not a grown man, who must know his mind? He had called her innocent. But she wasn't.

"Ye must ha' thought me churlish no' ta thank ye and yer father." He, too, looked out over the loch so he wouldn't have to look at her.

"No. I didn't think you churlish . . ." She took a step toward him in the darkness. She could feel his ragged breathing. And what of her own? She struggled to master the physical sensations and the emotions that rolled through her. She took a breath. *It is an experiment.* She only wanted to see how the physical act of making love with a vampire, in her new vampire state, compared with her experience, human to human, with Tom Blandings. That was all it was. She felt his reluctance, and yet she was sure he wanted it, too. Was it his honor that kept him from taking her in his arms?

She knew he was honorable, for all his pretense of callousness. "I thought you didn't think yourself worth helping. That's different."

"I might ha' been right."

Jane had to get some distance here, or she was going to just throw herself at him.

CHAPTER
Ten

The girl turned away from him with a suddenness that seemed to rip the bond of tension grown up between them. She pushed herself toward one of the window embrasures that overlooked the loch. Callan followed her. He seemed to be doing a lot of that. Lord knew he shouldn't, but he couldn't seem to help himself. She leaned against the wall. He managed to veer over to another window opening. Panting as though he'd just exerted himself he looked out. The waters of the loch below were ruffled with the wind.

"It's deep, so they say," she remarked. "Deeper than any other lake on earth. Probably just superstition. They say monsters live in it, too."

Was it deep? On the surface it looked like any other lake. But then, surfaces were always misleading. Beauty could harbor evil beyond belief, for instance. He stared at Jane Blundell instead of the loch. Her profile against the window embrasure was bold. No one would call her nose fashionably pert, for instance, and her chin . . . her chin was strong. She wore no rouge, and did not darken her eyelashes. She seemed to own naught but severe gray dresses.

It occurred to him that she had much in common with Scotland. No frills or lace, just a strong spine and features you might not appreciate right up until the point where you couldn't imagine them looking any other way. Only the violet eyes were a concession to conventional notions of beauty. But she was beautiful nonetheless. He looked away in disgust. He was lusting after her again. His loins tightened. Beauty was not a proxy for goodness. He knew that better than anyone. He shook his head against the dark water that began to rise inside his mind.

"What kind o' monster?" he asked, just to distract his thoughts from their direction.

"An orm. The great primeval worm of the world."

He drew his brows together. Superstition.

Suddenly she turned to him. "Why don't you go into politics?" she asked. "I mean after you're cured. Represent the Scottish interests in Parliament. You could make the English see Scotland as it is and what its people need."

He snorted in disdain. "All governments are corrupt."

"Not all," she protested. "Some try to do good."

Could a belly feel bleak? If so, his did. "Individual men doing small positive actions," he managed, turning out again to the cold, indifferent waters of the loch. "Sometimes those are possible. But no' societies." He had believed that one could create utopia once.

"Why not?" she challenged.

"Because they descend ta the lowest o' their members." He knew that to his cost. Maybe that would satisfy her. He could feel her eyes upon him, but he did not turn to look at her.

"What made you feel that way?" she pressed.

"Woman!" he objected. "D'ye never give a man peace?" He was *not* going into that.

She looked taken aback by his vehemence. Good.

Then he saw her gather her courage. "I have trod carefully on several occasions tonight in order not to frighten you because I can see you have some sorrow or some shame in your past. But that approach doesn't seem to be working." She stepped closer to him. "You give nothing of yourself, at least not if you realize you're doing it. And that doesn't seem fair, when I have told you about my work, and my hopes for being useful." She drew a breath, in spite of his glare.

"Frighten me?" he asked through gritted teeth. She was too close. "It would take more than a slip o' a girl ta frighten th' likes o' me." He turned back to the loch.

She turned to look out her own window with a humph of disgust. "Then maybe you're frightened of yourself. You are certainly afraid of allowing any kind of human contact."

They both saw it. Directly below them and not fifty yards away through the sheets of rain, a huge . . . something . . . like a gray hump of flesh, rose out of the water. Waves sloshed against the bottom of the tower. The gray hump seemed to slide in a never-ending length until it slipped under the water, only to rise in another place and another like an undulating . . . snake.

The girl gasped. Instinctively he strode the two steps toward her and took her in his arms as they watched the gray flesh, only slightly lighter than the black of the loch at night, disappear. They stood for a moment in silence. She was trembling in his arms. The feel of her slight shoulders against his chest, her arms around his body, made him tremble, too. The swell of his loins was almost painful. He felt her recollect herself. She straightened and stepped awkwardly away. He let her go, though every fiber in his body screamed at him not to do it.

"What . . . what was that?" she whispered.

He feigned a calm he did not feel for several reasons. "I expect it was yer monster."

She leaned into the embrasure, scanning the lake; yet another example of her courage. "Evie said that's what brought on her labor. But I was down near the loch that night and saw nothing. I thought she was . . . hallucinating."

"Apparently she was no' hallucinatin'." He calmed his breathing. Monsters could not frighten him. Was he not a monster himself? And a big animal, no matter how strange, could not hold a candle to Asharti, in terms of being fearful.

The girl turned to him, excitement gleaming in her eyes. "But this is wonderful! A creature hitherto unknown, and living right in Loch Ness . . . Why, this would make a marvelous paper for the Royal Society if one could only make some organized observations! My father would have an irrevocable place in history."

"Is that what he wants?"

That gave her pause. "Yes . . ." she answered slowly. "He wanted history to remember him for his work with transfusion. And now he has been sidetracked into finding a cure for me. I think he regrets it." There was hurt in her eyes. "They laughed at his paper on vampirism."

"Th' monster would be only a distraction to him, then." Callan managed a small smile he meant to be encouraging. "We must ha' all his intellect bent on finding th' cure."

She nodded. "Sorry." She smiled ruefully. "I appear to be easily distracted these days." She admitted what she considered her faults so readily. She made herself vulnerable, even laughed at herself. She'd made _him_ laugh tonight. He couldn't remember the last time he had really laughed, not at crude jokes in taverns, not at jibes by his once-followers. What she'd said tonight wasn't so much funny as it was . . . dear.

What was he thinking? He had no right to laugh, or to think her dear. She was prying and dangerous to his peace of mind. Did he possess any peace of mind? And the less time spent in her company the better.

And yet, there she was, not five feet from him, gone silent. He could see the heat growing in her big violet eyes. Callan stared at her and knew that he should have risked being burned to a crisp by lightning rather than come in here with her. His damned cock was stiffening and his balls ached. He'd tried to distract her. Hell, he'd tried to distract himself with talk of luck and such. But here she was with her violet eyes going dark. Now she was stepping closer to him. Didn't she know her danger?

And yet . . . she didn't know anything. She may have lost

her virginity, but the cad who took it had not cared enough to pleasure her or even be tender with her. She had no idea what sexual experience was like, let alone the sensory explosion of sex once a Companion circulated in your blood. There was no one to tell her about that part of being vampire.

He jerked himself over to stand in the embrasure of the window that looked toward the sleeping village, one palm on each side of the stone aperture. His body clamored at him, fully erect. He might burst right here. *Ye've held yerself away from women for two years,* he admonished. *Don't let a chit of an English girl lure you inta . . . inta what?* He swallowed hard. *Either being like Asharti or being reduced ta what Asharti made ye?*

That was the crux of it, wasn't it? He was afraid giving in to his sexual urges would derail his pitiful attempts to wrest his soul back from Asharti. He'd lose control and run amok or find out that his only means to pleasure with a woman was through pain. He closed his eyes.

Her palm on his side sent shocks directly to his loins.

"Time for us to stop running from it," she whispered as she pressed herself against his back and buttocks. He felt her breasts flatten against his soaking shirt. His private parts were so heavy they were painful. "I won't consider it a commitment. I won't cling."

He groaned and turned, his hands held out, away from her. He dared not give in to his body's screaming urge. But still she pressed against him. He felt her nipples against his chest through the fabric between them. Now she would know what she had done to him. His erection lay against her belly. His body was on fire. She ran her hands over his wet shirt.

God, but it was more than a man could resist!

He leaned forward and brushed her forehead with his lips as his arms found their way around her. He sought out her lips. The softness of them struck him to the core. She opened her mouth to him, and then his tongue was inside. He tightened his embrace . . .

"Jane," he whispered into her mouth. "Jane . . ."

God help him, her tongue searched his mouth tentatively in return and she ran her hands down over his buttocks. His cock was pressed between them, throbbing. She ground her hips against it. Bloody hell! He was lost . . .

Jane opened her mouth to the sweet penetration of his tongue. She'd never been kissed like that. The shared moistness was more intimate than anything she had ever known. She wanted to touch more of him. The hardness of his erection against her belly was a revelation. How long had he been that way? She knew what he looked like naked and aroused, and the thought of him lying on the table in the kitchen at Muir Farm three nights ago made her tremble inside. She needed something, not like what she had done with Tom Blandings—she didn't care about that—but something. She pressed her hips into his thighs.

He growled. But she was far from frightened. She pulled up his kilt and ran her hands over his bare buttocks. That was what kilts were for. His muscles clenched as he pressed himself into her. She could feel the raised ribbons of his scars. He pulled his lips from hers to kiss her neck. Would he bite her? She didn't care. He could have every drop of blood in her body and welcome if he would make the needing go away.

"Tell me ta stop now," he said, panting in her ear. "In a minute I'll no' be able ta turn back."

"Why would I want you to stop?" she whispered.

He swung her up into his arms and carried her to where her cloak lay spread on the ground. He laid her down gently then stood. He ripped the pins from his kilt and tore off his waistcoat, sending buttons popping everywhere. She tugged off her boots as he did the same. She pulled at the bodice of her habit where the military-style black buttons held the gray wool together. They too popped, and her breasts came spilling out of her torn chemise. His kilt pooled on the floor and he was naked except for his shirt. She tore at the ties that held her skirts to the bodice. He knelt and pulled her skirt free. She couldn't quite see the part of his anatomy she sought. It was revealed only by the bulge in his long shirt. She tugged at her drawers. They ripped in her hands. She wanted to be naked and see him naked, too. He pulled his shirt over his head. The enormity of his erection gave her a deep satisfaction. It would be demanding of her. She wanted that. It might begin to satisfy the need she felt tearing at her from the inside.

The scars stood out against his flesh, shouting that he had been abused. But that was behind him now. He was focused only on the present. Even in the dark, she took in every detail of his body; the veins over his biceps that fed the muscles, the bulge of his thighs, the thick dark hair in which his erection nested. He seemed so different than he had lying on the kitchen table, so alive, so . . . ready. Three nights ago her reaction to him was not likely to result in intercourse, whereas now . . .

He lay down beside her, pressing kisses on her throat. Then he fastened his mouth on her left breast and suckled there, gently. She arched, moaning, panting. Tom Blandings had never done that! She had never known how sensitive her nipples were. He fingered her other breast. She writhed against him. "More," she moaned. "I want more."

He pulled away from her breast and looked up at her. How had she ever thought those gray-green eyes were cool? They flashed with heat, even as he grinned, showing even white teeth. She loved that grin already though it was only the second time she'd seen it. "Are ye saying ye want my cock, lass?" His accent had grown thicker.

"Is that what men call it?" She mimicked his accent. "Then, aye, I want yer cock." To prove it, she reached down and circled his shaft with one hand softly. She reveled in his hissing intake of breath. Had she ever touched Tom Blanding's penis? She didn't think so, for the sensation of silken skin over such hardness seemed a revelation. She moved her hand up and down, as she had watched Meg Carruthers do with her customers, and he arched his back. His nipples were tight and pebbly. It must be with desire because he couldn't possibly be cold. She herself was burning. On impulse she licked his nipple and felt it tighten even further. She laid her thumb over the tip of his cock. Moisture oozed there. It made her ooze with him in a delightful shudder to know that this was a wet experience for him, as well.

Gently he took her hand from his cock. "Be careful, lass. Ye'll draw me too soon."

"Then get to yer work, lad." She grinned and spread her thighs to him.

Callan wanted nothing more than to shove his aching cock to the hilt inside her and pound against her until he came in a roaring gush of sweet release.

But he couldn't. Not yet. The girl had never even had her pleasure of a man. And he couldn't be certain she'd climax along with him, vampire or not. She hadn't had anything like a fulfilling experience with that cad she chose to receive her virginity. He must make certain she was the one who received pleasure tonight, hard as it might be to wait.

He put aside the feel of her breasts against his chest and mastered himself. He couldn't help the growl, low in his throat, as he covered her mouth with his, searching with his tongue. In spite of her challenge, he didn't move his body to cover hers. What he wanted most was to please her with his mouth, to taste the musky cream he could smell on her even now, but he wasn't sure she was ready for that, and the last thing he wanted was to frighten her. So it was his hand he put between her legs. His palm pressed against her mound and his fingers slipped inside her moistness. She gasped in surprise.

"What are you doing?" she moaned.

"No' taking any chances," he muttered.

• • •

Jane had no idea what he meant, but she lost all power to concentrate on anything but what his fingers were doing. They rubbed over flesh so sensitive she thought she might not be able to stand another moment of it, but she never wanted him to stop. He dropped his head and took her nipple in his mouth again, pulling gently on it with his lips. Sensation shot through her from her woman's parts to her breast and back again, cycling up until she wondered whether she would lose consciousness. The only other sensation there was room for in her brain was the feel of his throbbing erection against her hip. Somewhere she heard him whispering soothing encouragement between his bouts of sucking. He fingered her in circles and then gently back and forth over some swollen part she didn't know she had. She was panting and lifting her breast to his mouth, thrusting her hips up into his hand. Her world contracted. Her body contracted with it. She cried out in a continuous series of sharp gasps. And then she just exploded. There was no other word for it. He didn't stop rubbing her. She curled into him, her muscles contracting. Her body finally jerked away from his hand of its own volition as a shriek escaped her.

The air vibrated around her as the sensation between her legs slowly faded. She examined his face even as he was examining hers. His eyes still glowed with passion. His pale skin stood out against the darkness, his dark hair blended with it.

She shouted a laugh, but the laugh turned into a sob and then she was crying against his bare chest, the scent of cinnamon and male suffusing her. Nothing remotely like this had happened with Tom Blandings. She rocked and sobbed as he held her, and smoothed back her hair, whispering to her that it was all right.

"Don't mistake my tears," she gulped at last. "It wasn't painful, or distressing. It was wonderful. I don't know why I'm crying."

"I do. And I dinnae take it wrong," he whispered.

"Is . . . is it more intense for us?" It couldn't be like that for mere humans.

"Aye."

She realized that his . . . his cock was still throbbing against her bare hip. "And what of you?" she asked, suddenly shy. How could she be shy after what she had just done with him? She reached for his shaft. She wanted to give him what she had just experienced.

"Nae." His marvelous lips rolled the word out. His eyes were hot. "Ye ha' no' yet had th' whole experience. If I can last, God help me, ye'll peak again with me inside ye."

Impossible! It would surely kill her. But she didn't care. He kissed his way up her throat to her jaw, caressing her skin with those marvelous lips. His hands were big on her body, over her ribs, across her belly, around her hips, and down to her thigh. The throbbing began again between her legs. Her breasts grew heavy. He growled as he kissed her lips and she loved the fact that all he could do was growl. In spite of his protest she touched his cock again. Drops of moisture oozed from the tip onto her thumb. She rubbed the moisture over the head and down the shaft.

"Lord, woman!" he gasped. "I canno' hold it."

"Then don't." She put her lips on the place at the base of his throat where his pulse was pounding and licked the salty skin. She spread her thighs.

"Ye're ready so quick?"

She just nodded, thinking she might burst if he didn't bury his thick member in her right *now*. He moved into position over her. Her breasts flattened, her nipples just scraping the hair on his chest as he held himself with one elbow over her and positioned his cock with his other hand. "I'll go gently now," he whispered, easing into her.

She didn't want gentle. She wanted to feel that hard flesh slide in through all her wetness. She reached around and put a palm on each buttock and pulled him into her. The shock of satisfaction as he filled her made them both moan. He felt huge, and she impaled on him. Then he was moving in and out, the muscles in his buttocks bunching and releasing under her hands. Her entire nether region suffused with sensation once again. Could she stand it? He covered her lips with kisses even as he pumped inside her. His cock split her, demanded of her. She arched into him, all thought narrowing to the feel of his mouth on hers, his hand on her breast, the sensation of his cock driving into her wettest, most needy parts. She didn't have to think about the movements or wonder if they were correct. They came of wanting more of him inside her and arching to meet his thrusts, which were coming faster now. Then she couldn't think at all, but just said "oh, oh, oh," to match the grunts he emitted in time to his thrusts.

This time the world contracted to a tiny pinpoint of light . . . and then burst, like lightning and thunder all at once except inside her body, and she was keening as all her muscles contracted yet again. Then, wonder of wonders, he stilled, the muscles under her hands taut, and she felt him spurting inside her. They froze, immobile while the moment expanded and contracted.

They both tried to breathe. He swallowed and made as if to withdraw.

"No," she said, pulling him in to her. "Just a little while more." He eased himself over her, keeping his weight on his elbows, yet covering her with his body.

"Jane," he murmured, his bass rumble caressing her name.

So this was what all the fuss was about!

She felt transformed.

Wait! What was she saying? She had been possessed by a frenzy. It might have been demonic. She had lost all control, all objectivity. At the very least she had just worshipped at the altar of Dionysus, not Apollo. She looked up at him and saw a look of . . . of what? Possessiveness?

Kilkenny's weight suddenly seemed to pin her down. She pushed him off her, panting shallowly. He rolled away, startled.

She sat up, clutching her bodice together. Did she have no self-control, no decency? Even now just the sight of his . . . his genitals made her throb again. Where would this lead? Would she become just another silly female mooning after men? That wasn't what she wanted. And Kilkenny! What did he care for her aspirations, her true nature? He just took advantage of her lust. She wanted to burst into tears again. And they were not the same kind of tears she'd just shed against his chest.

What had happened to her?

Jane pushed him off her and sat up, flushed and breathing hard. Callan rolled away, shocked. He knew he had given her pleasure. The raw emotion in her eyes a moment ago was amazement, tenderness. But now her eyes sparked with anger as she pulled her clothing together.

What had he done here? Ravished her? No, she had been willing but she regretted it. She wrote in her notebook that she wanted transformation. But sexual intercourse did not transform. The act of congress always left one flat and yearning for something that didn't exist. That must be what she was feeling. He had felt it a hundred times. And he'd felt worse with Asharti. But that wasn't how he felt now. He'd thought . . . but the look in her eyes said he was wrong.

God, how had he sunk so low as to defile her? She hated him. He could see that. And if she knew what he had done in the desert . . . He squeezed his eyes shut. If Jane Blundell had even a hint of how evil and weak he was, she would spit on him and order him away.

He got to his feet somehow and turned away from her. They had used each other just the way Asharti used him to slake her lust. The tenderness he'd felt for her was an illusion. And certainly any feelings he imagined in her were only that—imagined.

The damned vampire lust! The Companion used them both. It wanted life, and sexual congress was the ultimate expression of creation and life. Why in God's name had he given in to it? The feel of her soft flesh against his had maddened him. Indeed, it wasn't safe to think about her even now. He might lose whatever small portion of his identity he had managed to scrape together since Asharti. Or worse, he might give it away.

He strode to where his wet shirt pooled on the floor. He stood frozen above it, the air in the tower chill now that the fire inside him had been doused. Outside the wildness of the storm had sunk to a steady, soaking rain.

What he felt tonight was far more powerful than what he had ever felt with Asharti. Why? Was it because for two years he'd not felt a woman's touch on his body, a woman's lips on his? They had offered. Women always offered to a well-made man. He wanted to claw at his face, to rend the flesh Asharti had found desirable. But he would just heal, and his Companion wouldn't even leave disfiguring scars.

He didn't need any more scars. He was disfigured on the inside. The face of an innocent man in the desert, begging for his life, flashed before him. All he had tried to do since he escaped couldn't change his true nature. Emotion whooshed from him, leaving his shoulders to sag. Jane was right to be angry. She must despise him.

"I can't believe I . . . I so lost my senses . . ." she muttered to herself.

"It will no' happen again, I promise."

"You're right, it won't." Her voice was tight.

He reached for his shirt. The sodden fabric slid over his head. He wrapped the kilt around his loins. Even now, imagining her behind him, he felt himself rise again. He had to get out of here. But he couldn't leave her to fend for herself. He must escort her back to the farm. God, what would he do, just knowing she was in the house with him, remembering her breast in his mouth, the way she spread her thighs so eagerly for him? He began to ache. He kept his back toward her as he snatched up the basket of the latest poison her father would use to torture him.

"Come," he said, his voice hoarse in his ears. "It's time ta brave th' rain."

He motioned her to the stairway. She glanced at him and then away. She was ashamed of what they had done here.

And why not? So was he.

The ride back to the farm was sodden and silent. Jane, once so eager to know about her condition, now felt a wall between her and Kilkenny she could never bridge. The horses trudged up the glen in the relentless rain. She had never wanted to be one of those frivolous misses who thought only about how to attract a man. She had more serious things to do with her life. She had no desire to cede control of it to a man. She had seen the possessive look in Kilkenny's eyes tonight. It was the look all men got in their eyes when they looked at a woman. Well, she would never be possessed by a man.

And yet, she had surely lost control of herself tonight. The feel of chaotic emotions and desire ripping through her unrestrained frightened her. She would have done anything tonight to make the needing go away. She would have abased herself, begged him, and played the wanton. Now that she thought on it, she *had* done those things. Where was her pride? Where was her purpose? If she wasn't careful, she'd end up begging any man she could find to rub her the way Kilkenny had tonight. She flushed with shame. How would she bear his presence in her house, knowing that he knew what she had done tonight? Could he be trusted to keep his distance? She cringed. It might not be Kilkenny who was untrustworthy, but herself.

CHAPTER
Eleven

Callan pulled the horses up to the barn, uncinched their saddles, slid their bridles over their heads, and tossed them some hay, then headed down for the house through the rain.

As he pushed into the kitchen, Clara was dishing up some vegetables around a pheasant that smelled wonderful. She glanced up at him and her eyes widened. Callan realized that his kilt was pinned awry and his waistcoat had no buttons. What must she think of him? Probably just what he deserved that she think. He pushed through the kitchen, past the dining room. He was about to go upstairs to change into something dry if he could find it, when he saw Miss Zaroff and Jane . . . Miss Blundell (damn it, he had no right to call her anything else) in the sitting room.

"My, but there appears to be so much you do not know," Miss Zaroff was remarking. "There you are, Kilkenny." She motioned him in. Callan had no desire to confront Miss Zaroff looking like he did. But he didn't want her badgering Jane about what she didn't know of being vampire. He set his jaw and ducked into the room.

Jane . . . Miss Blundell had already changed into yet another drab gown, black this time. She was looking flushed. He could smell what they had done together on her. He must exude a similar scent. He glanced to Miss Zaroff. She could not help but know what they had done. Indeed, her eyes narrowed.

"Kilkenny, I was just telling Miss Blundell she should proceed with caution when she is out alone with you." The woman already knew Miss Blundell had not proceeded with caution.

Callan went still and said nothing.

"After all," Miss Zaroff continued blithely, "it is not often one encounters so famous or so ruthless a criminal."

Callan had been a fool to think she would keep silent about his past. Why did she choose to reveal it now? Was it because she knew he had made love to Jane Blundell?

A ruthless criminal? What was Miss Zaroff saying? Jane looked at her stupidly. She glanced to Kilkenny, but he only set his lips and looked grim.

"Can it be you do not know who you harbor?" The musical laugh sounded like it should have been tinkling through a grand palace, not the humble sitting room of Muir Farm. "Callan Kilkenny is a famous fugitive. He made a vampire army and tried to take over the government of England, didn't you, Kilkenny? You wanted to create a vampire society to prey on humans. And the corpses he left in his wake! I have no idea how many."

The muscles in Kilkenny's jaw clenched, but still he said nothing. Jane was shocked. Was Kilkenny a criminal among his own kind? Was he making vampires, plotting treason, killing people? How little she knew of his past and that only what he had told her himself.

"The Elders want you dead, you know." Miss Zaroff put one lilac-gloved finger to her dimpled chin.

"Well, they'll ha' ta wait until th' cure is found," Kilkenny muttered. He turned on his heel and strode from the room. Jane heard the kitchen door open and slam shut. She stared at Miss Zaroff, who looked exactly like the proverbial cat who dined on canary. She couldn't face that expression. She wouldn't give the woman the satisfaction of being smug about knowing more about Kilkenny than Jane herself did. Was it even true? But Kilkenny hadn't bothered to deny it. She felt her anger rising in her throat. She'd just see about that.

She mustered a smile. "Won't you excuse me? I find I'm fatigued." And she too left the room, to Elyta Zaroff's widening smile.

Damned interlopers. He lit the lantern hanging outside the tack room. He might as well oil the saddles and bridles before they stiffened from their soaking. He got out some oil and rags, slung Miss Blundell's sidesaddle over a stall door. It smelled, subtly, of her, beneath the scent of wet leather. He found he couldn't face that smell, so he decided to rub down the mare and grabbed a curry comb.

Elyta Zaroff had put a wedge between him and the Blundells. The look in her eyes as she informed on him, so smug, so . . . ruthless. That look was familiar somehow. A powerful vampire woman . . . more powerful by far than he was . . .

He clenched his eyes shut and leaned on braced arms against the mare's barrel as the memories washed over him unstoppable.

Marrakech, March 1819
Callan hung his head, on hands and knees above her. His body was drenched in sweat, his cock still achingly erect, balls tight with need. A drop of his blood splatted on the golden skin of her thigh. She sighed in satisfaction and pointed to her side. He lay beside her and she licked at the jagged cut she had torn just over his nipple. His erection pressed thickly against her thigh.

She raised her head. Her lips were rosy with his blood. She was not human. He knew that now. "You made me force you again tonight, slave. You have not yet learned true submission."

He closed his eyes, exhausted. What did she want? He obeyed her. He had no choice.

"Ah," she breathed, tracing his lips with her long-nailed finger. "You must want to submit. You must want more than anything else to do what will please me."

How could one love such horror? It had been almost a month. All thought of escape was gone. She kept him chained whenever he was not in her presence, and in her presence, he could no more escape than he could vanish into thin air.

She sat up and arranged her silks. She usually remained clothed, except when he bathed her and she took him during or directly after her bath. "Stand to the strap," she said casually.

He sucked in a breath and pushed himself to his feet. He could only hope she would grow bored with whipping him. She grew bored easily. Two poles were set perhaps a yard apart especially for him. He stood between them, spread his feet and grasped the poles above his head. If he made her force him into position, she just prolonged the punishment. He heard her moving behind him. Her attention must be elsewhere, for his aching erection eased. He breathed in, and out. He could bear this. He always bore it. He imagined her picking up the broad leather strap fitted with a wooden handle at one end. His palms were slick and he rubbed them against the poles to get a better grip. If he fell, she would be displeased.

"Your countrymen are all so resistant. It's true, I find that stimulating," she remarked. "But I think you are capable of something more, with coaxing,"

What? What more? He dared not think what she meant by coaxing.

He heard the rush of air that preceded the snap of leather against his flesh. The sting made him jump. He should be grateful it was not the lash. But she liked to let the thin, bloody stripes heal before she used the lash again and his back was still raw tonight. The strap was painful but it didn't draw blood. It left only swollen red welts. She was strong *enough to maim him, even kill him, but she didn't. These sessions were controlled, designed to break him down, bit by bit. She worked his back and thighs, but she always beat his buttocks almost lovingly.*

The blows went on and on. He swayed as he struggled to remain upright. Sweat poured off him in the stifling tent. The rhythm broke. He felt her behind him. His knees were wobbling.

"Say you love it," she whispered in his ear.

He swallowed. God, she was bringing up his erection again. Maybe if she liked resistance, he should not resist. "I love it," he said before she needed to compel obedience.

"No, no, no. You must mean it. You must be stimulated by submitting to me." She ran her nails lightly over the welts and scabs on his back, down to cup his right buttock. "Mean it."

How could he convince her he meant it? He hated every moment of his servitude. He couldn't ask her how she'd be convinced. She didn't like him speaking, let alone questioning.

But, as often happened, she seemed to sense his question. "When you get a natural erection from submission to me, I will know you are truly mine."

He hung his head. Impossible! He would never satisfy her.

"Do not despair. You will come to it with training."

Callan wanted to scream. He began to fear he would *come to it.*

Callan moaned. He rolled his head on the mare's warm flank. He *had* come to it. He'd lost himself after months of abuse, until all he thought about was how to please her. Not that he could avoid the strap or the other "recreations" she devised for herself. But he avoided the pain inside his head she could create to punish him. And that was why he didn't indulge in sex with a woman. He was afraid of the twisted emotions it would engender.

He lifted his head.

But he had indulged in sexual relations tonight with Jane.

And it hadn't been like that. Yes, there was lust. Lord, how he had wanted her! He knew for certain she had wanted the same from him. And it was true that it was their Companions that goaded them to it. Yet . . . had there not been tenderness, too . . . ?

It didn't matter. He must keep away from her. He must never give in to those impulses again. He might betray himself. She might know the whole of what he had been, what he had done . . . And it was so much more than betraying England.

"Guilty memories?"

He jerked around to see Jane Blundell standing in the barn aisle.

The look of horror on Kilkenny's face almost made Jane take a step backward. She steeled herself and stood her ground. She had to know the truth. Could she have been so mistaken about him?

All emotion drained from his face and his eyes as he purposely pulled the mask down over his features. "Aye, guilty memories." He returned to currying the mare.

She would not let him escape so easily. "And are you a criminal?"

"Aye."

She was half surprised he'd answered her question. But it certainly wasn't a satisfying answer. She clenched her fists at her sides. "And a traitor?"

"Aye."

This was *not* what she had pictured on the way up to the barn at all. She'd imagined him telling her his past in detail, so she could judge him. Because if she had been so wrong about him then the world was a different place entirely and . . . and she didn't know what she'd do. But she couldn't judge his character if he was going to admit to everything in a single, unsatisfying syllable. "To England, or to vampire kind?"

"Both, I expect." His shoulders bulged with muscle under his half-dry shirt as he worked the currycomb over the mare's glossy hide. Missy stood quietly. As Jane watched, she touched her nose to Kilkenny's elbow and blew softly on him. Missy liked him.

God help her, so did she. That was why she couldn't quite believe Miss Zaroff.

"How about the corpses?"

He looked ill. "Aye, that too."

"Are you going to tell me about it?" she asked finally, in exasperation.

"Nae."

She sucked in a breath. "They implied that you're evil, and you don't even defend yourself, and . . . how is one to know what to believe?" She felt her voice rising.

"Believe them." His voice was so low even she could hardly hear it.

"Fine. I'll believe them." She turned on her heel and strode from the barn.

Callan snatched up the rag and the oil and began to rub her saddle with fierce strokes. She'd think the worst of him. What did he care? He had no business caring what she thought. He wasn't even human anymore. And it wasn't just because of the thing in his blood. He'd become less than human when he'd given in to Asharti, and all the useless efforts to deny his true nature that he'd engaged in over the last two years couldn't change his cowardice, his . . . aberration. He clenched against that pain. If he thought about that he'd go mad. He couldn't afford to go mad at the moment. He took a breath. He'd think about his current problem.

He didn't believe anyone from Mirso Monastery would want a cure for vampirism. The whole power structure of the Elders was built on the fact that vampires couldn't kill themselves. If they could simply take the cure and live a single mortal life, or even commit suicide, why would they need

Mirso's secret chants or the Elders? Elyta Zaroff and Brother Flavio, and perhaps Clara, too, had another reason for wanting the cure. Did it matter? Once he was cured, and he had a copy of the formula, they could do what they wanted with it. He'd copy the formula from the doctor's notebook as soon as he was cured. Then he'd be gone.

Could he leave the Blundells to the tender mercies of Elyta Zaroff and Brother Flavio?

Of course he could. Why not?

He refused to think about that. He worked on Faust's saddle, concentrating on the feel of the leather under his hands, the smell of the neetsfoot oil. He had to distance himself from the Blundell girl. When the time came, he'd take the formula and go. What he couldn't do was let her presence distract him into doing what they'd done tonight. He'd better stay up in the barn all night, to keep away from her.

Hell and damnation! What he needed to do was explain his crimes to her in detail. Then she'd know how bad he was and turn against him. She'd never want to be in his company again, and he'd be safe from her. He slung the saddle into the tack room and blew out the lamp. No time like the present.

Callan let himself into the farmhouse kitchen. He heard movement in the room at the far end of the hallway upstairs. The Zaroff woman in her room. Was Jane already asleep an hour before dawn? But either she wasn't here or she was already asleep. He couldn't hear her. He'd have to postpone his confession. The next best thing was to barricade himself in his room so he wouldn't have to see her. He took the stairs two at a time, not caring if Miss Zaroff heard him. He strode down the hall toward his room, past Jane's door. And stopped. Was she inside? Even if she was asleep he should be able to hear her breathe. Nothing.

He'd never actually seen her room. An impulse took him. If she were gone it would be safe. He turned the knob. The door swung open silently. For one brief moment of hope and dread he thought she might be there after all, laid out upon her bed, in her night clothes.

The room was empty. But she was there in every detail. More of her paintings hung on the walls. A tall shelf was filled to overflowing with books. The bed was covered with a richly embroidered coverlet in deep greens and blues like water in the evening just after the sun had set. He'd wager she had stitched it herself. She'd told him she could sew. Who else would be so bold as to use those colors when the fashion was for pastels and pristine white? He ran the tips of his fingers over the embroidery. Fishes and swirling kelp beds were stitched on rich brocade quilt blocks, an embarrassment of intricate design. Her bed was a vision of the sea. How was she capable of making such richness when she dressed only in black and gray? It was as if he was seeing her naked all over again. Being in her room, seeing her private things, was that intimate.

He should leave. And yet he wanted to breathe her in, know her. He turned his head. A magazine lay, open, on the little table next to a leather wing chair set by the hearth. He wandered over. It was open to a fashion plate. A frivolous dress in pink gauze with rows and rows of wide ruffles at the hem was drawn and colored in loving detail.

Jane read magazines with fashion plates? He picked it up, revealing a stack of several more. So her addiction to fashion plates was long-standing. He looked at the date. Six months ago. She couldn't get the latest *London's Ladies Magazine* up here in the wilds of Scotland. He flipped through the other illustrations of the latest fashions. "Straight from the Salons of Paris," one caption read. "Pomona Green Is No More. Ladies of Fashion Prefer Sea Foam." He dropped the magazine back to the little table and slipped hastily out the door. He must get out of here.

He was shocked. He was intrigued. He thought he knew her. He didn't.

Did she know, herself? It was of a piece, though. Her paintings were extraordinary. She loved beauty, wherever it was found, even in pretty dresses. So why did she deny it?

Callan took the beaker from Dr. Blundell. He didn't let his hand shake.

"If this doesn't work," the doctor muttered, "I don't know what will." The man looked old today and worried.

Callan was naked in the dim laboratory. The windows were draped against the sun. Candles lit the winking glass around them. "Well, then, let's hope this takes th' trick." Callan strove to sound more cheerful than he felt. He up-ended the flask and swallowed the thick, bile-green mixture in long gulps. It was sour, but he managed to get it down.

As he handed back the empty flask, Miss Zaroff pushed in from the sunlight outside. He cringed away, covering his eyes, and grabbed for his plaid.

"You new ones are so sensitive to a little sunlight," he heard her say. "I had forgotten."

Callan clutched a fist full of kilt to his loins. The door closed with a bang. Callan swung round. "What do ye want?" he rasped. A stinging feeling ran along his veins.

"To observe the results of the latest test, of course," she said. "Dr. Blundell, would you mind an extra pair of eyes?" She wore a deep purple traveling cape as a shield from the sun, but her face was uncovered and she wore no gloves. She had not blistered as he would have.

"Of course not, my dear." The doctor bustled to get her a stool. He called her "my dear" just because she looked younger than he was. Ludicrous.

Callan felt the familiar cramping as the poison took him. His skin broke out in hives. He sucked at air as his throat began to close.

"My! The effect is certainly immediate," Miss Zaroff remarked.

"To the pallet, Kilkenny," the doctor advised. "If you fall, you'll break my glassware."

Callan staggered a couple of steps and dropped to his knees, gasping. He tried to pull the kilt up about him so she couldn't see his bare buttocks, but it was beyond him. He doubled over.

"May I get you some tea, Miss Zaroff? This is likely to go on for some time."

Callan heard the words from a distance. He vowed not to groan. He hardly had air for it.

"Yes. Please. My, this is quite stimulating isn't it? Does he always suffer so?"

Callan clutched his stomach. It felt like his intestines were being ground up with glass. He wanted to vomit, but his throat was so closed he thought it would choke him.

"One hates to cause such pain. But I'm afraid it's necessary."

"Absolutely, Doctor. Without question."

Callan was writhing now. A strangled gargle issued from his throat. Sweat soaked him.

"Perhaps you'd better take that plaid from him. He'll only soil it."

"Dear me, I forgot myself. I should rather cover him, seeing as we have a lady observer."

"Never mind on my account. Feel free to have him naked as the day he was born, in the spirit of science, of course." That tone sounded familiar. But Callan couldn't think. He tried to breathe. His flesh felt like it was being torn from his bones. The pain in his gut was worse than it had ever been before.

"Thank you, Doctor," Miss Zaroff remarked. "Tea is just the thing." Someone pulled the plaid from his clenched fists. "What is your strategy today?"

"Three poisons in combination. This is the strongest potion yet."

The pain went on and on. He couldn't hear their words, though he knew they were talking. Breath grew harder to come by. Blackness ate at the edges of his vision.

Jane dashed up from the house with a blanket over her head. Her skin buzzed with irritation, though she was well covered. She'd spent the few remaining hours of night roaming the hills above the farm with her watercolors. But she couldn't paint. She could hardly even think. Was Kilkenny as bad as he said he was? Miss Zaroff and Brother Flavio thought so. They thought him bad enough to deserve death. And what of their interlude at Urquhart? She was torn between her resolution never to see him again, so that she would never run the risk of succumbing to her desire, and remembering the feel of his skin, the glow in his gray-green eyes. She was, in short, a hopeless muddle. She'd only come up to the house when the sunrise chased her in. It was when she was taking off her half-boots that she remembered her father would be testing a potion on Kilkenny during the daylight hours.

Strangled cries and her father's calm voice issued from behind the door as she burst through it. Kilkenny was writhing on the floor, naked, drenched in sweat, his face red and gasping. Veins stood out in his neck as he clutched his belly. Miss Zaroff sat on a stool sipping tea and her father peered at Kilkenny as he made notes.

"Jane!" Her father hastened up to push her back toward the door. "You mustn't see this."

She pushed past him. "What are you doing, Papa? He's choking!" She didn't wait for an answer but grabbed a rubber tube they used in transfusions and knelt beside Kilkenny. His breath came in horrible sucking sounds and his face was going purple. Welts stood out on every available patch of skin. That was the nightshade. Dear God, Papa had given him the root, raw!

"I think your poisons must have killed his Companion,"

Miss Zaroff remarked. "Else he would have healed the welts that are closing his throat."

Jane wanted to scream at her, but she had to save her concentration for Kilkenny. She pushed a hand under his head and clutched it to her breast. He struggled at first, but she could see his eyes swimming. She forced open his jaw and shoved the tube down his throat. She was probably damaging the tissue, but if this didn't work the only thing left was a tracheotomy, and she couldn't imagine thrusting a knife into his throat to open the airway. His chest went still. The tube pushed through the swollen tissue as she fed in more and more. She grasped the end and blew as hard as she could. His chest rose visibly. She took her mouth away and the air rushed out. She blew again, waited, and again.

His eyes jerked open and he began to choke on the thick tube. He flailed and struggled until his eyes focused. He quieted. Then his eyes went red. Power washed over Jane as his Companion surged into action. The welts on his skin faded. He scrambled to his knees, pulling frantically at the tube. When it was out, he stood, trembling, as he sucked in great breaths of air.

He should be angry. But he just dropped the tube on the floor looking . . . defeated. "Th' show is over. Dinnae think ye've got th' cure quite yet," he muttered between gasps.

"You could have killed him, Papa!" Jane got to her feet. While she feared for Kilkenny's life she'd paid no attention to his very impressive genitals, but now . . . She handed him the plaid. He had come to himself enough to color violently. She felt herself color in return.

"Always a possibility, my dear," her father said, pressing his lips together ruefully. He turned to Miss Zaroff. "I feel I'm so close! And yet . . ." His shoulders slumped.

Kilkenny clutched the kilt around his waist and reached for his shirt.

"I must adjust my poison mixture. Rather less of the nightshade, I should think . . ." He wasn't talking to them at all at this point. "Perhaps a soporific to depress the parasite's reaction?"

Kilkenny ran his hands through his hair. It was damp with sweat. His jaw was covered in dark stubble, and the scars on his throat stood out. Jane had no idea what to say to him. Was this the kind of torture he must endure by day while she was sleeping peacefully in her bed? No matter how much a criminal he was, he didn't deserve such treatment.

He bent and picked up a blanket from a pallet filled with straw and drew it around his shoulders. "I'll be getting back ta th' house."

Jane watched him push past her and saw that Miss Zaroff was watching him, too. Her eyes were hooded, speculative. Jane smelled . . . lust on her. Her eyes opened involuntarily. Did she smell like that when she wanted Kilkenny? If so, he would have known of her desire for him from the first. Could Miss Zaroff and her companions smell what Jane and Kilkenny had done at the castle? Dear God! She frowned. Or maybe that was just as well. She didn't like Miss Zaroff lusting after Kilkenny. Maybe she'd think he was already taken.

He wasn't, of course. Jane contracted inside.

Kilkenny stumbled out into the sunlight, drawing the blanket up over his head. What if he wanted to have sexual relations with such a beautiful woman? Jane wouldn't give in to her own sexual urges, but she didn't want Kilkenny giving in to his with Miss Zaroff, either.

She shrugged the hood of her cloak up and pulled it down over her forehead before she dashed out after him. By the time she reached the house, his door was closing upstairs. She thought wildly of offering him a soothing bath after his ordeal. But she couldn't go out to the well for water until dark. He'd have to wait for comfort.

Mrs. Dulnan arrived and seemed unfazed by the presence of so many houseguests. Jane passed them off as other patients and forced herself to give instructions. The woman seemed competent and sensible. Jane gave her a tour of the house, told her that she would take care of the bedrooms herself, since they'd be occupied during the day. But her thoughts kept straying to that scene in the laboratory, where her father and Miss Zaroff had watched so calmly while Kilkenny suffered. Would they have watched him die? She had no doubt about Miss Zaroff. She and the strange monk had been willing to kill him outright if he had not been useful to finding the cure. But her father?

She watched Mrs. Dulnan move about the kitchen preparing a meal for her guests, oblivious to the fact that they were vampires. Jane had to admit that her father had seemed like someone she didn't know up there in the laboratory. And Miss Zaroff had been nothing if not chilling. Jane was so tired she was almost dazed. Far too exhausted to figure out how she felt about all of this. She trudged upstairs.

The only thing she knew was that this situation was spinning out of her control.

CHAPTER
Twelve

Callan stumbled up the stairs, swung the door closed, and tumbled onto his bed. Was Blundell really close to a cure, or was he some mad dilettante who only sounded sane?

He groaned. He might not live through a test of the next dreadful concoction. Miss Zaroff's manner . . . There was something unsettling about the way she had observed that dreadful experiment so dispassionately.

He heard feminine footsteps on the stairs. They paused outside his door. Jane's scent drifted over him. Jane? Why could he not banish her first name from his lexicon? He had to forget the night at the ruined castle. That way lay madness. She probably hadn't saved his life today. The Companion would have saved him in any case. But her altruistic impulse in the face of his distress was . . . Well, it was tempting to think it was something it was not. She was generous, giving, courageous. She would have helped anyone she saw suffering. It was a testament to her nature that she helped him in spite of her revulsion at what they had done together, and her new knowledge of his crimes. His stomach felt bleak.

The footsteps moved off down the hall and he heard her door close. He imagined her in the room he had seen, with the things he had touched around her. Was she undressing? He tossed himself onto his side and put that thought away.

But others crowded in. Callan couldn't seem to confine his thoughts to achieving his own purpose. He kept thinking how important the cure was to Ja . . . Miss Blundell, as well. The vampires would not kill her while her father searched for the cure. But if the cure was found, what then? Would they let her take it? Callan would no longer be useful. They'd kill him. He didn't care about that. He had longed for death so many times. The world would not miss the likes of Callan Kilkenny. But Miss Blundell must take the cure and be set free. She could be no threat to them. Would they see it that way? He felt so helpless! He was no match for the newcomers. He could not protect Miss Blundell or force them to give her the cure.

He heard the bed in her room creak. He strained to hear her breathing. In time it became regular with sleep. Exhausted as he was, sleep still seemed far away for him.

Jane woke that evening with confusion still churning in her breast. There were three new vampires in the house who were absolutely ruthless and whose motives were suspect. Mrs. Dulnan had been here all day, while Jane slept, doing who knew what. And Kilkenny was, by his own admission, a traitor who had raised an army against England and humanity, and a killer. How could she have been so wrong about him? And killer or no, she realized that she was still incredibly attracted to him. She could not be trusted around Kilkenny. Rising, she slipped into her wrapper with a sense of foreboding. She needed a bath. She wouldn't think about why.

While she was in the little room off the kitchen that held the bath, she heard her father come in from his laboratory. At the same time heavy boots on the stairs were followed by the creak of the door from the hall into the kitchen, and the scent of cinnamon washed over her. Funny, she would not mistake that scent for any of the other vampires. It was Kilkenny.

"And how are yer potions this morning, Doctor?"

Kilkenny's voice held hope, in spite of what he'd gone through yesterday.

"Hard to say. Hard to say. Jane?" her father called.

"Just a moment, Papa."

"I need valerian and hemlock. Can you gather some tonight?"

"Certainly." Jane stood up. The water splashed off her into the bath.

Her father sat down, but she could feel Kilkenny go still. Was he listening to her, imagining her in her bath as she had imagined him? Nonsense. Of course he was not. She grabbed for the towel and began rubbing herself dry with unrelenting vigor.

She made certain she was presentable in a charcoal-colored morning dress very nearly black, her hair tidy before she emerged. Her father stood at the hearth, kettle in hand. Kilkenny stared from where he sat at the table. His gray-green eyes seemed . . . shocked. Shadows hung under his eyes and there were lines around his mouth. No wonder, after his experience.

"D'ye never wear anything but gray and black?" he asked, swallowing.

What? She drew herself up. "I am a serious student of science and a woman of medicine. Sober colors are appropriate to my calling," she said in a dampening tone. That she had grown to hate those endless gray and black gowns did not alter the fact that he had no right to criticize her.

He accepted the rebuke with a speculative look in his eyes.

"It's a little early for valerian," she said pointedly to her father. "But I might find some on a south-facing slope."

Her father poured water into his tea leaves. "Can you add some dill weed to your quest?"

"For your formula?"

"To add to tomorrow's leftover stew . . ." he muttered. She went to his side and checked the pot. A hearty chicken stew simmered there.

She cleared her throat. "It won't be necessary for Mr. Kilkenny to accompany me." She glanced to Kilkenny, who looked relieved.

"Jane, how can I work when I'm worried about you?" her father asked plaintively. "I've told you, he goes with you or you can't go and I get none of the ingredients I need. Kilkenny, promise me you won't leave her alone."

Kilkenny swallowed once, and nodded. "Aye. Ye can count on me."

Jane heaved a sigh. Kilkenny wanted nothing to do with her. She'd wait until her father went to bed, and then release Kilkenny from his promise. There was no use arguing with her father now. So she changed the subject. "Mrs. Dulnan seems to have done well by us." She looked around. The kitchen was spotless, potatoes peeled on the cutting board. Water stood in a pot ready to be boiled. She glanced to Kilkenny. His eyes had softened as he followed her movements. As she watched, they got that peculiar gleam in them. Was he . . . was he laughing at her? How could he after all that had happened?

"Oh, very well," she said, making her voice cross. "You were right on all counts."

"Right?" Her father jerked his gaze from the fire. "Not quite, my dear. The formula still isn't right. Still, the key is to depress the reaction of the parasite, I know it."

Jane suppressed a smile. Her father was oblivious to so much around him.

Miss Zaroff and Brother Flavio had not yet appeared, which was a relief, but Clara came downstairs, nodded once, and helped Jane set the table in the dining room. The two women were silent as they worked. Clara insisted on serving dinner, as Jane's father spoke of his dwindling supply of glassware, the boiling time required for his concoctions. Jane wasn't listening. She could not keep her attention from Kilkenny, though she did not look directly at him. She rather thought that, though he didn't look at her either, his attention was focused on her, too.

Her father droned on through dinner, not noticing the silence of his companions. But upstairs, all was not silent. Jane could hear Brother Flavio and Miss Zaroff talking in snatches around and between her father's monologue.

"I don't think I can last," Miss Zaroff said. "You can't expect it of me, Flavio."

"You have no choice, Elyta." Flavio's voice was stern.

What did they mean? Did she require blood? But Jane could provide for that need. There was some low conversation she couldn't hear over her father's voice. He was recounting the chemical properties of *conium maculatum*.

"How about Kilkenny? He'd serve nicely." That was Miss Zaroff.

"You need the old man, Elyta. He wouldn't like it if he found out."

Again she couldn't hear words, just Miss Zaroff's petulant tone. Found out what? She couldn't make out anything else until there was a cry of "Get out!" from Miss Zaroff. Kilkenny and Clara both glanced up. Was she the only one who had been eavesdropping?

"Mark my words, Elyta." A door closed.

For what would Kilkenny serve nicely? She glanced to Kilkenny, but his face was closed and frowning.

Clara cleared the table and Jane used water from the bucket by the door to wash the dishes. She hurried as fast as she could, wanting to be away before the two vampires upstairs made their appearance. Kilkenny grabbed up a cloth and wiped them. He stood close enough that she could feel the warmth of his body. He was wearing another tartan, Lachlan's blue and red this time, and a shirt open at the throat. She was acutely conscious that he was naked under his clothes. Lord. Couldn't he stand farther away? As if he knew her thoughts he began to fidget.

Clara returned. "I'm afraid I must hurry out to procure some new ingredients," Jane apologized. "Can I give up my place to you?"

Clara nodded silently and stepped up to the sink. Jane's father collected Rathbone's *Plants of Scotland* from the sideboard and went off to bed. She had to get out of the house instantly and away from Kilkenny.

"I'm certain you have better things to do than gather herbs," she said brusquely to Kilkenny. "I'm perfectly capable of going out by myself." She lifted her chin.

"I've bound myself ta yer father. I'll go."

"There's no need."

"It does no' seem ye ha' any choice." His lips were a grim line. "I'll saddle th' horses."

Well! Maddening man. He probably did it more to annoy her than from a sense of honor. Jane stomped up to the small shed that held her gardening tools with both dread and a strange excitement in her breast. But wait . . . why did she want to be rid of him? Weren't there still so many things she had to know about being vampire? That had not changed. He might be a traitor and a murderer . . . but she'd been alone with him before and nothing had happened to her. Except dissolving in lust and having sex with him. He wanted the cure, badly enough to subject himself to torturous experiments. He wouldn't risk alienating her father by attacking her. All she had to do was draw him out without letting her sexual urges get the better of her.

He was saddling the horses when she arrived at the barn, his worn German-made saddle for Faust, and her sidesaddle for Missy. He led the horses out, took her baskets with her trowels and tied them to Faust's saddle.

She put her foot in the stirrup and was about to haul herself up, when he took the reins from her roughly. "Can ye no' wait for a man's courtesy?" He bent and cupped his hands.

"A little surly today, Mr. Kilkenny?" she asked sweetly. He was too near—too near!

He straightened. "And ye're sa concerned with bein' as good as a man ye can no' be polite."

"It's the man who's supposed to be polite," she protested. "The woman receives."

"So ye think ta accept a courtesy is no' an act o' courtesy itself? Are ye that afraid ta receive? Ta always be giving is a kind o' selfishness."

She swallowed. He was talking about wanting to be in control. Was that so bad? "When you put it that way . . . But I think it's just as hard for you. You didn't like that I helped you that first night, or last night, either."

His lips clenched ruefully. But he jutted his chin. "Sa we're both selfish."

"The truth is I thought you might not want to touch me," she said, relenting. She wouldn't admit she didn't want to touch him, either. His gaze roved over her face for a moment before he bent again. She held her breath and placed her boot in his hands. The electric charge burned even through her boots. He tossed her up.

"It's hard, but I dinnae begrudge it." His voice was low, almost a whisper. He handed her the reins and swung up into his saddle.

She bent her head as they walked out the barn door. It *was* hard. The air vibrated around him. He smelled of cinnamon and something else and male musk beneath it. She had never been so aware of a man's . . . physicality. The very word "body" in reference to him made her want to shudder. Her female parts pressed against the subtle movement of the saddle and throbbed to life. Her feeling about Kilkenny seemed to have no bearing on her experiment with Tom Blandings. That had been a . . . a tribute to scientific method. This was fundamental, elemental, inevitable; wind and tide crashing against rock that did not yield but over time was worn away . . .

They trotted up toward the gate that opened to the track up the hill behind the farm in silence. It stretched, became painful. Finally, as he leaned over and opened the gate, he said. "Ye ride well, Miss Blundell."

"What an encomium from a man!" she exclaimed as she passed through the gate.

He glanced up to her, then leaned down and swung the gate shut. "Does a man's view of women fester with ye sa?"

That took her aback. "Like a wound," she answered lightly. Then she sobered. Criminal or not, she wanted information from him. Could she achieve truth and trust from him by giving him less? She took a breath, deciding, as he trotted up beside her. She'd tell him as much of the truth as she knew. "I suppose I'm preoccupied with whether the circumscribed role a woman plays in the world is dictated by her nature or society. Perhaps if I had known my mother . . . She died in childbirth, to my father's shame. He was afraid it would ruin his practice. Who would have a doctor who had let his wife die? So he worked twice as hard, and gained a reputation for his technique of transfusion." The path sloped up the hill that cradled Urquhart Glen. Fern and bracken grew on either side. The moon shone brightly. To Jane it was as bright as day. But it didn't make her way clearer. How could she explain the old problem? "I want to be like him," she said slowly, "to make him proud of me. He expected a boy to carry on his work, you see, but all he got was me. I've tried to be more . . . logical, more attentive to scientific method than he believed a girl could be. And yet . . . well, I haven't satisfied him." She smiled to force her tone lighter. It wasn't as strong a smile as it might have been. "He doesn't even let me help him with his work." She took a breath. "So, I suppose I have always been fighting against men's idea of women, wanting to believe it was not my nature that limited me, but their opinion."

He nodded, those marvelous lips pressing together.

"I know he loves me." She sighed. "I suppose that's why I don't want to disappoint him. And . . ." She hesitated, feeling the dread emotion welling up into her throat.

"And what?" he pressed.

In for a penny, in for a pound. This was a way to draw him

round to her true object. "And now . . . with this thing in my veins, I feel I'm drifting away from him." Her voice sank to a whisper. "Are we even the same species now?"

For a long moment he said nothing. Had she frightened him into retreating? But at last he said, "Ye are no' th' same anymore." She could hear him breathing, and the horses blowing, and the rustle of the larch leaves, the movement of some small animal off to their right. "But ye can be. Yer father will find th' cure."

She shook her head. "Can one go back? Is it possible, once one has been what we are?"

He pressed his lips together. "Ye can at least, Miss Blundell. Ye're an innocent. And ye'll stay that way until yer father finds th' cure."

He must have resolved to tell her no more, just to keep her from knowing the worst. "You of all people should know I'm not innocent," she protested.

He shot her a skeptical look. "It has nothin' ta do with virginity. Ye're th' cherished daughter of a London doctor ta th' *ton*." His tone said he thought that was something small.

She felt her anger rising. "I was delivering babies in the slums by the time I was twenty. I've seen the poor and the helpless, women beaten and abused, old before their time. I've seen death, Mr. Kilkenny. And tried to fend it off where I could."

He examined her briefly before he turned his eyes back to the path. "Did yer father approve o' ye venturing inta th' slums?"

She colored. It hadn't been right to fool Papa. "He assumed I was shopping." That proved she was sophisticated enough to lie by omission at least.

Kilkenny nodded. "I'll wager ye came back with an empty purse every time."

Worse! Did he know everything about her? She bit her lip, thinking of Mrs. Dulnan.

He glanced over to her. "Dinnae worry. Sometimes there's nae way around charity."

He had given money to those less fortunate, too. Many times. He must have. Look how expert he was at providing for Mrs. Dulnan without even seeming to do so. And he had provided for the unknown prostitute, Alice.

"I'm sure ye're a woman o' th' world." His expression was too serious to be truly serious. "As a woman o' th' world, d'ye believe in love, then?" It was as if he'd read her notebooks.

Was he trying to goad her into some sort of declaration he could point to as naïve? "No," she said lightly. "I think it's all a hum. People talk about transformation—that's just nonsense. The physical act is mildly pleasurable, but I can't see what the fuss is all about." He looked taken aback. Maybe what he wanted was some sort of paean to his skills in lovemaking. Well, he wouldn't get it. The part about it being only mildly pleasurable was a bald-faced lie, of course.

His expression closed down. "I agree with ye there."

"You've never been transformed by it?" She peered at him closely.

He cleared his throat. "If I was, it was no' ta my betterment."

"Ahh." What did he mean? Likely that what they had done together made him a smaller person. Was the insult meant to be personal, or did he just think that every act of such . . . intensity diminished one? Very well, they had gone this far, she would ask. "You mean what we did made you a worse person? It's not as though you raped me. I was willing, if you noticed."

He looked up at her sharply. "I was no' talkin' about us."

"Then who?" She was going to *make* him explain something of himself to her.

"Nae. I'll no' tell ye that," he said. His voice was flat. His profile revealed nothing. Then how did she know he was in pain? But she did. It was by his very blankness that she knew.

They broke out onto the crest of the hill that faced south. New grass poked up through a meadow of bracken. Moonlight made Kilkenny's black, curling hair gleam. Jane had learned a lot about him in the last three days, though it didn't clear up the mystery. He'd been hurt, badly. His spirit was as bruised as any man she had ever seen. But he still had the courage to believe you must use what gifts you had, even if they were onerous to you, to do good. He was exactly like Robin Hood, little as he liked that. He was still an idealist, though that idealism was battered. How did that fit with being a criminal and a traitor? Had he lied to her about what he'd done? But she didn't think so. Unless she was so truly naïve she didn't recognize a liar. What to believe about him?

The horses picked their way through the bracken. Much as she wanted to know more about him, her purpose was to find out more about being vampire. But how? If she was clumsy he'd refuse to tell her anything and the opportunity would be gone. To their left the mountain called Carn Nam Bad by the locals shot up starkly above the crest of the hill they had climbed. Below them on the right the dark waters of the narrow loch, filled with who knew what monsters, lay flat and ominous. Valerian would be hereabouts somewhere. They'd have to get off their horses and comb the meadow for the tiny pink flower whose root had soporific qualities. Not an easy task to find the plant since the flowers would be closed at night.

All right. She'd assume the little he had revealed about himself was true. And she'd use it to get what she wanted. If he'd been telling the truth, here was a man who did good deeds and was ashamed of the fact that he had enough idealism left to do them. He protected people. He'd committed to protect her and her father. That was her opening.

"I know you think vampires will come again to stop my father's work," she observed.

"Aye." He pressed his lips together grimly.

"And they'll try to kill us."

"Aye." His expression said he hated that he felt obligated to tell the truth. Was that why he spoke so little?

"Can you stop them?" This was cruel in a way. But she daren't back down. "Can those three that arrived last night stop them?"

He looked away. "I will no' lie ta ye. It is no' certain."

She took a breath. "Then I need to know what it means to be a vampire—what I am facing, how I can use what I am." This might work. Fear filled her throat. What if what he told her was so horrible she couldn't bear it?

He turned in the saddle and shot her a piercing look. Emotion flickered behind his eyes. Then he bent his head, staring at his thigh. Finally he took a deep breath. "Fair enough."

Jane's impulse to gloat at her victory melted away as the fear inside her rose. She unhooked her knee from the sidesaddle horn and slid to the ground. She wanted to walk beside him so when he explained she wouldn't miss a single word. He looked surprised, then swung his long leg over Faust's croup and jumped down himself. They pulled the reins over the horses' heads and walked in silence for a moment. He stared at the ground. She didn't press him. He had committed. He was a man who kept promises.

"This will no' be easy for ye," he muttered.

"No matter how horrible, tell me all." There was still a lump in her throat, though.

He took a deep breath. "Verra well, then." He looked out at the loch. "Ye know some already: th' heightened senses, th' strength, th' healing, th' sensitivity ta sunlight. What I dinnae think ye know is that th' thing in our blood has power and ye can use it, if ye know how," he continued. "Th' power is what makes th' vibrations. Ye've felt them."

She nodded silently, afraid her voice would betray her fear.

"Th' vibrations are faster th' more power ye ha'. And power grows with age. Verra old ones are stronger than we are."

"Like Miss Zaroff, and Brother Flavio and even Clara."

"Aye," he said grimly. "Now listen carefully. If ye call yer

Companion, it answers with power and a red film across yer vision."

"That's when our eyes look red to others," she murmured.

He nodded. "Th' power makes ye stronger yet. And it does other things." He paused.

He didn't want to tell her. "What? What other things?"

When they came, the words seemed dragged from him. "If ye keep askin', th' red goes black and ye . . . well, ye pop out o' where ye are and inta somewhere else." He glanced over and must have seen her incredulity. "If they come for ye, ye'll need ta know this, sa attend ta me."

"All right . . ." She was totally at a loss. What did he mean "pop out of where you are"?

Handing her Faust's reins, he walked four paces and pointed over to a slate outcropping that jutted through the meadow. "I'll go from here ta there." He stood straight, hands at his sides, legs apart. "First I call my Companion. Then ask for power. I'll do it slow, sa ye can see it."

Jane was braced for the fact that his eyes went demonic red. He pressed his lips into a thin line as he concentrated. But she was not ready for the black, whirling vortex that swirled around his feet and slowly rose up over his knees, his hips, his chest. Then things happened faster. He was enveloped in the blackness and . . . winked out. She was staring at empty space.

"Here," he called. He stood, with neither red eyes nor black vortex, near the outcropping.

Jane's mouth dropped open. She pulled the horses forward even as he strode back toward her. "What . . . ? What . . . was . . . ?" She felt like an idiot.

"It's called translocation. Comes in handy when ye need ta escape."

"How far can you go?"

"Two or three miles, as near as I can tell. I think people say we can turn inta bats because we disappear in th' night. It is no' true of course. Th' part about th' mirrors though . . ." He took the reins of the horses. They cropped the new spring grass eagerly, tearing at it with their great incisors, apparently oblivious to the miracle that had just occurred.

"But we do cast reflections, I've seen you in the mirror."

"True. But when we translocate, th' power gets denser until light does no' escape. Yer reflection disappears, just before ye disappear yerself." He motioned to her. "Now try it."

Excitement and a thrill of fear spun around her spine. She nodded. This was what she had wanted, a tutor. She stepped several paces away.

"Look at th' rock there," he instructed.

She glanced at the rock. It was about fifty feet away.

"Now, then, think about callin' to yer Companion."

She looked doubtfully at him.

"It seems verra silly. But do it."

Companion, she thought. An answering thrill along her veins startled her. She took her lip between her teeth. *Uh . . . Companion, may I have some of your power?* A red film slowly dropped over her field of vision. The moon glowed red. Kilkenny's face, too. The loch was burgundy-black. And she felt strong. Blood pounded in her ears. She took a breath and closed her mouth. Something sharp cut her lip on both sides.

She almost jerked out of her concentration, but Kilkenny said, "Call for more."

May I have more power? The answering surge made her gasp. She looked down. Her gown was red, not gray. Around her feet a blackness whirled. Some force within her pulsed.

"Think about th' rocks and call for more," she heard Kilkenny shout.

Rocks! More! Her thoughts were getting harder to control. The spiral of power went up and up, and she couldn't feel her legs and then her hips and she knew the darkness whirled around her and she was frightened, but there seemed no way to back down now without betraying his commitment to teach her, so she shouted in her mind, *More!* And the world went black and there was a shrieking tear that sent pain shooting through her body. She might have screamed but it was lost in the instant where she seemed to be rent into a thousand pieces.

And it was over. She swayed beside the rocks. Kilkenny and the horses were outlined against the loch, fifty feet away. She sank to the ground. It was either that or faint. Kilkenny dropped the grazing horses' reins and started toward her at a run. He threw himself to his knees beside her and grasped her upper arms.

"Are ye well, lass?"

"That . . . hurt."

Guilt washed across his face. "Breathe now. There's always a cost."

"You might have told me." She blinked.

"Ye might not ha' gone through with it," he said ruefully. "And ye did a good job convincin' me ye ought ta know."

She shook her head, trying to anchor herself. How could she do that when she had just come unstuck from where she was and maybe even who she was? Was she still Jane Blundell? "A scientist seeks knowledge," she managed. "I would have gone through with it. Is it always that painful? It didn't seem to affect you that way."

"There's always pain," he acknowledged. "But it gets easier, after a while."

As she came to herself, she began to feel the heat from his hands on her arms through her riding habit. He was so close. If she turned her face up . . .

Their lips were inches from each other. His eyes searched her face. They glowed in the darkness that was almost day to her, but more . . . seductive. She felt his chest rising and falling with his increasingly ragged breathing and the vibrations that called to her. Wet throbbing began between her legs. She wanted him. There were no two ways about it.

He took his hands from her arms as though he had been burned and stood. After a moment he held out his hand to help her up, but the action looked like it took all his courage.

It certainly took all her courage to place her hand in his palm. God! The feel of skin to skin was like scraping your shoes along a carpet when the wind was high and then touching someone unsuspecting, but a hundred times more powerful. She let him pull her to her feet and took her hand back before it was blackened with the energy coursing between them.

She had to face the truth. She had never felt so alive, so connected to another person as she did with him; not her father, not her friends, and certainly not with Mr. Blandings. The act of sexual congress with Kilkenny might not be exactly transformation, but it had changed forever her perception of pleasure and intimacy. And she had to admit she wanted it again. Now would be ideal. If she weren't careful she'd just throw herself at him. What was she becoming? Or what had she already become?

He cleared his throat and stepped back a pace. "Ye'll no' be able ta best an old one in strength," he croaked. "Sa ye call th' power, pain or nae, and go."

She nodded. Of course, she had no intention of leaving her father to the mercy of vampires if it came to that. But acquiescence was the price of more knowledge. That was what she was here for. It was why she didn't just run from the feelings gushing through her. She wanted to know more, no matter how horrible. She swallowed and tried to get some semblance of control over her body. "What do you call that . . . phenomenon again?"

"Translocation." He turned to the horses, still quietly grazing as if the whole world had not turned inside out, and she followed.

"How about the other legends? I tried touching garlic and crosses. Nothing happened."

He shook his head. "They canno' repel us. Though I can see where ye would no' want ta associate with anyone who eats a lot o' garlic." There was that gleam again.

"And what is the scent we have? I mean underneath the cinnamon."

"Ah, that'd be ambergris."

Ambergris. She should have recognized it. It was one of the rarest ingredients of perfume, taken from whales and worth a fortune. Echoes of the pain receded. Now she tasted the blood on her lower lip. As they rejoined the horses and she took up Missy's reins, she pulled out a handkerchief from the sleeve of her habit and dabbed at her lips. "Do you want to tell me how I cut my lips?" She raised her brows.

He looked guilty again and chewed his lip. "That's about feeding yer Companion when ye dinnae get yer blood from a cup." He looked over to her. "Are ye sure ye want ta know this?"

Definitely not. But she said, "Yes."

He ran his hand over Faust's neck as the horse grazed enthusiastically. "Fangs," he said at last. "The Companion's power runs out yer teeth. There ye have it."

An image of wolves flashed through her and the needle teeth of bats. She was breathing shallowly. "You rip, like . . . an animal?" she whispered.

"Ye dinnae ha' ta rip. Puncture and suck, though," he said grimly. "Like an animal."

She felt her eyes go big.

"Enough," he said roughly. "Let's find this root o' yers."

CHAPTER
Thirteen

Callan tried to break off her questions and get down to their task but she stayed rooted to the spot. She looked so horrified. And why not? She was right. She needed to know how to use the thing in her blood. She needed it against Elyta Zaroff and the others if not against the vampire faction out to destroy the cure. But he felt like he'd just destroyed whatever innocence she'd had. He hadn't even told her about the compulsion. What would she think of that?

"Come now," he said again, more softly. He kept himself half turned away. He wanted to take her in his arms to comfort her, but who knew what he might do if he felt her heart pounding against his? Even clasping her arms had stiffened his detestable cock.

"Are we evil?" Her voice was shaking.

He stared at the ground. Oh, yes. He was at any rate. Maybe he had always been evil and now he was just an immoral vampire instead of an immoral man. But he couldn't tell her they were evil. Maybe she could avoid it, with her sweet, generous nature. She was waiting for an answer. He raised his head. "Is th' thing in th' lake we saw evil?"

She shook her head, slowly. "It just is."

"People in th' village think it's evil." He had to give her hope.

"Yes." Her voice was more her own now. "They think that seeing it bodes disaster. The old biddies think Evie's baby is cursed because she saw it right before she gave birth."

"And what is it, really?"

"Just a big animal. It probably got trapped when the loch closed to the sea at Moray Firth. It just goes about doing what a big creature needs to do."

"We're like that."

"You mean we must do what our nature requires?"

"Close enough."

"Does it require that we kill?" Her voice was small, but resolute. That was the girl he'd come to know in the last days.

He shook his head. "Ye dinnae kill fer yer blood."

"Do you?" she whispered.

Ahhh. The pain jerked through him. He carefully closed down his expression, fighting back the guilt that drenched him. "Once." That was true. That was the only time he'd killed just for blood. He turned away before she could see the half-truth and grabbed the horses' reins. He wouldn't try to excuse himself by telling her he hadn't meant to kill that one. There were other inexcusable acts for which there had been no excuse. "Now will ye look for yer flower or no'?"

He glanced back and saw her decide to follow him. They combed over the meadow in silence. He put some distance between them to get a little peace from the importuning of his genitals. He had vowed he would never lose himself to a woman again. Yet he had lost himself with her last night. He told himself it had not been like it was with Asharti. But he might be wrong. He'd longed to please Asharti, and she'd used his lust against him. Last night had he not thought of Jane's pleasure first? Had he not lost all control of his lust? Just like with Asharti.

He watched her poke at a low clump of greenery across the meadow and stand to wave at him. She'd found the flower.

This was not love. Vampire to vampire, their blood called

to each other. He had told Miss Blundell they didn't need to be evil. But this dreadful sexual urgency could not be wholesome. Both churches he'd followed, Protestant and Catholic, would say they were possessed by the devil for the fearful longing in their loins. They were cursed. He'd never entirely escape the desert and Asharti. He knew that now. But if he gave in to his sexual urges, he'd lose whatever small shards of himself were left.

Jane waved to Kilkenny that she'd found the valerian. He was standing stock-still, staring into space. When he turned his eyes on her, she saw such pain there it was as if someone had dashed cold water on her. What had he been thinking? Or remembering . . .

Suddenly, knowing the new rules of her existence didn't seem enough. She wanted to know Kilkenny. What was his pain? *Why* had he killed and betrayed his country? Perhaps therein lay the key to dichotomy between what she'd been told and what she felt was true about him. She motioned again and this time, after some hesitation, he strode across the meadow. He stood over her, examining her as though his life depended upon it.

"Are . . . are you well?" she asked. At her words, he started, and then his face just closed down. It was the most amazing thing. He squeezed every drop of emotion from his expression.

"Well enough." He tore his gaze from her face and looked around. "D'ye need th' whole plant?" She didn't, just the flowers, but before she could say anything he had knelt and taken up a trowel. He had the small bush out by the roots and was shaking it in an instant. Jane watched his flat expression, looking for the emotion.

"There's another over there," she remarked, as much to buy time for her appraisal as a need to have more. He got up without looking at her and strode over to the clump.

Her mind strayed again to what he had said, how they got their blood. Something niggled at her brain. Punctures. Fangs. Horrible! She could hardly imagine . . .

The scars on his body! The twin, circular scars at his throat and on the inside of his elbows, and . . . Oh, dear Lord, his groin . . . They were the marks of puncture wounds made by fangs . . . before he was vampire and could heal without scarring. And that meant a vampire had sucked his blood, many times. What vampire would take blood by biting his groin?

A woman!

Even a strong man like Kilkenny would be no match for a vampire woman. The dreadful possibilities expanded in her imagination. He had other scars, the jagged ones. Vampires didn't have to rip and tear, he'd said, but that didn't mean they couldn't if they wanted. And the grim look on his face when he said it . . . A female vampire had torn his flesh and licked his blood. There was no question in her mind that it was a woman. The nature and location of the scars all spoke of some twisted sexuality and obsession. Revolting!

She watched Kilkenny kneel and dig at the valerian with his trowel. No wonder he was so grim and withdrawn. Not surprising that he hated what he was.

She almost gasped. The woman who gave him his scars was the one who made him vampire. She just knew it. She had seen the pain and longing in his eyes when he talked of the woman who made him that first night in the woods. Could he love someone who had done that to him? Perhaps the twisted sexuality and obsession was his as well as hers.

That made her blink. But then why did he want to be cured so badly? He would be reveling in what he was, devoted to the one who made him and shared his twisted pleasures.

Unless he had rejected that horrible part of him. That made sense. The only way to reconcile the honor and generosity, even the touch of self-deprecating humor she saw in him with twisted love, killing, and vampire armies taking over England was that he had changed, or recovered from a madness. And the madness might be a reason for his crimes, not an excuse, mind you, but a reason.

It still didn't ring true.

Dear me, she thought. *I still don't know what to believe about him.*

She shook her head. Scientific method. Were her conclusions about Kilkenny and the unknown woman mere imaginings? She would never be able to ask him. But the evidence of his scars and the clues inherent in his own words made her deductions seem logical.

He pulled up the plant and shook the dirt from the roots. "Enough?" he asked.

She nodded as he put it in the basket. "I think so."

He took the reins of the two horses. They turned back down the hill.

"Now for the hemlock by the little loch up the glen." She wanted to get out of here.

Another thought occurred. What if the lust she felt was the precursor to losing all control and becoming like that unknown woman who hurt Kilkenny? A chill ran down her spine, and it wasn't from the night air. She must absolutely not give in to her lust, lest she become the monster Kilkenny knew it was possible to be.

"Well, not a success." Miss Zaroff frowned as Brother Flavio, Kilkenny, and Jane stumbled into the kitchen from the laboratory. She was standing in the doorway in a lilac sarsenet walking dress with a matching reticule hanging from her wrist. She pulled out a small vinaigrette and held it delicately to her nose. Jane watched as Brother Flavio helped Kilkenny sit on one of the sturdy oak chairs. Kilkenny hadn't needed resuscitation today, but the process was still horrible enough. Clara, who had been peeling potatoes, went to the canister of tea and ladled some into a teapot.

"The valerian was not the answer," her father said absently as he wandered in.

Miss Zaroff threw up her hands dramatically and made a small sound of disgust.

"I thought surely . . ." Her father looked old today.

Miss Zaroff came to stand over him, hands on hips. "What is this . . . this valerian?"

"An herbal soporific." Her father's voice held exhaustion.

"Soporific? What is . . . soporific?"

"Valerian contains a sleep-inducing compound," Jane explained. "Sit, Papa, and drink some tea," Clara set a cup down in front of him with a tea-strainer over it.

"A narcotic to depress the parasite's reaction long enough to kill it." Her father sighed. "But apparently not strong enough." Clara poured tea into the cup.

"Narcotic?" Miss Zaroff asked quickly. "Like opium? Opium is one of the few ways to suppress our Companion, though I warn you, it does not kill it."

"Opium!" her father crowed. "Of course! It is stronger than valerian by a thousandfold. The apothecary at Inverness will have a tincture of laudanum at the least." He bustled to the door. "I'll go tonight."

"Not you, Dr. Blundell," Miss Zaroff called.

Her father stopped and turned at the sharpness in her tone.

"You are too valuable. Flavio will go as soon as the sun sets. It is what, fifteen miles?"

Her father nodded, turning back to his table. "Seventeen. I'll need to distill it . . . and . . ."

Opium. They were going to give Kilkenny opium as well as poisons. He would not meet her eyes. The cup clattered against its saucer as he raised it to his lips.

"At least I'll get some sleep," he murmured.

Jane sat writing in her notebook at the kitchen table, alone. She had slept a few hours. The sun was setting. Kilkenny was still asleep in his room. Brother Flavio had just departed for Inverness in the gig used by Mrs. Dulnan during daylight hours on a mission to acquire opium or laudanum in large doses. He'd have to brave the sun tomorrow to buy it. Jane's father had retired to his study, his nose in dusty herbal texts. Miss Zaroff was not yet in evidence. As soon as it was full dark, Jane would avoid both Kilkenny and the other vampires by going out into the hills alone. Her father never had to know. She would practice translocating until it was a skill she could rely on. She glanced to her notebook where she had outlined a practice regimen.

The thing she couldn't reconcile was how you actually directed your reappearance by thinking about where you wanted to end up. What interaction of the host's mind and the Companion's power did the trick? It was just like Kilkenny's luck, where the Companion's energy seemed to fuse with its host's knowledge and experience to produce a specific result, almost as though two beings became one. Perhaps the organism in her blood wasn't a parasite. Maybe the relationship was more symbiotic. That would account for the feeling of being more alive. Was that really a feeling of being more whole than she had been before the infection?

That was entirely subjective. But there might be objective consequences. For instance, if you could direct yourself to a new location, why couldn't you direct another object? Could one move objects with only the mental power lent by one's Companion? Intriguing thought! She scribbled furiously in her notebook. She'd never be able to ask Kilkenny. The experience that haunted him, the accusations Miss Zaroff had made, what they had done at Urquhart, all sat between them now like a hunched gargoyle, ugly and hard as stone. It watched everything each of them did, and glared at them. She felt it. He felt it, too, she could tell.

Above her she heard the click of heels across the scrubbed wood floors. There was a certain anxious rhythm to them. They came from Miss Zaroff's room. She must be hungry. It might not be for lamb and parsnips, no matter that she said she didn't need blood immediately. Jane should offer her blood. Now that Jane thought of it, Miss Zaroff too was a fount of information that should not be wasted. She headed up the stairs and tapped on her guest's door.

"Miss Zaroff? Would you like dinner?"

The door opened. Miss Zaroff wore a dressing gown of finest aubergine silk, patterned with pagodas and blossoming branches. It showed a fulsome cleavage to advantage. "Miss Blundell, do come in." She swung the door wide.

Clara stood by the window, brushing off a dashing riding habit of lavender gabardine. *Drat.* Could she pump Miss Zaroff for information with Clara in the room? She stepped inside . . . Again, she caught the scent of female musk. "I just thought . . ."

"Clara will provide for my needs," the woman said brusquely. "Won't you, Clara?"

Clara caught her intention, bobbed once and murmured, "I'll go immediately, miss."

"Do sit," Miss Zaroff said, motioning toward one of two chairs by the fireplace.

Jane cleared her throat. "If you have need of . . . blood . . ." The word caught in her throat.

Miss Zaroff waved a hand. "I fed in Inverness. But I thank you for your concern."

Jane sat on the edge of her chair. "You seem . . . agitated. Is there nothing I can do?"

Miss Zaroff gave a brittle laugh. "I can provide for myself if there are any comely males in this backwater."

"Oh." There probably were no men attractive enough for Miss Zaroff in the village. That left only one possibility.

As though she read Jane's mind, Miss Zaroff remarked, "Perhaps you'll share Kilkenny. He's strong enough to service us both, and Clara into the bargain."

Miss Zaroff knew that she and Kilkenny had . . . And she said it so matter-of-factly! Jane was shocked. She lowered her gaze. Was that all they had been doing, servicing each other? She flushed. She glanced up to see Miss Zaroff's knowing look.

"You *are* an innocent, aren't you?" The woman chuffed a laugh. "I'll wager you thought it was true love." She made it sound like a crime.

"No, Miss Zaroff." Jane felt her flush deepen. To conceal the arrow that had just been plunged into her heart, she asked lightly, "But is it possible for you to answer a question?"

"Call me Elyta. We are sisters in a way, are we not?"

Jane wasn't sure about that. But she wanted information. "Elyta, then. Is . . . is this heightened sexuality a normal part of being vampire?" There. Put it in the context of scientific research and the fact became almost manageable.

"Lord, yes." Miss Zaroff . . . Elyta rose and went to stand at the window, looking out into the night. "Surely you have felt the Companion's urge to life?"

Jane nodded.

"Our sexual needs are but another expression of that." She shrugged and turned back. "I need servicing several times a day. Which is why this journey has set me on edge so."

"Oh." Jane cleared her throat. "And it is the same for men?"

"Absolutely. And when two vampires come together . . . well, the result is inevitable. It doesn't often come up, since we live one to a city. To congregate would only draw human attention to our need for blood."

"How lonely," Jane exclaimed. "To have no one with whom you can share your secret."

"No one to challenge your power," Elyta amended. "Personally, I like Rome."

"You have lived in many cities, then?"

"It's a bit of a round-robin. When one leaves, a city is vacant, and another may decide to relocate, which leaves another vacancy."

"So you never have . . . relations with your own kind."

"Relations?" Her laugh tinkled merrily. "Occasionally. But let me advise you never to have sex with one as strong as you are. Pick those you can dominate. It's much safer."

Again Jane was shocked. "Why?"

"Because a woman exposes herself during sex. She is vulnerable to her own desires, and to her need for the male to plunge himself inside her. The only way to counter that is to be the one in control." She looked slyly at Jane. "You must be careful with Kilkenny. You are both new. You cannot control him during intercourse."

"It . . . it won't come up," Jane whispered. "I'm going to take the cure." The vision of sexual union Elyta had just expressed was so dismal it almost took Jane's breath away. Yet hadn't she experienced for herself that need to have Kilkenny plunge himself inside her?

"Still, if your father doesn't produce the cure tomorrow, you'll find yourself with needs. Come to me, and I will provide. You shouldn't be fucking Kilkenny alone." The word shook Jane. She had heard it only in the poor neighborhoods where she attended her charity patients. For a moment it distracted her. But then she frowned. Exactly what was Elyta proposing?

Jane's face must have shown her disbelief, for Elyta smiled again. "Have you never had a threesome? Well, well, another treat in store."

Jane swallowed. Kilkenny wouldn't fall in with Elyta's plans. Would he? Or would he have relations with anyone to hand, just because he was a vampire and needed sex? She wouldn't call it "making love." It obviously wasn't that. He hadn't been making love to her, either.

Clara came through the door with a tray.

Jane rose abruptly. "Perhaps you're right." She choked. "I must go now."

Elyta's attention had already shifted to her dinner as Jane closed the door. She hurried down the stairs and out into the night. She must get away from here. She'd practice translocation. Maybe she would try to move stones—anything to keep her distance from Elyta Zaroff and Kilkenny. Now if only she could escape the feeling that surged up from her stomach into her throat. No matter how she had castigated herself about what happened at the castle, she hadn't really thought it was the kind of experience Miss Zaroff had just outlined so bleakly. She had thought that perhaps Kilkenny . . .

She had been a fool.

CHAPTER
Fourteen

Callan trudged into the kitchen with a pail of milk and set it
by the sink. Clara had made a pie out of early gooseberries.
The smell of pastry and cooked fruit filled the kitchen. She
looked up as Callan entered. Her brown eyes were strangely
flat.

"My mistress wants to see you," she said.

"Your mistress can go ta hell," Callan muttered. He
pushed past, but she held his arm.

"Please," she said. "If I don't bring you, she'll be angry
with me."

Callan pressed his lips together. He wouldn't put it past
Miss Zaroff to say cutting things to her maid. "Verra well.
I'll see her."

The girl trailed him up the stairs. *She's no' a lass, but an
old vampire by her vibrations,* Callan reminded himself. She
tapped at her mistress's door. "He's here," she said, and
opened it.

Callan pushed inside. "What d'ye want?"

Elyta Zaroff sat brushing her long black hair in front of a
small dressing table. Her purple dressing gown with some
kind of flowering trees and pagodas on it gaped over perfect,
jutting breasts. Her eyes lifted to his in the mirror. "You were
made by Asharti, weren't you?"

Callan lifted his chin to hide his shock. "Nae." How did she know his shame?

"Don't bother to lie. I saw your scars. They are her marks."

He clenched his jaw. She'd seen him naked. What did he care if this woman knew? "Aye, th' marks are hers. But she did no' make me."

"Then one of her minions did, perhaps Fedeyah."

She knew! He didn't respond, but stood staring at her.

"She was a good student," Miss Zaroff remarked. "I'll wager she trained you well."

"What . . . ?" All that was implied in that statement washed over him. But even as he turned to plunge toward the door, her eyes flashed the deepest of reds and he was transfixed.

She rose, slowly, sensuously, and moved toward him, a smile spreading across her face. He felt the familiar helplessness like a black blot growing inside him. He tried to move, but she had him fast, transfixed like a butterfly in the collections displayed at the university so long ago.

"Poor Asharti." She pulled at his cravat and let it drift to the carpet. "She had been much abused by men. I met her in . . . let's see . . . the early part of the fifteenth century, in Florence. Delightful place, what with the Medici running the place and the Buonarotti boy carving those beautiful nude men and priests flagellating themselves. It was nearly perfect for us until Urbano threw us out." She pulled Callan's shirt off over his head. It turned inside out as the sleeves left his wrists. He was having trouble breathing. The vampiress could have popped the buttons on his breeches, but she slid her hand beneath the waistband and unbuttoned them carefully. "We traveled together. I taught her everything I knew." Her gaze held his. He wanted to shout in horror and protest. How could there be another like Asharti? And in the Highlands of Scotland, worse luck? He had *done* with Asharti.

"To the bed with you," she whispered, and enforced her

command with a push on his chest. He stumbled backward until he felt the bed against the back of his thighs. It was the same as the one in his room, high, with a carved oaken headboard sporting thick spindles at each corner. She pushed him onto it. He gritted his teeth as she pulled off a boot.

There were only three of them, though. They couldn't suppress his will twenty-four hours a day. He could escape. He *had* to escape. "Ye . . . canno' hold . . . me . . . forever," he managed.

Her chuckle chilled him. She jerked off his other boot. "But that is what is so delightful. I don't need to hold you. You will hold yourself at my disposal."

He gasped for breath, trying to resist her. "Th' minute . . . ye . . ."

"Nonsense." She pulled his breeches and smalls from his hips. "You want the cure too much. You won't leave." She surveyed his body.

To hell with the cure. He couldn't bear this! He felt the familiar tightening in his loins. His cock began to throb. He twisted his body as if that could loosen her hold on him.

"No wonder Asharti liked you. Even aside from the blue eyes, which she always favored of course, you are well made." She lifted his balls, stroked his newly rigid cock lightly. How he wanted to throttle her! But he, of anyone, knew how useless struggle was. She was old. She would have her way with him as Asharti had countless times. Something inside him died a little. He had thought to escape Asharti's effect on him. He'd tried to find a new life, not normal maybe, but something. And it had been all for naught. Blackness rolled through him.

"You will call me 'Miss Zaroff' in front of others, but 'Mistress' when we are private together," she murmured into his ear. She laid herself along his body, propped on one elbow, and turned his head toward her, exposing the artery in his neck.

This was it, then.

He had no hope of avoiding what she would do to him. He battered his mind against her will anyway. He felt her lips against his throat smiling at his resistance, and then the puncture of his carotid. She sucked lightly and pulled at his cock roughly with her left hand. He hated the desire he couldn't prevent from rising. Was she doing it, or was it his own weak nature? He couldn't even plead long celibacy as an excuse for his lust. He had given in to his needs only two nights ago with Jane Blundell. Elyta pulled her canines from his throat.

"My Companion is so much stronger than yours, I can drink your blood easily," she observed, whispering. "Vampire blood always has a special tang." Her tongue circled her lips. She drew the nail of her index finger across his chest, leaving a bloody gouge. He shuddered, not from pain, but from the horrible familiarity of it. She ran her tongue along the bloody furrow, using her saliva to keep the cut from healing, just like the vampire bats in South America Blundell had written about in his article. Then she sucked at it. His cock strained for release. When finally she pulled away, her robe fell open, revealing lush breasts with prominent nipples. "Delicious. When Jane joins us, we mustn't let her drink, though. Your Companions would be warring in an instant. Not fatal, but uncomfortable."

When Jane joins us? What . . . ?

"I've invited her to partake. Clara, too," the vile woman whispered, licking his jawline, even as she hefted his balls. "Clara declined. Quite the prude, Clara."

Callan swallowed hard, trying not to focus on the sensations ripping through him. Miss Blundell wouldn't join in these games . . . would she? Were all vampire women voracious spiders? He jerked his head away from Elyta.

She chuckled. "Grasp the bedposts," she whispered.

He struggled as he had struggled once before in the desert but Elyta's will was implacable, just as Asharti's had been then. He grabbed the posts. She hiked up her robe and straddled his loins, placing his cock at the correct angle and sliding onto it, sighing in satisfaction. He gasped. She pushed herself up off his chest and slid down again. The humming in his blood sang in time to the rhythm she created.

He groaned, but not with desire. He wasn't worth a ha'penny. His eyes filled. There was only one pinpoint of hope. Gathering himself somehow, he focused on it. When she was done with him tonight, she might ignore him, not believing he'd escape. But he would. He'd abandon both the cure and Jane. He had no choice.

Jane found translocation exhausting. She'd managed the feat four times already tonight. At least the concentration it required kept her from thinking about either Kilkenny or Elyta. Confusion rose in her breast. She looked around, wondering if she should try again just to keep it at bay. She breathed in and out slowly, twice. She must strive for scientific objectivity. Very well. She had a new theory to test. No time like the present.

Question: could the power of her Companion be transferred? Could she move anything else besides her own body? She spied a huge outcropping of rock poking through the heather. Too big. She wandered toward the bluff that rose practically out of the loch, searching . . .

There. That rock couldn't weigh more than four or five stone. She knelt about ten feet from the edge of the cliff in a bare patch among the scratchy bramble that by July would yield the delicate pink flower clusters of heather. She willed herself to release the tightness in her neck and shoulders. She untied the knot in her belly that related directly to Kilkenny. And then she called.

Companion!

Life surged up along her veins. Power. Connection. She felt the wholeness, right or wrong. She would use it. She stared at the rock at the edge of the cliff and tried not to think she wanted to go there, but that she wanted it to go.

Give me power.

The black surged up around her knees. This was the hard part. What could she do but try? The blackness wanted to rise round her but she pushed it down. She stared at the rock.

And pushed the power out. She imagined outthrust arms.

Ahhhh! A wrenching jerk of pain. Her eyes dimmed for a moment.

She blinked. The rock was still there.

She sighed. *The essence of experimentation is patience,* she told herself. But she didn't feel patient. She didn't feel scientific. All she felt was . . . small.

Still, she wasn't ready to return to the house. So she tried again. Again she fixed her attention on the rock at the edge of the bluff and called her Companion, again the surge of power, suppressed. She thought about pushing it out. This time she felt it flow in a smooth stream. She breathed out. As the last of the air escaped her lungs a twist of pain made her gasp.

She stumbled to the edge of the bluff. A ragged earthen pit gaped where the rock had been ripped out at the roots. The rock itself careened down the slope, tumbling over, shedding damp clods as it went until it sloshed into the loch below the little bluff.

Her eyes went wide. She'd done it. She'd moved something.

She grinned. The pain hadn't been as bad as when she jerked herself out of space and reappeared. She'd have to practice this, construct experiments to see how much weight she could move and how far and how many times in a row before she got tired . . .

Kilkenny hadn't said vampires could do this. Was he keeping something from her? Or perhaps he didn't know everything about his state. Perhaps she'd be able to tell him a thing or two eventually. That was certainly a satisfying thought.

Life careened around her veins. She was strong and more alive than she had ever been.

But not for long. Why should she practice throwing

stones about when she was only waiting for the chance to abandon that power forever? Sighing, she picked up the basket full of feverfew. What could her father want with that? She drew her power.

Behind her, she heard a slosh of waves. An eerie groan cut through the air. She gasped.

The blackness drained away as her concentration broke. Jane whirled. A hundred feet out in the dark gray loch a surge of flesh cut the churning water. Not again! She could see the skin rolling into view and sliding back into the water in what seemed a continuous loop. How big *was* this creature? And why did it keep appearing whenever she was near the lake? Another hump emerged, closer this time. Jane had the distinct feeling it was coming closer. Fear flashed through her. Instinctively, she called to her Companion. Darkness whirled up around her feet. She thought about the hill above the farm. A shock of pain and she was gone.

She wavered into space at the top of the hill. Three miles away, in the water, the creature submerged. She stood there, trying to breathe, for some minutes. There. She was better. She mustn't let fear rule her judgment. She'd just missed a wonderful opportunity for closer observation. Some student of science she was! She turned toward the farm. The house below was a stone miniature like the models of the Coliseum and the Parthenon in the British Museum. Dawn was only a couple of hours away.

She didn't have the strength or the will to translocate, so she trudged down the hill the way she had come. No one was about in the kitchen. Banked chunks of peat glowed in the great hearth in preparation for the morning meal. A slab of beef waited for the knife. The room smelled of burned peat and fresh bread.

Above her a rhythmic thumping echoed in the walls. What was that?

Her eyes grew wide in realization. Damn him! Did what they had done mean *that* little?

She stomped up the stairs. Anger flooded her, banishing reason. Outside the door to Elyta's room, she paused. There was no question; the banging came from inside.

She threw open the door. Kilkenny lay across the bed, naked, his fists clenching the spindles at the corners above his head. The dark hair across his chest and under his arms stood out against his pale flesh. He was slick with sweat. Elyta, silken robe open, her bare breasts bouncing, rode him vigorously. The base of his stiff cock was clearly visible where it was stuffed deep inside her. At the sound of the door, Elyta paused and turned, a slow smile spreading over her flushed face. Her eyes glowed red with the influence of her Companion.

"Care to join me?" she asked, her breath coming a little fast.

Kilkenny turned his head. The expression on his face was one of horror, shame, despair, all mingled in some complex mélange of distress, no doubt over being caught *in flagrante*.

What could she say? What right had she to interrupt them? Obviously, Kilkenny had made his choice. His choice was to . . . to *fuck* . . . whatever came to hand. She shook her head in answer to Elyta. Her eyes filled. She couldn't let them see her anguish. She spun on her heel and threw herself along the hall to her room. The door slammed with a satisfying bang. She only wished the door could shut out the emotions boiling inside her. To her dismay, the anger ebbed as suddenly as it had come. Tears overflowed as she threw herself on her bed. She tried to get the anger back. Damn him all to hell and herself into the bargain for imagining he might have cared.

Callan was not lucky enough to be called to the laboratory for testing formulas that day, since Flavio did not return from Inverness with the laudanum. Instead he spent the day in Elyta's room servicing her again and again. She had become Elyta to him, just as Asharti needed only a single name, no matter what she wanted to be called. The look of revulsion on Jane's face created a pain in his gut. Now her opinion of him was secured. She believed him not only a criminal and a traitor, but a fornicator with any woman available. She would think what they had done together meant nothing to him. He could be grateful only that she had refused to join Elyta.

He lay across the bed, the bedclothes in disarray, drained figuratively, but not literally. Elyta had not let him ejaculate all day. She curled against his side now, dozing. Even now, she might wake and rouse him. He felt defiled.

As he had defiled Jane Blundell? He clenched his brows together against the thought.

What he had done with Jane Blundell wasn't fornication, no matter that the church would call it so. The feel had been entirely different. Yes, there was lust. Lord, but he had wanted her! Yet there was another . . . undercurrent with Jane, one that he . . .

What was the use? Jane Blundell was lost to him. He was Elyta's now, body and soul, until he escaped, just as once he had belonged to Asharti. His chest felt heavy. He daren't draw his power to escape until Elyta let him out of her presence. Would she grow careless?

Asharti never had . . .

Atlas Mountains, December 1819
"Fedeyah, bring the generals to me at ten," Asharti commanded.

The eunuch Arab who had served her for centuries bowed and retreated. He was the one who made others as she was. She did not deign to use her own blood to turn them.

Callan blinked slowly as he stared at the fire in the middle of her tent. Outside it was a cold morning. They had made camp on the northern slopes of the Atlas Mountains. The army was on its way to Algiers, stopping at villages to take blood.

None of that mattered to him. He lived from her last

command to her next command. Inside he was filled with dust. She had what she wanted of him. Always. There was never any doubt. He knelt in sandy mountain soil at the edge of her carpets. The sand absorbed the blood that drooled from the wounds she had made on his body. He was wrong. He wasn't filled only with dust. He was filled with dust and blood.

The tent was quiet. Incense filled the air. Sandalwood. It almost obscured the scent of cinnamon. He could hear her quill scratching across a papyrus. Maybe she would be too busy . . .

"Slave!" The quill stopped. He scrambled over the carpets to crouch in front of her chair, forehead to the blue and red pattern. "How may I serve you, mistress?" he murmured.

"Pour me wine," she said, pushing her scroll away. He could hear the rasp of paper against the inlaid wood of her table.

"At yer command," he whispered. He rose. In truth he was a bit dizzy, so he placed his steps carefully. The amphora of wine sat on a small, low table along with a tray of fruit and a bowl of nuts. He poured the limpid red into her chased goblet. Her eyes upon him made him exquisitely conscious of his genitals. He felt himself tighten. Was it her will or his?

"Bring the whole amphora." He picked up the amphora and negotiated his way around the fire crackling under the smoke hole of the tent. He set his burdens upon the low table, inlaid with mother-of-pearl in complicated geometrics. She wore a wrapper of fine red wool against the cold outside. A golden amulet hung between her breasts, matched to gold rings sporting dozens of tiny, tinkling discs in her ears and a dozen gold bracelets circling her arms.

He ducked his head and knelt beside her so as not to let her see his dizziness. His cock was full, if not rod-straight. She sipped in silence for a moment. Was she reading the scrolls she had written, or was she thinking of the faults he had accumulated this day in serving her? Anxiety wound up around his spine. Had he been eager enough in her litter this night? He was so tired. She allowed him little rest. At night he walked beside her litter while the army was on the move, except for those times when she called him inside. She dozed and used him and dozed again. By day he served her in her tent until she slept. She allowed him to truly sleep in the afternoon as she slept, before she bathed in preparation for sunset. Sometimes he could catch some moments of sleep while she reviewed her troops in the evening. In the first months of his captivity, longing for eight hours of sleep in an English feather bed could bring tears to his eyes. But he hadn't cried in a long time. He existed now in a place beyond tears. He had crossed some line. He was not his own creature, but hers.

"Will you require compulsion tonight to serve me?" she asked, her voice silky.

"Nae, mistress." He swallowed the lump that choked his throat.

"How do you serve me?" She lifted a curl of hair from his shoulders. His hair and beard had grown during the months she had owned him.

"Willingly," he breathed.

"And why do you serve me willingly?"

He cast about, frantic. He didn't know the answer. "Ye're . . . my mistress." Did it come out as a question? She wouldn't like that.

She lifted his chin. Her grip was iron. "And you were made to belong to me. Serving me fulfills your purpose in life."

He lowered his gaze. "Yes, mistress."

"Suckle my breasts," she commanded, pulling aside the fine red wool.

He lifted his head to where she leaned over him, and first licked her left nipple and then fastened to it. He felt her arch into his mouth. Her nipples were very sensitive. Her long nails raked his scalp as he sucked, and stopped and sucked again.

"*How long is it since I have had to punish you with pain in your head for resisting me?*"

He didn't know! Weeks? A month? He sucked her right nipple until he heard her catch her breath. "*I dinnae count the days, mistress,*" he whispered.

She chuckled. "*You are intelligent. It makes you difficult. But you have come round to submission in the end. A pity the act of submission doesn't yet make you hard.*"

She asked the impossible! Would she punish him if he could not comply? The very thought of punishment made him soften. And she wasn't using her strange power to bring his cock to attention. He let his left hand drift toward his genitals, even as he cupped her breast with his right. He must raise himself in order to please her.

"*No!*" she barked. "*Too easy. I want it to rise of its own accord.*"

He slid his hand under her robe to caress her hip, hoping to distract her. Hadn't sex and pleasing her become his only reasons for being? He should be able to keep an erection. It was the fear that stood between him and the reaction she required. But someone who had only dust inside could not really be afraid, could he? He concentrated on his desire to serve her even as he kissed her belly. But thinking about serving her brought the fear.

Very well. He'd think of those lost times when he had enjoyed the sexual act. His thoughts slid to days in Edinburgh as a student, to a bonny wench called Megan . . . But how could a wraith of long-dead times rouse him?

"*You know, I consider it almost an insult that you need compulsion to achieve an erection,*" the hated contralto murmured above him.

God help him . . . she'd whip him, or create the pain in his head until he was hoarse with screaming. He took a dreadful chance. "*It . . . it is only that I am weakened, mistress. And tired.*"

"*You make excuses?*" she cried, pushing him back. He

sprawled on the carpet. It scratched at his raw skin. "There is no excuse for a slave not pleasing his mistress."

Callan scrambled up to press his forehead to the carpet, waiting for his sentence to be pronounced. There was a long silence. Callan licked his lips. What was she doing? He dared not raise his head. Was she thinking of some new, more terrible submission she could require?

"You do grow weak from my tasting," she said at last. "But there is a cure for that."

She sprayed him with compulsion. His cock grew painfully erect.

"Now come here and serve me, and then we will cure this exhaustion of yours."

A cure for exhaustion. That's what she called infecting him with Fedeyah's blood. It made him strong, all right. Callan rubbed his temples as if that would erase the thoughts that plagued him. And now he needed a cure for the cure. But the price for staying to partake of it, if and when Blundell produced it, was the very submission that had twisted his soul. He couldn't endure that a second time.

Yet would he really forgo the cure to escape Elyta? The cure was his only hope to escape his vampire nature. Only then could he retrieve who he had been before Asharti, before Elyta Zaroff, before his crimes against humanity and against himself. And if there was no retrieving what he once was, or if he had always been evil and debauched and Asharti had only released his true nature, then once he was human again he could end his suffering.

Maybe he could bear his slavery to Elyta just long enough to take the cure. The cure was no escape, though. She could still use him as a human. She could prevent his suicide and keep him alive for a long time. So he should go, tonight if he could manage it. If he went, he'd be doomed to vampirism forever. But he'd be his own man. Or his own monster.

And Jane?

He couldn't leave Jane to Elyta.

But Elyta seemed to like Jane. Jane was in no danger from her, surely. And Elyta ruled Flavio and Clara absolutely. Yet . . . women like Elyta didn't like rivals. She wouldn't like Jane's streak of independence. At the first of Jane's pointed questions, she'd lash out. Jane had already refused Elyta's invitation to partake of him.

Nonsense. Jane could take care of herself.

Yet she couldn't. She didn't even know about compulsion.

But what good was he to her? He couldn't protect her, whether he stayed or left.

The sun was sinking, somewhere outside the darkened room. He was sinking with it, submerging in a dark and oily sea. The water filled his mouth with the bitter taste of despair.

Elyta stirred from her sleep.

Jane couldn't bear to be in this house another second. She'd tossed and turned all day. They were only two doors down. The feminine moans of pleasure, the masculine grunts, the periodic banging of the bed against the wall tormented her. Pillows over her head couldn't shut out the sound. There was no use leaving her room. She'd be able to hear them all over the house. And she was trapped inside by the sun.

Lying there awake, she couldn't forget the arch of his ribs or the strong muscles in his thighs and buttocks bunching as he lifted himself in counterpoint to Elyta, or the way his biceps bulged as he held to the bedposts. *Have you no shame? No control?* She should only be horrified that she had been so mistaken about him.

Well, now the sun had set. She rose, dressed hastily, and pulled her hair up into a knot. She'd get away. The loch? No, she had no desire to see the monster again. The castle? Absolutely not! That was full of tainted memories. Up the glen, then, as far as she could go.

Hmmmm. She didn't want to miss Brother Flavio's return. Her father would try the experiment with laudanum immediately. It wasn't that she wanted to be there in case
Kilkenny needed her. He might choke to death this morning. She sighed and followed him
cared. No, it was only that she wanted to witness the break-
through, and take the cure herself immediately. She didn't
want this thrill of life in her veins, or the throbbing insistence
that had lured her into sexual encounters with Kilkenny.

She'd ride Missy. Just to get into the cool night air. Flavio
wouldn't be able to start back from Inverness until sunset,
and then it was seventeen miles of bad road. She had several
hours yet. She strode down the stairs, refusing to tread
lightly. Let them hear her. She didn't stop to break her fast
but went right up to the barn.

Before she could get there, her father leaned out of the
laboratory door and beckoned. His white hair stood out at
odd angles. His coat was stained in several places and he
hadn't shaved this morning. She sighed and followed him
into his workroom. Beakers bubbled merrily with decoctions
in shades of green and brown and even dull red. Steam
fogged the windows of the old creamery building. The
whole place smelled rather . . . decayed.

"Jane, my dear," he said, turning back to his beakers.
"Where is Kilkenny? Flavio could be back at any time." He
drained the contents of one beaker through a long glass tube.
The virulent green liquid turned several corners and drained
into a glass tub of sorts, where it joined a clear viscous fluid
and miraculously turned a sort of blue-purple color, like
aubergine.

"I've no idea," she said stiffly.

Her father scribbled frantically in his notebook, mutter-
ing. "Two powerful poisons paired with laudanum . . ."
When he finished, he looked up. "Can you see he's fed well?
I want him fit. I'll dose him as soon as Flavio returns."

Jane set her lips. "He seemed quite fit last time I saw him."

"He'll require lots of protein—a few eggs, some rashers

of bacon and a kidney or two, some biscuits or bread, something to provide energy."

"Clara can attend to it." She couldn't help her impatient tone. "I'm going for a ride."

"Now?" Her father raised his beetling brows. "Jane, this could be all we've waited for."

She blew out a breath. "Oh, very well, Papa. I'll make sure he's fed. *If* he deigns to come downstairs." She turned on her heel. Missy would have to wait.

It must have been the smell of eggs and bacon that brought them downstairs. Jane was willing to let the food get cold rather than knock on Elyta's door again. She was going to put out the food and leave. Clara insisted that Elyta be served in the dining room rather than the kitchen. Jane and Clara had worked silently together preparing the meal. Now they set steaming plates of food on the sideboard.

Elyta, trailed in, en déshabillé, wearing her lilac wrapper, her dark hair hanging loose. Kilkenny followed. He had pulled on shirt and breeches carelessly. He did not meet Jane's eyes but pulled out Elyta's chair. The woman sat languidly. Jane smelled sex on them both.

"Kilkenny, fetch water for my bath," Elyta ordered. "Clara, I'm starving."

Clara selected food from the trays. Kilkenny made for the door. He looked strangely determined. Jane should be glad to see him go. But she had a promise to fulfill.

"My father wants you to eat, Mr. Kilkenny. You need your strength for the coming trial."

He paused. But he still didn't look at her. "I'm no' hungry," he muttered.

"I had forgot about the test," Elyta exclaimed. "Sit and eat, Kilkenny. You can get the water after we sup." Her ordering Kilkenny about was a bit . . . disconcerting. Was that what it was like to be so beautiful men would do anything for you? Still, Kilkenny didn't strike Jane as the type to take orders. She was wrong. Kilkenny sat, his fascinating mouth a grim line. Jane filled a plate and set it in front of him. He stared at it. She put a slice of toast and jam on her own plate.

Clara poured tea. "Would you like some ale, Mr. Kilkenny?" Jane asked, half wanting to torment him by making him speak to her. He *should* be ashamed of his behavior.

"This'll do," he said softly.

"Of course he'll take ale. It's entirely more sustaining," Elyta contradicted. Clara went to get the ale. He still hadn't taken a bite. "Eat, Kilkenny," she said sharply.

Still staring at his plate, he picked up his fork. He cut a bite from his egg. The yolk poured yellow that seeped against his bacon and toast. Jane watched, beguiled, as he hesitated, then shoved a forkful of food in his mouth. He swallowed convulsively.

"Are . . . are you ill?" She asked it almost against her will. It was just concern for the test.

"He's not ill." Elyta answered for him. "He's just a little lazy and rebellious this evening. Aren't you, Kilkenny?" Her voice was sweet.

"Aye." He almost choked on the word. Or on his eggs.

Jane realized in disgust that she must watch for signs of illness. If he was ill, the test would have to be postponed. He got through his food though, while Elyta chatted on about how living "rustically" as she called it was so hard on one of her sensibilities.

Jane wanted to shriek.

When they had done, Elyta pushed back from the table. "Kilkenny, my bathwater?" She smiled at him. It was a knowing, superior smile just like the one Jane had seen when Elyta first ran her eyes over him the night the vampires came to Muir Farm.

Kilkenny looked up, a terrible indecision written in his gray-green eyes. What was the matter with him? Just refuse the order if he thought it such an imposition. He tore his eyes away from Elyta's and stared at his empty plate, smeared with egg yolk and bacon grease. Then he pushed himself up and strode from the room.

"Men." Elyta laughed. "Such strange creatures!"

Jane heard the distant clatter of the gig. Brother Flavio was back.

Now was his chance. He stood at the well some fifty yards from the house. Lights shone from the windows. He could see Dr. Blundell hurrying down from the laboratory and Flavio's silhouette at the kitchen window with the two small packages the monk had unloaded from the gig. No one was paying any attention to Callan.

He could go.

He could do no one any good here. If he stayed there was only abuse and degradation ending in death, regardless of whether the newest formula worked. He'd vowed he'd never put himself in anyone's power again. He could keep that promise. Today had been like a nightmare reaching out from his past to twist his heart.

He sent the bucket clattering down into the well a second time. He'd stacked the bottles of blood at the base of the stone wall that circled it.

And if he left now?

Aye, there's the rub, as Shakespeare would say.

It wasn't just that he would endure an eternity of being a monster if he left without the cure. True, he had wanted the cure more than anything. Who wouldn't? But he could continue shouldering the burden of his nature.

He turned the handle and watched the wet rope stretch onto the windlass.

The thing that rankled was that if he left now Elyta would have won, in a way. She wouldn't be able to torture him, but she would have sacrificed nothing else. She'd have the cure she came for, whatever the reason she wanted it. And he would have abandoned Jane and her father to the capricious whim of a woman he knew to be evil. He knew in the pit of his stomach that there would come a time when Jane would need protection against Elyta.

That would mean Asharti had won in some strange way, too. She had turned him into the man who would kneel at her feet, begging her to abuse him. He had committed . . . atrocities under her influence. He couldn't deny it. But he didn't have to keep being that man who didn't stand up to her, did he? A man could change. He wanted to change, to prove that Asharti did not control him even from her grave. He had to take a stand against her sometime. He'd tried to take back his soul by doing small good deeds, but still she sat in his heart. And he'd never confronted her directly. How could he? She was dead. But now she lived again, in Elyta. Now he had another chance to achieve a different sort of ending to his story.

There was no hope of helping Jane and the doctor escape, once the cure was found.

He had no plan.

But he couldn't run away, either.

He poured the water from the bucket attached to the well rope into the second of the two he had brought with him, then replaced the bottles of blood and lowered them into the cool water again. He turned back to the house and hefted the two sloshing buckets. He was going to endure what Elyta could compel, and all for some slender hope that he could change things this time, that he could take back what he was, and who he was.

Elyta was right. He wouldn't run away. He just hoped she was wrong about the reason.

CHAPTER
Fifteen

Jane watched as Flavio cleared the old butter churns from the laboratory and upended several wooden tubs as seats for Elyta and Jane. He stacked some of the milk buckets to make room. Several lamps flickered, bathing the laboratory in bright, golden light. Her father paced among his bubbling beakers, making last-minute preparations. Kilkenny stood, stone-faced, hands clenched. Only Clara had not bothered to attend the spectacle.

"Wasn't he to be naked, Doctor?" Elyta examined Kilkenny with a critical eye.

"I'll no' strip in mixed company," Kilkenny muttered, eyes fixed on the floor.

"Nothing we haven't seen before, yes, Jane?"

"Quiet now," her father ordered, waving a hand absently. Jane was glad her father was too distracted to realize what Elyta's comment might mean about his daughter. "Flavio, bring the opium. Are you sure about the dosage?"

Flavio set two packages wrapped in brown paper and tied with string on the workbench. "I'm sure. Our metabolisms run at a higher rate than humans'."

"Then I'm glad you stayed to get the powder. It would have taken a quart of tincture of laudanum." Her father lit a flame under a small metal bowl.

Kilkenny paled further as he stared at the bricks of white powder Flavio unwrapped.

Her father loaded four teaspoons into the bowl. "Jane, find my notebook." She could feel his excitement. He thought this was it. "I shall have to make several injections. Flavio, can I get you to stir this? I'll get the syringe."

Flavio stepped up to his task. Jane rummaged among the books on the table and found the leather-covered journal. Flipping the pages, she saw the endless recipes her father had tried. She turned to a clean leaf and rubbed her palm along the crease to flatten it. Now for a pen . . . How did her father find anything in this jumble? There, under the table. She bent to retrieve it, and held it to the light. It wanted mending.

Kilkenny took it from her. "Let me do that." He grabbed the knife her father used to cut herbs. It was much too big to mend a quill. She started to protest then realized that he wanted occupation. He cut his finger, but it healed even as she watched. He handed the quill back to her.

"Thank you," she murmured. She wanted to tell him he would be all right. Or maybe just that she wouldn't let him die just because he'd had sex with Elyta. She had no right to think it a betrayal. He'd never promised her a thing. How depressing . . .

Her father had assembled the syringe. He peered over Flavio's shoulder. "It's ready. Now just keep adding more, a spoonful at a time." He glanced to Kilkenny. "What, man, are you still dressed? The formula tonight contains an emetic."

"What's that?" Kilkenny asked.

"It makes you vomit," Jane whispered.

"I'm used ta that," he said grimly. "Just ha' one o' th' buckets handy and I'll do."

Flavio grabbed a wooden milk pail and set it next to the pallet on the floor.

"Very well, young man, but you must take off your shirt

at least. I'll need several injection sites." Her father filled
the syringe from the metal bowl. "I may want to use the
femoral artery, too." Kilkenny's countenance darkened. He
knew about femoral arteries. He had many circular scars
along his own.

Kilkenny pulled his shirt up over his head. The sight of
his strongly muscled torso stirred juices Jane would rather
suppress.

"Jane," her father said sharply, recalling her to her senses.
"The cord."

She grabbed the rubber tube her father used to aid in injections from the laboratory table. "Hold out your arm," she
murmured, tying it tight. "Now make a fist." His biceps muscle bunched. She caught Elyta's smirk out of the corner of
her eye. Elyta must smell the scent of Jane's reaction. Jane
stepped back, breathing slowly to calm herself.

Her father turned, the upended syringe spouting a tiny
fountain of liquid as he made sure the needle had no air bub-
bles. Thirty ccs? Could anyone take so much pure opium?
"If you're wrong about the dosage, Flavio," he remarked,
"we'll kill him outright."

"Nonsense," Elyta snapped. "He's immortal. Well, except
for decapitation."

"It's the right dose," Brother Flavio said quietly. "Enough
to stun his Companion."

"Relax your fist," her father ordered, his focus all for the
vein in front of him. It was a ropy blue shadow plunging
down Kilkenny's forearm. Her father took Kilkenny's elbow
to steady it and slid the needle into the vein, just below the
crook of his arm. Kilkenny didn't even flinch. Her father
pushed the plunger slowly home. "Number one." He pulled
out the syringe and turned to collect a small pad of gauze.
By the time he turned back, the puncture wound had closed.
"Well!" Her father raised his brows and tossed the gauze
away. "Jane?"

Jane repeated the process. At least there would be no need

to use the femoral artery. They could probably stick the same vein a dozen times with no consequence. This time she looked up at Kilkenny. He too was intent on the vein that even now bulged in his arm. The longing in his gray-green eyes was startling. He wanted the cure that much. He must have felt her gaze, for he glanced up at her, and the expression changed to one of shame. He looked away.

Her father stepped up with the next syringe and plunged it in.

Jane bit her lip when her father filled a third syringe. Surely no one could take so much opium, even a vampire! She peered at Kilkenny. Already his eyes had lost focus. As the third dose plunged home, he staggered. Flavio stepped up and steadied him.

"Lie down," her father ordered.

Flavio eased Kilkenny to the pallet. Her father took a candle and knelt beside him. He pulled up Kilkenny's eyelid and waved the candle in front of his face. "Pupils dilated," her father remarked. "The drug is taking effect." Indeed, Kilkenny seemed hardly sensible. "We'll wait a bit now before we give him the formula for tonight." Her father stood. He dipped the quill in the inkstand and began scribbling notes.

"What formula have you used?" Elyta asked. Her voice was almost too casual.

"Time enough for that if it works," her father muttered. "But the ingredients are common. We'll be able to produce a metric ton of it, if you've the need, and a source of opium."

"Excellent," Elyta murmured.

Callan felt heavy, his senses dull. He looked down on his body from somewhere above. They were all clustered round, peering at him, except Elyta, who fanned herself from her position on the periphery. His own gray-green eyes stared up, focused on nothing. Strange that no one seemed to notice their true color except Jane Blundell. There was Jane. How sorry he was she had to know the worst of him. But perhaps that was all there was to know.

Better she was disillusioned earlier than later. He wasn't worth her attentions. He knew that. He wasn't worth anything. The feelings he had tried to put by swirled around him.

There, the doctor was pouring out a cup of something of a strange purple color. He leaned over, holding it to Callan's lips. Callan felt himself choking. The liquid burned. But he felt it all from a distance. He watched his body convulse. Flavio brought the bucket. His body vomited until he spit up blood. There was pain. But it felt as though it belonged to someone else. This was not nearly as bad as before. He felt himself drifting. The connection with his body was growing longer, stretching until it was just a tenuous thread . . .

"Papa, do something!" Jane held Kilkenny's wrist. His pulse was faint, irregular. She looked back up at her father, accusing.

"What?" he asked, distracted as he looked up from his notebook.

"If you don't do something, he's going to die. The Companion isn't able to help him."

"But we must kill the parasite, Jane."

"Not at the cost of his life," she hissed. "A stimulant! Inject something with a stimulating effect to the heart."

"What? Pennyroyal?"

"Or tincture of foxglove. What do you have?"

Her father looked around vaguely.

"Papa! Hurry?"

"Uh, let's see. I might have some foxglove here somewhere."

"Get it," Jane ordered. She lunged for the syringe as her father emptied a tube of powder into a beaker of water and sloshed it about. She pushed the end of the needle into the beaker and sucked up the liquid. No time to administer it orally and have it absorbed through the stomach lining. Had

anyone ever injected the essence of foxglove directly? She
felt Kilkenny drifting away. She knelt beside him. No time
to bind his arm to bring up the vein. She felt for the vessel
and rolled it under her fingers. Thank goodness men had
such prominent veins. She glanced to his face, hesitating.
His eyes were half-closed, unfocused. The injection might
kill him.

But he was dying anyway. And no one else would care,
not even her father except that they would have no one to experiment on. She slid the needle slantwise into the vein.

She was all Kilkenny had. She pushed the plunger home.

"He'll require more opium at intervals."

The voice was far away. His body burned. Fire ate along
his veins, pumped by his heart. He tried to speak, but
couldn't.

"Reduce the dose, Father. He can't stand so much again."

Jane. That was Jane's voice. He wanted to reach out for
her, but something held him, just like he had been immobi-
lized by Asharti's compulsion, or Elyta's. He could almost
see Asharti's face, hanging above him. Asharti's almond
eyes resolved themselves into Elyta, and then the image
shifted back. Somewhere he heard someone groaning.

The faces above him were one, and both, and one again.
They held him imprisoned. His cock rose at their command.
He wouldn't, couldn't serve them. Could he? Would he?

"Well, we've seen this phenomenon before. He's a virile
lad, I'll give him that."

"Papa, he's suffering . . ."

The voice grew fainter. *Jane,* he wanted to call. But he
couldn't. There was only Asharti, and Elyta, and pain.

Jane wiped Kilkenny's naked body with a damp cloth. His
body had been racked with fevers for two days. His sheets
were constantly soaked with sweat. Flavio had helped her
change them twice already. They needed changing again.

It didn't matter whether he was a traitor now, or a murderer. Even one who was evil shouldn't suffer like this. She wouldn't think about that. She was so worried about him, his nakedness and his periodic erections didn't cause her as much distress as they once would have. She was too busy trying to balance her father's dosage of opium with tincture of foxglove. Her father was lessening the opium each time in a blind attempt to avoid killing his patient, should Kilkenny actually be turning human now. But there was no certainty about the program. Too little and the Companion survived, too much and the patient didn't. Kilkenny vomited up anything she tried to feed him. His urine output had been minimal, which said his body was in shock, his kidneys under stress. He was consumed with toxins he had no way of processing.

How much trauma could a man's body endure?

She shook out a clean sheet over him, then took up a little pot of cream and sat beside him. A fire crackled in the grate. Kilkenny had been alternating bouts of fever and chills, so she kept the room warm. Though he had been staying here more than a week, there was little to say it was his. No brushes were laid out on the dresser, no nail-paring knife. But he owned them. He had been well groomed before his illness. He must have left them in his valise, as though he was poised to leave at any moment. Only the great sword leaning against the mantel said a man occupied this space. She smoothed a finger full of cream across his chapped lips. How she wished to see the words ripple out through those wonderful, mobile lips again!

She rubbed her temples. Two days since she had slept. Her father didn't know she attended Kilkenny continuously. He thought Clara took a turn. But Jane would never trust Kilkenny's care to anyone else. Jane moved a wet strand of hair off Kilkenny's forehead.

All her anger at him, all her feeling of betrayal seemed silly now. Could she of all people not understand the internal fires that had driven him to bed Elyta? Surely the expression on his face of horror and shame when she had stumbled in on them went deeper than the fact that he'd been caught *in medias res*. He was ashamed of what he was, and what that made him do.

He didn't care for her, of course. He had been tender with her in spite of their driving lust at Urquhart Castle. But she didn't fool herself. The driving lust was why he was there. Who was she to cast stones at that?

The fact that she might be weak enough to care for him, beyond the simple fact of vampire lust, was her own failing not his. If he died, and she never got to . . . To what? She couldn't tell him any part of what she felt. She touched his three-day growth of beard. She wouldn't think of her feelings for him. She only wanted him to live.

The sun was rising. She glanced around. The curtains . . . She rose and felt the room waver.

"Miss Blundell, let me."

Flavio steadied her and sat her in a chair. When had he come in? He looked at her with concern until she smiled with what she hoped was reassurance. Then he pulled the draperies.

"I'll watch him." He came to stand in front of her.

"I'm fine," she said, shrugging her shoulders. "A momentary faintness."

"You haven't slept in days. What good will you do him if you collapse?" Flavio's brown eyes were soft with understanding.

She shook her head. "What if he should need a stimulant and there is no one here to administer it? You do not know how. Father is busy compiling his notes . . ." Indeed, the fact that her father seemed more interested in his records than the patient himself . . . disturbed her. Had her father become so fixated on the outcome he could not see a man's suffering?

"If his pulse weakens or becomes erratic I will call you."

"You're tired. You've been taking care of the animals . . . if you fell asleep . . ."

"I won't fall asleep. You can count on me."

Could she? She searched his face. She was perhaps no more reliable than someone else at this point, she was so tired.

"I . . . let someone down once. Kilkenny reminds me of him. Give me a chance to redeem myself." Flavio's voice sounded as though his throat was raw.

One couldn't deny that kind of plea. She nodded once. She would be better for some sleep. "Very well. You'll call me at the first sign of an erratic or fading pulse." It was a command more than a plea. She stood. Kilkenny's long black eyelashes brushed his ashen cheeks. *Don't die. I'd never forgive myself.*

"I'll change out his sheets," Flavio promised.

"And check his pulse every quarter hour," Jane instructed. Flavio nodded, smiling. "Now get thee hence."

Tears rose. They were just tears of exhaustion. "Thank you," she murmured.

A rhythmic thumping invaded Jane's dreams of monsters in the loch. She realized that she hated that sound, though she couldn't think why. She blinked, groggy.

Wait! She lurched upright.

It *couldn't* be! Anger churned up, banishing the vestiges of sleep. She threw off the coverlet and struggled out of the high bed. She did not stay to don slippers or wrapper but lunged for the door and strode down the hall. A low masculine moaning issued from Kilkenny's room and a higher-pitched panting. She didn't bother knocking, but threw open the door.

"What are you doing?" she shouted.

Elyta was straddling Kilkenny again, working herself up

and down over his stiff cock. She was naked this time. A heavy fall of dark hair concealed her back. Her narrow waist flared to buttocks like plump, twin teardrops. One hand rubbed herself between her legs. Kilkenny did not participate this time. He was barely conscious. His head lolled to one side. Elyta's yips cycled up into a continuous shriek. Jane strode forward and grabbed her shoulder.

But her orgasm was done. She relaxed, a smile of satisfaction on her lips.

"Get off him," Jane hissed. "What were you thinking?"

Elyta raised her head and shrugged off Jane's grip. Jane staggered back against the wall. Was Elyta that strong? "It's been two days since my needs were met. What did you expect?"

"I expected you not to abuse a man who is ill," Jane gasped, pushing herself up.

"What does he care?" Elyta dismounted Kilkenny's hips and reached for the lilac wrapper pooled on the braided rug. "And Flavio is not easy to subdue."

"Where is Flavio?" Jane's anger welled anew. Flavio had promised to watch Kilkenny.

"I'm still stronger than he is." Elyta shrugged her wrapper up around her shoulders.

Kilkenny looked entirely unconscious. How could he sustain an erection in his condition long enough to satisfy Elyta?

Elyta glanced back to him. "I'll keep him erect if you care to take a turn."

"You'll . . . You'll keep him . . . ? What do you mean?"

Elyta tied the belt of her wrapper. "Don't you know? Since I'm stronger, I can raise his erection and encourage or suppress his ejaculation. It's a matter of compulsion."

"What is this . . . compulsion?" She'd heard them talk about it. Did she want to know?

Elyta raised her head. The amusement in her eyes rankled. "But of course you don't know." She laughed that tinkling laugh. "He wouldn't tell you that, now would he? He might want to use it against you."

"*You* tell me," Jane said through gritted teeth. "Just tell me."

"Perhaps a demonstration . . ."

Jane wasn't sure she wanted a demonstration. Dared she leave Kilkenny? She was still trying to decide when Elyta's eyes flashed red.

Jane froze. She tried to turn and stride out the door, but . . . she didn't. She just didn't. Elyta's eyes were captivating. And then she felt it; the thrill between her legs, more intense than she had ever experienced. She had a terrible premonition.

"You see?" Elyta smirked. "I can make you want him. I can make you use him."

Jane found herself moving toward the bed and Kilkenny's insensate form. The need inside her was like to drive her mad. That didn't mean she'd do Elyta's bidding. She wouldn't!

But she knelt beside him, and reached out her hand. She knew without being told what Elyta wanted. She wouldn't do it! She struggled against the will that seemed to drench her. Slowly, her hand clasped his cock and began pulling on it. She wouldn't! But she was. This wasn't erotic. Yet she throbbed, wet and needing. She rubbed Kilkenny's cock. He roused himself enough to moan. His eyelids fluttered and his chest began to heave. Jane rubbed the head of his cock with her thumb. She didn't want to. She wanted to shriek.

"He's been erect for hours without coming. You have so much sympathy? Let's give him what he needs. Rub him harder." Elyta's voice was a sibilant whisper.

Jane slid her hand up and down Kilkenny's cock, even as he rolled his head. She hated herself for her complicity, but she couldn't stop. Elyta slid up behind her, watching.

It didn't take long. Kilkenny's abdominal muscles contracted. White fluid pulsed out across his belly. Jane was horrified. It seemed to go on and on.

When the last dribble had oozed out, he collapsed. Elyta handed her a towel.

Jane felt the bands of compulsion fade. Tears sprang to her eyes. She held one hand to her mouth. What had she done? Kilkenny was entirely slack. Shaking, she raised an eyelid with one thumb. His pupils were rolled up. She whirled on Elyta. "You . . . you bitch! Is this how you use your powers?" Her eyes widened in realization. A flash of Kilkenny's horrified expression filled her. "You . . . you *made* him service you before, didn't you?"

"Of course." Elyta shrugged. "Don't be so sour. I invited you to share. I was more than generous to one who was only made. How was I to know you were so ignorant?"

"That's vile!" And to think she believed he had done it on his own . . . The image of his expression at the dining table, the fact that he could hardly eat his food . . . She'd been right when she'd guessed that a female vampire had used him sexually, and drunk his blood. And now she knew exactly how in excruciating detail.

"You are hardly more than human," Elyta said with a sneer. "You have no right to judge one as powerful as I. We take what we want. Do men not take women if they are more powerful?"

"It isn't right no matter who does it." She wiped Kilkenny's belly. "You may have killed him. Then we'll never know whether this formula is your precious cure."

Elyta drew her delicate brows together. "Hmmm. I hadn't thought of that."

Jane picked up his wrist and felt the tiny, erratic pulse. His breathing was shallow.

"Oh, very well." Elyta pouted. Jane felt the rush of power behind her. She turned . . .

Elyta's eyes were carmine, her canines extended over her lips. But this time there was no compulsion. She raised her wrist to her mouth and used one of her own teeth to rip her flesh. She licked at the wound. Blood welled and then began to spurt.

"What are you doing?" Jane gasped.

Elyta made a face as blood splattered her wrapper and pressed her fingers against the wound. "Giving him strength from the blood of a very old vampire." She motioned Jane away.

"You can't," Jane said flatly. "You'll reinfect him with your Companion."

Elyta stopped and raised her brows. Jane saw acknow-ledgment pass through her eyes.

"Go. You've done enough harm."

Elyta hesitated, and then turned to the door. "I'll send Clara for blood from the well."

Jane just stared at her until she let herself out of the room.

But Kilkenny couldn't drink the blood. Hours later when Jane could finally rouse him enough to get it down his throat, he vomited it straight up. Her father came bustling into the room, his notebook under his arm.

"How is my patient?" he asked cheerfully, opening his notebook and laying it on the small secretary desk. The pen and inkwell still stood in readiness from his previous visits.

Jane stood, so he could see for himself.

"Hmmm. Skin clammy. Color not good. Has he been able to eat?"

Jane shook her head.

"Periods of consciousness?"

"Enough to sip a little water, but he doesn't seem to know me."

"Not lucid," her father muttered, scribbling. "Urine output?"

"None in the last eight hours."

He frowned. Taking the knife he used to mend his pen from one pocket and a handkerchief from the other, he wiped the blade carefully. He bent over Kilkenny and made a small incision in his forearm. It bled sluggishly. Jane held her breath. Blood dribbled down his wrist and dripped onto the floor. The wound showed no signs of closing.

Her father turned to her, eyes gleaming. "Get me some gauze, Jane. He's cured."

CHAPTER
Sixteen

Callan opened his eyes. Light streamed through the window. He blinked against the brightness. He'd been having horrible dreams where Asharti turned into Elyta who turned into Jane and they all tormented him. The dream clung to him though his eyes were open. He was propped up on pillows. It took all his strength to move his eyes and look around. Blundell slept in the chair by the remains of a fire. The color in the room was strangely flat, the house silent.

Sunlight.

That should hurt his eyes, burn his skin.

It didn't burn. It didn't even really hurt his eyes now that he was getting used to it.

He sucked in a breath and came to full awareness. His head throbbed. His body ached in every sinew. He tried to lift his head but the effort was too much and he fell back against his pillows. He seemed to be naked underneath the counterpane. There was no trace of either Elyta or Jane. The room was warm, and his bare arms lay outside the coverlet.

On one was a bandage.

Grunting with effort, he raised his hand and ripped the bandage from his other forearm, revealing a cut, its edges swollen together but not healed. Tears rose to his eyes.

He was human again.

• • •

When Jane woke she knew it was already dark outside. She'd slept all day. She and her father hadn't revealed that Kilkenny was cured. They'd decided to wait and see if he lived. For a while it had been touch-and-go. Jane was sure the ejaculation had killed him. She'd been consumed with guilt and anger at Elyta. It made her bold about keeping Elyta away from him. Flavio gave Elyta a soothing draught laced with laudanum to help her bear her privations.

Jane had watched over him all day, and then last night, Kilkenny began to rest more comfortably, his heartbeat regular if weak, his fever abated. Jane was so relieved. She finally felt able to entrust him to her father's ministrations during the sunlight hours.

Now she sat up in bed, her embroidered night rail of white linen tangled around her. The cure was real! She could hardly wait to take it. It would be an ordeal. But she was blessed with a strong constitution. She'd take it this very night. The whole experience would be behind her soon enough. She got up and threw on a wrapper of gray-striped lustring.

She had to see Kilkenny immediately. She paused, listening. Elyta and Flavio were down in the drawing room. She could hear the pout in Elyta's voice from here. Someone bustled in the kitchen. Clara. Mrs. Dulnan would have been here today and gone. She smelled the fresh-baked bread. She put on no slippers, but tiptoed barefoot down the hall, hoping to avoid their attention.

He was looking at her when she opened the door. The startling, translucent gray eyes with a hint of green blinked at her. How she had missed those eyes! Purple shadows hung under them. He was pale, unshaven, but still damnably attractive. That thought made her contract.

She hurried in and shut the door quietly, grinning. He gave her a tiny smile in return. It was a soft smile, warm. It made her feel her guilt at what she had done to him the more. Her father, asleep near the fire, began to snore. Jane sat on the bed. "How is it?" she whispered.

She didn't have to tell him what she meant. A little shadow passed through his eyes. "Good," he said softly. He always said it like the word ended in a *t*. She had grown fond of a Scots burr. How had she once thought it barbaric? But he didn't sound sure of himself.

"Well, you're still weak from your ordeal," she excused. "You can't expect miracles." She took his wrist. The shock of touching him returned, now that her worry had abated. It was all she could do to search for his pulse. It beat steadily back at her.

With a start she realized he might remember what she had done. She felt herself blushing to the roots of her hair. To cover her discomfiture, she rose and poured some water from the pitcher on the table by his bed into a glass. Even if he didn't remember now, he might recall as he recovered. She couldn't bear waiting for him to hate her. She'd have to take her medicine now.

She turned and cleared her throat. "I   I don't know whether you recall . . . what . . . happened while you were ill."

His eyes were wary. His examined her face carefully, questioning. Then his brows creased and disbelief chased pain across his face. Oh, he remembered all right. She searched for breath, shaking her head. "I'm so sorry. Elyta . . . but it doesn't matter. I did it."

"She used compulsion on ye?" he croaked.

She nodded, unable to speak around the great lump in her throat.

"Damn her! I should ha' told you," he managed.

Whether he meant about Elyta or about compulsion she couldn't tell. "I'm so . . . ashamed," she whispered.

"No' yer fault." His voice was hoarse with disuse.

"But I feel so . . . unclean." Tears welled up.

"I know."

He did know. Elyta had done it to him. And Jane had blamed him for it. "I'm sorry for what I thought when I saw you with her."

He was about to speak again, but he looked so exhausted she bent and laid her fingers across his mouth. "Save your strength." Here she was blathering on and wanting him to absolve her when he hardly had strength to speak. She looked down at the water glass in her hand. She was not exactly a paragon of solicitude. She sat beside him. "Drink now." She lifted his shoulders forward. His hands clasped hers on the glass as she helped him drink. The feel of his body against hers sent the familiar thrills down to her loins. Was she so far from Elyta? The man was ill, for goodness sake!

"Do you think you could stomach some broth? I had Clara boil the carcass of our chicken last night with some vegetables."

He nodded, swallowing.

With a start she realized he didn't smell like cinnamon and ambergris anymore. The only scents were of man, the cream she'd used to keep his lips moist, and the lavender water with which she'd bathed his forehead. She was too close, with her arm around his bare shoulders.

His gaze circled the room and came back to her. He looked . . . disappointed.

"What's wrong? Are you all right?" She laid him back down.

"I'm just . . . getting used ta it, that's all."

She managed a smile. "I can hardly wait to have that problem."

Behind her, her father stirred and woke. "Humph!" he snorted, peering about. "Kilkenny, you awake?" He pushed himself out of the chair and staggered over to examine his patient.

"He's better, Papa. I'm just going down to get him some broth."

"Well, well, my boy," her father chuffed. He leaned over and stared into Kilkenny's eyes, then examined the wound on his patient's forearm while he felt for a pulse. Her father nodded sagely. "Welcome back to the human condition."

"Thankee, both o' ye," Kilkenny croaked.

Jane smiled at him, then turned to her father. "So Papa, I think there's another dose left in the batch you made. We have more than enough laudanum. Clara can help with Mr. Kilkenny. So I can take the formula this very night."

Her father's beetling brows drew together. "I must mitigate the side effects first, Jane."

"I'll show you just the strength of tincture of foxglove I used to stimulate Mr. Kilkenny's heart. That helped counteract the depressive effect of the laudanum."

"Jane, I can't lose you. Let me refine the formula . . ."

"And who will you test it on, Papa? Mr. Kilkenny is now human. The other three like being vampire. They won't agree to take something that might cure them." She could see he had not thought of that. "I am your only test subject now. So you might as well give me the dose."

He rubbed his jowls, thinking. "At least let me do a bit of fiddling with it tonight, Jane. You can take it tomorrow . . ."

Light flared through the window. The night was lit by a red glow. A sound as of a growling breath shook the windowpane. Her father turned. Time slowed. Jane drifted to the window. "The laboratory," she murmured. Figures were silhouetted against an inferno.

"No . . ." her father whispered. "My notebook . . ."

Below them, the kitchen door swung open, casting a channel of light into the yard. Elyta dashed into the darkness, closely followed by Flavio and Clara.

"No!" Her father whirled and scurried from the room.

Jane looked at Kilkenny. "It must be vampires." She started for the door.

"Dinnae go!" he called roughly. "Ye're no match for them."

The implications hung in the air between them for a single instant. "I have to protect Papa," she said on her way out the door.

Outside, her father struggled up the rise to the laboratory, shouting in rage. Ahead, Elyta had already wrenched the head of a vampire from his body. Blood soaked the gravel path. Flavio grappled with another. Clara stood off to the side, wringing her hands. Jane could see at least two other strangers cast into relief by the flames that engulfed the laboratory.

"My notebook," her father moaned as he panted up the hill.

She grabbed his arm. "There's nothing to be done now, Papa. Come away."

A shadow loomed behind them. A huge, hulking man blocked their way back to the house. Jane gasped and stepped in front of her father. "What do you want?" she hissed.

"To finish what our brother started," the man said in heavily accented English. His face was set and hard. He had the Magyar features of the first attacker. His coat was of rough material, like that of a farmer or a poor tradesman. He hadn't made a move yet, though. Was he undecided about whether to kill them? She must keep him talking.

"Why would you destroy the only escape from your condition? It will be a blessing for some of your kind."

"Because of the way *they* will use it," he growled. His neck was as thick as a tree trunk, his hands large and gnarled with veins.

"Who? How?" Her father had gone still behind her.

"The Elders," he spat. "If they control both Mirso and the cure, they own our souls."

"They want to distribute it to those who need it," Jane protested.

"Who says that, Elyta? She's aligned with them." He shook his great, leonine head. "No, only those loyal to them will get the cure, just as loyalty is the price for entrance to Mirso. Either that or they will cure the rebels who do not want the cure by force. Khalenberg wants to go back to the way things were, when any could gain the refuge of Mirso. We struggle in his cause against the Elders. We do not want a cure. We do not need it. We embrace our nature."

She spared a glance to the flames now licking out the laboratory roof. "Well, it seems you've got your wish. The formula is gone."

The vampire stared at the burning building. The flames sounded like sheets flapping in the wind. Slowly his eyes turned back toward her father. "The cure exists as long as he's alive."

He lunged. Jane grabbed his coat collar and thrust with all her might. He fell back. "I won't let you kill my father!" she yelled.

"You're new," he said, recovering. He straightened. "You cannot stop me."

He swept her aside with one arm. She stumbled away. Her rage gushed over her. Bending at the waist, she launched herself at him, butting him in the stomach with her head. He staggered back. But Jane leaped on him, hitting his back with both fists.

"Leave us alone," she shouted.

It took her a moment to register the gurgle she heard behind her. "Papa?"

Everything stopped as she turned. Her father's neck angled horribly. A ferret-eyed man was just letting him go. He toppled slowly to the side.

"Papa!" Abandoning all thought of fighting, she ran to him.

Some part of her knew it was too late, even as she cradled him. His head lolled at an impossible angle. "Papa!" But his eyes saw nothing anymore. It happened so quickly! He couldn't just . . . die like that, could he? Did a man's life escape him so easily?

The ferret-eyed man grabbed her shoulders and jerked her to her feet. "Mebbe we could save this one for a while, Allya," he said, leering.

"None of them remains alive," the big one called Allya growled. His eyes were full red.

Red eyes! She had the same power. Kilkenny had taught her how to use it. The ferret-eyed man took her head in both hands from behind. *Companion!* Power raced up her veins. The world went red. She scrabbled at the man behind her but she couldn't get a grip. She tried to slip out of his grasp, but he was too strong for her. Very well. Kilkenny had taught her what to do.

Companion, now! She felt the whirling blackness sliding up. The vampire was twisting her head. She tensed her neck muscles, resisting.

"No, you don't, girl!" the hulking Allya threatened. His power showered over her, slowing the blackness at her hips. *Companion!* She thought about the well. A moment more . . . The blackness surged up. She'd make it now. She felt the triumph singing in her veins.

As her vision dimmed, she saw Kilkenny behind Allya with the great claymore raised in shaking arms. The world snapped to black with a sear of pain.

She popped into space next to the well perhaps a hundred yards from the melee. Kilkenny, dressed only in a billowing shirt that came to mid-thigh, hacked down at Allya. Blood spurted. But he had not enough strength to cut the big man's neck clear through.

Allya turned with a howl of rage.

No! she thought. Kilkenny mustn't die, too! Jane pulled up her skirts and took off at a run, wailing. Trying to draw the power again so soon would take her too long. The ferret-eyed vampire lunged for Kilkenny. Jane pressed her legs for speed. She was running faster than she thought was possible. Allya grabbed Kilkenny by the shoulders and hoisted him off the ground. The great claymore slipped from his grip and slid down the hill. Flavio appeared behind the ferret-eyed vampire and whirled him around.

No matter how fast she ran it wasn't fast enough. Allya shook Kilkenny, who flopped like a rag doll. Surely his neck would snap, just like her father's. Why had he come? He was no match for vampires either. Not anymore.

Allya was hissing something at Kilkenny. Jane was almost on them. Allya was so big! Her heart sputtered.

The claymore! She scooped it up as she ran up the hill. She swallowed, panting, as she raised it. Could she do this? Kilkenny's white shirt was covered in blood. *It's Allya's,* she told herself, pushing down panic. Allya half turned. A step more. She set her feet.

And brought the claymore down to finish the work Kilkenny had started. It slipped through flesh. There was a snap of bone. The tip of the claymore came around, nearly grazing Kilkenny. He dropped to the ground. Allya's arms clawed at his own wounded neck.

But it was too late. Allya's head toppled first and then his body. Jane watched, unable to look away. Kilkenny crawled to the body. She stood, immobile, as though she had been turned into a pillar of salt for the sin she had just committed. Kilkenny grabbed the head by the hair and tossed it down the hill. His gray-green eyes looked up at her with so much compassion she started to cry. Damn him! Why did he have to look at her like that? Slowly, she turned around.

The ferret-eyed vampire disappeared right from under Flavio's grip in a whirl of blackness. She didn't care about that. All she could see was her father's broken body. Flames shot thirty feet into the night sky from the charred black lattice of the laboratory roof. They cast the whole farm into red relief. Jane ran to her father's side and collapsed to her knees. Why she took his hand she didn't know, perhaps to jerk him back from the underworld by force. The very slackness of his muscles said her gesture was futile.

He was dead.

Tears splashed onto his waistcoat. They must be hers. Some part of her watched herself from far away. *So this is what grief feels like.* She'd thought she'd grieved over being a vampire. But that wasn't grief. She'd never known her mother, so she didn't grieve her passing. Grief apparently meant she couldn't catch her breath. Oh, those were sobs that choked her. She heard them as little brittle gasps. *That sound is really quite ridiculous.*

"Hell and damnation!" Elyta said. Jane heard her through the sobbing. She looked up. Elyta stood with hands on hips. "Well, we'd better find his notebook." She strode forward and stood over Jane and her father's body. "Where did he keep it?"

Jane heard the words, but she couldn't quite think what they meant. A voice in her head whispered, *Your father is dead. You have nobody now. You're all alone.*

Elyta pulled Jane up by one arm. "Where is the damned notebook?" she shouted.

Oh. That's what she meant. The sobs still racked Jane, though. She couldn't speak. So she just looked up the hill to the stone creamery building with the flaming roof.

Elyta and Flavio followed her gaze.

"Khalenberg and his minions have their wish. The cure is lost," Flavio said quietly.

Jane drew a breath deep into her lungs. Lost? She blinked against the flames. The air whooshed out of her. Glowing cinders drifted into the night sky. Snapping tongues of flame ate at the darkness. She turned her head to where Kilkenny lay, chest heaving, propped on one elbow in the grass. He had made it back to human. But now she never would.

Her father was dead. She was utterly alone in a world that held the kind of monsters who had attacked them tonight. She was a monster like them. Not only did she drink human blood, but she had killed tonight. She would be a monster forever, unless she was decapitated. The world was more horrible than she had ever imagined. She glanced to her father's body. Kilkenny was right. She had been innocent. But now her innocence was dead.

Down at the house, three carts filled with men and women

clattered up the drive. People spilled from them, shouting. Many carried buckets.

"Get ta th' well!" Mr. Campbell ordered. "Ye with buckets, form a line." He strode up toward Jane and Kilkenny, Elyta and Flavio. Clara disappeared quietly into the house. Jane heard the creak of the windlass as the bucket was drawn from the well, then the crash of glass. The bottles of blood had broken when the bucket was turned out.

As Mr. Campbell got closer, he slowed, taking in the carnage. His eyes darted from Elyta and Flavio to Jane standing over her father's body, across the decapitated remnants of their attackers to a half-naked Kilkenny, gasping on the grass. Blood was everywhere. It splattered the three others and soaked the ground. Jane looked down and saw that her wrapper was drenched in blood, too, as if they had all been painted by the same careless artist.

Now others were beginning to notice what the light of the fire revealed. A hush fell across the would-be rescuers.

"Come, Flavio," Elyta whispered as she stepped forward. "You know what to do." A threatening murmur rolled through the crowd. Elyta's eyes went the deepest carmine red Jane had ever seen. Flavio clenched his jaw and strode up to stand beside Elyta.

"Silence," Elyta hissed, and the word echoed in Jane's mind. The crowd's murmur halted instantly. Jane saw the ones who were looking at Elyta grow still. Others turned at the note of command in her voice and were caught by the red of her eyes. Flavio's eyes were red now, too.

Elyta glanced around. "Wet the roofs of the house and the barn," she ordered. The words seemed to come from the rocks and the trees, echoing out over the crack of the flames and back from the cloudy sky above. Elyta's voice trembled in Jane's lungs and reverberated in her mind.

To Jane's amazement the villagers formed two lines and began a bucket brigade. Elyta and Flavio moved off, eyes still red, to direct their work. Jane knelt beside Kilkenny.

"Are you all right?" she whispered.

"I'll do."

"You should never have left your bed," she chastised as she examined him for wounds. He was scraped about a bit, but seemed whole. "You aren't strong enough."

"I'll give ye that," he muttered. He lifted his brows and took a breath as though to gather himself. "Feels a bit . . . strange."

"Ahh." He was talking about being human again. She looked back at the burning laboratory. "I suppose I shall never know." Her voice was small. The night seemed infinite. Her father's death had stripped her of any light remark she might have made to turn away the emotion. She and Kilkenny were now stranded on opposite sides of a river, one cured, one not.

Jane realized all at once what she had been hoping, somewhere down so deep she could not even acknowledge it was there. She had thought that once she and Kilkenny were both human . . . maybe . . . maybe . . .

Tears welled again.

"I'm verra sorry, Jane." Kilkenny's voice was hoarse. "About yer father, and th' cure."

She nodded, unable to speak. She had no one who cared for her. Her father was dead. Kilkenny, who had so despised his own condition, would not be able to help but despise her for drinking blood, for her strength and her need for sex. Perhaps she'd become just as cruel and horrible as Elyta. How could he not despise her? For however long he lived. He was mortal now.

She looked away from him and watched the villagers saving the house and the barn from the infection of flying cinders. Anyone could see there was no saving the laboratory. With a great cracking sound, the blackened timbers slowly collapsed inside the soot-covered stone walls.

When they had worked for half an hour or so and the roofs

were wet, Elyta clapped her hands. "Villagers, go home. Forget what you have seen." Again, her voice reverberated.

And they left. One by one they turned and climbed back into the carts.

"Wait," Elyta commanded. "You in the red and yellow kilt—you remain."

A large man of middle age with a healthy beard stopped where he stood, his gaze fixed on Elyta. Jane recognized the keeper of the tiny tavern in the village.

"You stay." Elyta turned to Flavio. "We will need sustenance after our ordeal tonight, and that one"—here she nodded to Kilkenny—"isn't strong enough to supply us."

Jane contracted inside. Elyta would have no compunction about draining Kilkenny unless she had other plans for him. She hated to think what that might mean. The tavernkeeper, entranced, walked slowly up to the diminutive beauty.

Jane wasn't going to watch. She helped Kilkenny up, gently, so her strength wouldn't leave more bruises than he was likely to have from his encounter with Allya. He was shivering, probably with shock as well as cold. "Come into the house," she whispered. She pulled his arm around her shoulder and took his weight as they staggered down the hill.

CHAPTER
Seventeen

Jane and Kilkenny stumbled up the stairs. She lowered him onto the rumpled bed and swung his legs under the coverlet. Then she pulled off his shirt. Her spirit was numb. He made no demur at her stripping him. He seemed dazed. It was amazing that in his condition he'd been able to make it out of the house with the great claymore at all. She wrung out a towel and wiped away the smears of sticky blood on his chest that had soaked through the shirt.

Her brain felt dried out, like the inside of a walnut left too long on the tree. He should have stayed inside. Stupid man. Didn't he know he was human now? He'd nearly been killed. And there had been too much death tonight. She contracted inside. *Papa . . .*

She wouldn't think about that. She didn't have any sobs left inside her, and she couldn't think about her father without sobbing. So she'd just put it off for a while.

Kilkenny dragged himself into almost certain death just to help me.

The thought appeared inside her mind as though it was inserted by someone else. Why had he done that? His dark lashes lifted and his gray-green eyes looked into hers, examining her, even as she searched them in return. There was pain in his expression.

Downstairs, she heard a clatter. Kilkenny might not hear it at all.

"Elyta, you've drained him!" Flavio's voice rose in accusation.

"What does it matter?" Elyta, very angry.

"You tried." Flavio reasoned with her. "But now it is time to return to Mirso."

"I won't go back without the cure, Flavio," Elyta almost snarled.

"There *is* no cure. Not now."

Silence. Jane began to think again. *Would* Elyta and Flavio just . . . leave?

"Is that true?" This from Elyta, slowly, thoughtfully. Footsteps hurried up the stairs.

"Elyta . . ." Heavier footsteps thundered up after them.

The bedroom door banged open. Elyta stood there, a disheveled vision of lavender, now liberally splashed with blood. "You worked with your father," she accused.

Jane rose slowly. "I don't have the formula, if that's what you mean."

"Don't you?" Elyta's eyes narrowed.

"Believe me," Jane snapped. "If I had it, I'd be making up a batch right now."

"You might want to keep it yourself. What could you not ask in ransom for the formula?"

"Ye want it for yer personal power, dinnae ye?" Kilkenny had pushed himself up on one elbow. The bedclothes covered him to the waist, but the muscle of his abdomen and chest were revealed, the swell of shoulder and bicep, the soft nipples.

Elyta noticed, too. She smiled. Jane hated that smile. The eyes Elyta turned back on Jane were hard as well as avaricious. "Having the formula will guarantee me a seat on the council."

"I don't care about your vampire politics," Jane said. "The formula should be used to save those who were made vampire from a fate forced upon them."

Elyta snorted and started to reply, then stopped herself. "So re-create it."

"What?"

"Re-create your father's work. I'll take the formula back to Mirso so we control access to it for born vampires, and you can use it to save the ones who are made."

"But I don't know the formula . . ."

"You gathered his ingredients, didn't you?" Elyta's deep brown eyes were pools of covetous desire. Even without compulsion, Jane felt the push of her ambition.

Jane nodded slowly. "Yes . . . but . . ." She glanced to Kilkenny. He would be able to describe the taste, the texture, even the exact symptoms of the decoction he drank. She turned back to Elyta, her eyes flickering over the vampire woman's face.

"You don't remember what you gathered?" Flavio asked doubtfully.

Jane shook her head impatiently. "I have it all in my note-book."

"So there is no problem . . ." Elyta shrugged, but her eyes still burned with intensity.

"But I don't know which ones he was actually using in the end. I'd need someone on whom to test the trials . . ."

"Clara." There was not a moment's hesitation in Elyta's answer.

"She doesn't want to be human, does she?"

"And who else is there?" Elyta asked impatiently. "If we are to find a cure, there must be sacrifice. Kilkenny knew that."

"But it was my choice," came the gruff rumble from the bed behind her.

"Clara will volunteer, and if that isn't enough, there's always Flavio," Elyta said coolly. She put her hands on her hips. "You will try." It wasn't a question.

Jane glanced again to Kilkenny. His brows were drawn together in suspicion. But what did it matter? Jane wanted her humanity back. And what she did would serve others like her who wanted their humanity back, too. If it came down to it, she could test the formula on herself.

She nodded to Elyta.

"Excellent," the woman said briskly. "What will you need? Beakers and such? Flavio can take the carriage to Inverness and bring back whatever you want."

"Give me a list," Flavio said tightly. "I can return by tomorrow night."

"I might not be able to do this . . ." Jane felt the enormity of her commitment.

"Oh, I'm certain you will," Elyta cooed. "And you'd better do it quickly. I want to be gone by the time it occurs to Khalenberg that you may be able to re-create the cure."

Flavio and Jane were planning to use the kitchen as a laboratory as they went downstairs. Their voices disappeared. Damn his human hearing! He raised his eyes to Elyta. She was looking at him like he was the first course in a banquet for the starving.

"She thinks ye'll let made vampires live once they're human." Elyta was using Jane.

Elyta chuckled. "You know better. Once they know our ways they are a danger to us."

"That means she's a danger ta ye, too." His stomach twisted.

She nodded. "Yes." Her eyes were flat brown. Elyta would kill Jane the moment she ceased to be necessary. Anger rose up inside him. But anger would do him no good.

He pushed it down. "Sa what will it take for ye ta let her go once she finds th' cure and takes it?" Did he have anything he could trade for her safety?

"Nothing you can give me," she confirmed. "I'll take whatever I want from you."

His mouth went dry. He did have something to barter. He knew her. He had been trained by her acolyte. A plan circled inside his brain. He licked his lips. Could he do this? But

Jane needed protection from Elyta. And Elyta would exact a price from someone. Only he had the coin in which it could be paid. He knew how to do this, to his shame. He knew too that he might find out things about himself he'd tried for two years to deny. But what difference to anyone if the price exacted was the sacrifice of his soul? He wouldn't need to take his own life when it was over. Elyta would take care of that. His breath came shallowly. At least it was something he could *do* for Jane. He plunged ahead before he could change his mind.

"How about my submission?"

"You will submit in any case." Elyta shrugged.

"Willingly. Anything ye want. Far more satisfying than compulsion."

She lifted her brows. He'd caught her attention at least. The small smile curled only the corner of her mouth even as her eyes narrowed. "You love her, don't you?"

A weight sat on his shoulders. He shook his head. "It is no' for th' likes of me ta love a woman like her. She just deserves ta live. What happens ta me does no' matter."

"How delightful," Elyta purred. "An altruistic devil. You are a contradiction in terms—a puzzle, in fact. And how I like to unravel the knot of a mystery! Sometimes the only way to get the solution is to cut the knot, though. Would you like to be cut?"

He looked up at her. "If that's what ye want. Do we ha' an agreement?"

Elyta's smile was slow. She cocked her head. "We do. For her life only, not yours."

"I expected nothin' else. When do we start?"

Her smile widened. "Soon. First I must see that Clara has buried that man. You'd better get some rest. Your life is likely to be quite demanding in the very near future. I'll have Clara make up a restorative to strengthen you." At the door, she looked back. "Do I need to shackle you? If you try to escape, Jane will suffer."

"Ye dinnae need ta shackle me." His voice was steady as he said it.

She began to pull the door shut after her, a self-satisfied smile on her face, but she stopped. "One more thing. You don't tell her of our agreement. No matter what."

He took a breath. So if Jane found out what he was doing she'd think the worst of him. That wasn't new. And there was a horrible possibility that she would be right. "No' a word."

Flavio left with the carriage for Inverness. A leaden core weighed Jane down. Still, there was one task she had to face. Her father wanted burying. She headed up the hill. The creamery, a shell of blackened stone, still smoldered. Ash spiraled up on the draft where once live cinders had buzzed like fire ants. Inside the empty window frames, haloed with tongues of soot, coals glowed and tiny flames licked at the charcoal of the huge beams. Their crazy angles were like sticks from a game of spillikins abandoned by a thoughtless child. The air was acrid with smoke.

There were no dead bodies on the path. Where was her father? Trails of blood on the grass showed where they had been dragged up the hill. She followed the tracks up to the back of the creamery. Clara had her skirts tied up around her waist and was patting a mound of dirt with the back of her spade. There were four other fresh mounds. Her father's body lay in the wet grass. He looked asleep. Of all of them, he wasn't bloodied.

Clara straightened. "Go down to the house, Miss Blundell," she ordered quietly. "I'll soon be done here."

Jane stretched her hand out for the spade. "I want to do this."

"A fine lady like you shouldn't—"

"I *want* to do this." Jane's voice shook. She couldn't say more.

Clara nodded. She handed Jane the spade. "Do you want help?"

Clara's image rippled with the tears rising to Jane's eyes. She shook her head.

Clara nodded once. She was about to push past Jane when she stopped. "You'll want a marker, just until you can have a stone carved. Will a cross do?"

Jane nodded. Tears coursed down her cheeks.

Clara nodded in return and started down the hill.

Jane stabbed the spade into the earth and kicked it home with her sturdy half-boots. The wet earth was like butter to one of her strength. The smell of dirt and decayed vegetation and the fecund potential of growing things joined the smell of smoke and death. Ashes to ashes. Her life was full of ashes. She could taste them in her mouth. She threw the spadeful of dirt over her shoulder and stabbed the earth again. Why did he have to die? It wasn't fair! Just because he wanted to help her? Just because he was a brilliant man who *could* help her and others like her? Did nature abhor a man who stood above the rest? Well, then, damn nature all to hell. And if God was the progenitor of nature, then he might damn himself, as well!

She took her anger out on the soft, wet earth. The sides of the hole rose around her. The soil grew denser, but she didn't care. On one thrust of the spade the handle snapped off at the base. Shrieking, she thrust it into the floor of the grave as if to wound it. The Scots heavens opened and a leaden rain began to fall. She grasped the handle and let it hold her up until she couldn't stand at all and slid to her knees in the muddy hole. Heaving sobs, she dug at the mud with her hands, using them like claws to rip her father's grave into the earth. Droplets plinged against the water in the hole in a fierce chorus. No sobs of hers could compete with such an outpouring. She leaned against the muddy side of the grave as they washed her face.

Her sobs subsided with her fury. The rain was a flapping curtain of tears.

Oh, God, forgive me.

For long minutes she just knelt there in the rain, her body

heavy. But she couldn't just kneel here in an empty grave. It must be filled. She climbed out, her muddy dress clinging to her. She stood over her father's body. There would be no community of mourners, no sacred ritual, no coffin of carved oak to send him heavenward, no shroud, however little protection that would have afforded. He would go directly into the ground, to meld his flesh with the wet and rotting vegetation and the mud. Dust to dust, only wetter. He would become the peat that in centuries hence would feed the fire in the kitchen grate of a people who had long forgotten Muir Farm.

She picked him up, her arms under his shoulders and knees. How light he was for one of her strength. His head lolled against her shoulder. He seemed shrunken, as though the earth already had the part of him that pumped him up with life, and all that was left was this wasted husk. She splashed into the grave with him and laid him carefully down, arranged his limbs in a parody of dignity. The rain made rivulets down his cheeks, like tears. Her own tears were gone. She climbed out of the grave again, slipping, getting to her feet. Like a dream she took the metal spade in both hands and scraped mud back into the hole. The sound of the first splat into the grave was like a blow.

Doggedly, she worked. The rain settled into a sodden tattoo.

When it was done, she stood, swaying. She should say words. What words could she possibly say? Footsteps sounded behind her. She didn't turn. Clara, in a voluminous cloak, came to stand beside her. Jane turned her head, slowly. Clara held a makeshift cross; two sections of a fir branch, peeled of bark and lashed together with brightly colored braids of embroidery floss. They were absurdly cheerful. The ends were left long. The strands danced as the drops hit them.

"Here. Just until you have a stone made."

One end of the longer branch was sharpened. Jane took the cross and fingered the braid. "You couldn't find black?" *How ungrateful of me . . .*

"I had black. But black is for mourning," Clara said simply. She took the cross gently from Jane and went to the head of the grave. With a single powerful thrust, she plunged it into the earth. Jane stood like a statue, unable to move. That thrust had been so final.

Clara looked up at Jane, waiting for her to say something. But Jane had no words. She shook her head, her features threatening to collapse around her.

Clara nodded. She looked down at the grave and clasped her hands.

Jane closed her eyes, swaying.

"Return, on this happy day," Clara intoned, "to the one who made you, who knows you and yet loves you. The ones you left behind rejoice in your passing, and wait only to join you."

Jane opened her eyes. *Rejoice?* The rain subsided into a fine drizzle.

"You helped many. You left progeny," Clara continued. "Your mark on the wheel is distinct, and will last until you can return. Rest now. Suckle at the spirit of the world to refresh and enlarge your soul. You have earned it."

What a mélange of religions. She stared, wide-eyed, at Clara. Then she shook her head. *A little selfish, aren't you, Jane? Screaming and crying. Angry at God. Papa does deserve peace. What more fitting for a man so involved in the cycle of life than to return to God's earth?*

"Come," Clara said. "Let me make you some tea and heat you a bath."

The woman took Jane's arm and led her down toward the house. In the eastern sky, behind the house, a lighter band outlined the hills across the loch.

Atlas Mountains, March 1819
He knelt before Asharti, rock hard. Her gauzy dress was olive-green tonight. She wore copper armbands, loop earrings, a girdle tinkling with discs, and copper-colored sandals.

Now that he was vampire, she could devise more demand-
ing exhibitions of submission. She liked to see his blood flow
and since he healed so quickly she could make it flow as of-
ten as she wanted. She amused herself sometimes by sending
him into the sun naked until he blistered and oozed. But it
was only a matter of hours until he was whole again and
ready to serve her. And now there was nothing left of him. He
lived to please her and the thing in his blood made him hard
and needing. He was finally everything she wanted. He was
constantly inflamed, whether she abused him or not, and he
had begun to wonder if it was the abuse that inflamed him.

"So," she remarked, popping a date into her mouth.
"What next? The army moves at sunset. We have little time.
When we descend on Algiers, I will be too busy to enjoy you
for a while." She needed hardly any sleep. Her vitality never
seemed to wane. Some said she had taken strange blood of
some kind that gave her more strength even than others of
her kind.

"*I await yer command, mistress,*" he murmured.

"Well, you're certainly ready," She picked up a small
quirt. It was only perhaps eighteen inches, supple, with a
leather thong at the end. "But let us prepare your cock to
better please me." She nodded to him. He knew what to do.
He spread his knees, then leaned back and grabbed his an-
kles. His chest and belly, his loins and thighs were vulnerable to her. She leashed his bobbing cock with a looping
leather thong, so she could pull it down, away from his belly.

Standing, she popped another date into her mouth and
laid the little quirt across his inner thighs. He jumped. The
flesh there was almost the most tender. Almost. She struck his
belly, his chest. His Companion went about healing the welts
even as she laid them. As she worked, she jerked the leash
rhythmically. It was that which made him moan, finally. He
knew what would come. She took longer than usual getting
to his cock, but finally she knelt before him. She alternately
laid the quirt across his shaft and bent to lick the welt she'd

*made. Her saliva kept it from healing. The process was like
to kill him. Or no, to be fair, it only made him wish he were
dead. When she was done, she lay back on her divan and
beckoned. He knew what was required. He plunged his well-
ribbed cock into her moist folds until she writhed in pleasure. She could control his release. But these days it pleased
her to demand that he control it himself. To come inside her
without her permission meant a day in the sun . . . When she
had done shuddering, she lay back, looking dissatisfied.*

*He quickly knelt beside her, head bowed. The welts on his
cock slowly disappeared. "How can I please ye, mistress?"
Better to be punished for speaking than for failing to please.*

*Her brow furrowed. "I don't know," she said, pouting. "It
is all too easy with you now."*

*What? Did she want resistance? But when he resisted, she
punished him.*

*"Is sexual abasement all there is to require?" she mused.
She tapped a copper-painted nail against her ruby lips. He
saw it through his eyelashes, since he dared not look at her
directly. "But . . . I know!" She chuckled. How he dreaded
that laugh! She raised her head. "We stop at a village to re-
cruit our strength. A perfect test . . ."*

*Dread suffused him. A test? He knew she would ensure he
could not win.*

Callan woke from sleep with a start, Asharti's words still
echoing in his mind. He felt as though he had been drugged.
A figure was limned against the afternoon sun slanting
through the windows. Jane?

"You are awake." The figure twitched the draperies closed.

Elyta. Callan's intestines knotted. He knew what she was
here for. And his nightmare about the North African desert
two years ago was about to leak into the present.

She wore the deep purple wrapper. Her breasts moved
freely underneath the fabric. Clara came in with a load of
peat cubes dried at the hearth in the kitchen. She laid them

on the fire and withdrew. Callan sat up. He was stronger. Clara's vile potion had helped. There was no comparison, of course, to how he had felt when his Companion coursed through his veins. He was getting used to the dulled senses, the sharp sense of loss as his body yearned for the half of his being that had been stripped from his blood. Probably there would come a time when he wouldn't even miss the sense of being acutely alive. At least he was human. Poor Jane was not.

She would be soon, he told himself. And then he must trust Elyta to hold to her bargain. Not certain. But he had no alternatives. He could do this. He must do it. For Jane.

Elyta came to stand over him in the dimmed room. "Are you ready?"

"Aye. But there's one thing that's changed." Better to get it out in the open.

She raised her brows in threat.

"Nae, I'll submit ta ye," he hastened to assure her. "But I canno' guarantee th' stiff cock that comes with being vampire."

Elyta shrugged. "Well, as to that—I'll strike a bargain. I'll use compulsion only to keep you hard." She wagged a finger at him. "You must submit yourself, or your precious Jane dies the minute she has served her purpose."

"Agreed."

She sat beside him, sinuous, and ran her long-nailed hand through his hair. "And how are we feeling today?" She laid a finger lightly over the pulse in his carotid. "Much better. I knew Clara's potion would work wonders." She rubbed her breasts against his chest and kissed the hollow in his throat lightly. "We'll have to make sure you get one several times a day."

He shut his eyes, trying to breathe evenly, and lifted his chin to bare his throat.

"Excellent." She chortled. "I'll sip. But I won't feed from you. You wouldn't last. I'm going to savor you." She ran a hand over his chest and slid it down to his hip. "Kiss me."

Asharti had never allowed him to kiss her. She had considered it too intimate. He almost didn't know how to proceed. *Like you'd kiss any other woman,* he told himself. He lowered his lips to hers. *But not like you'd kiss Jane.* Elyta made a pout and he pressed his lips against hers. She slid her tongue inside his mouth, probing. From her it was a violation. His mind rebelled. *For Jane,* he thought fiercely. He ran his hands over Elyta's back, underneath her wrapper. He could do this. Soon she would compel an erection and it would get easier. She was a beautiful woman. Any man could do this, couldn't they? He tried to concentrate on her breasts brushing his nipples. Her hand had found his balls. She was squeezing. He opened his hips to give her better access. Now his cock was responding. Was that him, or was it her?

That way lay madness. Just respond. For Jane.

"Kiss me," she breathed into his mouth, "like you want to kiss that little slut."

Callan's chest tightened. He couldn't fail Jane. He thrust his tongue inside Elyta's mouth. It wasn't a passive act. Asharti would have punished him for that. But that's what Elyta wanted, wasn't it? She sucked on his tongue like a summer ice.

She pulled away. "Tell me how you'll demonstrate your submission."

Oh, God. "First I'll suck yer breasts," he whispered, bending his head. He pushed aside the neckline of her wrapper. His tongue flicked over her nipple. Her breath began to come faster.

"And later? Tell me what you'll do later."

"I'll lick ye between yer legs until ye come."

"Yes, but I won't be finished. I need release many times a day, and I've been deprived."

"You'll want . . . you'll want ta put yer teeth inta me, just ta taste th' blood even if ye dinnae feed." He pressed her buttocks to him so she could feel his erection against her mound. She slid along it and took his earlobe in her mouth. "I recommend th' inner thigh," he murmured.

"I'll take that under consideration. What else?"

"My cock. You'll want ta use my cock."

"Not yet. I'll want more submission first."

He kissed her throat, licking over the artery. His own breath was shallow and fast. He couldn't think. *Just use yer experience. Lord knows, submission is one thing ye're good at.* And Asharti had taught him much. He could do this. If only he didn't find out he liked it. "There are some whips in th' stable. I'll wager they'd leave good welts on my body."

"Ooh," she moaned, grinding against his erection, lifting her breast to be suckled. He did, swirling his tongue about her nipple assiduously. "The barn is a good idea. I don't want an audience. You'll moan, I know, as I lay the leather across your bare flesh. And then?"

He switched breasts. "I'll bathe ye."

"With your tongue." She sighed. "And then?"

What could she want? If she had coached Asharti, there was one thing she must like. Abasement. "I'll beg ye ta let me service ye again."

"I'd like to hear you beg . . ." she breathed as she rolled onto her back, spreading her legs. He lowered himself between them and flicked his tongue over the nub that thrust itself up between the folds of flesh. *I can do this.* He wouldn't think whether he was excited by her treatment. He pushed firmly on the door inside his mind as Elyta pressed his head into her sex.

"Flavio could be back with the glassware before morning," Jane said, "if he can raise a shopkeeper at night." She motioned Kilkenny to a chair at the kitchen table across from where she had her pen and ink and notebook laid out. His hair was damp from bathing. He wore one of the kilts and a crisp white shirt with a blue wool waistcoat. Clara had taken over laundry duties from Mrs. Dulnan, since Jane was sure they'd seen the last of any villagers. The vest made his eyes look almost blue. He moved stiffly to sit on the edge of the chair. She peered at him. He looked tired still, though he had slept away last night and the day, as well. She had thought he would recover quickly once the poison was out of his system.

"Do you . . . do you feel up to the interview?" she asked.

"I'll do," he said. But his tone was grim.

She herself had slept like the dead after Clara's warm bath and hot tea. And while there was a dull ache in her heart for her father's absence, she knew she must focus on the work at hand. Papa wouldn't have been so weak, and she couldn't be, either. The cure for vampirism existed. She had clues she could follow to find it. It must be found. She daren't let herself think about a life as a vampire, alone and ageless. Drinking blood. What would she become?

She had another problem. Her veins had begun to itch with need. Her Companion wanted blood. But there would be no more villagers sauntering up to donate blood. Could she hold it until she had reconstructed the cure? A day, two at most. Perhaps if her first trial hit the mark, she wouldn't need to find a way to fill her mother's china teacups with viscous, warm . . .

She pressed down the thought of blood, even as her Companion thrilled up in response.

Clara came up from the cellar with a tankard. "This will set you up, Mr. Kilkenny."

He took it from her and gulped from it. The sight of his strong throat undulating as he drank was . . . distracting.

What are you thinking? she admonished herself. *He's human now. He doesn't want you just because he's infected with the parasite anymore. You're the only one who's abnormal.* But not for long. She let resolution harden her. It would keep away the grief and isolation.

He put the sweating tankard down. It didn't smell like ale. "What is that?" Jane asked.

"Something to help him gain strength," Clara said. "Raw eggs, some herbs."

Kilkenny drained the remainder, without a word.

"Let us begin then," Jane said. "Close your eyes."

He looked up at her, suspicious.

"It will help you remember." A tenuous smile was the best she could do. "Trust me."

His expression softened. "Sorry. Trust is a little hard ta come by these days." His eyes gave that familiar gleam that was almost a smile before he closed his eyes.

"Excellent. Now think back to the time you took the potion. We were all up in the laboratory. And everything was bubbling away. You mended my pen. And then my father put that green mixture into the clear, thick liquid and it turned that strange purple-blue."

"Aye," he murmured. "And th' stuff smelled like . . . like damp leaves . . . in th' winter, after they'd been there for a while."

"Yes." She tried not to let excitement into her voice. He was good at this. She remembered the smell vividly now that he described it. "What of its taste?"

"I was feeling woozy from th' opium. But it seemed . . . thick. It slid down yer throat like . . . like aspic." She scribbled frantically. "It was bitter, too. I chewed some raw nettle leaves when I was a lad because some young ruffian said they made yer tongue go numb. They tasted a bit like th' potion."

"Anything else about the taste?"

"It seems strange, but it was kind o' chalky, too. All at th' same time. Bitter and chalky."

"Hmm. And when did you first feel the symptoms?"

"At once. My gut burned. I thought I'd bring it up and ruin th' whole. But it seemed ta get inta my veins and just . . . burn there."

"And what else?"

"I dinnae remember anythin' more, Miss Blundell."

It seemed odd that he called her that. Hadn't he . . . hadn't he called her Jane last night after her father died? For God's sake, she'd been intimate with him! But he still called her Miss Blundell. And she still called him Mr. Kilkenny. She shook herself. *Focus!* "Very well," she said, dipping her pen. "What can we conclude?" What could she conclude? Panic scuttled around inside her head and she slapped it away. "Well. The earthy smell. That's *Amanita*."

He lifted his brows.

"The mushrooms from the falls. But they wouldn't produce the viscous texture." She began writing. "One beaker was a virulent green." She tapped the pen against the page. "Could be anything herbal." She ran the feather of her quill along her jawline. "We gathered nightshade leaves. But I thought he'd given that over after your reaction. Valerian? But that's a soporific and he had the opium for that. Feverfew—is that so bitter? What else? What else?"

"What about tha hemlock we got from th' little loch up th' glen?"

"Yes! That's very bitter. I always wondered how Socrates got it down." She bent over her notebook. She could feel how his body occupied space, the scent of soap and wet hair. Wait . . . Did she smell . . . blood? She peered up at him. He glanced away. "Are . . . are you hurt?"

He shot her a startled glance. "Nae," he said quickly.

Hmm. She could swear . . . She examined him. Perhaps he had cut himself shaving? But no, she saw no cuts about his person. Well, it was none of her business anyway. The whole problem was that her Companion was hungry. Even now she could see his pulse throbbing in the hollow of his throat. Why did he have to wear his collar open today of all days? She cleared her throat. "Now, chalky . . . What plant provides a chalky taste?" She forcibly drew her thoughts away from blood and Kilkenny's body and racked her brain.

"Uh . . ." He chewed his lip. "Apples past their prime . . . nae, that's more mealy."

They sat in silence, frowning in concentration. At last Jane threw up her hands. "I can't think. Well, we'll leave that until later. There is always the problem of the clear liquid and the reaction between the two potions that generated such a change in color." She sighed.

"Th' clear liquid was th' thick one. Mayhap that was th' aspic. What *is* aspic?"

"You may never eat it again if I tell you," she warned, smiling.

"I dinnae frighten easily, lass," he said, "havin' been a vampire and all." The creases at the corners of his eyes and the gleam were the only things that betrayed a smile.

"Very well, then, brace yourself." She drew herself up. "One boils animal bones until they dissolve, leaving only a gelatinous substance."

He grimaced. "An' ye use that for jams, as well?"

"No, one uses pectin for that. It comes from apples and such."

"A relief, certain. Still, ye've ruined aspic for me forever." His eyes gleamed.

That was his smile. She made her mouth prim, but her smile would not be suppressed. It was so courageous of him to smile in spite of all that had happened to him.

"It's good ta see ye smile," he said, and his eyes definitely softened.

How could I smile? It was a complete betrayal of her father! Tears clogged her throat.

"I'm sorry," he said, covering her hand with his. "I should no' ha' said anythin'."

"It's all right. I must grow accustomed to missing him sooner or later." She blinked and tried to focus on the spidery crawl of ink across the page of the notebook. But all she could think about was Kilkenny's hand covering hers, how warm it was, how . . . comforting. Comforting, but still exciting. How could she feel like this even as she fought back tears? But she did. She wondered how long he would keep his hand there. She could feel him wondering why he had touched her, and how he could take it away. There was no way around the awkwardness, and he didn't seem to be doing anything except sitting there, staring at their hands just as she was. So she sat back and slid her hand from under his. She felt the loss of its comfort immediately.

He's a traitor. A killer. She shouldn't feel so comfortable around him. Or so uncomfortable for the wrong reasons. But she did.

A thought jumped into her mind unbidden, as though it had been pushed down for too long. She sat forward again and frowned. "But there is a problem with our theory. Gelatin isn't clear. It's brownish to varying degrees depending upon the kind of bones one uses." She tapped her pen on her notebook, leaving a distinct blot. "However, that would explain some of the vile smells up in the laboratory when Papa began his work here. And there is another issue. What point gelatin? It isn't really an active ingredient like nightshade or hemlock."

"Maybe as a stabilizer?" he asked. "It keeps whatever ye put in aspic from spoilin'."

"You're right." She started scribbling. "By suspending the active ingredients of either nightshade or hemlock it would reduce their volatility for a more predictable result." Jane heard the rattle of cartwheels. "Flavio!" She darted to the kitchen door, opened it and waited.

Kilkenny came to stand behind her. "Ye hear th' cart?"

She nodded, looking up at him. Was he . . . wistful? At last the cart heaved into view, pulled by two sturdy cart horses with their tails bobbed, the feathers on their fetlocks caked with mud. Faust pranced at the end of a lead rope tied to the cart. He neighed to Kilkenny.

"Did you get everything?" Jane called, stepping out onto the flagstone steps.

Kilkenny went to the horses' heads and held their reins as Flavio swung down.

"I think so, Miss Blundell. I bought the town out. When there weren't enough proper beakers at the three chemists, I visited the china shop and bought part of a table service, too. Mr. Kilkenny, can you stable these animals?" Flavio began handing Jane wooden crates.

"Aye." Kilkenny unbuckled their traces. "Stable is gettin' a mite crowded."

"It will take us hours to reassemble a laboratory." Excitement beat in Jane's throat. Hope warred with fear. Could she replicate the formula? There was only one way to find out.

CHAPTER
Eighteen

Callan led the second phlegmatic cart horse into a stall and forked some hay into his manger. The barn was lit by one lantern hung on a hook by the door and another by the tack room. They cast a soft glow over the old wood of the stalls. Faust and the other cart horse had joined Missy, the cow, and the two carriage horses in the loose boxes. The sound of grinding teeth could be heard up and down the barn aisle. There was an air of contentment about the animals Callan didn't share. Indeed, his stomach churned.

Could Jane reconstruct the formula? She seemed hopeful, but he was worried. The clues they had seemed so tenuous. Elyta wouldn't be forgiving if Jane failed repeatedly. His submission might prolong Elyta's patience, but not forever. Elyta wouldn't dare kill Jane if there was even a remote possibility that Jane could produce the formula. But what if she punished Jane to motivate her? He couldn't protect Jane, not really. Even when he had been vampire, he was no match for Elyta, and now . . .

Now he couldn't hear the things Jane heard, and couldn't see in the dark as she could. He wasn't strong like she was. She had carried those immense wooden crates as if they were sewing baskets. And he couldn't translocate, or compel, or . . . A chasm had opened between them.

Jane was hungry. He knew the signs well enough; a certain restlessness, the way she stared at his throat. She'd smelled his blood. He'd have to cut his forearm somewhere and roll up the sleeves of his shirt, so he could account for the scent. He didn't want her to know about the jagged wound on his chest, carefully concealed under a bandage. He didn't want her to imagine Elyta licking at it.

He felt a thrill of excitement in the air. He did not turn. He took a breath and gathered himself. "Mistress."

She chuckled. "I am eager for your services again tonight, Kilkenny."

He turned, and knelt, knees wide. The kilt left him feeling vulnerable to her.

"Too many clothes," she admonished.

He worked at stripping himself. The feeling of despair in his gut was not so bad tonight. He knew what she would do. He could bear it. He'd borne it last night. And he hadn't enjoyed his torment, thank God. Had he? He didn't know anymore. He felt his cock rise. It would be hard until morning now or until she had done with him.

"Up to the loft," she said. As he climbed the ladder into the dimness above, he saw her browsing among the leather traces and bridles hung on pegs at the end of the barn. She fingered a thick strap made to cross the draft horses' chests, and took up the long dressage whip Jane used to tap her mare. She flexed the supple, four-foot length. It had a small knotted leather strip at the end. She'd used that one last night. He pulled himself up over the edge of the loft into the piles of straw that smelled of summer sunshine. It scratched at his welts. Darkness whirled around her and she appeared beside him.

She tossed her implements into the hay, bent, and ripped the bandage tied diagonally across his chest. "You should know I want you entirely naked."

"Forgive me, mistress," he murmured. "I beg you ta punish me for my lapse."

"I will. First, I want to examine you. On your hands and knees."

He complied, his head hanging. He spread his knees. She ran her hands over his back. Her nails raked his welts lightly. Then with both palms she pushed apart his buttocks.

"Such pale flesh shows the bruising nicely," she remarked. "Asharti·was right about men from the north countries."

She squeezed his balls from behind and thumbed his anus. As she pulled on his sac, his hips changed angle. It was enough to madden him, but not enough to quench the need she raised in him. This need wasn't for abasement. He wasn't excited by pain and subjugation. He thought of making love to Jane in the castle. He hadn't wanted Jane to mistreat him. He'd wanted only to share the joy of passion with her. It hadn't been like this. So the erection that hung so stiffly into the straw was not of his doing but Elyta's. He was almost certain. It wasn't because of the submission. It wasn't.

She selected the dressage whip and laid it sharply over his buttocks. He flinched and gasped. That would leave blood. Her vibrations ramped up. It had left blood, all right. That was her Companion cycling up at the smell of it.

"Excellent," she breathed.

She rose and braced herself, feet apart, against the wall of the loft, still holding the whip. She parted her wrapper to reveal the dark mound of hair with which he was only too familiar. He crawled forward. She pulled her flesh apart with two fingers and he lifted his head to her slick folds. "Lick me," she hissed, and punctuated the command with the snap of the whip across his lower back. He grunted, and obeyed. "More assiduously." Again the whip snapped. He sucked on her nub, alternately thrusting his tongue deep inside her, anything to keep her from using the whip. But she used it anyway. He counted to distract himself. Ten stripes before her moans of pleasure cycled up into orgasm. He sucked her harder, trying to prolong it. She couldn't whip him when she was coming. The waves washed over her. He paused, and then began again. Again she yipped, and slid down the wall until she was on her back in the hay, moaning and writhing under his mouth as she pressed his head to her crotch. "Enough," she finally gasped.

He hung over her, braced on his elbows, his eyes squeezed shut against the humiliation and the need that still coursed through his loins.

"Oh, that was good," she murmured. She seemed to drowse.

He caught his breath and tried to press down thought. He'd done it. He'd submitted twice. And in some strange way it wasn't like what he had done with Asharti. Elyta hadn't compelled him. It had been his choice. The result was the same; humiliation, degradation—but different. It was his choice. For Jane. Now if only he was absolutely certain he didn't enjoy it.

Soon enough Elyta stirred, and rose, fingering the new welts she had made. "These will mark your shirt with blood tomorrow. Wear a waistcoat to conceal it."

"Yes, mistress."

"I would use your cock." She gestured languidly to a jar of oil Callan had used to keep his tack supple. She'd brought it up with her leather and whips. "Oil yourself."

He couldn't remember Asharti ever asking him to rub his own cock. In fact, he was expressly forbidden to touch himself. He swallowed and reached over to pour some oil into his palms. This was going to be exquisite torture. He spread his knees wider and cupped his balls with one hand, smoothing the oil over them. They were tight and high with need. With his other hand he grasped his cock and slid the oil over the shaft.

"Be sure to work it into the tip well," she ordered. He thumbed the head, shuddering.

Suddenly she rose. She picked up the strap as he pulled at his cock, head bent in shame. She stood behind and to one side where she could both wield the strap and watch his efforts. "Spread your knees wider. You're going to come as

I beat you," she said as the first stroke made the flesh across his loins jump. What? The heavy strap slapped across his buttocks, already bruised. He felt the control that both Elyta and Asharti always used to stop his ejaculations drain away. The strap struck his back and he groaned.

"Work yourself harder," she commanded. The strap came down over his buttocks and snapped at the back of his balls. He bent over in pain. She walked over and pulled him upright by his hair. "No one told you to stop working yourself. Cover your stones with your left hand." He cupped his hand around his balls to protect them from the strap and pulled at his cock. It was still stiff and thick, but that wasn't natural. She was keeping him hard. No one could keep an erection through a beating. Unless they enjoyed it.

"Don't forget the tip. More oil." She kept up both the instructions and the strap. He hunched his back and clenched his jaw, jerking at his cock and rubbing the sensitive head. He was sweating with effort. His cock burned, the need having crossed over into pain. Again and again the strap slapped across his body, and still he tugged at his cock. The loft seemed to swirl. The grunting he heard was his own. She increased the speed of her blows, urging him to be rougher with himself. And then the fire in his balls shot out through his cock in a searing stream of semen. The blows stopped as he spurted into the hay, teeth clenched in a grimace, on and on with pent-up fluid.

When it was done, he bent over, chest heaving. He wanted to sob. Maybe he was sobbing, he wasn't sure. The sounds he was making were dry and exhausted. He saw her lavender slippers come to stand at his head. The hem of her silken wrapper feathered his brow.

"I am pleased with you, slave. That will be the only way you are allowed to spill your seed in the future." To his horror he felt himself rising again. She rolled him over. He lay there, naked and erect in the straw. She took several small gold rings, in various sizes, all thin and delicate, from a pocket in the skirt of her wrapper. They glinted ominously in the dim light from the lamps below them. "Do you know what these are?"

He shook his head, afraid to know.

"They are symbols of your submission," she said, her voice deceptively sweet. She took a smaller ring and pulled it apart. A sharp point detached itself from a hole in the center of the other end. He blinked, frowning. She sidled up to him and put the other rings back in her pocket. "Lie still," she commanded, "or I'll tear you by mistake." She held the ring open with one hand and pinched his left nipple with the other. She was going to pierce him? His impulse was to struggle away. But he resisted the urge. He had committed to submission, for Jane's sake.

"I like to put them through the aureole," she remarked. The sharp end pricked his flesh. "The nipple itself is too small on most men." A stab of pain as she pushed it through made him tighten. She snapped the ring home and slid it round through the flesh. Then with a growl, she bent and sucked to get at the drops of blood. The bar of the metal through his flesh pulled against her lips. She sat back, licking her lips and smiling. "Very attractive," she said. Then she turned her attention to the other nipple.

When she was finished and had sucked the blood away, she pulled out a larger ring not quite so delicately made. "Spread your thighs," she ordered. "Now be very still."

He swallowed. His mouth was dry.

She pinched a bit of the skin on his sac to one side, pierced it and slid the ring through. It hurt enough, but worse, it made him want to shiver, and he dared not. She didn't pierce his stones, but slid the metal along under the skin and pushed the sharp end out the other side. When it was through, he let go his breath. Again she sat back, admiring. "Excellent. And it can be used to fasten you to a post, if your hands are tied behind your back, or a leash can be clipped to it."

The images she painted robbed him even of the power to blink.

She tugged gently on the ring. "There will be some swelling for a while, but I'll slide them through the flesh several times a day, and soon there'll be no pain at all."

"What do ye care if there's pain?" he asked, his voice a hoarse croak.

She laughed. "You're right. I don't." She fingered the bar under his nipple as she leaned forward and kissed him roughly.

He couldn't bear this! Elyta was worse even than Asharti. And he was worse, too. He had held an erection through Asharti's mistreatment, but he had never come to orgasm. Had Elyta forced him? He clung to that hope, because if she hadn't then he had become all Asharti wanted him to be and more, long after she was dead and gone.

Her breasts moved the rings that pierced his nipples as she thrust her tongue into his mouth. He didn't think he could endure more, either the humiliations themselves or his reaction to them. But he had to, for Jane's sake. He imagined Elyta chaining him, naked and erect, to the hitching post outside the barn by the ring in his balls for all to see his submission. She could make him masturbate in front of everyone, and he wouldn't be able to tell Jane that he wasn't so twisted as to want this, or so deviant that he could come to orgasm while Elyta beat him.

He wasn't, was he?

Jane stood back, hands on hips, as Flavio finished bolting the metal frame together. Packing crates were everywhere, their stuffing coming out like broken dolls. Glassware covered every surface in the kitchen. There were two new caldrons hanging from hooks in the grate of the great fireplace. Her father's laboratory was rising from the ashes here in the kitchen.

She carted crates out the back door. The night air was clearly redolent of spring. It was what, mid-May? Almost. It would be dawn soon. Where was Kilkenny? She glanced up to the barn and saw that the lanterns still gleamed feebly. Had he been up there all this time?

She frowned. She'd just go see that he was well. She listened for movement as she got closer. Was that the animals rustling in the straw of their stalls? She walked through the great doors. One lamp had failed, making the barn dim. Faust was indeed restless in his stall but . . . on the beaten earth floor of the barn aisle was a heap of clothing; a kilt, a shirt, stockings . . .

The noises were coming from the loft. And she smelled cinnamon.

Damn her! Hadn't she warned Elyta clearly enough? She didn't take time to climb the ladder. She pulled the darkness around her, waited the one long moment for it to coalesce, and then popped into the loft above her head.

Kilkenny hung above a naked Elyta, who sprawled on a wrapper spread over the hay. He was on one elbow, plunging his cock inside her, his right hand holding a breast while he sucked it. Elyta was arched in ecstasy. Jane couldn't make sense of a glint of gold in the darkness. What she could see was that his back and buttocks were both bruised and crisscrossed with welts.

"Stop it!" she shouted.

Kilkenny raised his head. This time there was no look of horror, only resignation.

Elyta laughed. "You do intrude where you're not wanted, don't you, Jane?"

"I'll not have you compelling him, Elyta. You want the cure, don't you?"

"I'm not compelling him. Ask him." She turned to Kilkenny. "You may withdraw."

Kilkenny hung his head and rolled off Elyta. To her shock, Jane saw that there were small gold rings right through his nipples, and . . . and a larger one through his scrotum. A tear across his breast bled. Elyta's lips were red with his blood. Jane felt sick. This had to be compulsion.

"Very well," she said, trying to control her anger. "You can answer truly."

"Nae." His eyes were flat, his expression dead.

"What was that?" Elyta asked sharply. "Am I compelling you to have sex with me?"

"Nae," he answered more clearly. "Ye keep my erection up so I can last, but that's all."

"You can't make me believe she lashed you, or . . . or put in those . . . rings with your permission," Jane sputtered.

Elyta smiled, wrapping her robe around her. "He suggested the whips himself."

Jane drew her brows together and looked at Kilkenny in disbelief.

"I let her do it." He looked down and away as he said it.

"You know . . . they come to like submission, and he's been trained by the best—an acolyte of mine, in fact." Kilkenny flushed scarlet. "He comes to orgasm under the lash."

Could that be true? Did he . . . did he want to be abused? She'd heard women in the brothels talk about clients who liked to be beaten during sex, but she'd thought . . . she'd thought those were weaselly old men, not young, handsome specimens like Kilkenny. "He doesn't look very happy about it," she said. But her voice was uncertain even in her own ears.

"What he's not happy about is you seeing it. That is quite a different thing."

Jane couldn't believe what she was hearing, and yet . . .

"Go, Jane," he said unevenly, his expression fierce. "Just go."

She didn't trust herself to draw the power, but scrambled down the ladder.

"Well," she heard Elyta say as she ran to the barn doors. "You are not quite done, slave."

Jane burst into the kitchen. Flavio was moving about in his room upstairs. Clara was trying to prepare food in between all the glinting glassware.

If Kilkenny wants to be abused, I'm the last woman in the

world to deny him. She paced the kitchen. When she looked up Clara was gazing at her steadfastly. The woman said nothing. Jane ran a hand over her hair. She must look a sight, disheveled, pacing about, distraught.

"Sit down," Clara said. "I'll get you some tea."

Clara, ever practical. She took a handful of tea leaves and poured hot water from a caldron into a tea pot, over the leaves. Jane sat at the table now arched over with tubes and flasks and metal struts. They'd *have* to eat in the dining room now. Jane found herself thinking that she would miss the intimacy of dinners in the kitchen with Kilkenny. Why? There could be no more intimacy with Kilkenny if she knew he was sitting across from her yearning to have Elyta whip him. Just like with that woman who had made him vampire and sucked at his groin. He liked that treatment. He must. How boring her simple idea of lovemaking must have been to him!

It just didn't *feel* right. Or true. Something was wrong.

If Kilkenny wanted to be abused, why had Elyta had to use compulsion on him before? The first time she'd interrupted them, when he was still a vampire, there had been no mistaking the fact that Elyta had to use her power to compel him. She'd had red eyes.

Clara brought a cup, and the kettle to the table. Her movements were deliberate. Jane stared as the tea swirled in the cup. Clara got a cup of her own and sat down at the other side of the corner. Their knees practically touched.

"Now, what is eating at you?" Clara asked calmly.

Jane thought about the last time she'd talked with Clara, or rather sobbed and shrieked at her father's grave. Clara must think her a near lunatic. She got a grip on herself and tried to answer calmly. "Kilkenny. He says Elyta isn't using compulsion on him. But whips and . . . and little rings pierced through his flesh and sex . . . She must be." She clutched her cup. "But she didn't have red eyes. Still, that kind of thing isn't *normal* . . . and I know there are different kinds of normal. But could he really . . . ?" She had lost all sense of calm.

"What kind of compulsion did he mean?"

"What?"

"Well, he said she wasn't using compulsion. Was it just the vampire compulsion he meant, or all compulsion?"

Jane's mind sputtered, and then went to work at the double. Wise Clara. There were other kinds of compulsion, weren't there, besides the kind that needed red eyes. But what did Elyta have that could compel Kilkenny? Jane raised her eyes from her cup to Clara, plain Clara, practical Clara. "Why do you stay with her?" she asked suddenly.

"Who says I stay with her?" Clara stirred her cup and sipped.

"Well . . . well, you're here, aren't you?"

Clara lowered her eyes. "I stay with Flavio, not Elyta."

Jane felt her eyes widen. Clara? Practical Clara loved Flavio? And he must not know . . .

"At home, in Mirso Monastery, there is not so much . . . freedom. I came . . . I came out that I might know of the world outside again. To see if it had changed since I had been in Mirso."

"How long were you at Mirso?" Jane held her breath.

"Four hundred years?" Clara considered. "Four hundred and thirty."

"Oh." And she came outside to see if love existed and to follow her lover.

"I felt compelled to leave Mirso. There was nothing for me there. Elyta was going on a mission with Flavio. Therefore, I chose to serve Elyta. Compulsion works in many ways."

Jane stood. She couldn't help herself. "But. what could compel Mr. Kilkenny to submit to her . . . her torture? Especially as I think he has been subjected to that kind of treatment before. He has been . . . damaged by it, I think." Could he have been damaged enough to want it? She turned on Clara. "Do you know about Mr. Kilkenny's past?"

"I know what is said."

"Tell me." Good or bad, she had to know.

"He was made by Asharti, an acolyte of Elyta's."

"Who treated him the same." She'd been right!

"Most likely. She made many vampires, some for an army to overthrow the Elders and rule the world of humans, some for more personal use. But she was stopped. And then the ones she made were hunted down and killed."

"Except for Mr. Kilkenny . . ." But the Elders still wanted him dead. Elyta said so.

"Stephan Sincai, Flavio's ward, was sent to hunt him down. Flavio says Stephan spared Kilkenny. Flavio thinks Stephan is a good man. Perhaps Stephan did not dispatch Kilkenny because he too is a good man."

"But then why would he serve Elyta in this twisted way?" Jane cried.

"I can think of several reasons," Clara said, in her calm way. "Sometimes we bargain with the devil as the lesser of two evils."

"You mean he thinks she will kill him if he doesn't submit to her."

Clara threw up her hands. "Does he strike you as a man afraid of death?"

No. Kilkenny wasn't afraid of death. Somehow she felt like Clara was backing her into a corner. Very well. He wasn't afraid of his own death. He might be afraid for someone else. Who else was there? He hardly knew Flavio or Clara. Her father . . . She swallowed. Her father was past all pull on Mr. Kilkenny. Who, then?

Oh.

But he'd never . . .

She was in no danger anyway. Not as long as Elyta needed her for the formula . . .

Oh.

Once she found it, Elyta would kill her to secure the formula for herself and make sure no one else could get it.

She'd been naïve to think that Elyta would let her save made vampires when the Elders wanted them all dead.

"Ask him why," Clara said simply.

"I can't ask him that. Any more than you can tell Flavio you love him."

Clara looked startled at that. "I'm not beautiful like you, Miss Blundell."

"Nonsense. I'm not beautiful. I can't hold a candle to Elyta Zaroff. Love does not depend on looks. How do you know how he feels until you tell him how you feel about him?"

"You counsel me to reveal myself, and you won't do the same?" Clara challenged.

"It's *not* the same."

"Isn't it? Can you say to me that you don't love him?"

Jane's world shifted. The kitchen still glowed with lamplight, Clara hadn't changed a jot. And yet everything had changed. She *did* love Kilkenny. She had to be honest with herself and just admit it. Her feeling for him wasn't only the vampire need for sex. She cared what happened to him, wanted to be with him, mourned that they were parted by two different natures. And one big reason she wanted to be human again was so *that* barrier at least wouldn't stand between them. The dichotomy of what she believed about him and what was said about him, including what he said himself, was illusory. He might be a traitor. He might have killed in his time. But if he had, there were reasons for it. She felt his center was good and true. She knew he was worth loving, because . . . because she loved him, and she believed in herself enough to think she couldn't love a man who didn't have that strong center of honor, one capable of great love in return. She did know that about Kilkenny. He had revealed his nature in how he treated Mrs. Dulnan, or how he tried to protect her from the distasteful details of her condition, or in the courage it took to try to find a good path forward when he had been so damaged.

But that didn't mean he loved her. So she didn't answer

Clara's question. She didn't say she loved him. "I just can't assume . . ."

"So it is the same." Clara had her backed well and truly in the corner now.

Clara was right. Neither woman had the courage to find out that their love was not requited. "Well, I can't, Clara, that's all. But I can refuse to think the worst of him." Jane started to get angry again. Elyta *was* compelling him, through a threat to her. In some ways Elyta had made her a party to the sick play she'd seen in the barn.

And . . . and *bloody hell* if she was going to take that sitting down!

"They are coming," Clara said.

CHAPTER
Nineteen

Jane whirled as Elyta pushed through the door, resolution rising in her breast. Her heart was pounding. Could she do this?

"A forest of glass has grown in our absence, Kilkenny," she exclaimed, smirking at Jane. Kilkenny hung back, his eyes on the floor. His shirt was bloodied in several places. Her Companion shivered inside her veins in reaction to the scent of blood. He held his plaid loosely about his loins and he was carrying his boots as though Elyta had not given him time to dress. Jane realized he had been bloody when they sat in the kitchen so many hours ago, waiting for Flavio and planning formulas. He must have been bandaged or his clothes concealed it. Now Elyta didn't care who knew what she did to him.

"Clara," Elyta barked. "Mix Kilkenny a draft of that tonic. He's going to need his strength. Is supper ready? Or should we call this breakfast? I never know."

Flavio appeared in the doorway. He froze when he saw Kilkenny. "Up to your old tricks, Elyta?" he said through gritted teeth.

"And what have you to say to that?" Elyta sneered. "I lead this expedition. And I require that my needs be met, so I may be strong and focused."

Jane saw in Flavio's eyes that he wouldn't stand up to Elyta.

Well, there were kinds of compulsion available even to those who weren't as strong as Elyta was. Jane went calmly to the sideboard and took her notebook from the drawer.

"Have you made progress today?" Elyta asked. "Clara, get some wine from the cellar."

"Oh, yes," Jane murmured, stalking to the great hearth as Clara headed to the basement stairs. "I've come a great way even in the last few minutes." She stirred up the fire with a poker until the flames blazed bright from the peat cubes and opened her notebook.

"Read to me of your conclusions," Elyta commanded, taking Jane's chair.

Jane smiled. "No, I think not." She took a breath. Then, abruptly, she tore out a fat bunch of pages from the middle of the book and tossed them on the fire. They caught in an instant. She cast the rest of the book on the flames. The pages curled and blackened.

Elyta jumped to her feet. "What have you done? You stupid cow!" Elyta raced to the fire and grabbed at the pages, but they crumbled in her hands. Big flakes of ash floated up through the flue. She snatched back her fingers, cradling them to her breast. They were red and blistered, but even as Jane watched they healed. "Were those your only notes?" Elyta asked, her voice as hard and cold as the stones at the bottom of Loch Ness.

"Yes," Jane said. Her heart felt light for the first time in some time. Kilkenny stared at her in consternation. "I think I have learned a lesson from you on compulsion, Elyta." She almost laughed. "Let's see if I have got it right." She glanced to the hearth. Even the leather cover of the book was only charred shreds now. "You want the formula. There is now no written record that can help you to it. Though my own notes were tenuous at best," she amended in the spirit of disclosure. "So all that is left to you is what is in my head."

"Not much has changed." Elyta said with a sneer.

Jane nodded slowly. "Except me. And now I say that you will not use Mr. Kilkenny so, or I will not help you to your formula."

Elyta shrugged her shoulders. "I will compel . . ."

"You can't compel creativity." Dear Lord, she hoped that was right. The compulsion she had witnessed produced physical actions. Could vampires compel a state of mind? Right or wrong, she had to bluff it through. "It's going to take lots of imagination, all my knowledge and Mr. Kilkenny's too as well my experience helping my father, to rediscover the cure. So, Elyta, how badly do you want it? Enough to forgo your 'needs' until it is found?"

"Jane," Kilkenny said quietly. "Dinnae do this. It's after ye ha' found th' cure ye need protection. Then ye'll ha' nothin' ta use against her."

Jane felt the breath sigh out of her body. He'd as much as told her she'd guessed right (with Clara's help, of course) about his motivation for consorting with Elyta. She smiled at him. "Let's cross that bridge anon. I can't let you—"

"It was nothin'. It meant nothin' in th' scheme of things."

"It meant something to me." She turned to Elyta. "Do we have a bargain?"

Elyta's eyes were black diamonds of hate. "You *dare* . . ."

"Yes. What do you say?" Elyta's reaction told her all. She could not compel creativity.

"If you think you can stop me from doing what I want with him—"

"Mr. Kilkenny will not leave my side. He'll sleep in my room and work with me and bathe in my presence. If you so much as speak to him, I'll stop work on your cure. Is that clear?"

Elyta bit back whatever words she would have said, and flounced from the room. They heard her stalking up the stairs.

"I'll take her supper," Clara said calmly. Jane saw her glance at Flavio.

"Let me," he said. "She's in a lather. And I have a few words for her myself."

Kilkenny and Jane watched Clara dish up food and hand a plate to Flavio. "I'll just set us places in the dining room," she murmured and withdrew.

Jane knew she couldn't avoid blushing if she looked at Kilkenny. So she looked into the fire instead. All that about bathing in her presence—it was another bluff; she'd probably go mad if he did. And it smacked of Elyta's air of ownership.

"Ye did no' ha' ta do that."

"Oh, yes I did." She gathered herself. "One has to make a stand."

He looked much struck. Then he raised his brows. "Ye did no' believe me when I said she was no' compellin' me."

"No." She chanced a glance at him. He still puzzled her. "You want everyone to think you're such a bad man."

"Ye've no idea."

"Case in point."

"Jane, ye dinnae know how bad th' world can be."

She liked it when he called her Jane. "You're right. I'm beginning to find out, though. Elyta is a very bad woman."

"I'm bad."

"You'll have to tell me more about that sometime. Right now I think you are generous and self-sacrificing, and courageous in the face of evil."

"Jane, ye dinnae know me."

There was such an air of resignation about him. "Mr. Kilkenny, do you want help getting those rings out, or not?"

"What?"

"Well, I assume you want them removed."

He straightened and held his marvelous lips together tightly. "Aye."

That was better. She hated seeing him despise himself so. "Do you want help?"

"Nae. I'll do it."

"Good. No time like the present." She pointed to the room that held the bath and the mirror. "I'll make up some salve using all this shiny equipment Flavio brought us."

He nodded once, his lips still a hard line, and moved stiffly toward the small chamber. At the door he turned and glanced back to her. "D'ye want me ta leave th' door open?"

She shook her head, embarrassed. "I think she's busy for a while." The sound of arguments upstairs must be obvious even to him.

His eyes softened. "Thankee."

Jane felt herself flushing. "Anyone would have done it."

"Nae," he murmured. "Anyone would no'. Ye're th' courageous one." He slipped through the door and closed it softly behind him.

Jane let out a breath she hadn't known she'd been holding. Clara appeared in the doorway. "Thank you, Clara," Jane said. "You were right."

Clara just smiled. They both heard a sharp intake of breath from the small room to the side of the hearth. Clara raised her brows in inquiry.

"She pierced his flesh with some rings," Jane said curtly. "He's taking them out."

Clara nodded. "He'll want a bath. And soap will keep his welts from festering. I'll put water on to boil." She poured a bucket of water into a caldron and headed for the well.

Jane realized she was shaking. Was it a reaction from facing down Elyta? Or was it the hunger of her Companion making her feel so tenuous? *Focus, Jane!* Very well, she'd not think of Kilkenny in the little room with the bath, naked, removing the rings from his nipples and his sac. She shivered. Not doing too well at focusing, at least on anything other than Kilkenny. She felt an itch course along her veins. She paced the room. She wouldn't be hungry now. She wouldn't!

All right. Kilkenny. If she was going to focus on Kilkenny, she should make something useful of it. She peered at the herbs above her. Ahh, woundwort. *Prunella*

Vulgaris. She'd make a salve. If she started now, it would be ready for him by nightfall.

Dinner was an odd affair. Elyta was fuming in her room. Kilkenny drank the potion Clara mixed him, designed to bolster his strength, though now it would not serve Elyta's purpose. He sat stiffly, because of the welts on his buttocks no doubt. Jane forcibly occupied her mind in memorizing possible combinations of ingredients for the formula tomorrow. She'd make up a batch and see how it looked. Still, she could hear the beat of Kilkenny's heart and smell the blood on him. And she realized she had no choice but to make good on her promise to keep him by her side if she was going to be sure Elyta did not slide back to her old ways, probably with Kilkenny's misplaced complicity. How could she bear having him near? Even now she felt inflamed, not only in her loins but in her veins and arteries.

Clara sewed up his chest after his bath, while Jane stole surreptitious looks at his strong torso as she worked on her salve. Jane could have done a better job, but Clara's was good enough and Jane didn't dare touch that chest. She might just burst into flames in some unlikely spontaneous combustion. Kilkenny was silent. Had her actions alienated him further somehow? Or perhaps he was just ashamed. Jane wanted to tell him he mustn't dwell on what had happened, but what right had she to advise him?

Flavio and Clara began to yawn. Jane watched Clara staring at Flavio out from under her short eyelashes. Finally Clara stood. "Flavio, let's leave these two." He was about to protest when she put her finger against his lips. This startled him so he just stopped in mid-breath. "Come upstairs," she commanded, drawing him from his chair. Flavio had an air of surprise and . . . speculation about him.

Jane felt the vibrations in the air ramp up. Two vampires were reacting to touching each other. She smiled encouragement at Clara. After all this time during the long journey together, she was finally making a push to achieve her goal. Clara looked embarrassed. The poor girl only lacked self-confidence. She was so self-effacing she made herself plainer than she was. Jane felt depressed by Clara's act of courage. Jane had faced Elyta, but she hadn't faced Kilkenny yet.

Flavio turned Clara to the door by her elbow. "You're right, Clara. It's time to retire."

Jane tucked an escaping tendril of hair behind her ear and began to gather up the dishes. She was tired, too. The sun was shining somewhere outside the darkened windows, and the days were getting longer. The last nights had been so wearing, she felt as though her bones had turned to lead in some kind of reverse alchemy. She stacked the plates. Kilkenny gathered up the silver and the trays that had held the chicken and the roasted potatoes. They carried them back into the kitchen and washed up in silence. Jane was nervous and dropped one of her mother's cups. It shattered. She looked at it with horror and began to cry.

"How clumsy! I have no idea what's wrong with me," she said, wiping her cheeks.

"Dinnae ye?" Kilkenny asked, his deep voice soft.

She jerked her stare away from the shattered china. How dare he challenge her? "You mean the fact that my father was murdered two nights ago and I have an evil woman waiting to kill both of us if I do happen to find the cure for the horrible disease that makes me a monster?" She didn't mention that she might not find the cure and would be separated from him forever by her condition, or that both humans and her fellow monsters wanted to kill her because she was a made vampire. Why heap on consequences?

"Ye need blood. I know th' signs." He held her with his gray-green gaze.

"Well, I don't think the villagers are going to line up to donate even if they don't quite remember why they think Muir Farm is evil. You noticed that Mrs. Dulnan didn't come today?"

"Ye dinnae need donations, Jane."

"I am not going to rip throats like Elyta. I'll . . . I'll find the cure before I need it too badly." She didn't believe that. He was standing too close. She could smell the blood on him.

He raised his brows skeptically.

"And . . . and now I'm going to bed." Here it was. "And you are coming with me."

"That is no' necessary . . ."

"If you think I'm going to let her talk you into some twisted act of submission, or worse yet, compel you, because she has some need to be serviced every hour on the hour, all while I'm snoring away, you have another think coming, Mr. Kilkenny," she snapped.

His face softened again. She liked when it did that. And unaccountably, creases appeared around his eyes. "D'ye snore, then?"

"Of course I don't snore. That was a figure of speech."

"I'll wager ye do, and I'll get nae sleep at all."

It was she who was likely to get no sleep. Especially if he insisted on touching her, as he was now, turning her around by her elbow and giving her a gentle push to the door. He blew the lamp out. She could feel him following her. She'd toss and turn with worry if he wasn't in the room with her and she'd get no sleep at all if he was. She sighed. Better he was in the room with her. He would be in no mood to repeat the mistake they'd made at Urquhart Castle, not after what he'd gone through with Elyta. All she had to do was to keep her hands to herself.

She closed the door to her room. "Turn your back," she commanded. Callan turned obediently. "And don't you peek."

"I ha' seen it before," he remarked.

"Don't remind me," she muttered under her breath.

He was bone-tired, or he wouldn't have said anything so casually crass. Stupid to remind her of something she regretted so. It still amazed him that she had taken his part against Elyta. The girl had incredible courage. He hoped to God she could find the cure without her notebook. Tonight she'd robbed him of the only way to prevent Elyta from killing her when the cure was found. What could he do to protect her now?

"Sa what's wrong with Clara tonight?"

"She loves Flavio. Always has. It's why she serves Elyta, just to be near him."

Well, that was interesting. "Lucky dog." If his hearing were better, he'd be able to hear them talking down the hall and know how her feelings were being received even now. Behind him Jane scampered from behind the screen where she was changing and over to the bed. "All right, you can turn around now."

She swung a quilt around herself, but not before he caught a glimpse of her form inside her thin linen night rail, backlit by the lamp. She curled up in the large wing chair and tucked her feet under her.

"What d'ye think ye're doin'?"

"I'm settling in for the day."

"And ye're wantin' me ta take yer bed from ye?" He snorted. "I dinnae think sa."

She looked exasperated. "So, you think you can sit in the chair all day, when you could barely sit through dinner? The only way you'll get any rest is on your belly."

She was right about that. "I'll sleep on the floor, on this rug," he said, pointing.

"You will not," she said indignantly. How her violet eyes flashed when she was angry.

He grabbed a pillow and the coverlet folded at the foot of the bed and knelt gingerly on the rug. "I will, unless ye use compulsion on me." She looked outraged. He turned his face away from her. That was unfair. "Ye might as well go ta bed and be comfortable."

"If you can be uncomfortable, so can I." She bit out the words.

"Verra well, then, we've got a plan." He felt his eyes closing of their own accord. He should be thinking of a plan himself. How to get Jane away from Elyta once she found the cure . . . If she found the cure . . .

Jane watched him fall asleep, almost while he was still talking to her. He'd pulled the coverlet over himself badly. She sighed, got up, and twitched it over his legs and his right shoulder. She glanced to the bed. She would be more comfortable there, and it obviously made no difference to him, but suddenly sleep was far away. The itch was back in her veins, and the place between her legs began to throb even as she looked at his face, softened by sleep.

And he thought he was a bad man! Stubborn? Yes. Exasperating? Absolutely. But he was so far from bad that he had made a bargain with the devil to save her. Maybe he would have done it for anyone. He might be that much of a knight errant. Or maybe . . . maybe he felt something for her.

But she couldn't think about that, not until she had cured herself and they were both on the same side of the chasm Until then, such thoughts were dangerous.

She curled up in her chair again, and kept her demons at bay by calculating percentages of each ingredient she'd use tomorrow. She'd try making gelatin, but dilute it with alcohol. That might bleach the aspic to the clear state she'd seen in her father's laboratory.

The liquid not only didn't turn magenta, it flamed and sent smoke boiling up to the ceiling to join the stains from the last two, similar results. Jane let out an anguished cry. "I'll never get this right at this rate!" It was perhaps two in the morning.

Kilkenny took her shoulders. "Calm down. Did no' ye say science takes patience?"

"I . . . I can't calm down. It's the chalky quality that's missing. I know it is and I just can't think what to . . ." Sobs were right there, just beneath her Adam's apple. And she couldn't let them come up any farther because scientists didn't cry. It was just that the itching in her veins had come round to something like pain. She couldn't think. And his hands on her shoulders weren't making things better. *Au contraire.*

"Ye know what's wrong." His eyes were serious, concerned.

She pulled away. "Let's not go into this again."

The fire had burned itself out, leaving a hard, blackened crust in the bottom of the flask.

Flavio wandered in. "My! That's certainly an interesting smell." His face glowed, as if all was right with the world. Jane would wager it was because he and Clara had come to an understanding. The thought made her annoyed when she should only be glad for them.

"I'm progressing just about as rottenly as it smells," she huffed, throwing herself down on a stool. "Which is what you want to ask." Was she jealous of Clara and Flavio?

"Nonsense, child. I came to say Elyta has gone out. You won't see her again tonight."

"She's probably draining every local in the village," Jane managed, thrusting up out of her chair and pacing the kitchen.

"I've warned her. And it's better if she sips a little every night, believe me."

Jane saw him glance to Kilkenny, who shook his head. "And don't you two conspire against me. I'll get this formula. I will . . . and . . . and then I won't need any of your damned blood." This would have been very dramatic, except that she burst into tears.

Flavio took her by the shoulders. "My dear, you're tired. Did you sleep well today?"

"No," she said between sobs. "I hardly slept at all."

"Give your experiments a rest. Go to bed early. Let your mind work the problem in your sleep. Haven't you retired with a problem, and when you woke up, the solution was right there?"

Jane nodded, sniffling.

"Well, just you go up to your room. And I'll wager when you awake, you'll see the problem in a whole new light." He guided her to the door.

Flavio glanced back over his shoulder as he took Jane out to the staircase. Callan nodded at the monk. He knew what he must do. There was no question of talking her into getting what she needed from some shepherd. He watched her wipe her hands on the white apron she wore over her gray dress as she trudged up the stairs. What would the dour dons at the university in Edinburgh think of a scientist with violet eyes and an apron over her dress?

"I'll watch Mr. Kilkenny for you," Flavio soothed from the base of the stairway.

"Yes, but would you ever set yourself against Elyta if she wanted him?" Jane fussed. "You'd better come get me if she returns." Flavio looked startled, then hurt at her lack of faith.

"I'll help Clara at the well," he said grimly as he pushed past Callan.

Callan set his lips and headed after Jane. He'd have to go carefully. He mustn't frighten her. If she would but let her instincts take over, everything would be fine. But Jane wasn't a woman to give in to instincts, at least not very often. The image of her, hair undone and wild about her face in the dim tower of Urquhart Castle, sprang to his mind. He pushed it down fiercely. He'd been vampire then and so was she. Now, until the cure was found, they were two different species. One of whom needed something from the other she wouldn't take. He had to show her what she must know, in case there was no cure. That meant blood and something more, as well. She had to find the joys of taking blood to balance out her horror.

He took off his boots and unwound his cravat. He'd worn

it so as not to distract her with the blood pounding in his throat. She was past protection, though. She'd been weakened by the energy she'd expended in the attack of the vampires. She required blood even then. He tossed the cravat on a chair and unbuttoned his waistcoat as he padded silently up the stairs.

She'd know he was coming, of course. There was no hiding from one with hearing as acute as hers. So she was staring at him from her bed as he opened the door. The light from the hallway illuminated her but dimly.

"Go away," she whispered, but her eyes weren't sure she wanted that. He closed the door. "I . . . I'm not safe for you right now." Her eyes were indigo reflections of the night.

"I'm no' lookin' for safety."

She jerked her gaze away. It darted about the room, looking for alternatives. She put her knuckles to her lips. He stretched himself out beside her. The bed creaked with his weight.

"I should have the strength of character to run from you," she breathed.

"Ye should ha' th' strength ta be who ye are." Now that she had removed her apron, the tops of her breasts were revealed by the neckline of her dress. They rose and fell, and his cock rose with them. God, but she was beautiful. And she didn't even seem to know it. Or maybe she just didn't value it. Being beautiful didn't fit with being a scientist.

"Why are you doing this?" she asked, panting.

"Because I know what ye need."

"Oh, very well," she said crossly. "I'll just drain a bit from Flavio's wrist into a cup . . ."

"Ye can no' drink from a vampire sa much more powerful. Which leaves out Flavio, Clara, and Elyta. I'm yer only choice, unless ye want ta roam th' hills lookin' for shepherds."

She looked around, wild-eyed. "I . . ."

"Ye canno' hold out and ye know it." He knew he was backing her into a corner. There appeared to be no choice.

He deliberately softened his voice. "Ye may need ta know how ta get what ye require." He leaned in and brushed his lips across hers. She shivered. "It can be pleasant for both th' giver and th' receiver. Ecstatic even."

"This is wrong," she said, moaning into his mouth as he kissed her again lightly.

"No' wrong. Natural. And with a bit o' compulsion you can leave them with good memories, thinking better o' themselves." He slid his hand around her back and kissed her. *Yer body knows what ye need, Jane. Listen to it,* he thought. He slipped his tongue inside her mouth, not probing, not insistent, but gently caressing. He dared not pull her to him or she would feel the hard shaft of his cock against her belly. So he ran his hand up behind her head. He pulled away from her kiss, lifted his chin, and gently guided her head toward his throat.

How many times had he been violated by Asharti and Elyta while they drank his blood? How defiled he'd felt. Yet now, it was wholly different. He *wanted* Jane to feed from him. He wanted to satisfy her every need. The only problem might be that she would rip his throat as the need overcame her. He couldn't heal that kind of damage anymore. And he didn't want to die.

That realization struck him hard. He had been dragging himself through life trying to find value, but not valuing his life, in a kind of joyless desperation. He'd wanted the cure so he could commit suicide if he couldn't find his way back to a time before he had been twisted by experience. But now, he didn't care if he could never be the charming rogue he'd been before Asharti. He wanted to live, even as he was. What had changed? He felt Jane's lips hovering above his throat and knew.

Her body began to tremble. Did she know where the carotid artery was? She had studied medicine surreptitiously by helping her father. She kissed her way round his throat until her breath came hot on his neck just at the right place, under his jaw. She knew, all right. He stroked her hair. She would be feeling the throb of his blood, pulsing against her lips. Her back was straight, tight. Still she resisted. "Ask yer Companion for help," he whispered. He'd take his chances with death to give Jane what she needed.

Her vibrations cycled up. If he could see her eyes, they would be red. Her canines would have elongated into fangs. He braced for her capitulation and the moment of life and death it would bring. He could feel her panting struggle. "I want this, Jane," he murmured. It was true.

She resisted for a single moment more before she went limp in his arms with a tiny moan. Her hot breath whooshed out over him and she sank her canines gently into his throat. The moment of pain subsided. She didn't rip, or tear. "Suck now," he whispered, relaxing against her body. She pulled him into her and began to draw at his neck. He could feel her hands on his welts but that was far away. Her body moved against his in rhythm to her sucking. "That's right," he murmured. She might not know when to stop. He should tell her. But the feeling of her suckling and rocking against him was so near to ecstasy he wanted it to go on forever.

She pulled away with a tiny cry and took his head in both hands. "Have I hurt you?" she asked, searching his face. Her eyes faded from red to violet.

"Nae, lass." He smiled tenderly. How like her to be only concerned for him, in spite of the demands of her Companion. It must have taken all she had to pull away. "I'm a full-blooded Scot, or maybe an Irishman. I've more in my veins for ye yet tonight, any road."

"Oh, dear." Her pain was palpable.

"Dinnae ye feel better?"

"I do. God help me, I do. The life is bursting in me."

"And now there's somethin' else ye need." He knew what she was feeling. He had felt it. She had an urge to life inside her that demanded fulfillment. He kissed her. He probed her mouth with his tongue and she kissed him back, still holding his head in her hands, even as he ground his groin against hers. Let her have no doubt he wanted her.

"Callan," she whispered. It was the first time she had ever said his given name. She said it as gently as she had taken his blood. He liked the sound of it on her lips.

"Are ye wantin' me ta make love ta ye, lass?" he asked her softly.

She nodded, a wicked gleam in her eyes. Then she collapsed in uncertainty. "If . . if you're up to it. I mean . . . and it wouldn't have to be actually making love . . ."

He silenced her with kisses. "Ye're th' one best ta get rid o' these clothes."

She raised herself on one elbow, her eyes now gleaming. "Best watch what you begin, Callan Kilkenny. You might not be able to finish it."

"Ye're talkative. But I'm no' seein' any results."

She sat up, then took her bodice in both hands and ripped it with a vampire's strength.

"I dinnae like all the gray dresses anyway. Ye should be clothed in red and midnight blue like yer eyes, with lace and jewels and silks."

"When you seem to like worn coats and boots that have seen better days?"

"Then how about us both bein' naked as babes for th' moment?"

"I won't sew buttons on these breeches yet again." She pulled the shirt over his head, and he unbuttoned his breeches with care. She thrust them down over his hips. He pulled them off. Her eyes widened at the sight of his erection, then darkened into the color of midnight.

All thought of going slowly was abandoned. She needed him and she needed him now. He rolled her on her back. She spread her thighs and put her hands over his buttocks to help him thrust inside her. But she must have felt his welts, for she jerked her hands away and placed them carefully on his waist. He plunged into her. The first thrusts were so satisfying! Then he stopped and lay between her legs, full inside her, propped on his elbows.

"Now Jane, drink again, and ye'll see what pleasure is." He turned his head.

He felt her power. She placed her teeth over his artery and slowly, tenderly, penetrated him. He began pumping inside her, in rhythm to her sucking. The feeling of essence being drawn from him seemed to extend from his throat down to his cock. He pushed the pace faster. He mustn't come before she did, but the pull toward orgasm was like a fast horse galloping, powerful, unstoppable. She felt it, too. She gripped his shoulders as she contracted, and he let himself go, arching against her sucking lips and her clenching womb as he gave his body's fluids to her body, spurting blood into her mouth and seed into her loins.

She pulled her teeth from his neck with a little moan and collapsed against her pillows. "Oh . . ." she said in a small voice.

He drew himself out of her. Weakness enveloped him. Breathing was a little difficult. It would pass. She was up on her elbows, bending over him. "Callan? Callan, are you well?"

He smiled at her. Dear Jane. Even in her ecstasy she worried about him. "Aye, lass."

"I'm so sorry. I took . . . I took too much."

"Nae. Did I no' tell ye there was an ecstasy of givin' as well as takin'? I would no' ha' missed that for th' world." He closed his eyes. It hadn't been the untamed wildness of the sex, vampire to vampire, they had at the castle. His senses had been dulled back into humanity. But the joy of giving to Jane had its own sweetness.

He loved her. That was what all this was. He'd never loved before, so it had crept up on him while he wasn't looking. He'd thought he just wanted to protect her. He wanted to live just to be with her. But if she required his death he'd give it. He cared about her more than he cared about himself. He was now pretty certain that was what love was.

She lay back and laid his head against her breast. He gave a little moan of satisfaction. "What?" she asked, worried.

"Yer hands are always sa gentle on my body," he murmured. Maybe that was what made his experience with Jane so fundamentally different than with Elyta or Asharti. He felt Jane's goodness immediately in her touch.

"Rest, Callan." She brushed her lips across his hair. Was it just her vampire needs he had felt? Was he only a victim her goodness demanded that she save from Elyta, or did she feel something like what he felt for her?

How could she? He was only mortal now and she was vampire. Worse, he was still tainted with evil from Elyta through Asharti and now round to Elyta again, while Jane was all light and goodness.

"Rest through the day with me . . . and we will start again tonight on the cure," she said.

She must find the cure. If they were both mortal, he would know how she felt about him. It wouldn't be all mixed up with being vampire. He'd find a way to save her from Elyta. He had to. He drifted . . .

CHAPTER
Twenty

Jane woke tangled in Callan's limbs. The sun had just gone down. Her blood thrilled through her body. How alive she felt! Sometime during the day he must have pulled the coverlet up over them. Dear Callan. He was lying on his belly, head pillowed on her breast, one arm thrown across her. She longed to touch the muscles in his shoulders. The welts that peeked from under the coverlet still made her angry. She lay still, drinking in his warmth, his weight across her body, the crinkly hair on his chest against her breast, his curling black hair with the twin streaks of gray on her shoulder. His breath was warm and moist on her neck. She felt her loins stir. His thigh was across hers under the coverlet. That soft flesh she felt must be . . .

They had had intercourse of several kinds in the wee hours of the night. It wasn't quite so . . . transforming as it had been in the castle. Maybe that was because he was mortal now. And yet, the feel of taking his blood had been so sexual, it heightened the act itself. The experience was certainly different from her intimate moments with Mr. Blandings. That might not be because of the blood. Perhaps no carnal relations with Callan Kilkenny would ever be like sex with Mr. Blandings, blood or no, vampire or no . . .

She had drunk his *blood*! How did she feel about that?

Guilty. She had lost all control. She had given it over to her Companion and to Callan. She had never believed in giving control to anyone. She was an acolyte of Apollo, not Dionysus. But in return for her lapse, she had been taken out of herself, to another level of *presence* in the moment. Sensation had been overwhelming. Wasn't that selfish, to have the moment of objective time so infused with yourself and vice versa? But it wasn't only herself in the moment. The experience of Callan's body, his sexual and spiritual essence, had infused the moment, too. She ran a finger lightly across that waving mass of black hair. He had given his blood so freely. He was a generous man. A good man. And mortal.

She *had* to find a cure. She didn't want to be a vampire when he was not. How could he . . . care for a vampire? True, he understood her. But he would grow old, and she would not. She would drink blood and be burned by sunlight. Who would give up daylight for a lifetime if one didn't have to? Would any man tolerate a woman with ten times his strength?

"Chalk," she said suddenly, as the thought popped into her head. That was it!

He stirred. "What?" he asked, groggy.

She eased him off her and sat up. He leaned on one elbow and rubbed his eyes. "Chalk!" She grinned. "Why did I think it had to be a chalky plant? Papa used chalks to write on his slate."

"Were they no' burned in th' fire?" He was wide awake now.

"He had spare chalk in his desk." She was out of the bed and striding to the wardrobe. She threw open the doors. "Let's see." The dresses hung in dreary similarity.

"Some choice." He stood behind her.

"At least I never have to worry about matching reticules or half-boots, or pelisses or—"

"And ye'll tell me ye wouldn't enjoy matchin' yer fripperies, too, I'll wager." He tried to frown at her, but his eyes were wry. "I'd call that a fabrication."

What? Did he know her guilty pleasure in planning wardrobes she never wore? How dare he laugh at her? "I'm a serious student of science, and working to bring modern medical techniques to midwifery," she protested as she pulled on her underthings. "Are you going to help me mix a new potion or not?"

"Aye, I'll help ye."

"Au naturel?"

He glanced down at himself, seemingly in surprise. It gave her stomach a turn to see his nipples still swollen where Elyta had pierced them. The wound Clara had stitched snaked up his chest. His scrotum must be sore, too, as well as his back and buttocks. But none of these injuries had affected his enthusiasm last night. He picked up his breeches hastily from the floor.

"Oh, dear." Jane sighed as she watched the mixture turn an unattractive mouse color. It was the fifth time tonight.

Callan squeezed her arm. "I'll chop more ingredients. Ye revise th' proportions."

"Persevere," Flavio murmured from a stool by the sideboard.

Elyta burst through the door, vibrant in purple silk, and glanced to the bubbling sludge in the beaker. Her eyes flashed with anger. "You're never going to find the formula at this rate! If I had known you were such a dullard . . . but what should I have expected from a girl?"

"Give me time," Jane said, trying not to let Elyta's barbs take hold, though it was just what she'd been thinking to herself. "I have the ingredients, or nearly. I just need the proportions, the right temperature. I'm close."

"You have no time! Vampires from Khalenberg's faction will come back just to make sure they have tied up loose ends. Who knows how many there will be?" Clara came up behind her with her shawl of Norwich silk.

"Elyta," Flavio soothed. "Shouting does no good whatever." He smiled at Clara, who returned it shyly. Come to think of it, Clara was fairly glowing, too. They looked happy.

"Science is a matter of patience," Jane said with more conviction than she felt. "One must work through all the possibilities methodically."

"There is no point in testing the formula on Clara until it looks right," Elyta fumed.

"Go away, Elyta," Flavio said quietly. It was the first time Jane had heard him give her an order. Love must agree with him. "Let them work."

Elyta turned on Jane. "You know you can't produce a cure, but you think to buy time to escape. Well, cunning minx, you could not run far enough. I would hunt you down. *They* will hunt you down. As long as anyone thinks you might *possibly* know the cure, whether it's true or not, your life is worth nothing. *Nothing!*"

"Thank you for making that clear, Elyta," Jane said. She hoped her voice was cold enough to illustrate that she was in total control. Elyta didn't have to know how frightened she was inside. "Now if you'll let me get back to work?"

Elyta narrowed her eyes. She was about to speak when Flavio guided her out of the kitchen. "Clara, just give your mistress a soothing draught and take her out hunting."

They heard the three moving about upstairs and then the front door slam. Callan went over to the cutting board by the sink and calmly began to cut hemlock.

"Am I really a target?" Jane asked in a small voice.

He turned, knife in hand. "We'll give th' formula ta anyone who wants it. When everyone has it, th' fact that we know it won't matter."

"What if I can't produce it?" she whispered. All her doubt assailed her.

Callan put his arm around her and leaned his cheek against the top of her head. "It's a matter o' patience. You've said so yourself."

"Elyta isn't looking very patient right about now." She

sighed and picked up a paper on which she had listed the last formula. She drew a line through it, and wrote out another with the proportions adjusted slightly. "Cut a bit more hemlock, Callan. I'll weigh it."

Callan felt totally helpless as he watched the next trial fail, and the next. It was a long night. He wasn't vampire. He wasn't strong, or keen of sense. He wasn't even a scientist.

And Jane was in terrible danger. Elyta was right. The vampires who wanted the formula destroyed would never let Jane live if they thought she had a chance of producing it. If she did produce it, Elyta would kill them both once she had it. And if Jane really couldn't produce the formula, Elyta would kill her in a rage. All roads led to disaster and Callan was helpless to prevent it. He was only a human and that had never felt so weak and half-alive as it did now. It would soon be time for the sun to rise, though he could no longer feel it in his veins as he once had. Jane looked tired and dispirited.

"Enough for tonight," he said. "I'll cook ye some eggs and a rasher of bacon. I might even be able ta find a pot of jam for yer bread. Safe enough, since it has no' got gelatin in it."

Her shoulders relaxed. She smiled, a little crookedly. "He cooks, too."

"Well, eggs and bacon are about th' limit o' my skill."

"That sounds wonderful to me."

He busied himself washing his hands after handling the hemlock, watching her surreptitiously. Her eyes darted over the glass forest of beakers and tubing. "It could take years," she whispered. "There are too many variables to control for. Too many . . ."

"One day at a time." Oh, *that* sounded inane. He found a knife and sliced the bread.

"I'm not smart enough." This time her voice was raw. "Not enough of a scientist." Her eyes filled. He wanted to go to her, take her in his arms and kiss away her tears, tell her it would be all right. But it wouldn't.

"Ye're smart enough, Jane. Ye're th' most intelligent person, man or woman, I've ever known. Ye said yerself it'll take time."

She rose. "Callan, look at me." She turned him away from the bowl where the five eggs he had cracked now swam. Her eyes were almost indigo and wet like a rainy night. "I don't think I'm going to find the cure. I'll spend my life looking for it, however long that life is. I won't give up. But any happy ending will be accidental. I didn't know enough of Papa's formula to complete the unknowns." She shook her head in self-recrimination. "I lied to Elyta. I am nowhere near a cure, and not likely to be so."

He couldn't tell her it would be all right but he could take her in his arms. The delicate scent of cinnamon and ambergris wafted over him, even with his dulled senses. He looked up at the ceiling and the bundles of dried herbs hanging from the beams. They didn't say anything. What was there to say?

Wait! The vampires were gone. Elyta's petulance had drawn her into carelessness. She believed Jane would stay for the sake of the cure and he would stay for Jane's sake. But there was no cure. And he didn't have to submit to Elyta or let Jane be killed. He *wasn't* just a victim anymore. He'd made a choice, but there were other choices. He could make them, too.

Bloody hell! Mortal or not, he still had a brain, didn't he? It spun now with alternatives. He went to the nearest window and pulled back the heavy blanket that covered it. An hour or more to sunrise. Plenty of time when one of them was vampire. Where? Possibilities cycled through his brain. Urquhart Castle. That would do as well as any other. This would depend on Flavio, and even Clara. Once he would have discounted them, but now, if what Jane said was true, everything had changed for them as well. His eyes darted over the kitchen, considering. He had only moments to plan. He let Jane go and whirled to the stairs that led to the cellar, grabbing the basket they used for gathering herbs and a lamp.

"What are you doing?" Jane called.

"Nae time . . ." In the cellar he swept up some carrots and parsnips, potatoes, a pot, and hen's eggs. There was some jerked beef. Perfect. No ale, the cask was too heavy. They'd get water from the loch. He took a flask. Rope? The barn. He took the stairs three at a time.

Jane stood at the doorway, looking startled. Lord help him, but he'd need all his Irish powers of persuasion to get her to go along with this mad scheme. He pushed past her and ripped blankets from the windows. "Go upstairs and get yer cloak and some night things." He wouldn't tell her anything else, least of all how long they might be gone. She could make do. She was hardy. "I'm goin' ta th' barn."

"Callan, what's this about? You're frightening me."

He looked back at her from the door and broke into a grin. In the end, he let his grin take the place of all those Irish powers of persuasion. Or maybe the grin was the essence of them. "Trust me, lass. I ha' a plan."

Callan ran into Flavio on his way down from the barn with a sturdy cord. Elyta hadn't been as careless as he'd thought.

"Whoa," Flavio protested. "Where away?" He frowned.

Callan stopped stock-still. The meeting might actually be fortuitous. Calm purpose filled him. Now he must plant the seeds of their success. They needed Flavio. "She can no' find th' cure." Callan set the words out there between them.

Flavio sighed. He knew what that meant.

"Sa we're goin'."

"She'll find you."

Callan was careful here. "Not if ye dinnae tell her we're gone. Give us a day's start."

"If she finds out I've helped you . . ."

"Go ta yer room. Say ye did no' know we were gone."

"She'll blame me."

They both knew what that meant. *He will no' do it,* Callan

thought. But he must. And in the end, more. "Ye *could* just do everythin' ye're told all yer life."

Flavio ran his hand over the rough wool that covered his thighs. "She has influence with the Elders. She can keep me out of Mirso."

"Th' choice is yers, that's certain."

"I have no choice." Flavio bit out the words.

"Ye always ha' a choice." Callan mustered his courage "Ye made a choice when ye did no' help Sincai against th' Elders."

Devastation flickered in the monk's eyes. Had Callan gone too far? "Th' Rules th' Elders make are no' infallible. One to a city, for instance. That does no' seem right." He let that sink in. Flavio might not be enthusiastic about that rule right about now. "But I canno' stand jawin' with ye." He pushed past the monk, who stood still, indecisive. "Ye'll tell her or no'. If ye care ta be o' service, ye'll suggest searchin' Inverness."

He didn't look back, but strode toward the kitchen. "Take care of Faust and th' mare. I'll be back for 'em." He hoped the seed he'd planted in Flavio would take root. If not . . .

He was stuffing their meager supplies into his valise when Jane came down dressed in her traveling cloak.

"Callan," she said "what do you mean to do?"

"I mean us ta go, Jane, before Elyta comes back. We canno' stay here and wait for more ta come after ye, or for her ta get impatient when ye canno' produce th' cure." He grabbed the valise and put the stack of blankets under that arm. She looked so forlorn.

"I failed us."

He shook his head. She had failed? Hardly. She'd stood up to Elyta for his sake. She bore being vampire far better than he had. She'd loved her selfish old fool of a father and slaved her whole life to be worthy of him when he wasn't worth half of her. And now she felt she'd failed because her father hadn't valued her enough to include her in his experiments? Callan slid his free arm under her cloak and pulled her gently to him. He could not help the smile that rose to his eyes and pulled on his lips. "Ye ha' no' failed. Th' cure was lost in th' fire without yer father tellin' ye enough ta allow ye ta reproduce it. That's different."

Her eyes were big with self-recrimination. She was about to speak . . . when he shushed her. "We must go. Now hold me tight and draw yer power."

"Can I . . . ?"

"Aye. Ye can move us both."

She pressed her lips together. The vibrations in the air ramped up. There was a tingling around his feet that swirled up around his knees. There would be pain, harder to bear than if he was vampire. "Where . . . ?" she asked.

Hips and loins were tingling now. Chest. "Think o' Urquhart Castle."

He screamed as the blackness enveloped them and turned them inside out in space.

The grassy sward inside the ruined castle walls shimmered into life around Jane. Callan fell to his knees, gasping, beside her. "Are you all right?" she asked, bending over him.

"Aye." He pushed himself to his feet, breathing hard.

The predawn gloaming was at hand. The sun would rise at any moment. Did he mean to hide here for the day? It was so close to Elyta! But she would be hemmed in by the daylight just as they were. For one day it might work. Callan took her hand and stumbled across the open bailey toward the tower that sat at the loch edge of the outer wall in a little depression. He turned in a circle surveying the place. What was he up to?

He turned to Jane. "This part is up ta ye. We need ta block this door and make it look like nae one has entered for a hundred years." He nodded to a great stone buried in the earth nearby. "If ye push that out o' th' ground, it'll roll right down. I'll get up on th' tower and shove down some stones around it ta make it look natural. We'll transport inside."

Jane surveyed the sky. They had so little time. Why did he think they must bury the doorway? But he did. And she had committed herself to follow his unknown plan. It was probably a mark of her despair to cede all control to him. "You go inside. I'll do this thing."

"Nae, I'll help ye."

"Transporting seems a little hard on you," she said doubtfully.

He looked away, exasperated. "Let a man ha' some pride, lass."

She raised her brows. Men's pride. At a time like this? And she *tried* to suppress the little smile around her mouth, but he was so dear she couldn't. She covered it instead by scurrying to the door and heaving it shut. Callan scrambled up the castle wall. She looked up to the great stone. Could she push it out of the ground? Was she that strong? He thought she was. And he thought this was necessary. She ran up behind it and placed her hands on the rough, cold surface.

This was ludicrous. She looked over to Callan who had climbed up onto the tower from the outer wall just where some crumbling crenellations began. He set down his valise and the blankets and moved along the ramparts, testing for places where the mortar had failed.

All right. She was on her own here. She heaved herself against the stone, grunting. It rocked forward and rocked back. She heaved again, using its own movement to increase the swing. She almost fell when it finally tore its muddy roots from the earth and went tumbling down the hill. It crashed against the thick wooden door and the whole tower shuddered. Callan grinned at Jane. She was a little stunned. Slowly she turned toward the east. She could practically feel the sun surging up toward the horizon. They had only moments to complete their task.

If she concentrated, she could bring down the stones of

the battlements from here, she was sure. But what if she somehow missed and threw Callan to his death? She drew her power. She'd have to go in person. As she materialized beside him, Callan pushed over a whole weakened section of the crenellations that formed a waist-high wall. Rocks tumbled over the great stone below. He turned, startled at her presence. She pushed at another section. It too gave way. Together, they heaved stones from farther away into the growing pile. It looked like a landslide. Not quite natural perhaps, but if it would rain and settle the dust . . . He grabbed the blankets and the valise.

The sun edged over the tops of the hills.

Jane gasped.

Callan took her in his arms, shielding her with his body. "Now would be good."

Companion! The power enveloped them both. She thought about the room where they had first made love.

They popped back into space inside the tower. Light came through the slits of window embrasures and the cold of the loch seemed to penetrate her bones. Callan dropped to his knees, gasping. The valise and the blankets slipped to the floor. She bent to him.

"We must get down ta th' verra bottom," he wheezed.

Well, she surely wasn't going to transport him again, especially to someplace she'd never been. What if she materialized inside stone or dirt? Could you do that? She jerked up the metal ring in the floor. Then she returned to collect him, the blankets, and the valise. She pulled him along as he scrambled to the stairway. *He'll probably fall and break his neck,* she thought. But he didn't. She lowered the trapdoor as she descended after him. Down and down they went, until they came to the base, four floors down, much nearer the waterline of the loch. Here there were only two narrow windows, perhaps twenty feet above the surface of the water. The floor was of earth. The room was dim and smelled of damp soil and cool stone. He took up two blankets from the stack and tucked one into the cracks between the stones in the arch of the window embrasure.

She watched him block the light. "It might be more comfortable up a floor or two."

"Th' smell of th' earth will help conceal us."

"What need for one day? She is trapped by the daylight, too. We'll go to Inverness as soon as the sun sinks behind the hills." As he got another blanket in place, he turned, tripping over a stone half-buried in the earthen floor. He couldn't see in the dark anymore.

"She'll search Inverness," he growled. "At least I hope sa."

"Fort Augustus then, down the loch."

He went still then. His gray-green eyes showed light in the darkness. His breath still came a little hard. He chewed his lip. "Jane . . ." he began, then couldn't seem to go on.

"You do have a plan, don't you?" Had she trusted him for nothing?

"Aye." He wiped his hand over his mouth. "I want ye ta make me vampire again."

"What?" She must not have heard him right.

"I know it's a lot ta ask of ye," he rushed on. "I'll need blood after th' first infection, but I'll try ta get by with verra little. Three days, nae more."

"But all we've wanted is to be cured." She wasn't sure which aspect of his plan she should protest first.

"I know. But that does no' look verra likely now."

"It's too late for me, yes." She let those words sink in. She was stranded. "But you are mortal again. Why would you give that up?" A part of her rose up in joy that she might not have to watch him grow old, that she wouldn't be separated from him by her Companion and all it brought with it. Hope flared that if they were both vampire, they could take the tiny flowering of intimacy she had felt between them and turn it into . . . But she couldn't trust to that. He'd never said he cared for her. It was wrong to assume anything.

But she found herself holding her breath, waiting to hear

what he would say about why he wanted to give up his mortal state.

Callan heard the uncertainty in her voice, though her form was indistinct in the dimness. He *had* to get her to turn him. It was the only way to save her. How would he convince her? Her question was the crux of the matter. But he had no idea what to tell her. Emotions he hadn't thought he owned anymore boiled up out of his belly and threatened to shut off his throat. If he told her he was doing it to save her she would never allow it. If he told her he loved her and wanted to be with her . . . she'd probably be appalled. She knew what he was, at least a glimpse of it. Elyta had told her. He had no right to claim her affections, she who was so intrinsically good.

But maybe her nature was the key. He could play upon her desire to help people. He took two slow breaths. He could do this. Could he make her believe his lies?

"I want it because bein' mortal feels . . . small, half-alive," he said. His voice was hoarse with strain. "I miss th' strength. I had ta let ye move th' rock, for heaven's sake. I miss th' heightened senses. I *want* that feelin' of bein' alive, and powerful. It . . . it was a kind o' joy. And I want ta be connected ta my Companion. It feels . . . whole and I miss that." With a shock he realized he *did* feel that way. He did miss it. And because it was true it might just convince her.

"But what about being a monster . . . outcast from society?" She took a step toward him.

"All ye have is who ye are, Jane. Ye're either a monster inside or ye are no'." Of course he was a monster, with what he'd done. Still, the statement itself was true. He pressed forward. "Ye ha' ta accept that. It is no' th' Companion that makes ye a monster." There, that was better. He believed that part too, as it turned out, because Jane was still good, regardless of the fact that her blood swam with the Companion.

"You *want* this?"

"Aye." He let his need for it drench that one word.

"But three days! Surely Elyta will find us," she worried.

"She'll think we left early last night." True, if Flavio lied for them. Callan wouldn't think about that. "She'd never think we'd hide sa close. She'll assume we went ta Inverness. By th' time they find we did no', we'll be gone."

"That only delays the inevitable. They'll hunt us down . . ."

He couldn't tell her his plan. It was so slender a scheme it would just worry her more. Let her think him in control for as long as she could. Had he made a mistake staking all on a plan so tenuous? But at least it was a plan. At least they were trying. "One step at a time, lass."

He held out his hand in the darkness. He couldn't see her features clearly, but he could feel her anguish. He'd be totally dependent on her for three days. Once he would have been horrified at the prospect. But not with Jane. He was only sorry she must be subjected to what would come. "Do this for me. Please."

She rushed forward into his arms. "Callan, Callan, are you sure?"

"I'm certain." He felt her vibrations wash over him as he gathered her into his chest. How he longed for her happiness! Before she could be happy, he'd have to save her life.

"I'm glad you've accepted who you are. You aren't a bad man, no matter what you say."

He stiffened. Not true. But he couldn't disabuse her of that notion, or she'd never share her blood with him. He cleared his throat. "Jane, do it now, before ye lose yer nerve."

Jane felt him tighten. She looked up and saw the pain in his eyes. She'd seen that pain many times now, right before he closed down emotionally. She searched back over the conversation. He'd never said he wasn't evil. He only said the Companion was not what made you so. And he'd been very careful to skirt the issue. Which meant he was trying not to lie to her. He would let his guilt, his shame over whatever he'd done, stand between them. The core of him was true and good. She felt it. She believed it. And if he'd made mistakes, well, they were past, and he had to move beyond his guilt. Whether he was vampire or human, that guilt would be a barrier to what she wanted. What did she want? She still hardly dared admit it, even to herself. But he had sacrificed himself for her. That said he cared for her, didn't it? Yet would he ever act on that feeling, even if he felt it? Not if he kept thinking the worst of himself, thoughts so painful they put up a wall that kept everyone away, including her . . .

She moved out of his arms. She had to think.

"Jane?" The desperation in that one word ate at her. He *did* want to be vampire again. She could be sure of that. She turned to look at him. What she was sure of was that if he locked himself away from her there was no possibility for them. Whatever he had done, it had festered within him until it turned him against himself. The only hope to achieve her end, and maybe the only hope for him to achieve any kind of peace with himself, whether he wanted her or not, was to clean out the wound and expose the infection to light and air. He needed to tell someone about it. He wouldn't want to do that. He'd probably go monosyllabic and retreat again.

But she had something he wanted. She could use that. It was for his own good. And it might be the only chance she had for him to love her.

There. She'd said it. A weight dropped from her shoulders, in spite of all the uncertainty around them. She knew she loved him. Now she wanted him to love her in return. And she was going to have to make a push to get what she wanted. Clara had been right.

"Are you evil?" she asked calmly, though her heart was thumping. It didn't matter. He couldn't hear it. "I mean, apart from whether you're vampire or not."

He blinked but said nothing.

Ahh, she'd been right. He didn't like to lie, but he was

afraid if he admitted he was evil she wouldn't turn him. Then she had to make it an ultimatum. "Before I turn you, I want to hear what you've done."

"Why would ye want that?" he growled.

"To make sure the man I'm turning is the man I think he is."

"Who of us is what others think us?" His expression had already closed down. His mobile, lovely lips thinned. Had she overplayed her hand? "Are ye what ye want others ta think? Was yer father?"

"What do you mean?" She was taken aback.

"Well, let's just use him as an example." He'd gone on the attack. "Th' world thinks he's a caring humanitarian who saves women's lives. But I saw him keep his daughter in virtual slavery, without valuing her as he should. He cared for women in general but wasn't generous with them in th' particular, apparently. And he was th' kind of man who could watch suffering pretty dispassionately as long as it was in th' name of science."

"Leave my father out of this," she cried. "How dare you?"

"Well, let's take ye, then." He folded his arms across his chest. "Are ye what ye seem? Ye wear those dour gray and black dresses like it was a funeral, trying to be sa scientific. But I've seen those magazines with lace and folderols and th' latest fripperies in yer room."

"You looked in my room?" Her voice was rising, out of her control.

"I did. And ye say ye hate that men want control, but all ye do is try to be one o' them, with more control over yerself than they ha' over ye. Ye deny yer a woman, Jane. Ye dinnae like ta be soft or pretty. But ye do love beauty, else ye could no' paint those flowers as ye did. All ye want is control, yet ye hate what ye are sa much, ye ceded control ta yer father by lettin' his goals in life be yer goals." He frowned at her.

"Not true!"

"Tell me ye did no' try ta be like a man just because yer father wanted a boy."

Jane didn't respond to that. She couldn't. "And *you* know so much what women are?" she mocked. It was the only defense she had. "They aren't all Elyta." That had made a hit. She could see it in his eyes.

He pressed his lips together. "I know ye, Jane. Ye're warm and passionate. Ye're givin' and hardworkin'. Ye never think of yerself and ye've got a laughin' way about ye . . ."

He trailed off and stood there, looking vulnerable. Jane felt her anger wash out of her. Did he hate what she was, or not? That last description, delusional though he was, made that stubborn gleam of hope flare up. She held on to the fact that he had struck an awful bargain just to protect her. There had to be a reason for that beyond just his honor. He was right about one thing. She had denied her femininity. But she'd already abandoned that tactic to pursue what the female in her wanted. Her female part wanted to be loved by one Callan Kilkenny. She pushed away the fear, the anger. He was trying to make her forget her purpose. She gathered herself. "You're right." She looked him in the eyes. "About all of it." This was going to hurt her. "Even about Papa. Perhaps it was that he was so single-minded. He could sometimes ignore almost . . . anything in pursuit of his aims, even me." She took a breath. "I went through a time when I hated him for it. All the while I was trying to get him to notice me, to take me into his confidence, let me be like him. Strange, yes?"

"Nae." It was a soft rumble in the darkness. "No' strange at all."

"So, you are a perceptive man. But it doesn't change what I want from you. I want to hear why you are bad. All of it."

His brows contracted, half in consternation, half in pain, if the expression in his eyes was any indication. "Nae," he said, a little raggedly.

"But turnabout is fair play, if we're to trust each other." Her relentlessness almost frightened her.

He didn't answer.

"If you want me to start guessing, as you did, I will." She went to the pile of blankets and shook out two upon the earth. She sat down on one and gestured to the other.

He stood, irresolute.

Would he be able to tell her the truth?

CHAPTER
Twenty-one

"Ye drive a hard bargain, woman," Callan said through gritted teeth. Jane watched as he strode across the space between them and threw himself down on the other blanket as far away as he could get from her, his wrists clasped about his drawn-up knees. She heard him take in a breath. He didn't know where to begin.

"Why don't ~~you start with why~~ you're a traitor to England and to vampires?" She saw his shoulders relax. He felt he could tell her, so that must not be the worst of it. "I know part of it. Clara said a woman named Asharti made you vampire. She made an army. You followed her. Is that what made you a traitor to vampires?"

"Aye," he murmured after a moment. "Though I was no' a regular member o' her army." Here he grimaced.

"Is that the only reason you're a traitor?" she pressed. If he was to get any relief from confession, it had to be thorough.

He gave a bitter chuff. "Nae," he said, and took another great breath. "After she was killed, th' army disbanded. Th' Elders sent powerful old vampires ta massacre all those she made. I escaped in th' chaos through th' desert. But they hunted us down. It had nothin' ta do with whether we were good or bad. It was no' about justice. I thought . . . if made vampires with true hearts had a homeland, a refuge, we could stand against th' Elders. I guess I was lookin' for another cause ta give my life meanin'."

"England was going to be your homeland?"

"Aye."

So he stood against vampire kind and was a traitor to his human government all at the same time. "What happened to your cause?"

He lifted his chin as though his cravat was tight, though he didn't wear one. "Pretty much what happens ta every cause. I tried ta pick virtuous men who wanted ta use our powers for th' good of both races." He looked away. "It did no' work out sa well."

"They weren't good men?" she asked softly.

His lips curled in self-abnegation. "Some killed for their blood."

She shrugged. "You aren't the first to believe in utopia. Or the first to have their ideals stripped from them."

"People died, Jane." His voice was raw. "Is no' that bad enough for ye?" He was angry at her for making him do this. That was clear.

But she couldn't lose her courage now. That hadn't been the worst and she wanted the worst. "You're obviously trying to frighten me," she said as calmly as she could. "But you'll have to do better than that."

He had a tight grip on himself. "Verra well. I said I was no' a regular member of her army." He cleared his throat. "In fact . . . I was her slave."

Jane nodded. Her guess was right. It didn't give her satisfaction.

"If I'd been a man I would ha' found a way ta make her kill me before I let her do . . . what she did."

Jane kept silent. She knew what Asharti might have done. No man could stand against compulsion. But she dared not comfort him. If she sympathized he might lose his nerve.

"In th' end, I did whatever she wanted." His voice was flat. "And I wanted ta please her. She did no' need ta use

compulsion on me. After she made me vampire it was all
tied up with how much I needed sex." He looked down at his
knees. "It was no' pleasure, but I could hold an erection
through anythin'." He stared at her, challenging. "Worse
than ye thought, I expect."

He didn't need compulsion? He held an erection through
the kind of abuse she had seen on his body? But . . . his situation wasn't unique, just hard to comprehend from the outside. "I can see how it disturbs you. But I've seen the like
before; women who won't leave the husbands that brutalize
them, people who don't press charges when they've been
kidnapped. Victims can get tangled up emotionally in their
situation. The powerful ones take over their victims' lives
and the victims want to please them. They hate themselves
for not being as ruthless as their tormentors. Some even become tormentors themselves of those weaker than they are."
She would wager he hadn't done that.

"She was th' center of my life. When I escaped her, I had
nae center, nae purpose." His shoulders sagged.

"So you tried to build a new society," she whispered.
"You can't tell me you had no courage, no ideals."

Callan looked at the compassion in Jane's eyes and it all came
flooding back to him. Damn her for feeling sorry for him!

*Screams filled the outskirts of the village as the army herded
its people into the market square. Callan shuffled beside
Asharti's palanquin, naked except for his chains. She liked
to see him dressed only in chains. His veins itched with
hunger that bordered on pain. Distracted as he was, he
smelled fear along with the dung of animals, dusty streets,
dates and onions and rancid sweat. Asharti called a halt at
the market square. Slaves drew back the draperies of her litter so she could watch the proceedings. Callan watched with
dazed dread as the adults were separated from the children.
Those of Asharti's army who had been turned, as he had*

been, hovered avariciously around the edge of the frightened crowd. Asharti gave the signal and the vampires moved in, compressing the throng. Wails and ululations rose from the mass. The milling children in one corner of the square screamed and cried. Those adults on the outer circle were the first to go. Vampires clamped their victims' necks. Red eyes glowed. Screams echoed and were silenced. There was a universal slurping sound that made Callan want to retch. It had been two weeks since Asharti had allowed him blood. The thing in his veins smelled the blood in the air, and demanded of him. How he hated what he was! Several strong young Arabs were brought to Asharti. She held them with her red eyes, and sucked them dry. They fell in a heap next to Callan, flesh sunken because it was no longer supported by full capillaries.

When Asharti had drunk her fill, she motioned to one of her lieutenants. "Bring one for my slave. Not too lively."

It was a boy, sixteen, perhaps seventeen. One of them had already been at him, for his neck drooled rivulets of blood from twin wounds. His great dark eyes were so suffused with fear Callan was afraid he'd lost his mind. The vampire pushed the boy to his knees in front of Callan.

Callan swayed. The thing in his veins shouted at him. The itch inside his body made him want to scream. He wouldn't do it! He clenched his fists against the roaring in his ears.

"Do it," *Asharti commanded. He could hear her in his mind, if he could hear nothing else.* "Else I'll think up new punishments for you."

He didn't care. He wasn't an animal, to feed on humans like an animal. His blood rushed about in his body. His vision dimmed.

And went red.

Nae, *he thought.* I'll no' tear a human throat. *His breath wouldn't come. He bade the thing in his blood stand down, but it wouldn't and the red film would not clear. He stood, trembling with effort, but he felt his canines lengthen. There* is such a thing as free will, *he told himself.* If ye do this thing, yer just as bad as they are.

With a rush the world went carmine. He stood shuddering against the demand of the thing in his blood as it suffused him with power. He wrenched his head away.

Then, as though pulled by a force a thousand times stronger than he was, he slowly turned back toward the boy. The boy lifted his chin. Callan bent, so slowly, and felt his canines pierce the throat. He cried out as he gripped the boy's shoulders and sucked. Blood flowed in over his teeth and tongue. The thing in his blood rejoiced. It sang in a great chorus through his veins. Alive! it sang. Alive! The blood is the life. *On and on he sucked. A little breath crossed his face, a sigh almost. The boy slumped in his arms.*

Callan blinked as the red drained away. The boy's doe eyes stared up, unseeing. He had a sunken look about his face. The singing in Callan's veins sank to a satisfied hum.

The boy was dead.

Callan let him drop with an anguished cry.

Behind him, Asharti laughed, a deep contralto chuckle. "Ahh, we think there are things we will not do. But are there?"

Callan's stomach rebelled. He vomited blood onto the hard sand of the market square. But as quickly as the spasm came, something suppressed it. He knew he would not retch again. A sob caught in his throat.

"Come, slave," she said, alighting from her litter. "I am not done with you." She reached for the chain that hung down from the ring at his neck. He stumbled to his feet, dazed.

Asharti took him to the cluster of remaining villagers, cowering, their screams now swallowed and gone. "You there!" she called to one of her lieutenants. "Bring me a man."

I will no' suck another one, *he thought. Now that his terrible hunger was assuaged, he could resist, could he not? He must. And if she made the pain inside his head, he'd still resist. He'd grown too afraid of that pain. It was time to challenge his capacity to endure.*

The lieutenant grabbed an older man, his beard just going gray. His burnoose was ragged, his sandals worn. A woman screamed and tried to pull him back into the circle, but another of Asharti's minions jerked her away. She fell to her knees, sobbing. The Arab was pushed to his knees in front of Callan.

"Now your sword," Asharti commanded. The lieutenant hesitated before he pulled his great scythe of a curved blade and handed it, hilt first, to Asharti. He was afraid she would decapitate him. "Not to me," Asharti barked. She gestured to Callan.

The man held out the weapon to Callan.

Callan shook his head, horror blossoming in his heart. "Kill me then. I will no' kill him."

"But you will. Because it isn't you I'll kill if you refuse. I'll kill the children."

Callan looked up at the clutch of children in the corner of the square. There must be twenty. "Ye canno' mean it."

She smiled. "What are they to me? Kill him and I'll spare them."

He turned on her, sword in hand.

She pursed her lips in disgust. "You know I'd never let you kill me."

He did know it. But she wasn't bringing up her power. Her eyes weren't red. A knot twisted his stomach. She wouldn't grant him the refuge of compulsion. She required him to choose the evil. The sword hilt seared his palm. He shook his head. "I will no' choose."

She chuckled, low in her throat. "Even refusing to choose is a choice, slave." She nodded to the lieutenant. "Kill a few of the little ones."

Callan spun. "Nae! Ye canno' kill bairns!" he cried.

The lieutenant paused, glancing to Asharti.

"You can stop it," she whispered. "A single thrust. A quick death. He's an old man."

Callan felt himself go slack, in mind as well as body. He

stared at the man, burning the frightened features on his psy-che. The man began to murmur prayers. He clasped his hands convulsively at his chest and put his forehead to the sand at Callan's feet. Callan couldn't swallow. He couldn't breathe. How would he bear what he would do here? He glanced to the crowd of children, quiet now except for the wail of a babe in an older child's arms. "Dinnae make me do this," he whispered, knowing it was hopeless.

"But I shall."

Those three words damned his soul more surely than the thing in his blood.

He raised his sword.

Jane was about to reach out to touch his arm when he turned on her. The look in his eyes was so fierce she sat back, sur-prised. It was as if he wanted to punish her for excusing him. "If ye want th' truth, Jane, then here it is and ye'll be sorry ye asked." The words were ripped from a raw throat. "I killed for her. No' in battle, no' as justice or retribution, and no' be-cause my life was threatened. I executed innocent people just because she told me ta do it. Explain that away."

Jane felt her mouth fall open. He'd killed innocent people?

His breath was ragged now. The words pent up for years seemed to tumble out as fast as he could make them come. "She did no' use compulsion on me. She gave me a choice. She wanted my soul, no' just my body, and she got it, Jane. She got it. At first she just gave me a boy, maybe sixteen, when I was sorely in need of blood and others had been at him first. I sucked him dry. That was bad, certain. But I did worse. There . . . there were men, with their wives wailing as I hacked off their heads. And I did no' even drink from them. I used a sword. I did *anythin'* for her. I . . . I killed fathers, brothers, husbands. I destroyed their families' lives."

He'd killed wantonly just to please a woman? Jane felt nausea pour bile into her throat. *This* was evil! How could it not be? And she *was* sorry she'd asked him. How could she know he'd done something so horrendous? She imagined he'd killed in battle or in a hand-to-hand contest—some conflict where there was an equal chance for his opponent or at least some reason for the death. But there was no honor in killing unarmed peasants, no reason.

But . . . wait. She swallowed and licked her lips. She mustn't just give in to disgust. He couldn't really be blamed for draining a boy when the need for blood was on him. She knew that firsthand. And this was Callan, who had put himself in Elyta's power to protect her when he knew only too well how horrible that would be. This was the man who told the truth even when the truth was incredibly hard. And this was a man who never forgave himself. He was worth reserving her disgust until she knew more about the circumstances.

She steadied her breathing. "Did . . . did you want to kill them?"

His head shook as if words were too much for him.

"But you were afraid of what she would do to you." It was hard to imagine him afraid.

"Nae. I mean I was, but it had gone beyond that. She'd kill th' others. She had nae compunction about killin'."

Jane leaned in. "She would have killed others if you hadn't?"

"They always rounded up th' village children while they fed from th' parents."

Jane sat up. "And why isn't that compulsion?" She was so glad she had not given in to her revulsion.

"I'm damned, Jane. She gave me a choice and I made it, every time."

"Instead you should have let her kill—how many children were there?"

He raised his head. His eyes were dead and flat. "Twenty sometimes. And aye, I should ha' let her kill them. Her soul would ha' been damned, no' mine."

"Well, the God I know doesn't damn someone's soul for saving the lives of children. Your only recourse was to kill yourself and the church would damn you for that, too."

"But I could no'," he muttered, looking around wildly. "I had tried. Th' Companion, it will no' let you kill yerself once it has firm hold on ye. I managed to put a stake inta my heart when she first infected me, but I healed and then I found out it takes decapitation ta kill us, which is hard ta arrange, and . . . by then I could no' let it happen anyway. After th' first time I killed a man, I begged Fedeyah ta do it. But he would no' help me. He said th' Companion would make me defend myself, and he did no' care ta bleed."

To think he had been so despairing he had driven a stake into his own heart made her clench against tears. There hadn't been any choice for him about killing those men. She had to make him see it rationally, unclouded by the emotion twisting in his heart.

"Clara says there are all kinds of compulsion," she said, almost conversationally. "The kind vampires have and the kind that anyone can bring to bear. Asharti compelled you to kill those men. She just didn't use her vampire powers to do it."

"Ye've a generous spirit, Jane," he muttered.

Why couldn't he see in himself what she saw in him? "What did you do when you discovered the vampires in your cause were killing for blood?" she pressed.

He shook his head, looking bewildered. "Nothin'. Stephan Sincai killed them. When he spared me, I . . . I wandered. All I could do was . . . sometimes . . . use my strength . . . small acts . . . inconsequential . . . I did no' make a difference."

"You used your power to help the powerless."

"It did no' stop th' cruelty or th' avarice for long. It was all stupid. Useless."

"You are the one with a generous spirit, Callan." Too direct!

He chuffed a bitter laugh. "I'm no' ye, Jane. Dinnae try ta make me over in yer image."

"Was it not you who submitted to Elyta in a bargain for my life?" she cried. She'd pushed him too hard, and now all she could think to do was push him harder.

"It was nothin' I had no' done before." His voice was bleak. "Ha' done now. I told ye about th' evil in my past. Keep yer bargain."

Her belief that if Callan could talk about the wounds festering inside him he could overcome them seemed suddenly naïve. Probing them only made him suffer more. And he was too damaged to make peace with himself. But she couldn't let it go without making one more try. "Asharti compelled you to kill those people as surely as if she had red eyes at the time," she said as clearly and as seriously as she could. "Even good men can be made to do bad things."

"Believe that, if it will make ye give me yer blood."

Jane felt as if she had been slapped. She sucked in a breath involuntarily, then let it out slowly. Very well. If blood was all he cared about, he would have it. "Give me your knife."

He felt in his pocket and came out with a small utility knife that folded in on itself. He pried it open and handed it to her. She snatched it from him and grabbed his hand. He held it out, palm up. Before she could lose her courage, she sliced across the pad just below his thumb. Blood welled immediately. The smell of it was intoxicating. Then she held her own hand out and did the same. "It's yours, if you want it so much," she said, holding out her hand.

He hesitated only a moment before he pressed his palm to hers.

Their fingers twined, pressed the wounds together and sparked with that familiar tug, one to one, flesh to flesh, blood to blood.

It was done.

He sat huddled under the window, silent, as the fever came on him. He couldn't speak to her, not after what she'd made him do. Did she have to rake through the ashes of his soul as the price for infection? Recounting all his failures as a man, all his crimes . . . And in the next days, he'd have to drink her blood. He'd wait as long as he could, take as little as he dared, just enough to give him immunity once more to the parasite.

If only Flavio didn't tell Elyta when he'd seen them leave. Would he find the courage to lie to her? Then if Elyta assumed they'd gone to Inverness . . . if it took her two days to search for their trail . . . if she believed Callan's planned lie when she finally did find them . . . if Flavio felt guilty enough about abandoning Stephan Sincai to help them when the final confrontation came, as come it must . . . if Clara loved Flavio enough to take his side against Elyta . . .

A lot of ifs. And if the ifs failed, his rash action in escaping would have doomed them to death. He didn't care for himself, of course, but Jane . . .

He glanced over to where she was using the little knife to cut up carrots. He wouldn't be able to eat soon, but she would. He hoped he'd brought enough to sustain her . . .

He stood, a little shaky, and went over to the valise to retrieve the leather waterskin. She looked up at him with hurt in those big violet eyes. Well, she'd best get used to hurt. There was a lot of hurt in the world and she was going to live for thousands of years if they survived Elyta. So was he, if he survived the first infection. He'd teach her, tell her everything of course, set her up in a city . . . there was no vampire in Edinburgh, was there? She'd be the toast of the town in no time. As for him . . . it didn't matter. He had half a mind to go north, where it was frozen. The Orkneys, or the land of the Finns. Cold might suit him after all that time in the heat of the desert. Bleak might suit him. He wouldn't think about why.

He unbraided the cord and tied the frayed ends around a rock he pried out of the earth. Then he wrapped the rope around the neck of the waterskin. "Get drinking water from th' loch with this. Lower it only in daylight sa Elyta will no' see it."

"The villagers . . ."

"Canno' scale th' sheer wall up from th' loch. Canno' move th' rock from th' door."

She nodded and peered at him. "Do you want some jerked beef or one of these carrots?"

He shook his head and turned abruptly. He swung a blanket around his shoulders before he sat down. He didn't want her to see him shiver. The fever was starting in earnest.

She watched him alternately shaking and sweating as he lay huddled under the blanket. It had been twelve hours since they'd pressed their palms together. "Do . . . do you need blood?"

"No' yet," he managed.

She rose and took the last blanket from the pile they'd brought. She laid it gently over him. He turned his face away. She could understand that. He resented her bargain. He had only wanted to be vampire again. She should have given it to him without a price, especially one that had caused him so much pain.

But he'd gotten what he wanted. He was going to be vampire again. Now Jane was not sure that being on the same side of the chasm was enough to bring them together, though. And there was still Elyta and Flavio to contend with. She didn't count Clara. Clara wouldn't kill them. She hoped to God Callan had a plan for escaping Elyta's wrath. Her rashness in escaping without going more particularly into the likely outcome seemed foolhardy.

But what choice was there? Elyta would have killed them when she failed to produce the cure, or in Callan's case perhaps something worse.

Daylight was edging into twilight, so she took her last opportunity to run the waterskin down the rope into the loch.

While she waited for it to fill, she ripped a wide strip from the linen night shift she'd brought. She'd use it to make a compress for his forehead. He wouldn't let her touch him yet, but if his experience was like hers when she had turned, he would soon lose all power of resistance. He seemed hardly to notice her as she moved about the packed-earth floor.

When she went to pull up the waterskin, her eye was caught by a roil of water about forty yards away on the surface of the loch. The monster again? She stopped to watch as first one hump and then two of heaving flesh slide through the black water. Was that a fin slapping the water at the side there? She wasn't sure.

Something was happening on the loch these days. Something brought the monster to the surface when it hadn't been seen for twenty years and twenty before that. How often had it been seen of late? Five times? Seven? There was some unseen force afoot. Weather cycles? But this hadn't been a year either particularly wet or dry. Had some small fish or plant on which it fed died out? She had no explanation.

She watched it roll closer. The skin was slick but not scaly, unless the scales were extremely fine. If she could study it, she might connect it to other creatures and know its nature. Slowly the humps of flesh submerged, one after the other. What kind of thing had two humps? An invertebrate? She turned from the window. This was not a problem for now. Now she must pay attention to Callan.

She knelt beside him. He was sweating. His eyes were half-closed, unseeing. "Callan. Callan!" He rolled his head toward the sound of her voice. "Should I give you blood now?"

"No' yet," he murmured.

She sat back, frowning. She had suffered much until her father had discovered she needed blood already infected to give her immunity. He added blood to the infected vial, so that the parasite might propagate and create a supply. When he had finally given it to her, it had helped almost immediately.

Callan must be afraid she wouldn't have enough to last through his ordeal.

And what if she didn't? What if she had to watch him die because she hadn't saved enough for him when he needed it most?

She steeled herself to wait.

CHAPTER
Twenty-two

The darkness of the tower was almost impenetrable. Jane stòod at the window that looked down toward Drumnadrochit. Callan moaned softly behind her. There, on the road coming up from the village, was a barouche with a lantern swinging at each corner. She drew back into the darkness. Only one carriage in the area was so light and well-sprung. As it came closer, she could hear the hiss of the wheels on the graveled road. The figure driving wore a monk's cowl. Its head turned, once, toward Urquhart before the carriage swept up the hill and past the castle.

Callan had been right. They were going to search Inverness.

She came away from the embrasure and rubbed her temples, staring through the darkness at Callan. His hair was soaked with sweat, its twin gray streaks clearly visible. His chin was stubbled with two days' growth of dark beard.

"I canno' . . ." he muttered. "I canno' . . . Dinnae make me . . ."

That was it. She wasn't going to wait any longer. *Companion!* The rush of power filled her and his form went red-black in the darkness. She'd been thinking just how to do it. He didn't have elongated canines . . . (Oh, very well! They were fangs.) He couldn't take her blood himself. She took the little knife in one hand, then knelt on his left side and slid her right hand under his shoulders to lift him. She cut her left wrist. She licked the wound to keep it open with her saliva. That was the property her father discovered she had in common with South American bats, the anticoagulant in her saliva. Blood welled. She pressed her wrist to his lips.

He did not suck, though his lips were smeared with her blood. Was it too late? She pressed his jaw open with two fingers and again held her wrist to his mouth. She willed her blood out through the wound until she could feel it spurting sluggishly down his throat.

There. His Adam's apple moved as he swallowed in reaction. "That's right," she cooed. "Drink, Callan."

Her wound closed and she cut again to open it and licked it. He swallowed convulsively. This time she let the wound close.

He sucked in a breath. His chest filled against her breast. His eyes opened, swimming with . . . what? Fever? Ecstasy? "Th' blood is th' life," he murmured. "Thankee."

"The blood is the life . . ." She smiled. "I like that."

"A saying of our kind." He grew more alert.

Our kind. The nature she shared with him. She had explored so little of it. She had been shocked that he wanted to return to being vampire. But was he not right about the feeling of being alive and whole? Would she not miss the heightened senses if they were taken from her? It was a realization that made her blink. The answer was yes. She would miss it.

She reached for the waterskin and let him drink. Then she lowered him to the blankets. But he tried to get up on one elbow. "It is night. They may come for us . . ."

She pushed him back down. "They've gone to Inverness. I saw their carriage."

He collapsed upon the blankets. "Good. Good."

Those lovely *d* sounds turned to *t*'s. She adored a Scottish burr. "Sleep now," she commanded softly. But she needn't have bothered. He was already sinking into oblivion.

• • •

Jane woke gasping for breath. She'd been dreaming of blood and monsters submerged in dark water and Elyta's laugh. She blinked, willing the dreams to give way to reality. Daylight leaked in around the edges of the blankets. Callan lay beside her. She could feel his heartbeat, faint, sputtering. He was naked beneath the blankets. She had stripped him in order to wipe the sweat of his fever from his body.

She sat up and felt her head spin. How long had she been asleep? She hung it down until the spinning slowed. Just loss of blood. Her Companion would make more. She needed to feed, but that was impossible. She couldn't take from Callan. How strange that the Companion must feed on human blood taken from others and yet created blood and repaired flesh for its host.

She shook her head, trying to focus. She must keep ahead of Callan's need. It had been prodigious. She'd had to give him blood every few hours no matter how much he tried to refuse. She'd had to force him several times. His erratic heartbeat told her he needed it again.

She'd had plenty of time in the last two days to think about what he'd said about her. She'd told him he was right about her more to press her argument than out of real conviction. But in the long hours in the tower, his accusations had rolled around in her mind. She had to admit she'd spent her life trying to be something she wasn't. She'd become a midwife not only to help others but to be more what her father wanted her to be, since she couldn't be a doctor. And hiding her love for fashion, being ashamed that her botanical studies tried to be beautiful in spite of her best intentions; all that smacked of denying who she really was. She was no better than Callan. If she wanted him to come to grips with what he was, could she do less?

And what was she? Female. She sighed. First and foremost she was female. Sometimes chaotic, more emotional than science cared for, seduced by beauty, all the frightening female qualities were hers and she had no choice but to acknowledge them.

Maybe she should claim them outright. Why should botanical studies not be beautiful, too? Why should scientists be male? Why should females dress in gray and black to be taken seriously? Why couldn't someone love her if she was a midwife? Why did she have to be a midwife, but couldn't be a doctor?

Hmmm. She paused, struck. She was thinking about all the things people wouldn't let her be. Perhaps she was looking at this the wrong way around.

Maybe it was she herself who wouldn't let her be those things. What did she want to be? Well, she *wanted* to be a midwife. It was a good life's work and gave her satisfaction. Let the doctors look down at her and welcome. She didn't care for their opinion. But she wanted to be a midwife who didn't wear gray and black, who loved and was loved, had children and painted, too. Maybe she should be those things and let other people be damned. Or perhaps *try* to be those things. Certainly she could paint what she wanted, even if no one else appreciated the results. Lord knew there was always so much work for a midwife among the poor that she wouldn't be turned away if she wore something more stylish. And love and marriage and children? Well, she . . . she could try her best there, too. Maybe not marriage. But love at least. Could Callan love her? Who else could, if he could not?

Funny, she hadn't even thought about being vampire . . . either as a plus or a minus . . .

Above her she heard voices. Elyta! Her heart jumped.

No. It was Mr. Campbell, Jamie, others. She held her breath.

"I dinnae remember this door being blocked up sa," Mr. Campbell said.

"Look, th' rock must ha' fallen from up there." She didn't know that voice at all.

"Well, there's nae gettin' in there now." Jamie sounded disgusted.

"But who put th' rope out o' th' window?" asked the voice she didn't know.

The rope! They'd seen her rope. Was Callan right? Could they get in?

"I dinnae see any rope, McKenna." Mr. Campbell was very definite, and very skeptical.

"But it were there. I seen it." McKenna was the voice she didn't know.

"Ahh, yer imaginin' things. Naebody could be in there." A fourth voice rose plaintively.

"Could if they'd got sealed in by th' rock slide. Travelers maybe." McKenna was unfortunately stubborn. "Anybody in there?" he called.

Jane held her hand to Callan's mouth lest he groan at the worst time.

"Well, if they're in there, they're goin' ta die there, for there's no getting' in with that great boulder blockin' th' door." This was a fifth voice. How many were there?

"Grapplin' iron up from th' loch, maybe." Jane held her breath.

"Try it if ye like, McKenna. Methinks yer imaginin' th' lot o' it." *Good for you, Jamie.*

Muttering. Grumbling. "Well, if ye're all too cowardly, I'll not break my neck alone."

"I dinnae think there's anybody in there. Tell ye what, McKenna, I'll buy ye a wee dram ta comfort ye."

The voices retreated. Jane exhaled. Reprieve might be short. Surely Elyta would retrace her steps when she realized they were not in Inverness. How could she not light upon Urquhart Castle as a perfect hiding place? The stones wouldn't fool her. Nor would they stop her. Elyta would tear them limb from limb in anger if she found them. Or . . . Jane's threat against Elyta could actually be turned back upon her. Couldn't she threaten Callan to force Jane to work

on the cure? And even if Callan were vampire again, he and
Jane were no match for Elyta.

It all seemed too much. She should eat something. She
looked around vaguely. In the beginning she'd eaten reli-
giously: jerky, carrots, parsnips, raw eggs, anything to help
her Companion keep her strength up. The food was gone
now. The valise looked emaciated, folded in upon itself in
the dimness over at the center of the tower room. But it
didn't matter. The ordeal was almost over, one way or another. This was the third night, wasn't it? She wasn't sure. If
he got through the third night, he'd live. And if he was going
to die, it would be tonight.

It was that thought that stirred her from her lethargy.
Callan needed her. She was the only thing standing between
him and death. It didn't matter if she was tired. What mattered was Callan. "Companion," she murmured aloud. She
didn't bother with the knife. The thrill of power was faint but
it washed her vision with red. Her fangs sprouted. She bit
down on her wrist and scooted against Callan, opened his
mouth, felt the spurting. *Swallow*, she thought, *or the blood
will choke you.* Finally his throat worked feebly. *That's better.* Maybe she would just go to sleep beside him, her wrist
against his lips. *To sleep, perchance to dream, Aye, there's
the rub.* But even the threat of dreams seemed unimportant.
If Elyta found them, she found them. Jane watched Callan
swallowing. That was what she must focus on . . . but focusing was getting . . . harder . . .

Callan snapped his eyes open. It was dark, but he could see
anyway; every detail of the rough stones, the minute splin-
ters of wood feathering the ceiling . . . And smell! Damp
earth, cool stone, the water of the loch outside, and . . . cinnamon and ambergris.

Jane. She lay against him, her arm across his chest. He
was naked under the blanket that covered the lower half of
his body. His chest and shoulders were bare. He wasn't cold,

though. Jane's body warmed him. He picked up a strand of the hair that lay across his chest, caressing it. Her tresses had escaped their knot and were spread in golden glory over the shoulders of her damnable, dear gray dress. How could a creature of the night have hair like the sun?

A thrill of life snaked along his veins and made its way to his crotch. Jane. He felt the curve of breast and hip. She was sleeping, pale in the dim light.

She had given him her blood many times—sweet, generous Jane. That's why she was so pale. His brows contracted. He could feel her breathing. It was steady, calm. But was she well? She stirred. He hadn't meant to wake her. She should rest. There was an ordeal ahead.

Life thrilled along his veins. He had a Companion again. But this time it was Jane's Companion that infected him. He liked that thought. The joy that sang in his veins was familiar, treasured more since he had lost it, but also frightening. His feelings were so complex he could hardly sort them out. He had abandoned all thought of going back to what he was before Asharti had infected him. The charming rogue was gone for good. He found he didn't care. All he knew was that he had to be vampire for Jane. He had to be strong. They both had to be strong or they would not win through.

The very fact that he was vampire meant they had survived three nights. Elyta would be wondering where the search had gone wrong. Sooner or later she and Flavio would come round to Urquhart Castle. That was good. The confrontation was necessary. He and Jane would risk all on a single throw of the dice, betting on Elyta. And Flavio. Even Clara. Would he were as lucky at that moment of truth as he was at cards or dice. There would be one chance only.

Jane's breasts under the bodice of her gray dress pressed against his chest. Even through the cloth, they were soft, yielding. He felt his genitals swell. His vampire nature was asserting itself, longing for the life that surged in Jane's veins. Like to like.

She stirred again and his cock rose. He stilled himself, willing her to sleep on. But she raised her head and turned sleepy eyes toward him. Dark smudges hung under them. How much she had given him! "Ye always seem ta be takin' care of me," he murmured.

Her eyes were soft. Now, with his new sight, he could see how violet-indigo they were even in the dim light. "Welcome back," she whispered. "I might say the same, you know."

Would that were true. Still, he smiled at her. She would think it was a smile of reassurance. She wouldn't know that he just couldn't help smiling when he looked at her. He'd never seen a more beautiful woman. Perhaps it was the goodness and the intelligence that shone from her eyes. It occurred to him that men had thought Asharti the most beautiful woman in the world. And almost anyone would consider Elyta beautiful. But neither Asharti nor Elyta could hold a candle to Jane, because of who she was.

Her eyes darkened. A faint whiff of woman's desire wafted over him. His balls tightened. His cock stiffened with need. It was his Companion calling to Jane's. And hers was answering. A little contraction rippled through his spirit. It wasn't that she loved him. How could she? But she wanted him. Her Companion demanded the most elemental gesture of life and living, as did his.

Once he'd thought he'd never have sex with a woman again, that the sexual act had been spoiled by Asharti forever. He'd gone more than two years without a woman, with help from his left hand. Until Jane. With Jane, the act was joyous. Was it just because she was vampire that he couldn't resist her? Probably. He couldn't resist Asharti in those first days of being vampire.

And yet . . . he wanted more than sex with Jane. He wanted to give something to her, anything. For him it *wasn't* just the urging of his Companion. After all, he'd made love to Jane when he was human. It hadn't been as explosive as vampire-to-vampire sex. Yet how sensual and satisfying it was to give her blood as they made their way toward climax. He had never felt anything like it. It wasn't like Asharti drinking his blood at all.

But he had to face the fact that for Jane, the only reason to want him now was the need of her Companion. She hadn't had release in days. *That does no' hurt me. It's just th' way things are.* What other way could they be, she being who she was and he being who he was?

"Why do you look at me so strangely?" she whispered, her eyes still dark with desire.

"I ha' new eyes ta see ye with."

"I must be a sight . . ." She ran a hand through her hair self-consciously.

"Aye." His voice was so husky, he cleared his throat. And he knew he couldn't keep the desire out of his eyes any more than she could. His genitals were so swollen they were painful.

"Do . . . do you need blood?" she asked.

He did. Her blood, even though it was vampire, would be necessary for several more days. After that, it would no longer sustain him and he'd need human blood. But how could he take more from her? He avoided her gaze. "Ye've given me enough." That was certainly true.

She ran her hands over his chest. As always, her touch was gentle. "You're healed."

He glanced down. There were no marks at all where Elyta had pierced his nipples. The jagged cut on his chest was gone, the stitches shed. He felt no raw welts on his back. He would still have his old scars, but all wounds he'd had three days ago were healed. The feel of Jane's hands on his body made his cock throb, straining against the blanket. And she was not immune, either. Her breath quickened. She would be wet between her legs. She glanced down at the blanket. He felt her own need ramp up. Even if she only wanted him because she was vampire, still she had needs, and he would do his best to fill them. He covered her hand with his own.

• • •

Jane leaned down. Callan's breath was hot on her throat. Lord, he was only just awakened to his Companion, and she . . . she wanted to make love to him so badly she could taste it. What kind of a woman was she? The feel of his chest beneath her hand, his hand, warm and dry, covering hers, knowing that his shaft was hard against his belly under the blanket, all made her crazy with desire. She so wanted to kiss him. She held herself forcibly in check. He might want her but it couldn't be good for him to expend so much energy so soon.

He reached up to her, and touched his lips to hers. Jagged bolts of heat shot to her most moist parts. His eyes widened. Did he feel it, too? His tongue slipped between her lips, and she was lost. The sensuality, the sheer physical joy of that intimacy, drenched her. She leaned in and kissed him back, searching his mouth with her tongue. His arms came around her and crushed her to his chest. She couldn't breathe. She didn't care. As a matter of fact, what she wanted most was to rid herself of this stupid gray dress. She pulled at the ties, never letting her mouth stray from Callan's. He worked at the buttons on her bodice and helped her shrug out of it. She pulled her skirts down and kicked off her slippers. Her breasts felt swollen. He freed them from the light chemise that rose up to cover her nipples under her half-corset. She tore at the corset and threw her remaining underthings away. He thumbed her nipples lightly and she had never felt so sensitive. She arched her back and presented her breasts to his mouth. He was not loath to take the suggestion, and fastened those wonderful lips onto her right nipple, sucking gently. The moist feel of his mouth on her breast, sucking, made her want to experience another kind of sucking. He had said that there was a joy in giving as well as taking. In these past days she had felt that satisfaction, even though it was but her wrist that he sucked at. But now, as she remembered him baring his throat to her while they were joined, she wanted the intimacy of his teeth in her throat as much as she wanted his cock inside her. She slid under the blankets with him, and pressed her body along his flank. With her left hand she grasped his cock. How she loved the little growl he gave as she slid the skin up and down over the hard shaft.

"Tell me you're going to put that inside me," she said, panting.

"Aye," he rasped. "I'll fill ye."

She straddled his loins, opening her flesh against the thickness of his cock. She slid along it, wetting it with her cream. He hissed in a breath and then grasped her waist and helped her move back and forth. When she could stand it no more, he lifted her as though she weighed nothing and she pulled his cock up. He lowered her onto his rod, slowly. But she didn't want slow. She pushed herself down on him. "Ahhh," she sighed, impaled. A feeling of completion filled her along with his flesh. The blanket slipped from her shoulders, unheeded. She put both palms on his pectorals and pushed herself up and down, reveling in the feeling of being filled. His lips were drawn back from his teeth, in something that was neither a snarl nor a grin. His breath hissed in and out as she thumbed his hardened nipples.

And then she raised herself up off him. After the first satisfying thrusts, she felt strong enough to make it slow. He looked surprised.

She smiled. "Drink from me."

"Jane . . ." he protested.

How like him to be concerned for her. "I'm strong enough. My Companion has been making blood at a furious pace. Do you mean to be the only one who has felt the joy of giving?"

His expression softened. His eyes creased. Had there ever been a time when she didn't recognize that as a smile? "I canno' deny ye anythin'," he said softly.

She lay down over him, pressing her bare breasts to his chest. He rolled her gently to one side, cradling her head with his biceps. She lifted her chin and looked into those gray-green eyes, baring her throat. "From my throat, as you took it from me." She rolled onto her back.

The throb of his Companion said he yearned for the blood and for the completion of their act. The life within her veins answered. His eyes went red. His canines slid out. Would this hurt? She, who was made from a beaker, knew so little about living as a vampire. A thrill of fear mingled with the throb inside her. That delicious half fear, half need made her own eyes go red.

As he bent, his black hair with the gray streaks at his temples fell forward. His canines scraped upon her throat. "Sweet Jane, generous Jane," he murmured.

And then she felt the twin pricks, hardly more than the piercing of her finger by a rose thorn. Was it her Companion that made the pain seem so unimportant? He sucked gently. With his other hand, he took his cock and slipped it back inside her. His body contracted as he thrust and now pulled at her throat more urgently. A feeling of total completion filled her, even as her hips thrust in counterpoint to his. She moaned as she held his head to her throat, feeling the pull of his lips at her neck. Her other hand splayed over his back as the muscles moved under the skin. Her hand strayed down over his loins to his buttocks. The bunching of the muscles there only served to heighten her excitement. Their Companions' vibrations ramped up some scale toward insanity. Energy seemed to pass between them, reverberating back and forth, growing with each round-trip. Jane opened her eyes, sure she would see a glow of light around their bodies. Instead the air seemed thick and full of power. It was almost buoyant. They seemed to drift on a bubble of energy. She had never felt so potent, so strong.

The wave burst over them without notice. The darkness of the tower around them disappeared. She screamed. Callan shuddered. The pulsing of his cock inside her pushed his seed into her core. It was as if she gave him strength with her blood and he returned the strength with his seed. They clung to each other, the ecstasy pulsing on and on until it wrenched them onto some higher plane. She glimpsed . . . something— a blinding light.

Then it was gone. A curtain closed and she was falling, falling back down into her body. The vibrations of her Companion cycled down, even as Callan's echoing vibrations slowed. Callan withdrew his teeth from her throat. She felt the wounds close. He held her, gently now, to his chest. His cock was still inside her. The thump of his heart against her ear was comforting.

Jane had never felt so satiated. But she didn't feel weak. Far from it. Their joining seemed to have increased her energy tenfold. That energy was now latent within her, waiting to be called upon.

She had been transformed.

It wasn't shocking. She thought back. She had been transformed when she had made love to him and sucked his blood in her tiny room at Muir Farm, too. How had she not recognized it at the time? And that was when Callan had been human. She had been transformed even the first time, when they had made love here at Urquhart Castle. What was it but a transformation which could induce her to cede all control over her body and let it do what it wanted, what it was made to do? And tonight? Tonight the whole world had changed. Transformation had been coming on in great bounding leaps, like a great Dionysian beast. Not a beast she was afraid of. Not anymore.

Or maybe it had been gaining intensity slowly as she grew to love Callan. She realized that in order to love someone else, one had to give up controlling everything oneself and cede some control to another. Was that why she had trusted him enough to simply transport out of the kitchen at Muir Farm because he said he had a plan? Yes. And she trusted him enough to abandon all defenses and let the sexual demands of their Companions burst over them in transforming ecstasy she could only experience by reveling in being female.

But what about Callan? Had he felt it, too? If he had, then nothing would ever be the same. He would know they belonged together. He would embrace the love she knew he had inside him. Their joining seemed the seminal purpose for their lives that enabled all their other purposes to flower. They were meant to be together, taking and giving strength and joy, spending their strength on others, recklessly, and on each other. She lifted her head from his chest.

And she almost lost her nerve. What if he hadn't felt it? What if she had been transformed and he had not? They would be stranded on opposite sides of a divide again. She remembered the fierce look of dislike he had given her when she forced him to reveal his past. There was a chance she had killed his love. She couldn't meet his eyes.

Forced him.

Ugly-sounding, isn't it? She had forced him to give up his secret self, the one he never revealed to anyone. It suddenly felt like rape, no matter her good intentions. Was she any better than Elyta? Her eyes drifted closed. She never wanted to open them again. But she had to. She must apologize to him, admit her guilt. She owed him that.

She looked up at him. His eyes were full of tears. They gleamed in the darkness. Even as she watched she saw one slide across his cheek. His teeth were clenched against the emotion, and his lips pressed together firmly. Oh, God in Heaven. Had she caused him so much pain? "I'm so sorry I made you tell me about your past," she whispered, her own eyes filling.

He blinked, spilling more tears, and put his lips to her forehead, gently. They were trembling. "Nae, lass. Ye were right . . ."

"Kilkenny!"

The hated voice seemed to reverberate around the tower room. Jane and Callan stared at each other, eyes wide. Jane realized the voice came from outside.

Elyta.

CHAPTER
Twenty-three

Callan withdrew from Jane quickly, rolled to his feet, wiping his hand over his face, and went to the window. Elyta stood on the shore of the loch in the moonlight just near where the road began to wind up toward the castle. The full moon cast a glittering path across the waters of the loch. Flavio stood behind her. Clara was there, as well. Callan's eyes were drawn to the water. Out on the loch, moonlight glistened on a smooth rolling hump. Another hump broke the surface and then submerged.

The things must be attracted by the vibrating energy of vampires. Maybe they were maddened by it. That's why there had been so many sightings whenever Jane was at the loch.

"I know you are there, Jane."

Callan jerked his attention back to Elyta. So this was it—a moment of truth that would change the rest of his life and Jane's. Their lives would be either very long or very short.

"I can feel your vibrations," Elyta called. "Now do you come down with him or do I come up and get you both?"

He mustn't lose his courage now. For Jane's sake. There was a slender chance of success here, but he must thrust himself through that narrow opening. He couldn't hesitate. He couldn't think about failure.

"You can't escape now. It takes much power to translocate. Together we can block you," Elytá threatened.

"We'll be down," he called. He turned to Jane, who stared up at him with big eyes. "Trust me now, lass. There is a way through this tangle."

She nodded, her big violet eyes serious. She still had the flush of their lovemaking in her cheeks and on her breasts. Callan had never felt anything like what he'd just experienced with Jane. All he could think about was that phrase in her notebook where she had talked about being transformed. He'd never been sure what that meant until now. Now he knew it in his bones and sinews, in a place so deep that the knowledge could never be eradicated. What had happened? That wasn't just vampire sex. Was it because he loved her that he had glimpsed that other world that hung behind some veil all around them? Had she felt it? Probably not. Especially if it required love to see it. She had apologized for making him talk about Asharti, about his sins. He knew why she had done it. She had thought to pry him out of the shell that always threatened to close down on him entirely. He hadn't treated the action as the kindness she meant it to be. He'd been angry. What mollusk likes to be pried from its shell? And he was a very ugly mollusk that should never see the light of day. He'd seen the horror in her eyes at what he'd done, no matter that she tried to gloss over it later with excuses for him. That was just her generous nature.

The sad truth was that if her vampire nature had not required the use of his body just now, she probably would never have brought herself to be anywhere near him. He felt an emptiness come to crouch in his heart where so lately there had been an incredible fullness.

That didn't matter now. What mattered was that he saved her life. He shook himself.

"Get dressed. We must go down ta her." He reached for his own clothes and dressed hastily as she searched for her shoes and scattered clothing, then turned to help her tie her bodice. It was an intimate action but one that felt comfortable now between him and Jane. She looked up at him when they had done.

She was about to speak, then thought better of it, and just smiled a fragile little smile at him. He couldn't smile, not in these circumstances, but he did feel his features soften. How could they not, looking at Jane?

"Just trust me, lass." He hoped he wasn't leading her to her death. That thought shook him. Was he bringing on the very tragedy he so wanted to avoid? And why should she trust him? But he held out his hand and for some unknown reason she took it. He pulled down the ladder to the floor above and handed her up. As she climbed, he gathered up her cloak and headed after her. When they came to the fifth floor, they were confronted by the great wooden door now blocked outside by the huge stone and the fallen crenellations. Callan gripped the great metal strap bolted to the wood that served for a door handle with both hands. The door was meant to open out, but those heavy metal hinges could be bent inward instead. He pulled, straining with thighs and back against the thick metal straps. They creaked and then bent. The door opened slowly inward, cascading in a fan of small stones.

"Stand back," he said sharply. Jane skittered back until the scree settled. The huge stone, irregularly round, blocked the entire entrance. Callan found purchase and put his shoulder to it. His thighs and shoulders strained. It was uphill outside the door. Too difficult. Perhaps he could roll it to the side. He changed angles and put his shoulder to it again. Two small hands appeared beside him.

"Let me help," Jane murmured.

"On three, then. One, two, three." They shoved and the stone rocked. They shoved again and watched it roll away from the door. The moonlight shone into the tower, bathing them in light much gentler than daylight. Callan plunged through the rubble and turned to hand Jane out.

"On the third day, they rolled the stone away," she said softly. She picked her way among the stones. She was so dainty, so ultimately feminine. He hoped she realized how wonderful that was someday. He only hoped he could make her reference to being reborn come to fruition.

They climbed the rise up to the broad sward of grass inside the castle.

"I half expected her to be waiting here," Jane said, looking around.

"She likes ta ha' th' prey come ta its own fate," he said grimly. God, what was he doing? There was so little chance that they would live through the night. And all might depend on a cowardly man finding courage and the love of a woman for that man in spite of all odds.

He grabbed for Jane's hand and they started across the ruins to the road. He could see Elyta clearly now. She hadn't moved. She stood, waiting, imperious, sure of herself. Movement caught his eye out on the loch, but when he glanced toward it there was nothing there. Must have been the moonlight glittering on the choppy surface.

He turned to Jane. She must play her part here. He took her by the shoulders. "Now lass, ye must ha' courage. Ye did no' make me. I relapsed. Stick ta that story nae matter what she says. Ye're grievin' because there's nae hope for ye ta make it back ta human. There is nae cure. That should no' be sa hard, since it's true. For th' rest, ye'll ha' ta lie. Can ye do that?"

He saw her processing all the ramifications. Her eyes searched his face. She was not the kind to lie. He knew that. But this was life or death. Then she nodded. Just that. Now she seemed to be the silent half of their pair, and he the one whose words tumbled out, unbidden.

"And if it comes ta that, remember—if we join our power we ha' more chance against them." He couldn't make his mouth anything other than a grim line. "Just think about our Companions joinin' forces and they will."

They walked down the road until it dipped to the shore of

the loch. He saw Elyta's brows contract. She had just realized he was vampire again.

Jane's heart was in her mouth. She'd always heard that saying without thinking much about it. It seemed ridiculous
on the face of it. But now she understood what it meant.
Her throat was closed. It throbbed with her pulse. She didn't
like the feeling.

Callan was going to try to fool Elyta into thinking there
was no cure and never had been. That must have been his
plan all along and why he wanted her to make him. All that
about wanting to be vampire again must have been a lie, no
matter how sincere he had seemed at the time. Even if Elyta
believed their ruse, she didn't see how Elyta wouldn't just
kill them both in outrage. They were made vampires, after
all. He had asked her to trust him. And there really wasn't
any other choice. They couldn't escape. They had to face the
vampires from Mirso Monastery. So she hoped to God
Callan knew what he was doing.

They walked down toward the shore of the loch under the
tower with its roots in the water which had been their refuge
for three days. The crenellated, crumbling stone now rose
above them. At the edge of the water they halted. Elyta was
frowning, as she thought over what Callan's being vampire
again meant. Flavio looked pained and Clara had eyes only
for Flavio.

"What have you done, you little bitch?" Elyta spat. "Well,
it doesn't matter. I'm taking you two back up to that house
and every day you don't produce results I'm going to torture
him. I can't imagine how I let Flavio talk me into being le-
nient with you when you challenged me, but I shan't make
that mistake again." She glanced to Callan. "And I'll enjoy
myself, too."

Jane let her shoulders sag. "But I have done nothing," she
said sadly.

Elyta advanced on them. "You made him . . ."

They all felt the new presences. Just down the lochside, three vampires stepped out of the trees. Elyta, Flavio, and Clara turned as one to face them. Jane recognized the ferret-faced man who had escaped the night her father died. The other two were strangers, one a gaunt, hawk-faced man, the other so baby-faced and rotund he looked a little like partially risen bread dough. They approached along the rocky shore, the tall, gaunt one leading. The ferret-faced one seemed afraid. The short, doughy one scrambled to keep pace with the others.

"Oh, dear," Jane breathed. Now there were six vampires who would want them dead. No words seemed adequate to express how bad this was. She glanced to Callan.

"I dinnae know . . ." he muttered. She could feel his brain racing behind his eyes. "Maybe it's better this way, at least if . . ."

A wave sloshed over their feet and Callan drew Jane a little farther up the pebbled shore.

"She's the one, his daughter," the ferret-faced man cried, pointing. "And the traitor Kilkenny was human last time I saw him. They'd cured him."

The three interlopers stopped, the other two flanking the tall, gaunt one, who was clearly the leader. His vibrations were tight and high, almost a hum. He was old. The others vibrated at different frequencies, younger. Together with those from Muir Farm they created a chorus of energy. It filled the air. How could she and Callan prevail against all this power?

"Khalenberg." Elyta sneered. "Come yourself at last?"

The gaunt one with the hawk nose and salt-and-pepper hair nodded. "The Elders must not be allowed to possess a cure. You know how they would use it." His accent was Germanic.

"And who says I want them to have it?" Elyta asked, speculating. She took a step toward the newcomers. "Anyone who has the cure will have power. You want to stand against the Elders? Don't destroy the cure—join me. We will control it together."

"And use it as a weapon against our kind? I know you too well, Elyta."

"And you are so pure with Treadwell and Russo as followers? I know them, you forget. We all make our armies of the stuff at hand."

"I hate ta spoil this delicate negotiation," Callan said. The new vampire faction flicked their eyes to Callan and Jane. Elyta and Flavio turned their heads slightly but only Clara took her eyes off Khalenberg. "We were tryin' ta tell ye, there is no' a cure."

"What do you mean?" Elyta barked. "We all saw you turn human."

"He isn't human now," Khalenberg pointed out.

"She made him again."

"I didn't. He . . . he relapsed." Jane protested. "The effect was only temporary." She thought of her father, and how he had died for nothing really, since the cure he was seeking had now helped no one, and was lost forever. Tears welled in her eyes.

"His Companion was gone!" Elyta protested. "He had no vibrations at all."

Another wave sloshed up, bigger this time.

Flavio and Clara had both drawn their brows together, wondering what to believe.

"It wasn't gone. It was . . . neutralized, for a while." Jane improvised frantically. "I began to smell cinnamon and ambergris and knew what was happening."

"Sa we went," Callan finished. "We did no' know how ye would react ta th' failure."

"I don't believe you," Elyta said. "Why didn't you run farther? You stayed because you made him and you needed someplace to go to ground with a sick man."

"We knew you'd search for us in Inverness," Jane said.

"You could have gone to Fort Augustus to the west, then."
Elyta advanced on them.

"Th' process o' reawakening was no' a picnic. But she did
no' give me blood."

"You're lying. There is a cure. She just has to find it—"

"Look," Jane said, growing desperate, "I'll never find
Papa's formula again, cure or not. There are too many variables, too little information on how Papa did it. You could
torture Callan every day for years and I wouldn't be able to
find Papa's formula. And now, even if I found it, it would be
temporary." She could feel her face begin to crumple. "So
what's the use? I'll never be human again. And neither will
Callan." Tears rolled down her cheeks as she tried to master
the sobs. Some part of her asked if they were real. Another
part answered that they were connected to emotion, if not
the right emotion. She was frightened and tired and she'd
lost her father. And she would never be human again, even
if . . . if that had stopped being quite so horrific lately. She
let the sobs shake her.

Elyta frowned.

Callan put his arm around her shoulders. His energy
spoke to hers, reverberating between them as he tucked her
in against his side. "I wish ta God there *was* a cure."

Silence stretched as all six vampires stared at them and
tried to decide. This was the moment that would settle their
fate.

"I tend to believe her," Khalenberg said finally, in a voice
that was used to command. "Which aligns all our interests,
Zaroff, and leaves one final action. They must be killed."

"You aren't lying, are you?" Elyta asked Callan and Jane
with something like wonder in her voice. Then she exploded. "Zeus and Hera!" She advanced, her fingers curling
into claws, her lips drawn back. "I'll rip you apart myself."

"Why?" Jane shouted. "Why must we be killed?"

Callan pulled Jane behind him. His body was tense, ready
to defend their lives as long as he could. Jane had no illusions

that just because he was male he could win out against Elyta. She was a very old vampire. "What would it cost ye ta let us go?" he reasoned, as though Elyta was not past reasoning.

"Leaving aside your traitor state, since I myself might be called that by many these days, you must be killed because you are made." Khalenberg's clipped tone sounded like a sentencing judge. "Russo?" The doughy vampire nodded and strode forward to join Elyta.

"Which side are you on, Flavio?" Callan shouted. "The choice is yours."

Would Flavio help them? Callan seemed to think so. But Flavio just stood, immobile, as Elyta advanced on them.

Jane looked around wildly. The water of the loch was frothing about a hundred yards away, but she didn't care about a water monster when the land was filled with monsters all trying to kill her and Callan. She glanced up at the tower. If they just transported . . .

"Callan! Let's get out of here," she hissed.

"Do you think I'd let you escape?" Elyta sneered.

"You said we could join our power . . ." Jane whispered to Callan. She felt his vibrations ramp up. *Companion!* she called, and felt its answering buzz in her veins. She dared not break her concentration by looking down, but she could feel the tingling pool of blackness gathering at their feet. The power sang in her veins.

Elyta's eyes went red even as she lunged for Callan. Jane's power cycled down as though a blanket was thrown over the flame. The blackness dissipated. Elyta grabbed for Callan's head. Jane felt his power ebb, too. He managed to push Elyta's chin up. Jane couldn't get enough power to transport, let alone to take Callan with her. And he seemed totally occupied with trying to keep his head. Panic clawed at her throat. What to do?

A hand grabbed her arm. Russo! The doughy vampire jerked her away from Callan. With a grunt, she struggled away from him and scrambled, stumbling, over the pebbles of the beach. What could she *do*? Her eyes lighted on the crumbling crenellations above them. She couldn't raise enough power for translocation, but what about transporting stones? Maybe they didn't know she could move rocks. Maybe she could surprise them and distract Elyta.

Callan grunted behind her. She glanced back. Elyta had him by the head, twisting as Callan pushed her chin up. Callan was calling his power, but Elyta's eyes were carmine-red. She was stronger. It was only a matter of time. The doughy vampire was trying to pin Callan's arms. But they didn't have him yet.

Give me just a little power, Companion. The world went red. Blackness pooled about her feet, then washed away. The red film faded. *Focus!* she commanded herself. She stared at the stones above. She daren't try to hit those attacking Callan. She might hurt Callan himself. But by hitting others maybe she could distract Elyta, and Callan could escape. A stone wobbled loose from mortar powdery with age. She thought about the ferret-faced vampire. "Go!" she yelled.

The great stone flew from the battlements, followed by another and another. She watched them arc down and hit the ferret-faced one in the head, the chest. They knocked him to the ground and pinned him there. He wouldn't be down long. Khalenberg glanced at his compatriot and then stared at Jane. "How did you do that?"

"Would you like to see?" Jane whirled. Elyta lost focus, distracted by the hailing stones. Callan struggled away from her and Russo. Callan and Elyta circled each other until her back was toward the loch. Jane stared up at the tower and willed a shower of the great stones. They rained on Khalenberg and the other one, Treadwell, who had pushed his way out of the pile of rubble. But the two vampires still stumbled through the hail of stones toward her, grunting and staggering as they were hit. It wasn't enough!

Waves splashed over her feet. Some great stones plopped into the water with a spray.

Flavio lunged toward them. Not Flavio, too! But he pulled Elyta away from Callan. She turned with a growl and back-handed him. He sprawled across the stones.

"Still," Elyta commanded to Callan, her eyes deepening to burgundy. And Callan did go still. Now she would kill him with ease.

"No!" Jane cried. The stones stopped showering as she lost concentration.

But Callan was staring at the loch. His eyes too had gone deep red. His power ramped up. Focus on Elyta, not the loch, she wanted to shout.

Khalenberg pushed past Callan and lunged for Jane. She stumbled backward and sprawled on the stony verge. Khalenberg loomed over her, a look of grim determination on his face. "I'm sorry," he said and reached for her.

Then they felt it.

The air was filled with a great gasping intake of breath and a shushing spray of water. Waves sloshed up the gravel strand. Jane turned to see a gargantuan head with tiny eyes rise from the water on a thick and supple neck, limned by moonlight and pouring water. The snout had a wide mouth that flapped open now. A roar issued from the creature's throat high above them. It must be twenty feet out of the water. Behind the undulating neck was a great body with limbs like oars beached in the shallows of the loch. The creature seemed maddened, its head casting about for the source of its misery.

And there! Behind it was another, and another, all rising from the cold black depths of the loch. Water sluiced off their gleaming, slate-gray hides. Someone was shrieking. Jane could not take her eyes from those great beasts to see who it was. Clara perhaps, for Elyta was turning toward the creatures, her eyes going wide as she released Callan. Even Khalenberg backed away.

Only Callan stood calmly, dwarfed by the monsters. Their necks swayed, their heads, however big, absurdly

small for their massive bodies. The very quality of the air
was changed by their immensity. Callan held out a hand to
Jane without taking his eyes from the monsters that writhed
above him. Elyta stood, frozen, between him and the creatures. Jane hurried to take his hand. He drew her into his side
even as he called the power. The darkness whirled up in a
flash. Jane felt the popping pain and the world shivered back
into view around them.

She and Callan were standing on the parapet of Urquhart
Castle.

Below them the scene dissolved in chaos. Elyta drew her
power, apparently in an attempt to use compulsion on the
beasts. That seemed only to enrage them. One heaved itself
onto the beach using its stubby, flipperlike appendages.
Treadwell of the ferret face was crushed beneath it. His
scream floated into the night.

Another was bearing down on Flavio.

"Callan," Jane whispered. A flipper caught Flavio and
smacked his head against one of the great stones Jane had
showered on the beach. He seemed stunned. Russo turned to
run from the onslaught, his pudgy limbs pumping with effort. One of the monsters opened its mouth wide. The huge
head was propelled with surprising speed by the great neck.
One moment Russo was there and the next all you could see
were his legs, kicking frantically from the great mouth. His
screams were horrible. Callan held Jane tightly. The creature
raised its head to the sky, opened its gullet, and gulped the
rest of Russo down. Jane wanted to cover her eyes, but she
couldn't look away. Flavio! Where was Flavio?

Clara was running toward the beasts. No! She was running for Flavio. The monster heaved its bulk up and forward.
Flavio's body was lost in the darkness beneath it even as
Clara bent and snatched at him. The bulk came down. The
earth shuddered. But Flavio was clear. Clara heaved him up
and half dragged him up the shingle.

Elyta shouted at the creatures. From this angle Jane could

see that her eyes were red. "Go from here!" The words
echoed up to them. She was trying to compel them.

"It will no' work," Callan muttered. "The power is what
attracts them."

Jane looked out across the loch. Callan must be right, for
the surface of the water was choppy with rising humps. "My
God," she murmured. "How many are there?"

By the time she turned back to the narrow beach, Elyta
must have realized her mistake. Her eyes faded. There were
five of the great creatures struggling up the beach, their
heads undulating above their bodies. Clara and Flavio had
reached higher ground. Khalenberg transported to a point
high on the little cliff Jane had once stood upon, overlooking
the scene. Only Elyta now remained in range of the monsters. Her eyes lifted to the parapet where Jane and Callan
stood.

"You won't escape me," she yelled.

"Come away, Elyta," Flavio called. "It isn't worth it.
There is no cure."

Elyta was forced to scramble back as another monster
heaved itself forward. She blinked out of view in a whirl of
blackness and reappeared next to where Flavio and Clara
huddled together on a grassy knoll. She turned back to
Callan and Jane. "I'll find you," she shouted.

From the village, a group of men brandishing torches and
whatever weapons they possessed swarmed up the road.

"No you won't," Flavio said, rising. Jane could hear him
clearly, because of what she was. "You're going back to
Mirso where you belong, Elyta. There is nothing more to be
done here." He took one of Elyta's arms and Clara took the
other. Their eyes were red.

"You'll pay for this," she shrieked at Flavio and Clara.

"I don't care," Flavio said as he reached for Clara's hand.
Darkness swirled up around them and engulfed Elyta, too.
Just before he blinked from view, Flavio looked up at Jane
and Callan. "Thank you," he called, "for the reminder."

And they were gone.

The mob from the village lunged off the road and onto the knoll where the three vampires had just stood. Jane looked around for Khalenberg, but he was nowhere to be found. The waters of the loch quieted. Humps of flesh slid beneath the surface into the darkness below, now that the vibrations of the vampires had quieted. The villagers waved their torches at the creatures on the shingle. They seemed to take no notice. But they too heaved themselves back toward the water as if listening to some unheard call. In a matter of minutes, only the villagers were left on the shore of the loch shouting and brandishing their weapons. The choppy waters smoothed themselves. It was if the whole thing had never happened, except that the body of Treadwell, or more accurately, the crushed pulp of Treadwell, was still smeared across the beach.

"Come, Jane," Callan whispered, and pulled her in closer to the tower. "We dinnae want th' villagers ta see us."

They peered around the edge of the tower and watched the crowd mill disconsolately about. Finally the men broke away in ones and twos.

When Callan and Jane turned from the dispersing mob, they almost bumped into Khalenberg. Jane gasped.

"Was this your plan, to kill all in your path?" he asked Callan in his clipped accent.

Jane felt Callan draw himself up. He examined Khalenberg's face for a moment before he spoke. "Nae. I knew Miss Blundell and I would ha' ta fight Elyta. I hoped Brother Flavio would help us, since he regretted no' helpin' someone before. And I thought Clara might support Flavio, whatever he decided. With four ta one, I thought we could prevail against her."

"But you called the monsters."

"I dinnae count on ye and yers comin' in on her side," Callan said calmly. "I realized th' monster was attracted ta our power. It maddened them. Sa I used compulsion ta bring it in, as a distraction. When Elyta tried ta use compulsion on them, she only made them angrier."

"Got a little out of hand," Khalenberg observed.

"Aye," Callan answered. He was so brave. He looked Khalenberg straight in the eye, regardless of the fact that the man was so much more powerful than they were. "I did no' know there was sa many."

"And you!" Khalenberg turned on Jane. "How did you move those stones?"

Jane lifted her chin. "Well, if we can direct our own bodies in translocation, I thought we might be able to use the power to direct other objects, as well. I conducted experiments until I mastered the technique." She glanced to Callan. He looked proud.

"I guess Jane showed ye somethin' about being vampire ye did no' know. Maybe she's a better vampire than ye are." The two men stood there, glaring at one another. "Sa d'ye still want ta kill us?" Callan asked at last.

"We'll join our power against you," Jane threatened, though the threat was surely empty.

Khalenberg's brows drew together over his hawk nose. His face looked like it had been cut with a blunt chisel. He frowned. "Are you going to make an army, Kilkenny?"

"There were twelve," Callan said, exasperated. "How does that make an army?"

"Whole religions have been started with twelve."

"They're all dead, and some deserved ta be. Nae. I'll no' be makin' any more."

Khalenberg's eyes flicked from Jane's face to Callan's, examining them. Callan moved to stand in front of Jane. She couldn't have that. She took his arm and stood beside him. Khalenberg looked disgusted. "I hardly credit the fact that I am going to do this yet again. What is one more pair when there have already been three to my personal knowledge? And I'll wager Flavio and Elyta's servant are well on their way. My God, what is the world coming to?" His eyes went red. Jane braced herself to call on her Companion and add its power to Callan's.

But the red eyes did not shower them with compulsion. "You must show me how to move objects sometime, young lady." The words echoed and blackness whirled up around his lean form in an instant, and he was . . . gone.

Jane turned to Callan, who looked just as surprised as she felt. "He . . . he let us go?"

"Apparently sa," Callan muttered.

The wind off the loch took her hair and blew it about her face. She turned into the wind. The crisp cold air felt clean. The moon had risen until it was a tiny silver coin flashing a beacon of glittering light across the water. Around the loch, hills furred with trees rose protectively. It was beautiful in its own sere way. She had always known that. She had suppressed the pleasure it gave her, because to be moved by natural beauty seemed a violation of the discipline of science she aspired to embody. Tonight, that didn't seem so important. She was alive and the world held wonders that might never be entirely explained. Oh, someday people would know what kind of creatures lived at the bottom of Loch Ness. They would be catalogued and categorized. Someday science would know perhaps even how the creature that shared her body metabolized the blood she drank, or why she could blink out of space using its power.

But for now, those mysteries weren't important. She was alive, and the world was beautiful. Even Scotland, so poor and so sere, had beauty.

Far away to her left, lights flickered in the cottages of Drumnadrochit. The villagers would be gathered, telling and retelling the tales of the beasts that rose from the sea. This night would live in their stories, growing and changing until it became a myth, perhaps unrecognizable to any who knew what actually happened here.

In times to come, of course, no one would know. Everyone would be dead.

Except her. Except Callan.

Life stretched ahead in an unbroken sweep of years. There was time enough for everything. Frightening . . . exhilarating. What would she do with all that lay in front of her? That was a more important mystery. Sorrow lay ahead, perhaps jaded disinterest. A tiny hope of ecstasy. Who could know?

She felt Callan moving in to stand behind her. The pull of his body on hers was like the pull of the moon on the ocean; a tide rising deep inside her, irresistible. And that was the mystery she found more compelling than any. They had unfinished business. When Elyta had called his name, she thought he had been about to . . . to embrace what he felt. She wanted that. She would fight for it. Why else had she been transformed?

He wanted to touch her. He wanted to touch her so much his heart was slamming against his rib cage and his mouth was dry.

But he didn't. She was free now. She had eternity ahead of her. She was resourceful, intelligent, strong-willed, beautiful. And good. Jane was intrinsically good. She'd find new ways to help people, women and their babies first, but then, who knew where it would end? She believed in goodness because she was good herself, and gave herself unstintingly. His own doubts seemed a reflection of the defects in his character.

He cleared his throat and licked his lips. The wind blew her hair back against his shoulder. "I'll . . . I'll see ye ta Fort Augustus, or Glasgow if ye like. I dinnae think we should trust ta Inverness. It's likely she'll ha' gone that way."

She turned shocked eyes on him.

"I . . . I ha' plenty o' money. I'll see ye're well off, and there's whatever yer father left ye." The words tumbled out. "Ye can set up a clinic for birthin'. Maybe in th' New World. They will no' bother ye there."

Her face closed down. She looked away, toward the village. Then she looked around, at the loch, at the moon, then down at the stones of the parapet. Her silence was a rasp raking his flesh. She pulled her cloak around her. A distant smile curved her lips. Why didn't she speak?

"You were right about me, Callan," she said at last. To any who did not have the gift of vampire hearing, her words would have been lost in the wind. "I've spent my life denying who I am. I lived to please my father. I carved myself into who I thought I should be. I don't know exactly who I am, but I want to find out." She turned to confront him. "Now, who are you?"

"I told ye that," he said. His throat was full. She'd ripped it out of him in the tower.

"You only told me what happened to you. Are you Scots? Irish? Catholic? Atheist? Idealist, cynic?" she prodded. Her voice sank. "Who?"

"I'm a monster, Jane," he said. He made his voice as hard as he could.

"You said that we were monsters not by virtue of our condition, but by the condition of our souls." Her eyes blazed now.

"Aye," he barked. "And I told ye the condition of my soul."

"You told me you'd suffered. That you'd been compelled to do horrible things."

He turned away. He couldn't stand the intensity of her gaze.

"Let me tell you what I see in you, Callan." She stepped in closer. "I see a man who came back to sanity from treatment that would have broken any other. I see a man so courageous he took on England and vampire society in order to carve out a haven for lost souls, a man who believed in the intrinsic goodness of men so much he tried to create utopia."

"I was a fool," he rasped.

"And then, I see a man who, with no thought of reward, tried to use his powers to help those weaker than himself. You called them small acts. Were they? Not to those you helped. You never lost your ideals or your honor, in spite of all that's happened to you. I call that courageous. More than that, I call it good." She took him by the shoulders and tried to shake him, though the principal effect it had was to send the shooting fire of attraction careening through his body.

"Jane," he said, restraining himself with the last ounce of his will from taking her in his arms. "You want me ta be worth your . . . attentions, but it's all th' power of our Companions usin' us, willing us ta acts that affirm th' cycle o' life. Dinnae mistake lust for anythin' more."

Anger glinted in her violet eyes. She slapped him, hard. His head snapped to the side. "How dare you belittle what I feel for you! I *love* you, you prideful idiot! And don't tell me you didn't feel what I felt down there a few hours ago. I saw your tears. And that's not just lust. I think it requires love to reach that . . . transcendence." Her voice had sunk to a whisper. She looked frightened.

His cheek stung, but he hardly noticed. Loved him? Was that possible? "Ye've known me about two weeks, lass. That is no' love."

Her eyes got big and even more uncertain. "So . . . you don't . . . don't feel . . . it?"

He couldn't let her doubt herself like that. "Of course I love ye," he whispered. "I think I loved ye from th' first days."

They stood, looking at each other, wondering what came next.

A wicked grin struggled to reveal itself in her expression. "Sa," she mocked his accent. "I canno' ha' th' same feelin's ye take for granted in yerself?"

When she put it that way . . . He cocked his head, trying to decipher her expression as though it was writ in hieroglyphics. Uncertainty, covered by mock courage. Her mockery was her defense against the fear.

He stretched out one hand to her. It was the hardest thing he had ever done, or the easiest. She pushed herself into his arms and hugged him, fiercely. He ran his hands over her back, and kissed the sweet abandon of her hair. But he had to tell her. He couldn't let her make the mistake without warning her. "Jane," he murmured. "Jane. We are sa different."

"And more alike than either of us care to admit," she said, raising her head to look up at him.

"Ye're talking about th' evil part?"

"I was thinking more of the stubborn, prideful part."

"And what about th' qualities we dinnae share? Generous, giving?"

"I think we may share those, too."

"I dinnae yield on that point."

"I'll have to convince you."

His heart began to lighten, almost of its own accord. "It might take a while."

"Well, I think we have forever," she said reasonably. "That seems rather nice."

"Nice? I never thought o' it that way." But suddenly living long did not seem a trial.

"Maybe that's the wrong word." She paused, thinking. "But don't you think, all in all, we get a fair exchange? You said you wanted to be vampire again. And I think you want to believe that you were only trying to convince me to make you. But I think you were telling the truth. The feeling of being alive, whole, the strength, the energy inside us . . . I think we get the better end of the bargain, and I think you think so, too."

"How about th' need for blood?"

"You said we could make a fair trade for those who give to us by leaving happy memories and feelings of self-worth." She glanced up, reproachful. "You might do at least as much for yourself."

"You're a strong person, Jane. Stronger than I am."

Her brows furrowed. "You *chose* to give yourself to Elyta in one of the most courageous acts I've ever seen. You chose to be vampire again. You had the resolution to escape Elyta. You had the plan. You called the loch's monsters. You aren't a victim, not anymore, not of the Companion, not even of your own nature. I've never met a man so strong of character."

Deluded girl! She believed in him in spite of all evidence to the contrary. He *had* chosen. But she was wrong about what he had chosen. He didn't choose any of what she said. He chose her. And everything else followed.

"I'll never be th' charming rogue I was before that time in th' desert," he warned her.

"I'm glad I didn't know you then. I couldn't have loved that man the way I love you."

He bent and brushed his lips against hers. His Companion surged up along his veins as he deepened the kiss. Out on the water of the loch, a surge of flesh broke the water.

Jane gurgled a laugh into his mouth. "I think we'd better go collect our horses and leave these poor creatures alone. They couldn't stand us disturbing them constantly."

"Ye're right," he agreed, grinning. The way her eyes lighted when he grinned was a revelation. He resolved to do more of it. But right now he wanted to get somewhere where he could do this moment of decision justice. Jane's room at Muir Farm would do nicely. He wanted to make love to Jane in the twilight and at midnight, in the long slow ebb of night toward morning, in darkened rooms before they slept, in moonlight. His insides felt like some of Jane's aspic. Could it be that she wanted to be with him? He had to warn her. "Forever is a long time, Jane. Who knows . . . ?"

"Who knows, indeed?" She stretched up for another kiss. "We must take our chances."

A flare of hope shot through him, mingled with the electric charge of her touch. "I warn ye," he said slowly, pulling away from her mouth. "I am verra lucky at games o' chance."

She smiled. That expression in her eyes—he'd seen it before in recent days. Could it be . . . could it be love? The flare of hope leaped into a burning flame.

"I warn ye. I'm going ta buy ye dresses, Jane Blundell. Red and violet like yer eyes."

She nodded, tears filling her eyes. "I'd like that."

"If ye dinnae mind, I'd like ta settle in Edinburgh, at least for a while."

She raised her brows, not doubting, just curious.

He took a breath. "I'm a Scot. Edinburgh might actually be home."

Her smile kindled something inside him, in his heart, in his loins . . . "Edinburgh it is." She swallowed, and he knew what she would say next came hard for her. "Do you think it's possible . . . that we could have a child?"

Of course she wanted a child. She'd been a barren spectator in the world's cycle of fecundity for too long. "I dinnae know." He moved a strand of hair from her lips and tucked it behind her ear. Jane should have lots of children rather than just birthing other women's babies. "Anythin' seems possible." He grinned at her. "It'll take lots o' effort, of course."

He saw the gleam of mischief in her eyes. How she would torment him in the coming years with that dear mockery! "I think we should get started right away." She took his hand.

"Back ta th' farm then, first, before anythin' else." He smiled. He was going to show her the other things he could do with his mouth besides grin, this time at a long, leisurely pace.

They drew their power, together.

$\mathcal{L}$ook for the next two novels in this spellbinding series from *New York Times* bestselling author
SUSAN SQUIRES

One with the Shadows
Coming in Fall 2007

One with the Darkness
Coming in Spring 2008

FROM ST. MARTIN'S PAPERBACKS